THE BOLD AND THE BEAUTIFUL

RENNO—Born white and raised a Seneca, the pale warrior who is master of the forest must wage a strange new battle—at the Court of the King and Queen of England.

ADRIENNE—Trapped between French and English—a Huguenot beauty threatened by King Louis's foul prisons—she asks one night's protection from Renno, and in that night, changes her life and his.

JEFFREY WILSON—Once Renno's violent rival, he has become the Seneca's truest ally only to find himself once more drawn to Renno's woman.

NETTIE—Branded a harlot and witch by the contemptuous colonists, she would always be faithful to Renno.

ALAIN DE GRAMONT—His soul has been bought for gold by the French; he burns with hellfire to crush the mighty Seneca.

The White Indian Series
Ask your bookseller for the books you have missed

The White Indian Series
Book II

THE RENEGADE

DONALD CLAYTON PORTER

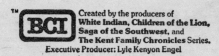

Created by the producers of
**White Indian, Children of the Lion,
Saga of the Southwest,** and
The Kent Family Chronicles Series.
Executive Producer: Lyle Kenyon Engel

BANTAM BOOKS
TORONTO • NEW YORK • LONDON • SYDNEY • AUCKLAND

THE RENEGADE

A Bantam Book / published by arrangement with
Book Creations, Inc.

Bantam edition / March 1980

2nd printing .... March 1980	7th printing ..... July 1981
3rd printing .... March 1980	8th printing .... April 1982
4th printing ..... April 1980	9th printing . December 1982
5th printing ... January 1981	10th printing . September 1983
6th printing .... March 1981	11th printing . November 1984

Produced by Book Creations, Inc.
Chairman of the Board: Lyle Kenyon Engel

Cover art and illustrations by Louis S. Glanzman

ISBN 0-553-25020-5

Published simultaneously in the United States and Canada

Bantam Books are published by Bantam Books, Inc. Its trade-
mark, consisting of the words "Bantam Books" and the por-
trayal of a rooster, is Registered in U.S. Patent and Trademark
Office and in other countries. Marca Registrada. Bantam
Books, Inc., 666 Fifth Avenue, New York, New York 10103.

PRINTED IN THE UNITED STATES OF AMERICA

H   20 19 18 17 16 15 14 13 12 11

"The white Indian has fought well against us," said the commander in chief of French forces in the New World. "Obviously he is courageous, resourceful, and skilled in the arts of war. But now he has been disowned by the Seneca and has become a renegade. We can use a man of that caliber in the campaign that will determine whether all of North America will belong to France or Great Britain."

THE
RENEGADE

Chapter I

The quiet in the vast forest of the Seneca was deceptive. Lurking unseen in the thick tangle of oak and evergreen, maple, elm, and birch were creatures dangerous to man—wildcats, bears, and wolves, with teeth as sharp as a Seneca spear. Underfoot were silent copperheads and the larger snakes that warned their victims by making a sound like a medicine man's rattle. But the most dangerous predators in the forest were two-legged—Erie warriors, the traditional enemies of the Seneca and their brother nations in the proud and powerful Iroquois League. Also, after the recent victory of the English colonists and the Iroquois, stray bands of braves of the Huron and Ottawa, allies of the defeated French, might have made their way south seeking revenge.

But Renno was at ease in the wilderness—relaxed yet ever-vigilant. He had quickly recovered his strength after his heroic march from the French town Quebec. And today, he was enjoying the mildness of this late autumn outing.

1

He was tall, with no fat on his lean frame, his step was silent, confident. In his scalp lock were the feathers of a senior warrior, at twenty-two summers the youngest Seneca ever to have achieved such rank excepting his distinguished father, Ghonka, the Great Sachem who ruled not only his own nation but all the Iroquois tribes.

It was regarded as extraordinary that an adopted son could follow so closely in the footsteps of Ghonka. Renno's mother, Ena, and his aunt, Sah-nee-wa, were convinced that the manitous, the spirits of the wilderness, had chosen the young man as one who would stand above all others.

Today Renno had come hunting with his brother El-i-chi, two years his junior. He was deeply troubled, and only in this endless ocean of trees could he find the peace to solve his dilemma.

In spite of his accomplishments as a warrior and leader of men, Renno knew he was unlike all other Seneca. His skin was bronzed only where it was exposed to the sun. Even his eyes were a pale blue in color, like those of so many of the English colonists who lived at Fort Springfield in Massachusetts Bay, a four-day march away. He had learned their tongue, he had fought beside them in battle, and for a time he had even imagined himself in love with an English girl. Colonel Andrew Wilson, landowner and commander of the western Massachusetts Bay militia, believed Renno had been kidnapped by Seneca twenty-two years earlier when they had raided Fort Springfield and he was right.

Even though Renno felt he was a Seneca, he knew he was different, and was conscious of his uniqueness.

On a day such as this, however, it was difficult to worry about problems he could not solve. The air was cool, redolent of pine and wildflowers; the sun filtering through the trees was warm and the forest teemed with game. The manitous would lead him to his destiny, guiding him in his future dreams as they had guided him in the past. This was a day intended for pleasure, and Renno carried Seneca weapons instead of the English musket and pistol he had learned to handle expertly. No man except Ghonka was his equal with bow and arrow, tomahawk and knife.

Renno halted on the narrow trail for a moment and looked back over his shoulder at the shorter, more slender El-i-chi, also a full warrior. The brothers' faces remained immobile, but each could sense the other's excitement. Colonists would have spoken at length about their feelings, but braves could express themselves without words.

The pair started forward again, effortlessly observing every aspect of the ground underfoot and the clumps of brush nearby, while listening for the faint sounds of game. After a time Renno halted again and pointed at two small patches of slightly crumpled autumn grass, signs of deer.

El-i-chi nodded almost imperceptibly.

A salt lick frequented by deer was nearby, and they turned toward it, slowing their pace. Renno drew an arrow from his quiver and notched it in his bow, as did El-i-chi. They could feel the mild autumn breeze on their faces, so they were in luck; their quarry would not catch the man-scent that would reveal them.

The lick stood at the base of a small cliff, about fifteen or twenty feet high, with sheer walls and no trees. The brothers halted and peered out into the open, but the deer was not there. Bent blades of grass indicated that it had left only recently.

Renno and El-i-chi moved into the open to investigate. The silence was so overwhelming that the buzzing of an insect sounded loud in their ears.

Suddenly Renno froze. His keen eyesight detected a very slight movement near the top of the cliff, and he knew at once why the deer had fled.

Poised for a leap to the ground below was a great wildcat, its teeth bared for a snarl. The powerful beast was gray, its fur streaked with tan, and a red gash in its side indicated it had recently been fighting. It was angry as well as hungry, and its eyes gleamed as they fixed on El-i-chi.

Renno had no time to warn his brother. The wildcat leaped, claws extended and ears flattened against its head.

Renno raised his bow, took aim, and fired an arrow in that fleeting moment, hitting his moving target. The shaft's impact knocked the animal off course, and it landed a short distance from the startled El-i-chi, wounded but still snarling viciously.

Without hesitation Renno moved in for the kill. Drawing a steel English knife, the one white man's weapon Renno carried, he advanced cautiously.

The wildcat swiped at him and attempted to rise to its feet, the arrow still protruding from its side, its fur matted with blood. Renno halted, aware that the beast was gathering for a last, desperate leap. Then his knife flew through the air, and buried itself to the hilt in the wildcat's throat.

El-i-chi bowed his head for a moment. "Always I am in your debt, brother," he said.

"You would do the same for me," Renno replied.

The wildcat's pelt was badly slashed, so Renno retrieved his knife, and decided to leave the carcass for the vultures. Within a day or two the bones would be picked clean.

A faint sound from the heights indicated that the wildcat had not been alone, so the pair returned to the forest to where the rise was gradual, and then slowly moved forward toward the lip of the precipice.

On the bare rock surface near the edge of the cliff they were surprised to see the bodies of three other adult wildcats all badly mauled and battered.

Beyond them lay the body of a huge brown bear.

Renno was able to identify him, even from a distance. It was Ja-gonh, whom he had named and taken home with him as a tiny cub more than fifteen years earlier. For two years Ja-gonh had lived with the family, which was proper because Ghonka and Ena were members of the Bear Clan. After Ja-gonh had returned to the forest, he and Renno had seen each other frequently.

Ja-gonh had once saved Renno's life, and also had driven off an older boy who had been tormenting El-i-chi. The bonds that tied Renno to the bear had been remarkable, but he had always regarded the relationship as normal and natural.

Grieving now, his heart heavy, Renno looked down at his animal friend and realized that Ja-gonh must have been attacked by the wildcats. Ill and almost incapable of defending himself, he still made his attackers pay dearly for their boldness. Three had died, and the fourth had perished at Renno's hand. Others, perhaps, had fled the scene.

"Ja-gonh," Renno murmured.

The great bear slowly and painfully opened his eyes. It was difficult for him to see clearly, yet he knew the warrior who stood above him.

Renno knew Ja-gonh was dying. El-i-chi had to use all of his will power, for even in moments of great tragedy, a Seneca did not betray his feelings.

Renno and the bear looked at each other for what felt like an eternity.

"I hear you, my brother," Renno said softly, "and I will do as you wish."

Ja-gonh closed his eyes.

Thumping himself three times on his bare chest with his fist, Renno raised his voice to a shout. "Hear me, oh manitous of sky and earth and wind. The spirit of my brother Ja-gonh is in your care. Always he has been loyal to you and to the trust you have placed in him. Take his spirit now to the land of our ancestors and his, so he may live there in peace for all time."

The breeze seemed to grow stronger.

Renno dropped to his knees and again drew his knife. "Good-bye, my brother," he said softly. "Wait for me. We will meet again when I come to join you." Taking a deep breath, he plunged the knife into the bear's body.

The wind sang through the nearby trees, rustling the dying leaves.

Renno cleaned his blade, then stood and looked up at the sky. After some moments he saw a hawk circling overhead.

A hawk had appeared at a number of critical moments in his life. One had circled above him during the worst of the ordeal he had undergone in his manhood trials. Another had helped him during the attack on Quebec, making it possible for him to lead his comrades into the supposedly impenetrable inner city. Renno knew that hawks were the messengers of the manitous, who guarded and protected him.

The hawk swooped lower for a few moments, then flew away.

Renno felt the crushing burden of grief dissipate. The manitous had answered his prayer, and were conducting the spirit of Ja-gonh to the afterworld.

Working swiftly and efficiently, Renno and El-i-chi skinned the bear. Then, carrying the hide with the head still attached to it, Renno led the way home.

Noting the bear's blood Renno had smeared on his forehead, cheeks and torso, the sentries stationed in the forest respectfully lowered their heads. Old men sitting outside longhouses stopped smoking, and small children fell silent. Fellow warriors folded their arms over their chests in the Seneca gesture of mourning. Women and girls silently moved out of his path.

He carried Ja-gonh's remains to the house of the Great Sachem, where Ena was grinding corn and Sahnee-wa was scaling a fish for the family's dinner. Ba-lin-ta, Renno's round-faced little sister, just thirteen, clapped a hand over her mouth and ran off weeping.

Renno deposited the remains on the ground.

El-i-chi explained what had happened to his mother and aunt.

Only Ena's eyes betrayed the anguish she felt for her older son. "We will treat the skin for you, Renno," she said. "So you can hang it on the wall in your own house. You will be reminded of Ja-gonh for the rest of your days on this earth."

The white-haired Sah-nee-wa, of whom even Ghonka stood in awe, smiled at her nephew. "You did that which was right, Renno," she said. "You did as Ja-gonh wished. Now he is in the care of the manitous. You showed even greater courage today than you have shown in battle. It is right that you belong to the Bear Clan, and I am proud of you."

"Go, my sons," Ena said briskly. "Wash yourselves in the lake, and rejoice for the spirit of Ja-gonh."

The brothers obeyed, moving off in silence.

Several hours later, the family sat down for supper around the stone pit outside the Great Sachem's hut. No one would mention the bear in Renno's presence until the hide had been cured and was hanging on the wall of his hut. Only Ba-lin-ta betrayed any emotion, but she was bolstered by the presence of Walter Alwin.

Three years her senior, Walter had never lived a normal life in the white man's world because he was a deaf-mute. He was the younger cousin of Deborah Alwin, Renno's first love. The boy's mother, Ida, had put aside her own prejudices and allowed him to come to the land of the Seneca because of her great fondness for Ba-lin-ta.

Although Walter ate most of his meals with the Great Sachem's family, he slept in the boys' lodge and spent most of his days with them. His lack of hearing and speech was no drawback in a civilization where the spoken word often was superfluous. He could hunt, fish, and play games; he was learning to handle weapons and was completely at home here. Previously as plump as Ba-lin-ta, he had grown lean and sinewy. Above all, he now carried himself with an air of confidence for the first time in his life.

After dinner, Renno lighted a long pipe with a coal from the fire and, after puffing on it, passed it to El-i-chi. It was now time to talk.

Ba-lin-ta, as usual, broke the silence and asked the question that her equally curious brothers were too polite to raise. "Where is our father?"

Ena exchanged a quick look with Sah-nee-wa. "He meets with the council," she said.

Renno was surprised. The council, comprised of the elders, war chiefs, and principal medicine men, advised Ghonka on matters of state, and usually was convened only in a time of crisis. The young senior warrior wasn't aware of any reason for the meeting, but his superiors didn't tell warriors everything.

Again the two women looked at each other. "Jeffrey, the son of Wil-son," Ena said, "came today to the land of the Seneca. He brought a message from his father, and he gives it now to the council."

Renno was elated. Jeffrey had become his close friend during the campaign in Canada. The young militia officer, once an arrogant and lazy boy, had been transformed by combat. Renno had saved him after he had been wounded in battle, and the two had become blood brothers.

"Jeff-rey will sleep in the house of Renno," he said.

His mother was quick to rebuke him. "If that is the wish of the Great Sachem," she said, "it will be done." Jeffrey Wilson had not come on a private visit, but was an official emissary from the colony of Massachusetts Bay, an ally of the Iroquois, and had to be treated accordingly.

"Wal-ter," Ba-lin-ta said, "hopes he will see Jeff-rey, too."

The boy nodded eagerly.

Ena smiled. "I am sure that can be arranged," she said.

Ena turned to Renno. "It may be," she said, "that you will be called to appear before the council. It is the wish of the Great Sachem that you stay nearby."

Renno remembered that soon after the attack on Quebec, he had promised that he would go as emissary to the English Great Sachem, King William, if necessary. Perhaps Jeffrey had come to say that this mission was at hand. But Renno refused to allow himself to wonder. Since earliest childhood he had been taught to be patient, and at the appropriate time he would learn whatever he needed to know.

The family scattered. Ena and Sah-nee-wa went off to a small shed behind the hut to treat the hide of Ja-gonh, and a protesting Ba-lin-ta went off to bed. El-i-chi wandered away in search of fellow warriors to accompany him on a stroll by the longhouse of the maidens. And Walter hurried back to his own longhouse.

Renno remained cross-legged before the fire, unmoving except to raise the long pipe to his lips. A sense of restlessness stirred within him, and he tried to tell himself it was because he wanted to see Jeffrey Wilson, but he knew better.

Once again, he guessed, his destiny would be joined with that of the English settlers. The manitous who watched over him obviously had decided that his life was to remain intertwined with the people into whose race he had been born. Surely it was no accident that he had rescued Deborah Alwin after her capture by hostile Huron from Canada. Surely it had been predestined for him to bring her back to the land of the Seneca and to learn her language during the months she had lived with him as his woman.

Since that time Renno had paid several long visits to Fort Springfield, and in the war against the French, he had been the vital link between the Iroquois and the colonists from Massachusetts Bay and New York. It was strange, he thought, but as he came to know the white man better, he began to understand and sympathize with them.

Not that he wanted to become one of them. As long as he lived he would be a Seneca, proud of his people and of their heritage, proud of the role he himself was playing as a warrior.

A quarter moon was rising high in the sky by the time the council meeting ended, and the Great Sachem returned home. A burly man with a huge chest, Ghonka had a light step that belied his advancing years. He exuded an aura of authority and dignity, making superfluous the buffalo cloak and elaborate featured headdress that he wore on state occasions. Ghonka was the chief of chiefs of the entire Iroquois League, chosen because of his unparalleled skills and valor in combat. His reputation was so great that not even the mightiest of the Iroquois' foes, the Algonquian, would declare war against him. But he had become far more than a field commander, and the colonists in New England and New York knew him as a wise statesman as well as a faithful ally.

His eyes grew brighter when he saw his elder son, and he slowed his pace.

Renno rose to his feet effortlessly and inclined his head in a respectful gesture of greeting. He never forgot that his father was the Great Sachem.

"You have heard that Wil-son has come to us with a message from his war chief father?" Ghonka never wasted words.

"I have heard," Renno replied.

"He waits for you in your house. When he speaks you will learn the reason for his journey."

"I will listen, my father."

"Listen well," Ghonka said. "And when the owls cry out in the night, think of what he has told you. When the great spirit of the sun returns in the morning, you and I will speak of these things."

The young warrior nodded.

The Great Sachem's manner softened. "You have fought with valor and cunning for our people, my son. Soon the women will sing songs about you that their children and their children's children will sing after them. I remind you of this so you will not forget what you have already done. No sachem and no conncil will force a senior warrior to do that which does not please him. You are free to make up your own mind." He raised a hand in dismissal.

Renno turned and walked slowly toward his own small house.

Jeffrey Wilson awaited him outside the hut. Almost as tall as Renno, he had lost the petulant expression that had marred his appearance as a youth. The lines in his forehead and at the corners of his eyes were proof that he had grown wiser through suffering, and at the age of twenty-two had become a real man.

He grinned broadly when he saw his friend.

Renno raised his hand in the Seneca greeting, then shook hands English-style, even though Indian custom normally prohibited such physical contacts. "Why you didn't come first to me when you get here, Jeff-rey?" he demanded, speaking in English.

"I had my orders, as you can imagine." Jeffrey stood with his booted feet apart, his thumbs hooked in his belt as he looked at the white Indian. "You've gained weight, Renno."

"Too thin before. Just parched corn and jerked venison on the march." Renno remembered his manners as a host. "You have food tonight?"

"Some of the women brought a meal to the council lodge." Jeffrey was too polite to say he had found the Seneca stew unpalatable.

But his expression betrayed him, and Renno laughed. "In the morning we eat breakfast my mother cooks. Much better."

They sat on the ground outside the hut and leaned against the wall. Renno reached into the pocket of his buckskin shirt and offered his friend a pipe. Jeffrey shook his head, reluctant to admit that the stench of Indian tobacco made him ill.

"Colonel Wil-son and your mother feel all right?"

"They're fine, thanks. Pa soon will be made a brigadier of the militia."

Renno admired Andrew Wilson and was pleased. "De-bo-rah feel all right?"

"She's prettier than ever, now that she and Obadiah Jenkins are going to be married."

"Good! Reverend is strong man. Make good husband for De-bo-rah."

11

"You're invited to the wedding, Renno, and Deborah is hoping that Walter will come home for it, too. I gather he's becoming a man here?"

"Soon Wal-ter be man. If Wal-ter come for wedding, Ba-lin-ta come, too."

"Of course she's expected. They're still close?"

Renno pressed two fingers together.

"I haven't traveled all this way for personal gossip," Jeffrey said abruptly. "The time has come for you to know of our plans for war with the French and Huron. Now you must fulfill your promise made to our fathers after the battle at Quebec."

"Speak on," Renno replied diplomatically.

"This coming year, sixteen hundred ninety according to our calendar, will be very important for England, for our New World colonies—and for you Seneca, too. King Louis XIV of France is a greedy man. He wants to dominate all of Europe, and England stands in his path. So he's building a huge army and navy, and intends to wage a major war against us."

Renno spat on the ground. "Seneca warriors and English soldiers fight better than French!"

"I quite agree, but there will soon be many more of them. They're increasing their artillery and cavalry, and the reports that reach Boston from London say that their navy soon will be enormous, too. But their activities aren't being confined to Europe. They're making major efforts here in the New World. Have you ever heard of Cape Breton Island?"

Renno pondered the question. "Big island of Algonquian and Abnaki."

"That's the place. It not only controls shipping on the St. Lawrence River, but ships stationed there could menace trade between England and her colonies. Well, the French are building a huge fort on Cape Breton Island that they're calling Louisburg, after their King. Soldiers are already being sent there from France, and by the time they're done with it, the place will become the most powerful fortress ever constructed in all of North America."

"Not good for English."

"It can be catastrophic for us," Jeffrey said. "The governors of all our colonies have been bombarding our King, William III, with pleas for help to counter the French threat. Well, King William is an able man, but he's short-sighted. He's so concerned about the safety of the British Isles that he doesn't give a hang about what happens in the New World. Governor Shirley of Massachusetts Bay has been writing to him continually, saying in so many words that the war will be won or lost in America, and that the winner will take possession of all colonies here."

Renno had heard all of this before. Nevertheless he remained puzzled. "Why King William not understand?"

"Only because his own interests lie elsewhere and he knows almost nothing about the colonies. That is why our governors and their advisers developed a new strategy. They decided to send a special envoy to London to see the King and explain our situation to him. This appeal *must* be different, Renno. It must come from someone who knows the ways of the Indian. That's why you were chosen as the ambassador. They want you to go to London and appeal to King William!"

Renno shrugged. "I'm a warrior," he said with a laugh. "I'm no speech maker!"

"Think of the advantages. You're indeed a warrior. You can show him how you use Seneca weapons. And forgive me for saying something I've never heard you discuss, but you're not only an Indian—you're a white man. I doubt if there's anyone else like you in all the tribes of North America."

Renno wasn't sure if his situation was unique, but he didn't want to dwell on it.

"In addition to everything else," Jeffrey continued, "you speak a passable English and you'll be still better by the time you reach London. You won't need an interpreter when you try to convince King William that his colonies here are in great danger."

Renno was quiet. He still had misgivings about the mission. London was the capital of the British Empire, and he didn't want to be regarded as a freak there simply because he was a white Indian. He recognized the truth of his friend's words, but he had no desire to be ridiculed.

Something else bothered him, too, and he found it difficult to admit, even to himself. A journey to London would take a long time on board one of the great white birds of the sea that he had seen in Boston harbor. And he might have to stay in London for a long time, far longer than the few weeks he had stayed at Fort Springfield. Would he, during this time, fall prey to the soft living and the diseases of the white man, because his skin was white? The very thought of losing his identity as a Seneca made him uneasy.

In any case, it was all too important to be decided on the spur of the moment. "We sleep," he said, rising abruptly. "In the morning I'll talk with my father. Then I tell you yes or no."

Jeffrey Wilson was tired after his long journey and his session with the Seneca council, and soon dropped off. But Renno stayed wide awake, tossing on his hard pallet. He hated to admit he was fearful but knew that a courageous man was wise to fear the unknown. Boston, with a population of ten thousand, had overwhelmed him, and it was impossible for him to picture London, a city of so many hundreds of thousands they could not be counted.

The food would be strange, and he hated to wear English clothes, which he regarded as ludicrous and constricting. He wouldn't mind carrying a brace of pistols, having become expert in their use, but he would need instruction in the handling of a sword like the colonists wore.

In London, too, he felt certain, there would be more attractive young women than he had ever encountered, and that thought disturbed him. He would never forget Deborah, and he also had warm memories of Nettie, the Fort Springfield harlot with whom he had also gone to bed. He was reluctant to admit to himself that his memories of those two white girls were far sharper than those of the various Indian girls he had bedded. A permanent attachment to some girl he might meet in London could destroy his future as a Seneca.

Obviously he would require stamina and self-control as well as courage if he hoped to survive the ordeal.

It was very late when Renno finally fell asleep.

He was wide awake at dawn, and after shaking Jeffrey, took him off to the lake beyond the palisade. There they coated their faces with venison grease and shaved, then swam in the cold waters of the lake.

Jeffrey's teeth were chattering as he dressed again. "I thank the Almighty I'm not a Seneca," he said. "I'd be ill with the ague half the year if I had to swim regularly in this icy water."

Renno laughed. The pair walked back slowly. The scent of autumn was still in the air, and Renno wished desperately that he could spend the next two weeks hunting with El-i-chi and some of his friends. First, however, a momentous decision had to be made.

As the two young men approached the house of the Great Sachem, Ba-lin-ta threw herself at Jeffrey with such force that she almost knocked him to the ground. Her mother and aunt frowned, but Ghonka smiled indulgently. It was plain that his only daughter held a special place in his heart.

Jeffrey had the good sense to bow to Ena, Sahnee-wa, and Ghonka, but his exchange of greetings with El-i-chi was as one soldier to another, with a forearm clasp.

Everyone was curious about Deborah's forthcoming wedding. Reverend Obadiah Jenkins had visited the land of the Seneca with Colonel Wilson, but Sah-nee-wa and Ena didn't remember him clearly. Jeffrey tried to speak in the tongue of the Seneca, but his speech was so halting that he reverted to English, and Renno translated for him.

The clergyman, he assured the women, was a man of integrity and strength, a worthy mate for Deborah. Ghonka knew him from the expedition into Canada, and the Great Sachem confirmed Jeffrey's estimate with a nod. His wife and sister were somewhat mollified.

Ena glanced briefly at Renno.

He knew what that look meant. His mother was berating him for not taking Deborah as his own wife. It was beneath his dignity to explain that their approaches to life had been too different.

Everyone knew the purpose of Jeffrey Wilson's mission, but during the meal Ghonka remained silent on the subject, so no one else mentioned it, either. Jeffrey brought Walter up to date on the news of Fort Springfield, and Ba-lin-ta passed the words along to the boy, her fingers flashing in a code that only the two of them understood.

When the meal was finished, Ghonka nodded at Renno, and they rose, then walked together through the town. Not until they were a considerable distance through the forest in a small clearing did they halt. The Great Sachem seated himself on a flat-topped boulder, and Renno made himself as comfortable as he could on another, slightly less elevated rock.

"You have thought of the offer that Wil-son brings?" Ghonka asked.

"I have thought long and hard, my father."

"The council thought hard, also. All agreed that the Great Sachem of the English would give you many muskets, cooking pots of metal, soft blankets, and other things which our people can use."

"The English are generous and give freely to their friends," Renno said.

"They are generous," his father said dryly, "because the French give so much to the tribes that have become *their* allies. For more than twelve summers the Ottawa and Huron have been in their camp. Now the French seek the friendship of the Algonquian. It is this that worries the council and the sachems of all the Iroquois nations."

"The Seneca alone can win a war with the Algonquian," Renno declared.

The older man was far more cautious. "If the Algonquian are armed with the muskets of the French, the Seneca and all of the other Iroquois, fighting together, would find it difficult to beat them. Remember that the

Algonquian are as numerous as the kernels on all the ears of corn in our fields at the time of harvest. Only the Great Sachem of England has storehouses filled with muskets and could give them to us."

"Then you wish me to go to the English sachem and tell him our needs," Renno said.

"My wish is not important," Ghonka said. "I cannot ask you to make this sacrifice. You did more than any other warrior to win our victory at Quebec. You have won the right to make your own choice."

Renno hesitated.

His father's eyes bored into him. "You are afraid to make this long journey. Why?"

Renno felt compelled to admit to him what he could confess to no one else. "My skin and eyes are like those of the English. If I stay too long with them I may become like them."

The Great Sachem astonished him by sighing. "I have had the same fear for you, my son, since the English colonists first came to the land of the Seneca and offered us the wampum of peace."

"I see the dangers ahead for us and for the other Iroquois," Renno said, speaking slowly. "Gladly will I risk my life in battle. I know what to expect in war. But I do not know what awaits me at the end of a long journey to the land of the English. It may be their Great Sachem will close the door of his longhouse to me."

Ghonka nodded. "I cannot see your future clearly. And I knew you would feel as I do. So I spoke with your mother and your aunt last night. They are wise. They hear the voices of the manitous when no one else hears them. Often they dream, and in their dreams they see the Great Faces that bring us the wishes of the spirits."

Renno folded his arms over his chest and waited. The ultimate decision had been taken out of his hands.

His father unfastened a small pouch of worn leather attached to his belt. "Sah-nee-wa gives you this gift," he said. "Perhaps you will dream. Perhaps you will learn in the dream what you are to do."

The young warrior took the pouch.

Ghonka rose and, not looking again at his son, left the clearing, making no sound as he walked rapidly away.

Renno inhaled deeply. He opened the pouch and, as he had anticipated, it contained a mixture of dried herbs. The recipe was a secret known only to Sah-nee-wa and Ena.

Not since the grueling retreat from Canada, after marching day and night without rest, had Renno dreamed. He feared no man other than his father, but the spirits and their interpreters, the Great Faces, made him apprehensive.

All the same, he knew what had to be done. He took a pinch of dried herbs, which he allowed to dissolve on his tongue. Moving to the flat-topped rock on which Ghonka had sat, he folded his arms and waited as he sat cross-legged. A stiff breeze blew, sending a shower of yellow leaves to the ground, and the young warrior suddenly felt cold.

But he remained clearheaded and alert, his vision unimpaired as he stared at a shaft of sunlight at the far end of the clearing. Steeling himself, he took another pinch of the herbs, carefully closed the pouch, attached it to his belt, and then laid his bow and arrow close at hand on top of the boulder. Grasping his tomahawk in one hand and his knife in the other, he stretched out on top of the rock.

For a long time nothing happened.

Then, even though the sun still shone and the breeze grew no stronger, in Renno's mind the clearing became as dark as a cloudy night, and the wind began to howl.

The signs were good, and Renno knew he was starting to dream. He seemed to be walking through a black, murky cloud, unable to see more than a few feet in front of him. Beneath his moccasins were smooth rocks of identical size, placed side by side. They reminded him of the cobblestone streets he had seen in Boston.

Then, suddenly, the cloud cleared away, and a full moon shone on a huge longhouse. It was unlike any of the Seneca, and Renno was puzzled; it was similar to the house of Governor William Shirley in Boston. But it was far larger, and a flag attached to a long pole flew over it.

Two sentries in scarlet and white uniforms stood at a gate of metal grillwork, but as Renno approached them, they opened the gate and vanished.

He walked inside and found it deserted. Wandering from stone chamber to stone chamber, he discovered that all were bare. They stretched ahead endlessly, and although no man was more expert at reading a trail, he was not sure he would be able to find his way back to the gate.

He entered a room larger than all the others, and there he halted abruptly. A fire burned in a huge hearth, and on the wall opposite was a carved wooden mask like those used by the Seneca witch doctors.

Here, truly, was a Great Face.

"Do you come in war or peace?" the Face demanded in a harsh, croaking voice, its lips unmoving.

"I come in peace," Renno replied.

"You are a senior warrior of the Seneca?"

He was annoyed. Any Great Face should know from the green and yellow paint on his forehead, cheeks and torso that he was a Seneca and held the rank of a senior warrior. "Of course," he said.

The Great Face became mocking. "Are you sure you are a Seneca?"

"Very sure!"

"Then why are you here, warrior?" The Great Face began to laugh, and the sound became louder and louder in the stone chamber.

Renno's eardrums ached, and he fled into the next room, the laughter halting abruptly.

He saw moonlight filtering in through an open window, and there was a strong scent of flowers in the air. In the far corner stood a bed with a canopy over it, a bed similar to Nettie's in Ford Springfield.

A young woman arose from the bed, and he thought at first she was Nettie, but she wasn't, and neither was she Deborah. Her skin was similar to theirs, very pale and unblemished, but this girl had red hair that tumbled almost to her waist, and her eyes were green, so clear and

bright that he stared at her. Only with a great effort did
he succeed in tearing his gaze from her.

She was wearing a gown of a soft, shiny white
material. The low, square-cut neckline partly revealed,
partly concealed the girl's high, perfect breasts. She had a
tiny waist and her skirt was very full, with frothy white
material edging the bottom.

Renno's throat felt dry. He felt rooted to the spot.

The girl spoke to him.

But he couldn't understand a word. She wasn't addressing him in the tongue of the Seneca or of any other
Indian language he had ever heard, and he knew she
wasn't speaking in English, either.

He strained harder, trying in vain to make sense out
of the gibberish.

The girl stopped speaking, and her full lips, painted
a bright red, curved into a smile.

Feeling foolish, Renno grinned back.

All at once she spoke to him in a heavily accented
English. "Come to London, Seneca warrior," she said. "If
you have the courage to face the muskets of the French
and the arrows of the Ottawa, let us see if you have the
courage to make the journey."

Courage? His exploits spoke for themselves, and no
warrior had achieved more. No warrior except Ghonka
himself carried a greater number of scalps on his belt. She
was mocking him, and a cold fury possessed him, making
it impossible for him to reply.

She backed away slowly toward the far end of the
room, then spoke to him again in the strange language he
could not understand.

He glared at her, and wondered what would happen
if he threw a tomahawk at her. No, such gestures were
futile in a dream—she would vanish into the air, un-
harmed by the weapon.

"If you dare," she said, "come to London. That is
your destiny, Renno of the Seneca, and you can escape it
only if you are afraid. But you would be miserable for the
rest of your days because in your heart you would know
you were a coward."

He was so furious he reached for the tomahawk in his belt.

The girl laughed and melted away before his eyes. Then the building disappeared, the wind grew stronger, and only the wilderness remained.

Renno opened his eyes. Dusk had come, and he realized he had slept all day. He slowly gathered his weapons, jumped to the ground, and trotted home.

Renno's family, Walter, and Jeffrey Wilson sat around the fire in front of Ghonka's house, calmly eating. No one mentioned his tardiness, and as he sat cross-legged beside El-i-chi, his mother handed him a steaming bowl of stew.

Jeffrey looked at his friend surreptitiously, but understood Indian manners enough to say nothing. Ba-lin-ta started to speak, but Sah-nee-wa glared at her, and the child fell silent again.

Renno ate heartily, his appetite unimpaired by his disturbing dream. When they were finished with the food, Ghonka lighted a pipe and offered it first to Jeffrey. Then Renno puffed on it and handed it to El-i-chi, who followed his example. Walter was eager to be treated like a man, so Eli-i-chi handed him the pipe.

The boy drew on it, then coughed as he gave it back to Ghonka. Only Ba-lin-ta smiled, and the adults knew she would tease Walter when they were alone later.

The moment had come for Renno to speak. "I will take Wal-ter and Ba-lin-ta to the wedding of De-bo-rah," he said. "We will go when the sun awakens in the morning. Eli-i-chi will march with us, and will bring three other warriors with him."

"Why will you take El-i-chi and the other warriors?" Ghonka knew the reply, but the ritual had to be observed.

"Ba-lin-ta and Wal-ter cannot march alone," was the quiet reply. "They will need protection on the trail when they return to the land of the Seneca after the wedding."

Ghonka well knew that Walter was capable enough to take care of Ba-lin-ta on the return trip, but chose not to say anything. Instead, he concealed a smile, but his eyes grew brighter. "You will not return yourself?"

Renno looked first at his father, then in turn at his mother and aunt. Finally he turned slightly so he faced Jeffrey Wilson. "It is decided," he said. "I will go with you to see the Great Sachem of the English."

Chapter II

Deborah Alwin was radiant, as befitted a bride-to-be, and she was the natural center of attention as she sat beside her future husband, the Reverend Obadiah Jenkins, at the head table in the dining room of Andrew and Mildred Wilson's farmhouse outside Fort Springfield. There were some in Massachusetts Bay who called the place a mansion, and perhaps it was, by frontier standards. But the Wilsons and their friends thought of it as the headquarters of a large, working farm. The whitewashed clapboard building was plain, and the furnishings were utilitarian except for a few family heirlooms brought from England two decades earlier.

Thanksgiving was a special holiday for everyone living in New England in November 1689. The big house was so crowded with dinner guests that tables had been crammed into the parlors and passageways separating the dining room from the other chambers. A few of the women wore gowns of silk or bombazine, a mixture of silk and worsted, but most, like the men, were dressed in the simple linsey-woolsey that was the everyday colonial attire. In fact, a number of the men even wore buckskin shirts and trousers, their only clothes.

The harvest had been bountiful this year. The settlers had ample quantities of vegetables and sufficient grain, but the meats were the real glory of the Thanksgiving feast. Colonel Wilson and his farm foreman, Tom Hibbard, had gone hunting every day for a week, and a dozen roasted wild turkeys were proof of their success. Quarters of buffalo had been cooked in outdoor pits, and for those who wished other delicacies there were duck, goose, and quail.

Friends, neighbors, and prominent members of the Massachusetts Bay militia were on hand for the celebration. The only person missing was Jeffrey Wilson. No one but his father knew he had been sent to the Seneca on a secret mission.

The people of Fort Springfield had become a closely knit community bound by the strong ties of frontier hardships and dangers. They had endured Indian raids together, and many, Tom Hibbard among them, had lost loved ones. The men had marched together on the Quebec campaign, and during lean years they had shared meager food supplies and somehow had staved off starvation.

One person did feel out of place, however. Nettie sat near the foot of the main table in the dining room. Penniless when she came from England, she supported herself in the only way she knew, and both the clergyman and his future wife were convinced that her good qualities far outweighed the stigma of the profession that necessity had thrust on her.

Certainly Nettie looked as demure as the other women. Her red hair was pulled back and tied in a neat bun at the nape of her neck, and the neckline of her bodice was modest. Although she knew many of the men present, Nettie took pains not to greet them with familiarity, and she was surprised that most of the women, entering into the spirit of the holiday, greeted her courteously if not warmly.

Nevertheless she was uncomfortable, principally because the man on her right was a recent client. Jack Davies, a newcomer to the area, was a burly farmer in his mid-twenties. Experience had taught Nettie he was demanding, crude, and selfish, and worse when he drank to excess. She had misgivings when she noted that he came to the table carrying a half-empty pewter cup of Colonel Wilson's rum punch, a potent libation. He took his place, dropping a hand to her thigh and squeezing hard.

Nettie was too embarrassed to make a scene. Reverend Jenkins inadvertently saved her from further mortification when he rapped on his cup for attention and then asked the entire company to stand.

Colonel Wilson bowed his head, and everyone followed his example. Obadiah Jenkins recited passages from the *Book of Psalms*, his voice ringing with sincerity.

The "Amen" of the assembled company was heartfelt. Although there were no survivors of the Indian massacre that had destroyed the original Fort Springfield twenty-two years earlier, most of those present had lived through hard times. Now, at last, they could begin to feel secure. Farms were flourishing, and storehouses were filled with grain, smoked meats, and other food. Every month newcomers from England swelled the ranks of the pioneers, and land on the east bank of the Connecticut River was growing scarce. The great fortress on the heights overlooking the river boasted a half dozen sixpounder cannon and was manned day and night by militia volunteers. No Indians dared to attack the town, even though outlying, isolated homes sometimes were still raided. There were a dozen shops now on King William Street, and it was rumored that Colonel Wilson intended to invest in a foundry as soon as he finished building his sawmill and the small factory where cloth would be woven.

No one knew better than Ida Alwin how Fort Springfield had grown. Marked by tragedy, she had lost her husband soon after giving birth to her son. Since that time she had worked for survival, aided in recent years by her orphaned niece, Deborah. But today Ida was able to thank the Almighty for his blessings. Deborah was about to marry a man admired by the entire community. Walter was thriving in the land of the Seneca, according to reports by Obadiah after he saw the boy several months earlier.

The man seated on her left interrupted her reverie. Leverett Carswell, a recent arrival in town, had become a man of consequence in only a month. In his early fifties, a widower whose grown children had remained behind in Yorkshire, he had come to the New World with a bulging purse. He was building a house in town, and his new general store, filled with merchandise that in the past had been difficult to obtain, was already doing a thriving business. It was said that he was about to become Colonel Wilson's partner in several new business ventures, but that story had not been confirmed. Ida, who didn't believe in prying into other people's personal affairs, had no intention of asking any questions on the subject.

The wrinkles in Carswell's lined, tanned face deepened as he grinned at her. "Ma'am," he said, "I'd be much obliged if you'd tell me the name of this soup I'm eating."

She was surprised that he could be so ignorant. "It's pumpkin, of course."

Leverett Carswell was incredulous. "Pumpkin soup?" He filled his spoon and held it out for her inspection. "It looks to me like there's meat in it. And onions and carrots."

"Quite right," Ida said, her voice growing sharp. "If you don't care for the taste, there are plenty of others here who'll enjoy it!"

"I think it's wonderful," he protested. "In fact, I never tasted better."

Ida sniffed aloud.

"I just wondered, that's all." He ate with obvious relish, then turned back to her as a thought occurred to him. "Am I right in assuming that you cooked it?"

"Well, I supplied the recipe, which happened to be my own, and I helped some in the kitchen." His scrutiny made Ida nervous. No man had looked at her that intently for many years.

"You're talented as well as attractive, Mistress Alwin," Leverett said, looking and sounding as though he meant it.

Ida was startled. In her own opinion she looked like an elderly, scrawny hen. Her late husband had never been free with compliments, and she couldn't remember a time when a man had flattered her. "Rubbish!" she replied firmly, and wondered about his ulterior motive. Certainly there was nothing a poor woman in her position could do for a man of Carswell's stature.

His steady smile indicated that he didn't take the rebuff seriously. "Your niece looks lovely," he said, nodding in Deborah's direction, then pausing for a moment. "Andy Wilson tells me your son has handicaps, and that he's trying to overcome them by living with an Indian tribe."

Ida nodded stiffly. She had no intention of discussing Walter with a stranger.

"My daughter was born deaf," Leverett said quietly.

Ida raised her head and turned to him. Obviously, he wasn't being casually curious, and the unexpected bond thawed her. "Then you know."

"Indeed I do," Leverett said. "She suffered torments for many years, and so did her mother and I. But she's overcome most of her difficulties, thanks mainly to the sympathy and patience of her husband. She has two healthy children and leads a normal life."

"That's good to hear," Ida murmured.

"Ordinarily I don't talk about her problem," Leverett said. "When will you see your son again?"

"I'm hoping he'll come home for the wedding next week." The dam broke, and Ida found herself unburdening her innermost fears. "Right from the start I haven't been able to see how life with the Seneca could help Walter. All Indians are dirty, pagan barbarians, and I'm afraid my boy will become a savage. The only reason I've let him stay on with the Seneca is because Andrew Wilson and Obadiah insist he's doing really well with them. I just can't believe it, and I'll have to see him and judge for myself."

Leverett became thoughtful. "I've had little to do with Indians since I've come to Massachusetts Bay, although they interest me. But I urge you to feel encouraged. Andy Wilson's judgment is sound, and Reverend Jenkins is sensible. So, even though I've never as much as set eyes on a Seneca, to my knowledge, I think you can rely on their advice."

"How could that be?" The chip reappeared on Ida Alwin's shoulder.

"One of our troubles," he said, "is that we're too civilized. I've noted in the short time I've been here that the people who seem the happiest and the best adjusted to life in the New World are those who have cast aside many of their English ways. Living so close to the forest can be good or bad, depending on a person's approach. What I'm trying to say to you, Mistress Alwin, is that the Indians lead less complicated lives. They're much closer to nature than we are. So they're better able to accept your son's handicaps and to deal with them naturally. At least that's my guess."

"You do make a body feel easier in the mind," she said.

"I just hope I'm right," he told her. "For years I prayed that my daughter would be cured, and it took a long, long time for me to realize she was adjusting to her condition far better than I was and was making a happy life for herself."

Ida tried to absorb what he was saying.

"But a Thanksgiving dinner celebration," Leverett said, "is no place to discuss such matters. Allow me to drive you home in my carriage later, and we can talk in more tranquil surroundings."

"Deborah and Obadiah will take me home," Ida said, stunned by his unexpected offer.

He refused to be shunted aside. "Young people don't

marry every day of the week," he said with a smile, "so I'm sure they'll want to visit with their own friends." His voice became firm. "We'll consider it settled, ma'am, that I'll escort you home." Giving her no chance to reply, he started talking to someone sitting across the table.

Ida felt conflicting emotions raging within her. No one had dared to give her orders for more years than she could remember, but this stranger seemed to take it for granted that she would obey him. Yet she also realized he was truly interested in her, which she found incredible. She had been without a man since the death of her husband, and she had assumed that no one would ever look her way again. Her mirror told her she was old and homely, and she couldn't imagine why the wealthy, personable Carswell should be so attentive. She thought it impossible that he was truly interested in her as a woman, but at the same time she couldn't help feeling flattered.

Farther down the table Nettie was having an even more difficult time. Jack Davies had refilled his mug with punch, and his attentions were becoming increasingly obnoxious. The miserable Nettie tried to concentrate on her meal.

But Davies gave her no chance. Sipping his fresh drink, he leaned toward her. "Nettie," he muttered, "there must be at least a half dozen bedrooms upstairs in this house. Let's you and me get away from these folks and put a feather mattress to the test."

Pretending she hadn't heard him, she continued to stare down at her plate. Unfortunately this lout was spoiling what was perhaps the most sumptuous meal she had ever eaten.

Davies peered hard at her, then his large hand vanished beneath the table. Nettie felt him grasp her thigh. With as much composure as she could muster she lifted a piece of turkey to her mouth.

Chuckling to himself, Davies squeezed.

The girl's discomfort gave way to pain as the man's grip became tighter. "Leave me alone," she told him, speaking in a low tone.

"You took my money fast enough a couple of nights ago," he replied.

"Please," she said, aware of her precarious position as a guest in the home of Fort Springfield's leading citizen. "This is no time to speak of such things."

"You got your eye on somebody else, maybe," Davies said. "I ain't good enough for you now you're trying to act like a great lady." His hand slid higher on her thigh.

Nettie gasped. Running the risk of creating a scene, she caught hold of his wrist and tried to remove the offending hand. Davies held firm.

Neither realized it, but their unequal struggle was being watched by Colonel Wilson's foreman, forty-year-old Tom Hibbard. Lean and angular, with hair that had turned white when his wife was killed in an Indian raid a year earlier, Tom had come to America as an indentured servant in the Wilson household. He had served his time with distinction, staying on as head of the field staff, and in the campaign against the French he had won a commission as a militia officer.

To most, Tom Hibbard appeared taciturn, and even the few who knew him well realized he was a man who preferred action to words. He was slow to make up his mind, but once decided, he moved swiftly.

Now he rose silently, made his way around the end of the table, and leaned down between the man and the girl, his manner so unobtrusive that no one realized there was anything out of the ordinary.

"Are you in distress, Mistress Nettie?" he asked softly.

The girl reddened. "I—I don't want to make a fuss, Master Hibbard." Her acquaintance with Tom had been slight, and she had sometimes wondered why he had never become one of her clients. Now, however, she could only think of him as Colonel Wilson's close associate, and her embarrassment became even more acute.

Tom turned to the smirking Davies. "I reckon you and I should have a little talk out in the open."

Jack Davies knew he was being challenged and his

laughter turned into a deep scowl. "Glad to oblige," he replied, and rose to his feet.

"I don't want to be the cause of any trouble," Nettie said faintly.

Tom led the young farmer to the rear of the dining room. They slipped out into the open, avoiding the kitchen, a spacious, separate building. Tom walked quickly past the barns and storage sheds, and when they could no longer be seen from the main house, he halted.

"Now, then," he said. "What was that all about?"

"I was teasing the little whore, that's all." Davies's manner became sullen.

Tom remained polite, and did not raise his voice. "The little whore, as you call her, happens to be the guest of Colonel and Mrs. Wilson. I neither know nor care what she does elsewhere, but in their house she's entitled to be treated with dignity."

Davies laughed harshly. "Don't tell me you're sweet on her!"

Tom refused to dignify the comment with a direct reply. "It was plain she was in distress. After this, Davies, mind your manners in the Wilson house."

"Do you aim to teach me manners?" Davies planted his feet apart and became belligerent.

"I don't make it my habit, because most who come here are gentlemen."

Davies cursed him and lunged.

Tom stepped aside easily and simultaneously landed a heavy punch that caught the younger man on the cheekbone, splitting his skin and drawing blood. Davies roared like a wounded animal and charged forward again, his thick fists flailing like hammers.

Tom had spent his youth in the rough neighborhood behind the London docks, and for the past fifteen years had lived on the edge of the wilderness. Even if Davies had been completely sober he would have been no match for the cool, methodical man who wove back and forth, avoiding punishment while taking the measure of his opponent.

Tom lashed out suddenly, catching Davies in the eye

and halting him. Before the astonished young farmer could recover, a succession of jabs peppered his face. He raised his arms to protect himself.

Putting his entire weight behind his next blow, Tom caught the younger man in the pit of the stomach.

Davies doubled over.

The next and final blow landed on his chin, momentarily straightening him, then sending him toppling backward. He landed on the hard ground with a thud and lay there in a daze, trying in vain to clear his head.

"Get off this property and don't come back." Tom's tone was calm and low. "If you do, you'll be trespassing, and next time I'll fill you with buckshot. What's more, stay away from Nettie. If you go near her again, you'll find you've had just a small taste of what will be coming to you."

He turned on his heel and strolled back to the main house, ignoring the curses that followed him.

Only Nettie saw him slip back into the dining room, and guessed what had happened. Tom accepted a heaping plate of food from one of the women, then sat down next to Nettie with a quiet smile. "You won't be troubled again," he told her.

She watched him as he took a thin knife with two tines at the end from his pocket, cut his meat with dexterity, and then began to eat. He seemed unconcerned.

Nettie reached out and touched the back of his hand. "You cut your knuckles," she said.

He seemed surprised as he glanced at the back of his hand. "I must have grazed them against a rock without knowing it," he said.

He was unlike any man she had ever before known. He had saved her from her tormentor, but his attitude made it plain that he wanted nothing from her in return.

"Thank you," was all she could say.

Tom shrugged. "Don't mention it," he said with sincerity.

Nettie was overwhelmed.

"Like I said before, I don't believe that lad will annoy you again," he said after consuming most of the food on his plate. "If he does, just let me know. He's been warned."

She couldn't recall a time when any man had raised a hand to protect her. All her life she had fought and struggled alone, on her own, and this experience bewildered her.

"Come to think of it, how did you get out here from town?" Tom asked.

"I—I walked," Nettie confessed, too embarrassed to offer the fuller explanation that she'd had no choice.

Tom became thoughtful. "It don't pay to take chances," he said. "I don't reckon there's much fight left in Davies, but he has enough rum punch in his belly to act mean. Let me know when you're ready to go back to town. I'll escort you myself to make sure there's no problem."

As Nettie thanked him she thought his motives were becoming clear. He would escort her into Fort Springfield, and then want to make love to her without paying a fee, a fair return for the service he had rendered her.

Tom misinterpreted her expression. "If you're thinking you'll be imposing on me," he said, "I give you my word that you won't. I've volunteered to take command of the militia night guard at the fort tonight. That way the officers with families can spend the whole holiday with their wives and young ones. So I'll be riding right past the center of town on my way to my duty station."

Nettie felt thoroughly ashamed of herself. Her first reaction had been right: this kind and gentle man really wanted nothing from her. For a long time she had despised all men, thinking they were selfish brutes, but here was one who really seemed different.

There was genuine warmth in her smile as she looked at Tom Hibbard.

Ida Alwin was annoyed with herself. Acting on sudden impulse, which she rarely did, she had invited Leverett Carswell to Deborah's wedding. Now, with the ceremony only twenty-four hours away, she was having second thoughts. Leverett was pleasant, but she didn't want him to get the wrong idea. And she could only hope he didn't think she was forward for having extended the invitation. Well, what was done couldn't be undone.

She wielded her broom vigorously, sweeping out the main room of her small log house even though it was already spotless. Deborah had gone into town for a wedding rehearsal, and Ida hated to admit to herself that she would be even lonelier after her niece moved into the new parsonage that members of the parish had just built.

A faint tap sounded at the door, and Ida answered the summons, the broom still in her hand.

A very young Indian brave stood in the entrance, his shaved head gleaming on either side of his scalp lock. His doeskin shirt, loincloth, and leggings were clean, but Ida vehemently distrusted most Indians and was on the verge of slamming the door when the young brave grinned at her.

"Walter!" Her heart stopped beating for a moment as they embraced.

Then Ba-lin-ta materialized out of nowhere and wanted to be hugged and kissed, too. "My brothers and the other warriors left Wal-ter and me here," she said. "They went with Jeff-rey to the house of Wil-son."

Ida was still almost speechless. Ba-lin-ta had grown taller, but it was her own son who fascinated her. He had sprouted, lost weight, and looked fit and hard. But his expression told the real story of the change in him. No longer shy and bitter, he stood confidently, and his eyes reflected the new sense of security he had acquired in the land of the Seneca.

The boy quickly demonstrated his talents. While Ba-lin-ta chattered, showing off her improved command of English, Walter went out to the woodpile, returned with an armload, and built up the fire, then filled a kettle and placed it on the fire.

He and Ba-lin-ta communicated swiftly, signaling to each other with their fingers. Then the girl opened a pouch on her belt and dropped the contents into the kettle.

Meanwhile Walter astonished his mother by picking her up and depositing her in her rocking chair.

"Wal-ter says we will let you do no work while we are here," Ba-lin-ta announced.

"How long will you stay?" Ida asked eagerly.

"Many days," Ba-lin-ta declared. "Renno will go very soon after the wedding, but he has told El-i-chi and the others to wait until Wal-ter and I are ready to go home."

A pungent, pleasant scent filled the cabin as a Seneca herb tea brewed. When it was ready, Walter, displaying a dexterity he had rarely shown, filled three cups with the tea. Then he went out into the open, returning with a pack made of buffalo hide, and from it he removed an object that resembled a thick sausage. Using the knife he carried in his belt, he cut off three generous chunks.

Ida had never eaten Indian food, and braced herself, but took care not to show her apprehension. A surprise awaited her. The roll, held together with cornmeal, contained dried venison, raisins, and chopped nuts, and was sweetened with maple syrup. It was delicious.

Again Walter reached into the pack and removed a dress of doeskin, which he presented to his mother. His gestures told their own story, and there was no need for Ba-lin-ta to interpret for him. He had shot the deer and cured the hide himself, and then, with Ba-lin-ta helping him, he had decorated it with porcupine quills he had dyed.

There were tears in Ida's eyes as she hurried up to the second floor of the log house to try on the dress. It fitted her almost perfectly, and her dislike of Indian attire suddenly vanished.

When she came back she hugged Ba-lin-ta again, then turned to her son.

Walter stood erect in the approved Seneca style, his arms folded across his chest, his face impassive. Then he read the disappointment in his mother's eyes, and knew that, even though he was becoming a warrior, he had to treat her in the only way she knew. Enveloping her in a fierce hug, he kissed her.

Ida made no attempt to stem the flow of tears that streamed down her face. Her son had been helpless in many ways. Now, almost three years later, he was self-reliant, well able to look after himself, his talents were developing, and he had acquired a great sensitivity to the people around him. It just didn't matter in the least anymore that he resembled an Indian brave rather than a white man.

If he continued to make progress, there was every reason to hope he would be able to lead the useful, happy life that had been denied to him before Ba-lin-ta had come into his world.

Mildred Wilson struggled into the snug-fitting dress of green velvet, trimmed with lace, that she saved for very special occasions. Her husband, already dressed in his militia dress uniform, sat in the most comfortable chair in their bedroom, watching and admiring her, even as his mind raced.

"How much time do I have?" Mildred demanded.

Andrew glanced at the clock on the mantel that had been in his family for generations. "Ample," he said. "Jeffrey has already gone, but Renno is waiting to ride with us."

"Will Walter Alwin be dressed as a warrior?"

"Of course, my dear. When I saw him this morning I realized he's already almost as much a Seneca as Renno and El-i-chi."

"Oh, dear," Mildred said with a sigh. "I feel sorry for poor Aunt Ida."

"Don't waste your sorrow," Andrew said. "She's so proud of her son she's ready to burst."

"Then you and Obadiah were right to urge that he go to the Seneca country." Mildred stood with her feet apart, her head cocked to one side as she put on her diamond earrings.

"Thanks to the Indian girl and the influence of

Renno. Walter patterns himself on Renno." Andrew paused. "In fact, I was just thinking that our Jeffrey does, too. It's Renno who has transformed him from a sullen ne'er-do-well into a responsible man."

"I've grown very fond of Renno," she said, "even though I must admit he makes me a little uneasy. It's so obvious, with his blue eyes and his fair hair—what there is of it on his scalp lock—that he's one of us. But at the same time he's so Indian, he sometimes confuses me."

"Just so he doesn't become confused himself," Andrew Wilson said.

Something in his tone caused his wife to glance up at him. "What's wrong, dear?"

"Yesterday, when Renno walked in with Jeffrey and announced he's willing to undertake the mission to London, I rejoiced. Just as Governor Shirley will rejoice when we reach Boston. Massachusetts Bay—and all of the other colonies—couldn't find a more perfect envoy to convince King William and the Privy Council that we need a great deal of help if we're to stave off the new French threat that Fort Louisburg will pose. But this morning I'm not all that happy."

Mildred dusted a light coating of rice powder on her face. "You no longer think Renno and Jeffrey will be able to accomplish what's needed at court?"

"I have confidence in both of them. But watching Renno at supper last night, seeing him doing his best to sit on a chair and use one of our tined knives as an eating utensil, well, it was almost too much."

Mildred dabbed light rouge on her lips, then looked at her husband in the reflection of her mirror. "I'm afraid I don't understand what you're trying to say, Andrew."

"Deborah knows Renno better than any of us. How well I'd rather not guess, particularly on her wedding day. But she has made it very clear in conversation with me that Renno realizes he's not an Indian by birth. He's very much conscious of the fact that he has white skin. And Obadiah says he actually discussed the problem with Renno many months ago."

"Why should it be a problem?"

37

"Watching Renno last night as he tried to conform to our ways made me aware of the inner struggle that must be tearing him apart." Colonel Wilson stood and buckled on his dress sword. "Frankly, the thought never crossed my mind during the campaign into Canada. Renno was the complete Seneca. That's how he thought, fought, acted, and lived at all times. But last night was different. He wanted to behave as we did."

"Then he *is* conscious of his unique position!"

He glanced at the clock and saw they still had a few minutes to spare. "I'm not suggesting that he broods. Jeffrey doesn't think so. We had a few private words after everyone else went to bed last night. It's Renno's future that concerns me. Massachusetts Bay needs him. So do Connecticut and Rhode Island and New York. But it strikes me we may be shortsighted. And damned selfish. What will we be doing to this young man who is still so impressionable?"

"I see now. You're wondering how he'll react to London." Mildred became grave.

Andrew nodded solemnly. "Yes, London—with a million people bustling through the streets. With its nose-in-the-air aristocracy, contemptuous of everyone below their own level, the relatives and so-called friends you and I escaped by coming here. London, with its merchants and bankers and fishmongers, its trollops and gamesters and highway robbers. Its earnest, hard-working people who know nothing about the world beyond the confines of the British Isles and hate all foreigners. Yes, and with the men and women of at least twenty other nations living or visiting there. Not to mention the taverns and other low places that came close to destroying Jeffrey."

"You're afraid that Londoners of every level will think of Renno as a freak."

"Of course they will, from King William to a chimney sweep, but that's the least of my concern. No man likes ridicule, so he'll be under pressure to change, to conform, to make himself like everyone else there. What I fear most is that if he tries to adapt himself to English civilization, he'll destroy his Seneca core—and in doing that he'll destroy himself."

"Then you mustn't send him," she said.

He shook his head. "It isn't that simple. If the French remain unopposed in the development of Louisburg and are allowed to strengthen their army and navy in the New World, it will mean the end of our own colonies here. What's more, their alliance with the Algonquian will become so powerful that the Seneca and the other nations of the Iroquois League will be defeated and become subject people. Through Renno we have our best chance, perhaps our only chance, to persuade the Crown to give us and the Iroquois the financial and military help we need to preserve our freedom. Renno will be running a risk, but the odds against all of us will be far greater if he doesn't go on this mission!"

The troubled couple went downstairs, and found Renno awaiting them in the largest of the parlors.

He sat cross-legged on the floor, ignoring the many chairs in the room. His head was shaved on either side of his scalp lock, he had smeared glistening oil on his face, arms, and body, and in spite of the cold weather he was wearing only a loincloth. Not only had he dressed as he would for a Seneca wedding, but he had smeared ceremonial green and yellow war paint on his face, torso, and arms. His tomahawk and knife hung from his belt, and his bow and quiver of arrows rested on the floor beside him. He was the complete warrior, the ultimate savage Indian.

Mildred smiled to herself. Her husband's fears were justified, she knew, but Renno appeared far from succumbing to the pressures of the white man.

The Wilsons rode into town in their carriage, flanked by Tom Hibbard and Renno, both mounted on geldings.

The wedding party was assembling, and Andrew, who would give away the bride, went off to join the others. His wife entered the church. Most guests had already taken their seats.

There was a stir when Ida Alwin came down the

aisle, followed by Ba-lin-ta and Walter, whose attire—or lack of it—resembled Renno's. The boy had insisted on appearing as a Seneca, and his mother was so grateful for his improvement that she made no objection, no longer caring what others thought.

Renno joined El-i-chi and the other warriors of the escort party. Wanting to remain as unobtrusive as possible, they perched uncomfortably on a bench in the rear pew. But it was impossible for the near-naked Seneca to remain unobserved. Members of the militia who had served in the Quebec campaign with Renno and El-i-chi left their own seats and came to greet them. Other friends Renno had made in Fort Springfield waved to him. But it was the newest immigrants who reacted the most strongly. They were startled by the presence of the savages, and took care to choose seats as far from them as possible.

Tom Hibbard deliberately moved toward a place beside Nettie, who sat alone. Afraid of being conspicuous, she was wearing a plain dress of dark gray wool, her makeup was subdued, and she stared straight ahead, paying no attention to the conviviality of others. As she felt someone slide into the pew beside her, she cast an oblique glance in that direction. Recognizing Tom, she felt relieved. There was one person in Fort Springfield, other than the bride and groom, who did not think of her as a pariah. She smiled in greeting, and impulsively touched Tom's arm to thank him.

He grinned at her in return, reddening when her fingertips brushed his sleeve. He felt sorry for the girl, and knowing the gnawing, bleak poverty of the London from which she had come, he understood her position. If he was any judge of character she was a decent person, and the least he could do was help her to hold her head a little higher.

Others were moving into the pew, forcing the couple to edge closer to each other until their shoulders touched. It appeared that they were attending the wedding together, and Nettie began to worry, afraid that Tom's proximity to her would injure his reputation.

He himself remained unconcerned. He was his own

master, beholden to no one, and people could accept or reject him, as they wished. Seeing Nettie frown apprehensively, he bent closer to her and whispered, "Don't you fret. Who cares what folks with mean souls and small minds think? I'll be happy to escort you to the reception after the wedding, and we'll really give them something to talk about."

She nodded and, afraid she would weep, turned away.

The side door of the church opened, and Reverend Obadiah Jenkins appeared, with Jeffrey Wilson as best man beside him. Both of them solemn, they walked to a place near the altar and waited there. Obadiah's eyes were bright, but he looked pale, and every married man present understood his nervousness.

The clergyman who would perform the ceremony, a visitor who had traveled more than sixty miles for the occasion, came in through the side door and stood behind the altar.

Two fiddlers began the strains of "Greensleeves," and Deborah Alwin, dazzling in a white gown, came down the center aisle on the arm of Colonel Wilson. Ever beautiful, she was a radiant bride.

Something stirred within Renno as he watched her move down the aisle. For months she had been his woman, and he felt a pang of regret that they had decided to part. That decision had been right, he told himself. Even though Deborah had lived as a Seneca, these were her people and she belonged here. Never could she have been as happy in the land of the Seneca, where she would have always been an outsider.

Just as he was an outsider here.

The ceremony was brief, and when the clergyman pronounced Obadiah and Deborah man and wife, Aunt Ida sniffed aloud. Walter grasped her hand and patted it.

Immediately following the wedding, the entire congregation adjourned to the parsonage, where the ladies had prepared refreshments. People formed in a long line and waited patiently for their turn to congratulate the groom and wish the bride happiness. Renno and his companions were unfamiliar with the custom and stood together outside the church, uncertain what to do next.

They were saved by Tom Hibbard and Nettie, who greeted Renno with the broad smile she reserved for real friends. He was delighted to see her, too. She had changed, and seemed far more reserved, but her eyes were still lively and warm.

"Come with us," Tom said. "First, we'll wish the bridal couple well, and then everyone will eat and drink."

Renno's face cleared. The ways of the colonists were more like those of the Seneca than he had realized. At home feasts also followed weddings, with warriors and women engaging in ceremonial dancing.

Tom offered Nettie his arm. She hesitated for a moment, then slipped her hand into the crook of his arm and walked beside him, her head high and her cheeks burning red.

The Seneca followed them, and when they moved inside the parsonage Renno caught a glimpse of Ba-lin-ta and Walter devouring slices of juicy meat served on chunks of the white wheat bread that had been unknown to the Indians until the English settled here. He saw that the two were completely at home, enjoying themselves thoroughly, and he envied them. They were as much at ease as they would have been at a Seneca festival in honor of the moon spirit.

The receiving line moved forward slowly. At last it was Renno's turn, and he raised his hand, fingers extended but together, in the traditional Seneca greeting of friendship.

Deborah Alwin Jenkins looked at him for a long moment. This was the white Indian who had saved her life, the man with whom she had lived and for months had believed she loved. He was still dear to her, even though she saw him differently now.

Obadiah knew of the affair and Deborah turned to him for an instant. He knew her intention and silently approved.

Deborah placed her hands on Renno's shoulders,

then kissed him full on the mouth. Her gesture was far more than it appeared to those who witnessed it; she had exorcised a ghost of the past and was free now to give herself to her husband without reservation.

Renno realized that something out of the ordinary had happened, but all he knew for certain as he shook hands with Obadiah in the English manner, then moved on, was that the newlyweds were his good friends. If they called on him for help he would gladly give them all he owned, and they would be equally generous if he found himself in serious difficulties. Obadiah had become his brother and Deborah was his sister.

He realized, too, when he saw Nettie standing shyly in a parlor corner, sipping wine with Tom Hibbard, that she was another with whom his relationship was forever changed. He had needed Nettie at a time when the ways of the settlers had confused and disturbed him, and she had needed him, too. He would always be her friend, but she seemed to have found a protector in Tom, and he approved. Hibbard was a cautious man, but in battle he was ferocious, a natural leader, and Nettie deserved a warrior on whom she could depend.

Renno's comrades-in-arms in the Quebec compaign greeted him vociferously, and offered him ale and wine. But he declined. He disliked the taste of the alcoholic beverages the settlers drank, and he hated the feeling of dizziness they caused.

Jeffrey Wilson was engaged in a discussion with a pretty girl, a vivacious newcomer to Fort Springfield, and Renno's instinct told him his friend would not welcome an interruption. Feeling he had no real place at these festivities, he slipped out into the open, where the air was cold and clean.

Walter and Ba-lin-ta had gone outside also, and the girl was being initiated into the mysteries of rolling a hoop, an art that Walter performed with great skill. Ba-lin-ta learned quickly, and soon they were engaged in a race across the frozen ground on the parsonage lawn. Renno watched them with amusement.

A burly young man in linsey-woolsey, obviously not

an invited guest, moved slowly down the dirt street, then halted as he listened to the laughter and talk coming from the house.

Renno didn't know Jack Davies, but guessed from the man's walk that he had been drinking quite a bit.

Walter and Ba-lin-ta were concentrating so hard on striking their hoops that they failed to see Davies, and Ba-lin-ta crashed into him, almost knocking him down.

The startled girl apologized at once. Davies stared hard at her, then at Walter, his eyes glittering. "What are you damn little savages doing in this town? Get out before I skin you alive!"

"De-bo-rah is the cousin of Wal-ter," Ba-lin-ta explained. "We saw her marriage."

Renno, concealed by a bramble bush, made no move, but watched closely. It was obvious to him that the drunken man was hostile and Renno was prepared to intervene.

"This half-naked barbarian is Deborah Alwin's cousin?" Davies demanded. "Is that true, boy?"

Walter, lacking the power of speech, could not reply.

Ba-lin-ta moved between them. "I have spoken the truth," she said quietly.

Davies raised a hand and tried to slap her. Renno's hand crept to the handle of his tomahawk. He could throw it with sufficient force to knock the bully unconscious without doing him permanent harm.

Ba-lin-ta ducked and avoided the blow. Davies cursed her and would have tried to strike her again, but suddenly Walter acted.

Drawing his Seneca knife, the youth leaped forward and held it close to the man's throat. The menace was real, and Davies knew from the expression in the savage's eyes that he would gladly kill him.

Renno waited, his tomahawk in his hand, a half-smile on his lips as he watched the incensed Walter.

Davies took a step backward. "You're mad," he said. "Go away before I do you real harm."

Walter caught hold of the man's short jacket, preventing his escape, and again brandished the knife, holding it close to the man's throat.

Davies's fear turned to panic when Walter disarmed him, snatching the man's pistol from his belt with his free hand and throwing it far from Davies's reach.

Using his superior strength, Davies broke away and ran off, hoping to retrieve his pistol before anyone saw that he had been disgraced.

Renno laughed aloud. Only two years earlier, Walter would have been helpless, but now he was well able to take care of himself and protect Ba-lin-ta, too.

Addressing them in the tongue of the Seneca, Renno called, "Come." The young ones saw him and, picking up their hoops, obeyed at once.

"You have done well," Renno, told them. "Now go into the longhouse before there is real trouble."

They grinned at him, then hurried into the parsonage.

Davies's courage returned when he picked up his pistol, and he decided to teach the little savages a lesson they wouldn't forget. He changed his mind, however, when he saw the tall brave daubed with war paint, a tomahawk in one hand, silently observing him. There were Indians everywhere today, he thought, and promptly forgot his intention of attending the reception as an uninvited guest.

Renno watched him as he hurried away, weaving from one side of the street to the other.

It was moments like this that made Renno despise the white man's ways. No Seneca warrior would have behaved as Davies had done. Had children injured the dignity of a Seneca, he would have either ignored the incident or reported them to their mother, leaving their punishment to her. Certainly it was beneath the dignity of a grown man to threaten a boy of sixteen summers and a girl who was even younger.

He had the consolation of being able to rejoice at the change in Walter. If the boy's mother allowed him to remain with the Seneca, he would become a true warrior, expecting no favors because of his disabilities as he took his place with his peers.

The incident disturbed Renno's calm. In two days he and Jeffrey would accompany Colonel Wilson to Boston, and soon thereafter he and his friend would sail on a great ship across the great lake of salt water to England. Perhaps the scene he had just witnessed was an omen, a sign warning him not to make the long journey.

Then he remembered his dream. He recalled, too, the relief and pleasure the colonel had shown when he had learned that Renno had consented to become a special envoy.

It was impossible to refuse to go. Too much was at stake, including his own honor.

Chapter III

English visitors to Boston often said they knew the town was provincial because it came alive so early in the morning. An hour after the sun rose, cowherds driving cattle to the Common to graze often argued heatedly with shepherds already there with their flocks. Merchants and ships' brokers, attorneys and importers rode up and down the narrow streets, their horses' hooves clattering on the cobblestones as the men made their way to and from meetings on which the commercial life of Massachusetts Bay depended. Housewives and maidservants were already on their way home with their day's purchases of meat and fish, greens and other foods procured at the markets that opened before dawn.

In the harbor, visible from the peak of Beacon Hill, ships prepared to sail on the morning tide, and fishing boats returned with their day's catch. The town's trollops, heavily painted, roamed the streets looking for trade, and constables armed with long staves patrolled in pairs, duti-

fully visiting banks, inns, and taverns to make certain all
was well.

Members of the Assembly, the colony's legislature,
gathered in the new brick building that had just been built
for them and would spend the day arguing issues of war
and peace and taxation that they had no power to
resolve. And in the handsome residence of white clapboard known as the Governor's House, a meeting of
importance to the future of all English colonies was
taking place in a second-floor office.

Florid, square-faced Governor William Shirley, his
wig hanging far below the collar of his silver-buttoned
coat, sat behind his desk of gleaming oak and, after
talking steadily for a half hour, wondered what he could
say that would impress the impassive young Seneca who
sat opposite him.

The governor glanced at Colonel Andrew Wilson,
whose relaxed air belied the tension he felt, then rose to
his feet, suddenly inspired. Crossing the room, he pointed
to a copy of a portrait of King William III that had
arrived in Boston only recently.

"This," the governor said, "is the Great Sachem of
the English."

Renno thought it remarkable that these people could
make drawings that looked like a man's reflection in the
smooth surface of a lake.

"What do you think of him?"

Renno shrugged. "I do not know until I meet him."

"He is a good, honest man." Shirley knew it would
be useless to explain that William had been the Prince of
Orange, ruler of the Netherlands, and that he and his
wife, Mary, the daughter of Britain's James II, ascended
the throne when James had been deposed. William was
conscientious and hard-working, but he was not English by birth and consequently lacked instinctive sympathy for the nation's New World colonies. "He knows
as little about Indians as you know about him. He has
never visited Boston or New York or Fort Springfield,
so he does not understand our problems."

"Jeff-rey and I will speak with him and will tell him," Renno said.

Again Shirley glanced at Colonel Wilson. The governor was hesitant to explain that it might require many weeks to arrange an audience with King William. Not wanting to discourage the envoy, he remained silent.

Colonel Wilson intervened. "I have brothers and cousins in London who will help Renno. They are members of William's council." His implication was that the King listened to advice, which wasn't necessarily true.

The governor turned to Jeffrey Wilson. "There are complicating factors in the situation. Louis of France is a bigot who has revoked the Edict of Nantes, which guaranteed religious freedom to French Protestants. Since the Toleration Act gave nonconformist Protestants the freedom to worship on British soil, these people, who call themselves Huguenots, are coming to Massachusetts Bay by the hundreds. In the next few years we expect to receive several thousand refugees. William is so incensed with the persecution going on in France that we hear he's thinking in terms of a holy war against Louis. As someone who spent his entire life—until recently—on the continent, he thinks only in terms of waging war in Europe. No one has been able to convince him that the stakes on this side of the Atlantic are also enormous."

"We'll do our best to persuade him, Your Excellency," Jeffrey said.

"That won't be necessary," the governor continued. "We have powerful friends at court who will do the necessary talking after we win King William's attention. You'll also be amply supplied with letters to people in high places who will help you. Renno isn't being sent to court to speak. He's being sent to attract the King's attention."

Colonel Wilson nodded. "That's precisely what I've been telling you, son. Use Renno for purposes of pure drama, and William will listen to us. Try any other method and you'll be wasting your time."

Jeffrey nodded.

Renno understood only a portion of the discussion. He took it for granted that, as the son of the Great Sachem of the Iroquois, he would be made welcome and courteously received by the Great Sachem of the English.

The governor walked to the door and shook hands with the two young men. "Succeed," he said, "and the English colonies in America will flourish. Fail, and the governor of New France will sit in this office."

They went straight from the Governor's House to the waterfront. There Colonel Wilson pointed out their ship, riding at anchor, to Renno.

The white Indian marveled at the vessel, which was many times larger than a Seneca longhouse, and wondered how it stayed afloat. But his friends had assured him it was safe and he had to trust them.

The sea chests and several boxes of provisions that the colonel had bought for them were already loaded into the ship's gig, and now it was time for the pair to depart. Andrew Wilson embraced his son, then hugged Renno. Rarely one to display emotion, he spoke huskily. "May God go with you," he said.

Four sailors manned the oars, and the gig threaded her way through the harbor to the waiting ship. She was a square-rigged brig of almost three thousand tons, the *Elizabeth Louise*, and her hold was filled with a cargo of timber and furs, New World products in great demand in England.

A rope ladder was lowered from the main deck, and Jeffrey climbed it, followed by Renno, who scaled it with ease.

The ship's master, Captain Edgar Winslow of Boston, a red-faced man in his thirties, awaited them. He raised an eyebrow when he saw the pale-eyed savage but made no comment. He was being paid a handsome sum for taking these passengers to England, and he knew that Governor Shirley himself was interested in their welfare. "Welcome aboard, gentlemen," he said.

"The Atlantic kicks up her heels at this time of year, so I hope you're good sailors. You'll eat in the saloon with either Mate Watts or me, whichever of us doesn't have the watch. Skinner!"

The bo's'n, a lean-faced, exceptionally tall man with a toothless grin, materialized from the direction of the aft deck.

"Show the passengers to their quarters and see to it that their gear is properly stowed. We sail within the hour."

Skinner led the two young men to a tiny cabin furnished with double-decked bunks, a shelf that dropped from a bulkhead to make a table, and large slop jar. The sea chests, already in place, would serve as chairs.

Bo's'n Skinner pulled off his knitted stocking cap to scratch his balding head. "If ye think this here is cramped," he said, "wait till ye see the crew's quarters. At least ye have a window." With the sailing imminent he was busy, and with these words he took himself elsewhere.

"Ordinarily," Jeffrey said, "I'd flip a coin to see which of us takes which bunk. But I've been to sea and you haven't, so I'll give you the dubious privilege of sleeping in the lower."

His tone, like that of the bo's'n, indicated that neither entertained a high opinion of the cabin, but Renno was impressed. Although it was only a fraction of the size of his own hut, it was nevertheless a private room with two beds in it, and it astonished him that there could be such quarters on a ship. He reached up to touch the lamp hanging overhead and again was impressed when he discovered it was remarkably similar to a contraption in the Wilson home that shed light at night. The sea chests were far more comfortable for sitting than the deck, and the boxes of provisions slid neatly out of the way beneath the lower bunk.

Nearby, down a narrow passageway, was the saloon, a truly large cabin furnished with a dining table, armchairs, and a spittoon. Several lamps hung overhead.

Behind the cabin was the galley, which boasted a wood-burning stove that stood in a box filled with sand. Renno realized the sand was to prevent a fire from spreading, and he was again impressed by the ship designer's ingenuity.

The passengers went onto the deck, and Captain Winslow invited them to watch the sailing from his quarterdeck. "Just stay out of the way when we're busy," he said brusquely.

Soon the brig came alive. The captain barked orders that were incomprehensible to Renno. Mate Watts, a short, stocky man, stood nearby, keeping a close watch on the activity, while the helmsman waited patiently at his wheel. The auxiliary sails were unfurled, making a loud, flapping noise before they became fully extended and filled with the wind. Then, under Bo's'n Skinner's direction, the anchor was raised and the mainsail was hoisted. As it, too, caught the breeze the brig tacked and began to make her way rapidly out of the harbor.

Renno marveled at the ability of the helmsman to avoid hitting other ships that were riding at anchor. It was miraculous that men could control the movements of this great bird.

The open Atlantic was choppy, with whitecaps creating a froth on the crest of waves, and the *Elizabeth Louise* began to pitch and roll. To Renno's surprise he felt queasy.

Jeffrey saw that he was becoming pale. "Don't go to the cabin to lie down," he advised. "Stay out here in the open."

Renno watched the seagulls circling overhead and envied them because they were not subject to the erratic motion of the brig. He hadn't known what to expect and found the sensation distinctly unpleasant. When he became chilly he went to the cabin for his cloak of buffalo hide, but immediately returned to the deck.

The land that lay to the west slowly vanished on the horizon. The frail brig was at the mercy of the elements. Renno hoped that the ship's master and crew could find their way to England across the vast expanses of water, which had no trails and no landmarks to guide them.

Shipboard routines were established within twenty-four hours of the brig's departure. Renno was awake at dawn, and to the astonishment of the crew he drew a pail of cold water from the sea and washed in it without showing any signs of discomfort. Meals were more than adequate, as they would be for several days until the supplies of fresh meat, bread, fruits, and vegetables ran out. Then everyone on board would have to eat pickled meats, smoked fish, and biscuits known as hardtack, which had to be dipped in water, rum, or steaming mugs of tea to make them edible.

Restless in the ship's limited space, Renno spent long hours roaming the deck. The two officers and fourteen members of the crew accepted him with some reservations. All were colonials and consequently were accustomed to the Indians of various New England tribes. But this tall, powerfully built Seneca with blond hair and blue eyes who spoke and understood English had them baffled. He was the good friend of the renowned Colonel Andrew Wilson's son, however, so they refrained from passing judgment on him. Experience had taught them that a man's true character would inevitably be revealed on a six-week ocean voyage. Renno had just such an opportunity sooner than anyone anticipated.

At midday of the third day, shortly before the noon meal, the lookout in the crow's nest called down to the quarterdeck, "There's a ship off to port, a-heading toward us!"

The captain cupped his hands. "Has she identified herself?"

"Not yet, sir. She's a sloop, and from the looks of her, she's very fast."

"Mr. Watts," Winslow said, "be good enough to run up our pennants."

The British Union Jack and the Massachusetts Bay flag were hoisted to the brig's yardarm.

The sloop continued to draw closer, and Renno watched in fascination as it seemed to fly across the surface of the sea.

Suddenly a cannon roared, and a six-pounder ball of iron crossed the bow of the *Elizabeth Louise*, falling harmlessly into the Atlantic. At the same time the stranger hoisted her own flag, a white banner dotted with rows of golden fleurs-de-lis.

"She's a French privateer!" Captain Wilson shouted. "All hands to arms."

Jeffrey and Renno hurried to their own cabin for weapons. "It's plain the French are already operating out of Louisburg," Jeffrey said. "A privateer supposedly has no official connection with the French government, which can deny she's under their protection. But that's nonsense. I'm afraid we're going to have our hands full." He loaded his pistols, filled his pockets with ammunition, buckled on his sword, and slung a powder horn around his neck.

Renno, who always carried his tomahawk and knife, silently selected his strongest bow and took a quiver filled with arrows from his sea chest. He hated to admit that the unexpected prospect of a battle pleased him, that the lack of activity at sea had begun to bore him.

The sloop was much closer when they returned to the quarterdeck, her own deck lined with men carrying pistols, knives, and cutlasses.

Captain Winslow described the situation briefly to his two passengers. "We're outnumbered about two to one, as near as I can make out," he said. "If they can, they'll kill every last one of us and send our ship back to Louisburg with a prize crew."

Several shots sounded from the sloop, but the aim of her sailors was faulty.

"That's a waste of powder and ammunition," Jeffrey said. "They need arms more powerful than pistols at this distance."

Renno nodded thoughtfully, tested the strength and direction of the wind with a moistened finger, and notched an arrow into his bow. The others on the quarterdeck watched him curiously.

He waited until the brig descended into the trough of a wave. Then, taking careful aim, he let fly.

Bo's'n Skinner shouted in triumph. "You hit one of the bastards, Indian!"

A faint smile touched the corners of Renno's mouth when he saw a man on the privateer's quarterdeck stagger to the rail with the arrow protruding from his body and fall before he could steady himself. A battle at sea was remarkably similar to one in the forest, except that here there was no place to hide.

Well, that couldn't be helped, and he calmly took another arrow from his quiver. The Frenchmen began to fire at him, but their bullets fell far short of their target.

Renno studied them briefly and selected a man who towered above his companions and was conspicuous because he wore a bandanna of red silk on his head. Again testing the capricious wind; he let loose his second arrow.

There was a moment of shocked silence on both ships as the giant crumpled, the arrow landing between his eyes. Then the New Englanders cheered.

But the battle was just beginning. Several members of the privateer's crew, grappling hooks in their hands, leaped to the rail as the vessels drew close together.

Even Renno realized they intended to lash the two ships together.

"Prepare to repel boarders!" Captain Winslow shouted.

Mate Watts raced to the main deck rail, as did Jeffrey, who drew his sword as he ran.

Renno remained on the quarterdeck with Winslow and the helmsman. The difference in height of about five feet made it possible for him to look down at the enemy, an important advantage.

Wood ground against wood as the ships came together, the grappling hooks were made fast and held, and the invaders began to swarm onto the *Elizabeth Louise*.

Renno unleashed a stream of arrows into the milling, struggling throng below. Steel clashed against steel, pistols were fired, and men on both sides shouted and screamed.

But Renno remained calm, as befitted a senior warrior of the Seneca, and sent arrow after arrow into the ranks of his foes. He felt a grim satisfaction as he saw that he killed two more of the attackers and wounded a third.

Jeffrey, wielding his sword with skill and grace, was engaged in a desperate duel with one of the privateer's officers, and for a moment Renno paused to admire his finesse. Suddenly there was a break, and the Frenchman staggered backward, severely wounded. He had to be helped to return to his own ship.

The men fighting below were packed together in such a dense mass that it was becoming difficult for Renno to distinguish friend from foe. The time had come for him to join in the hand-to-hand combat. He laid aside his bow and arrows, then drew in his breath as he took his tomahawk and knife from his belt.

Suddenly the ferocious war cry of the Seneca sounded above the din of battle, and the savage hurtled into the melee.

The startled attackers had enough. This half-naked demon destroyed what was left of their nerve, and they retreated to the privateer, leaving their dead behind and allowing the wounded to follow as best they could.

Within moments the fight was at an end. The French hastily cut the lines that tied the two ships together, and the sloop moved off in retreat.

A proud Bo's'n Skinner reported to the captain that none of the crew had been killed. Two of the seamen had suffered wounds, but neither was severely injured.

Renno paid no attention to the hubbub around him and methodically scalped the two Frenchmen he had killed, then heaved their bodies overboard. No one tried to stop him.

Captain Winslow ordered the brig to resume her

course, then joined Renno. "Indian," he said, "thanks to you we beat them. I've never seen anything like your performance."

Renno shrugged. He had done his duty, nothing more, but his spirit was troubled. For the moment, however, he said nothing.

The wounded were attended, the crew scrubbed away the marks of battle, and after everyone on board had congratulated and thanked Renno, officers and sailors ate their delayed noon meal.

Not until later, when Renno stood alone with Jeffrey on deck, did he unburden himself. "You are a fine warrior," he said. "I watched you drive your sword into the body of your enemy. No one could have done it better."

Jeffrey laughed. "Well, he extended me, I must admit. But I can't help wishing I could use a bow and arrow as you do. What you did was astonishing."

The praise fell on deaf ears. "I have learned to use the firesticks of the English," Renno said. "I like my arrows and my tomahawk more, but I can hit the target with a firestick." He stared down at the deck and lowered his voice. "I do not know how to use the long knife that you use so well."

"Forget it," Jeffrey said. "With all of your other skills, you don't need a sword."

"A true senior warrior," Renno replied stubbornly, "needs to use every kind of weapon. You will teach me use of the long knife."

"All right," he said. "After we get to London, I'll either give you fencing lessons myself or hire a teacher for you."

"No," Renno replied, his jaw jutting forward. "On this ship we have nothing to do. We start now!"

A short time later the first lesson began and lasted the better part of the afternoon, until Jeffrey's arm became so weary he could no longer raise it.

Thereafter, regardless of the weather, the pair spent hours on the aft deck every day, their blades clashing.

Members of the crew watched in fascination as Renno's skills improved, but he himself was never satisfied. He was a natural athlete, his eyesight extraordinary, and his sense of balance better that most, but he still knew that only incessant practice would enable him to act and react instantly and instinctively when he held a sword in his hand.

"I go to land of the English," he said repeatedly. "So it is right that I use the long knife in the way the English use it."

Jeffrey was convinced Renno would eventually become a truly superior swordsman. And he had to admit that, in the meantime, he was sharpening his own skills, as well.

Alain de Gramont shaved his head on either side of his scalp lock, stared out of the window of his quarters in Quebec's Citadel, and then reluctantly donned his uniform as a colonel of light infantry in the army of His Christian Majesty, Louis XIV. Left to his own devices, he would have preferred the loincloth of the Huron.

For twenty years, ever since his wife and baby daughter had been killed in a Seneca raid on his farm near the village of Montreal, Alain de Gramont had been leading a double life. He commanded the most efficient, best-disciplined regiment in New France, twice receiving official commendations for his superior unit. At the same time he was a leader of the Huron, living with them for months at a time, leading warriors on raids and in battles against their joint foes.

Today Alain de Gramont was the complete Frenchman. The new commander in chief of all French forces in the New World, Lieutenant General Etienne de Martine, had arrived the previous night from Fort Louisburg on Cape Breton Island and wanted to confer with him. French generals rarely earned Alain's respect, but de Martine was different. He had arrived at Louisburg with four thousand veterans of his own command, and his record as a soldier was brilliant. For once Paris had given the highest post in America to a man who knew how to fight.

Alain hoped that General de Martine would grant him a furlough to complete some unfinished business of his own, but that was unlikely. Well, if need be, he could postpone his feud with the young Seneca known as Renno. It was odd that their paths had crossed so often, but perhaps it was destiny, since both were white Indians.

When Renno had been very young, Alain had spared his life, content to wait until he grew older and more skilled. Then, in the attack of the English colonists and Iroquois on Quebec, Renno had had the upper hand when Alain's pistol had jammed, leaving Alain totally unarmed. Alain had retreated, and his humiliation still smarted.

Next time Renno would not escape. Somehow he had become the symbol of all that Alain hated, and not until his scalp was hanging from Alain's belt would he feel that his wife and daughter had been avenged. Damn the generals who interfered with the all-important vendetta that would give him peace of mind after two decades of torment.

But there was no way to avoid the inevitable. Colonel Alain de Gramont clapped his plumed helmet onto his head, adjusted his sword belt, and walked across the parade ground to the quarters that, prior to the building of Fort Louisburg, had been the permanent headquarters of the general-in-command.

The grizzled Etienne de Martine, his face as wrinkled and leathery as an old boot, read a sheaf of regimental reports as he sat in front of a roaring fire. Alain stood at rigid attention before him, saluted, and waited to be recognized.

"Good morning, Gramont," the general said, not looking up from his papers. "Do sit down and make yourself comfortable. I'll give you my attention shortly."

Alain sat opposite him, stretched out his legs, and studied his new superior. Thank God the War Ministry had chosen a real commander for the New World forces instead of another simpering fop who had ingratiated himself with King Louis. The only decoration that General de Martine wore was the broad, pale blue ribbon of the Order of the Golden Fleece, France's highest award. His boots were polished, but were not new, and the buttons on his tunic were made of brass, not the gold that his predecessors had favored. The sword that rested beside him was a real combat weapon, not an ornamental toy.

Lieutenant General de Martine put down his papers, looked hard at the younger man, and said curtly, "We meet at last."

"I'm flattered, sir, that you've heard of me."

"Rubbish. I've read every report you've written in the past five years, including your frequent resignation threats. Why didn't you like any of our previous commanders?"

"Because they weren't soldiers, General. They were Versailles courtiers masquerading as generals."

A faint hint of a smile appeared in de Martine's eyes. "What makes you think I'm any better?"

"I've been following your career since I was a lieutenant." Alain matched his superior's bluntness.

"Yet you ask to remain in Quebec for the present rather than accept a transfer to Louisburg."

"I'm closer to the enemy here, General. And closer to my Huron."

"Ah, yes, the Huron. Please remove your helmet."

Alain had to obey.

"It's true, then. You do assume the guise of an Indian," the general said, looking at the younger man's scalp lock.

"Allow me to correct you, sir," Alain said crisply. "I assume no guise. When I join my warriors, I become a Huron. I am one of them."

"I stand corrected," the general said gravely. "For the present, Gramont, I've granted you a respite and won't bring you to Louisburg."

Alain inclined his head in a gesture of thanks.

"When I plan my major campaign against the English colonies and their Indian allies, however, I'll send for you. No one else appears to understand the savages and the best way to use them in a campaign."

"Then I'm free to follow my own inclinations for a time, sir?" Alain asked eagerly.

"Not so fast. You are not. I sent for you because I have another assignment for you."

Alain swallowed his disappointment. "Yes, sir?"

"For the past two months, I've been negotiating with the Algonquian. It's my understanding they're the largest tribe by far on the North American seacoast."

"They are, General, but they've fought no war in a long time, and too many years of peace have made them soft. They'll need motivation if they're to be of any use to us as allies."

"I charge you with the responsibility for finding ways to inspire them. But first we must bind them to us with a treaty. They've agreed to the very generous terms I've proposed to them, including giving them arms and supplies of all kinds. But they won't sign a treaty with me. They insist they'll only exchange wampum with you. Why, I don't know."

Alain laughed. "Meaning no disrespect, sir, but your predecessors formed the bad habit of breaking their word. The Algonquian, like so many other Indian nations, know that when I make a promise, I keep it."

"Very well. I direct you to go to the country of the Algonquian and conclude a treaty with them. My aide-de-camp will give you the complete terms."

"Yes, sir." Alain debated whether to ask for extra time to raid the Seneca and, hopefully, confront Renno, but thought better of it. It would be necessary to pass through the lands of the Mohawk and Cayuga, then thread a retreat through hostile Iroquois country, and the venture might take as long as a month. His rendezvous with Renno would have to wait.

"I suppose," the general said, "you have some notion of how you intend to inspire the Algonquian."

Alain's eyes gleamed. "I have very definite ideas, sir. But I believe you might prefer not to know them."

General de Martine knew that Gramont could be utterly unscrupulous. King Louis, on the other hand, sometimes displayed unexpected sentiment, which he conveyed to the War Ministry, particularly at moments when his conscience bothered him. Consequently it might be best to remain ignorant of unethical acts performed by his subordinates. "You'll do whatever you feel is right and proper, Gramont," he said. "When I trust a subordinate, I believe in giving him his head."

"Thank you very much, sir."

The general dismissed him with a curt wave. "We'll meet again late in the spring or early summer," he said. "That's when you'll join my staff at Louisburg."

Alain obtained a copy of the proposed treaty with the Algonquian, then changed into Indian attire and left without delay for the main town of the Huron.

Arriving there a scant day and a half later, he was greeted with great warmth by the sachem and the elders of the tribe. He then amassed a patrol from the scores of warriors who volunteered to accompany him. Alain selected only veterans who had served with him previously, men who he knew would obey him without hesitation or question.

They marched south through snow and ice, their destination the main town of the Algonquian, located in the Maine District of Massachusetts Bay.

The march was arduous, but the Huron warriors encountered few difficulties, living on the supplies of jerked meat and parched corn they brought with them. It was said that only the Seneca could go on the trail with success at this season, but the Huron were often able to match the feats of the people who, in the distant past, had been their cousins.

One morning, an Alonquian sentry appeared from behind a screen of evergreens. The Huron scouts greeted him with the sign of peace, and Gramont immediately came forward from his place in the column.

"Golden Eagle of the Huron," he said, "comes in friendship to greet Lo-Ronga of the Algonquian."

It quickly became obvious that other sentries were lurking nearby. Hidden drums announced their approach, and the first sentry conducted the visitors another five miles. At last they came to the palisade of the Algonquian town, and the residents turned out in force in spite of the bitter cold.

The Huron were taken to the longhouses, and Alain became the guest of the sachem, Lo-Ronga, in his smaller, private dwelling. There they followed the Indian custom and did not discuss business immediately. A special meal was prepared, and later a sister-in-law of Lo-Ronga was summoned to sleep with Alain.

Not until the following morning, after breakfast, was the treaty discussed. The Algonquian examined each clause, and only twice did Alain correct his interpretation. Late in the morning the alliance was formalized by the exchange of wampum made of mussel shells.

The visitors remained for another day and night, then departed at dawn, heading north. They marched steadily, but late in the afternoon, after they had moved far beyond the screen of Algonquian sentries, Alain gave an abrupt order.

His surprised warriors instantly started off in a new direction, toward the southwest. They stayed on this course for the next three days. Then, early one morning, Alain told his men to wash off their war paint with snow.

The request was extraordinary, and they looked at each other uneasily, but they did his bidding.

Alain then daubed himself with red paint from a pouch he had carried from Quebec, and then passed the container to his men.

Again they followed his lead, but one senior warrior protested. "This is the color of the Algonquian!"

"That is true," Alain replied calmly, and continued to smear streaks on his face and forehead.

"It is the wish of Golden Eagle that we appear as Algonquian?"

"For the next half-moon," he replied, "the whole world will think we are Algonquian, especially the English colonists. We will make our way down the Connecticut River through the lands the English call New Hampshire, Massachusetts Bay, and Connecticut. In the towns on the river we will make many raids. We will burn houses and take much booty. When a man stands in your way, kill him. When you see a woman you want, do what you wish with her."

The idea appealed to the warriors, and they applied the red paint with greater enthusiasm.

But the senior warrior was puzzled. "Why do we not wear our own paint? Why do we wear the color of the Algonquian when we raid these towns of the English?"

"The Algonquian," Alain said, speaking slowly, "have been at peace for many years. Now they are the allies of the Huron, the Ottawa, and the French. But they have no hate in their hearts for the colonists who have come here from England."

"The colonists," the senior warrior said, "will think we are Algonquian. They will be very angry, and they will send their warriors who carry firesticks to punish the Algonquian. Many Algonquian will die!"

Alain chuckled and nodded. "It will be as you say. And the Algonquian will believe that the English colonists have attacked them without reason. There will be much hate in the hearts of the Algonquian, and then they will fight hard, with much valor, at the side of their new brothers, the Huron."

The warriors laughed aloud, pleased by the cleverness of the deception.

Alain told himself the scheme could not fail. He had found a way to guarantee that the largest of the Indian nations would do its utmost to help win the new war that would erupt within a few months.

Everyone in Fort Springfield was interested in the newest arrivals in the community. Rene Gautier was a carpenter. His wife, Louise, was clever with a needle, and it was obvious to all that they were devoted to their two small children. They established a claim to land adjacent to Ida Alwin's property, and in spite of bad weather, Rene began at once to cut down trees to build a house. Tom Hibbard and half a dozen other men helped. In the meantime the Wilsons insisted that the newcomers stay with them.

The Gautiers created a stir because, unlike everyone else in the area, they were French rather than English. They had spent only a year in the south of England before coming to the New World, so they were still struggling to master their new language. What aroused the sympathy of the community was that they were Huguenots, living proof of the anti-Protestant prejudice that King Louis XIV had unleashed when he revoked the Edict of Nantes several years earlier.

"At first," Rene told his new acquaintances, "we try to stay in Rheims. We have many friends there, many good neighbors. But the King, he does not want these people to be our friends. He send soldiers to tell them they will go to prison if they speak to us. Still we stay. Then an old friend tell us we will go to prison if we stay. The King, he will take our children away from us. What can we do? We sell everything and go to Southampton. There we work for a year so we can earn the money to come to America. Here we start a new life."

Almost everyone pitched in to help the newcomers. Rene was enrolled in the militia, and the colonel promptly issued him the musket he needed to defend himself and his family. Leverett Carswell quietly made Louise a gift of several lengths of cloth so she could make some new clothing. Ida Alwin contributed a kettle and frying pan. Deborah and Obadiah Jenkins invited the family to the parsonage regularly for meals, and tried to think of some way for them to earn a steady income while they established their farm. Nettie joined in the community's spirit, too, and discovering that she and Louise wore the same size shoes, gave the Frenchwoman a pair of her own, claiming they pinched her feet.

Only Jack Davies and a few of his cronies remained aloof, refusing to join in the work on the cabin and clearing of the land, saying they hated all foreigners. But Tom Hibbard generously gave two afternoons of his time every week along with many others.

It was Deborah who thought of an income-producing plan and set it in motion. She was sparked by the discovery that Nettie could sew, and she went to her husband with the news.

"Nettie is trapped, you know," she said. "She can't afford to change her vocation until she develops some other means of earning a living. I'm convinced she wants to change and I have a simple idea. There are many women in the area who are so busy helping their husbands on their farms that they have no time to make clothes and curtains and bedspreads and sheets. And some of them are very clumsy with a needle and thread. Aunt Ida and I can't help all of them. So I'm wondering if it might be possible for Louise Gautier and Nettie to go into business together as seamstresses. They could work together at Nettie's place until the Gautier house is ready to be occupied."

The clergyman heartily approved.

"The only problem is that I don't want to appear to be interfering or pushing. I'm learning that people think a minister's wife likes to carry a halo around her head."

Obadiah laughed. "It should be easy enough to arrange. Speak to Louise and Nettie separately. Be casual about it, and just drop the idea into your conversation. If they like it, they'll get together in their own time and their own way."

Deborah followed her husband's advice, and both

young women responded eagerly. It was Nettie who took the initiative. Knowing that Louise brought Rene his lunch every day as he labored on the new house, she decided to meet her there.

The weather was raw and a bitter wind blew across the Connecticut River from the limitless forests that lay to the west, but Nettie was warm in the lynx coat given to her by a trapper in return for her services. Only her footgear bothered her; she owned no shoes with sensible, low heels, but she managed to walk briskly.

Nettie came to the top of a hill, and from there she had a clear view of the half-completed Gautier house. Rene was hard at work, sawing lengths of wood with the expert ease that only a man who had been a carpenter all his life could achieve. Later in the day, when various friends arrived to help, they would add these planks to the growing skeletal framework of the structure. Others might be content to live in log cabins, but Rene's professional pride compelled him to build a more elaborate house. As he had explained to others, he and Louise would spend the rest of their lives there.

He was so busy that he failed to see a horseman ride up and dismount behind him. Nettie's blood froze when she recognized Jack Davies. He was the last person on earth she herself wanted to see, and she couldn't imagine that Rene would be pleased, either.

"What gives you the right to think you can build a house that's fancier than mine, Frenchman?" Davies demanded in a loud voice.

The surprised Rene stopped sawing and looked up.

"Frenchman," Davies said, towering above the slender Rene, "from my property I can see this place o' yours a-building, and I don't like it. Honest folks who work hard are happy enough to live in log cabins, but you ain't. You foreigners come here and start a-putting on airs. Well, there's folks who won't stand for it!"

Nettie was terrified. Even at a distance Davies's menace was plain.

But Rene Gautier had no intention of backing down. Standing with his hands on his hips, he stared up at the bully. "Davies," he said, "you live any way you like. I live the way I wish. That is why I come to Massachusetts Bay. Here people are free."

"Are you a-telling me to mind my own business?"

Rene nodded.

"Well, I'm making what you're a-doing my business!" Davies roared, and drove a knee into the smaller man's groin.

The attack was totally unexpected, the pain was excruciating, and Rene doubled over. Nettie had to clap a hand over her mouth to prevent herself from screaming. Davies measured the smaller man, then felled him with a brutal punch to the cheekbone.

Nettie had seen enough. She turned and fled down the trail, running as fast as she could.

Luckily she had gone only a short distance when she saw two riders approaching, and soon she recognized Tom Hibbard, en route to work on the new house, and Louise Gautier, carrying her husband's meal.

Nettie began to babble her story even before they stopped. Tom heard only a fraction of her story before he lifted her into his saddle and spurred forward to the Gautier property.

Davies was gone, but Rene lay stretched on the ground. All three raced to the stricken man.

Rene was conscious but dazed, and there was an ugly welt on one side of his face. While Louise sat on the ground and took her husband's head in her lap, Nettie hurried to a small stream that ran through the property and wet a handkerchief.

"You ladies attend to Rene," Tom said in a clipped voice. "I'll be back."

He leaped into his saddle and headed straight for the nearby Davies cabin.

Davies was pumping water from a well, looking pleased with himself, and his expression did not change when he saw his visitor. "Well now," he said. "You're about the last man in Fort Springfield I'd expect to come a-calling on me."

Tom dismounted, walked toward him, and wasted no words. "Davies," he said, "we may live near the wilderness, but we're a civilized people in Massachusetts Bay. There are laws that protect a man from unprovoked assualt."

"Unprovoked, huh? Name me a law that says a fellow can't protect his good name when he's been insulted!"

Tom realized Rene would have a hard time proving he had been assaulted without cause. Nettie was the only witness, and she would probably be branded as unreliable.

All the same, Davies couldn't be allowed to go scot-free. "You and I both know what happened just now at Gautier's," Tom said. "And you can't get away with it."

"Who are you to come here and threaten me?" Davies demanded.

Tom reached out and grasped him by the front of his linsey-woolsey shirt. "Hear me plain," he said. "Stay away from Rene Gautier, now and for all time. I beat the living tar out of you once, but that's nothing compared to what I'll do to you if you ever molest him or his family again. Remember that!" He emphasized his point by shoving suddenly.

Davies staggered backward and sat down abruptly on the ground. Tom did not bother to glance at him again as he mounted his horse and rode away. If he had, he would have seen murder in Jack Davies's eyes.

Instead he rode rapidly back to the Gautier property. Rene, still somewhat groggy, had recovered enough to eat. Not wanting a fuss made over him, he had ordered his wife and Nettie to talk about something else.

The young women, relieved because he had suffered no serious injury, were busily discussing going into business together.

"Davies won't trouble you again," Tom said as he

approached the trio. But Tom failed to recognize the extent of his own danger.

Deborah Jenkins greeted her aunt at the door of the parsonage and accepted the pumpkin pie that was handed to her. "I wish you'd stop bringing us food every time you come for dinner, Aunt Ida," she said.

The older woman sniffed. "I don't want Obadiah to waste away while you practice your cooking on him," she said.

The clergyman appeared and kissed Aunt Ida. "Everybody in the parish seems to feel as you do, and we're fully supplied with several meals a week. I'm trying to keep it a secret that Deborah is one of the best cooks in the colony."

They went into the parlor, where Obadiah poured them cups of cranberry juice. Almost immediately the conversation turned to Walter.

"I miss him something terrible," Ida said, "but I'm much happier about him now. It's astonishing that he should show so much improvement living with those savages."

"It's partly the Seneca way of life," Deborah said. "They accept his handicap as natural, and he's learning to cope as a normal person. And Ba-lin-ta, of course, is contributing more to his well-being than anyone can measure. It's remarkable how those two read each other's minds."

"Even if I had never been ordained," Obadiah said, "a miracle like that would convince me of the Lord's existence. I felt the same way when Renno accepted the assignment to go to London. He showed great personal courage, of course, but more than that was involved. He was responding to Divine guidance."

"Then you think his mission will be successful?" Deborah asked.

Her husband's smile was gentle. "I try not to anticipate what Providence has in store. Obviously it was right for Renno to make the journey. But I can't try to predict what may lie ahead for him—or for all of us—as a result of his journey."

Ida looked at him anxiously. "Then you have no way of knowing whether Walter will want to return home eventually, or whether he'll insist on staying with the Seneca. If he does, he'll turn into an Indian himself!"

"I think not," the clergyman replied. "But try to look at it this way, Aunt Ida. Walter is becoming completely self-reliant. He's becoming a man who will lead a productive, useful life. And if he chooses to spend his days with the Seneca, he'll be far more content than he ever would have been in a society that thought of him only as a cripple."

Ida sighed. "I tell myself all those things, but I still worry."

"Of course you do," Obadiah said sympathetically. "It isn't easy for any of us to put our trust in the Almighty in all things at all times. I devote my life to His work, but I still find it very difficult to practice what I preach."

Deborah thought it was time to change the subject. "Help me set the table," she said, and led the way into the small dining room, which was simply furnished with a table, chairs, two sideboards of unpainted oak made by parishioners, and a rug that one of the ladies of the congregation had hooked as a wedding gift. Three chairs were already in place, and Obadiah, following the ladies, brought another.

"We'll need one more setting, Aunt Ida," Deborah said casually.

"Who else is coming to dinner today?" Ida asked, a hint of sharpness in her voice.

Deborah glanced at her husband, making it plain that she wanted him to reply.

Obadiah cleared his throat. "We've asked Leverett Carswell," he said, and waited for an outburst.

Ida Alwin stared at the clergyman, then at her niece. "Well, I never," she murmured.

71

Seemingly unaware of her reaction, the couple busied themselves setting the table.

"Was there any special reason you chose to invite Master Carswell?" There was a distinct edge to Ida's voice now.

Obadiah's manner was soothing. "He's a splendid person, a gentleman, and we enjoy his company. There you have three very good reasons, but there's also a fourth. He lives alone and has no housekeeper, so he eats many of his meals at Donald Doremus's Inn. Far too many, I daresay."

Ida's voice grew tart. "Not as many as you might think. Lately Master Carswell has taken to showing up at my house about an hour before supper time. He always brings something with him. A beefsteak, venison chops, a Connecticut River salmon. Far too much for me to eat alone, so I'm always obliged to ask him to stay to supper with me. I know he does it on purpose, but it wouldn't be proper—when a body is being generous—to tell him I see through his trickery."

Deborah was making an effort to keep a straight face. "It would be my guess that Leverett likes you, Aunt Ida," she said.

"Rubbish, girl! I'm an old scarecrow who doesn't have a ha'penny to her name!"

"Evidently Leverett doesn't think you're a scarecrow, and he's so wealthy I'm sure he doesn't care if a lady has or hasn't money."

"He's romancing me, that's what he's doing. And it's utterly ridiculous!"

"Not at all," Obadiah said mildly. "He's been a widower for a long time, and you've been a widow for years. I know of no injunction in Scriptures that restricts romance to the young."

Ida could only sniff.

"No one is expecting you to behave like a young girl," Deborah said. "But it can't do you any harm to come to know Leverett better and discover for yourself whatever you may have in common with him."

"It isn't bad enough that he comes to my house all the time. Now my own flesh and blood have joined in a conspiracy with him!" Ida's voice was acerbic, but her expression indicated she was more pleased than she cared to admit.

Chapter IV

Lord Beaumont, the elder brother of Colonel Andrew Wilson, was a prominent member of the court of King William and Queen Mary, a high-ranking official of the Royal Treasury, and a patron of the arts. Urbane and cosmopolitan, he had traveled extensively throughout Europe and spoke several languages. He was delighted when his major domo told him that his nephew Jeffrey had just arrived from the American colonies, but he stopped short and gaped when he entered his library and saw Renno sitting cross-legged in front of the hearth.

His lordship's bewilderment increased rapidly. When a footman offered refreshments to the new arrivals, the white Indian refused spiced wine or tea laced with brandy, Spanish sack, or even a mug of ale. Instead he asked for a cup of water, which not even the lowliest servants in a nobleman's household drank. Then a platter of cold meats was served, and Renno, ignoring the plates, knives, and forks, rolled several slices of beef into a tubelike shape and devoured them.

The startled Lord Beaumont read the letters sent to him by Colonel Wilson and Governor Shirley.

Meanwhile, Renno examined his surroundings. Only an hour earlier he had disembarked from the *Elizabeth Louise,* and London stunned him. He couldn't have imagined a city of this size, with its towers and church spires as high as mountains, its streets teeming with more people than there were in the whole Iroquois League. Crowds had gaped at him, following him through the cobbled streets as he and Jeffrey walked to this place, and he had returned their stares.

It was all very confusing. Everyone appeared to be wearing too many clothes, and he wondered how they avoided stifling themselves. Only some of the women wore paint on their faces, and members of both sexes wore shoes with such high heels that they walked like the medicine men who wore stilts at the festival of the harvest. Horses and carts and carriages were everywhere, and some were carried in boxlike contraptions by uniformed bearers.

Renno wondered why Lord Beaumont poured a scent on himself that drowned out natural odors and made the young warrior's nostrils sting. He had to admit he admired the gold medallion that Beaumont wore on a heavy gold chain, but the man's coat with double rows of silver buttons, ruffled lawn shirt, waistcoat of yellow silk, and snug-fitting black breeches looked very uncomfortable. The marble statuettes, the boxes of sandalwood or ivory inlaid with mother-of-pearl, and other ornaments that decorated various tables were very pretty, but they served no purpose that Renno could see. He wondered if they had magic powers.

The windows were tightly closed, and so much heat was generated by the coals burning in the marble hearth that breathing was almost painful. Only scattered trees and small patches of lawn could be seen from the windows, and Jeffrey explained that trees in significant numbers and expanses of grass could be found only in what were called parks. Almost no one in London went hunting, and deer could be found only in private woods belonging to King William at a longhouse known as Hampton Court. It was strange to think that Londoners grew to manhood knowing nothing of outdoor life, hunting, fishing, or the mysteries of following a trail through a wilderness. It was small wonder that the people the young Seneca had seen were very pale and had pinched, worried faces. The members of his tribe, he reflected, would refuse to believe that so many people could live such confined, restricted lives.

Lord Beaumont finished reading the letters, glanced at the warrior, then smiled wryly at his nephew. "It was Andrew's idea to send this very special emissary here, I take it," he said.

"It was, sir." Jeffrey felt uncomfortable.

"Your father has always had a romantic streak in him, Jeffrey. That's what led him to migrate to the New World in the first place." His lordship sighed gently. "We shall see what can be done, but it won't be a simple matter."

"All we ask is that Renno be received by King William and—"

"All, you say?" Beaumont laughed aloud. "His Majesty is an orderly man who is trying to make up for the deficiencies of his Stuart predecessors. All of his appointments are scheduled many weeks in advance. Except for emergencies."

"Our governor, my father, and many other people in the colonies believe we face a very grave emergency."

"Quite so," Lord Beaumont replied quietly. "But there is no emergency until His Majesty determines that one exists. There's the rub. But I shall do what I can, and I'll enlist the aid of friends who have voices heard at court."

"Thank you, Uncle Philip."

"We'll see what develops before I'll accept any thanks. Now to practical matters. I own a small house on the River Thames, off the Strand, that's fully staffed. You and this—ah—Indian will make your home there while he acclimates to England and our ways. I'll send him to my tailor immediately." He turned to Renno. "You'll like that, I believe. I'm going to get you new clothes."

"I have plenty clothes," Renno replied, his manner courteous but firm.

"If we try to transform him into an Englishman," Jeffrey said, "he'll be just like everybody else here by the time he meets the King."

Beaumont had to agree. "A point well taken, and you may be right. But I don't envy you shepherding him around town."

Jeffrey grinned at him. "I'm looking forward to that experience."

"You're Andrew's son. But I'll give you a taste of what's ahead. Both of you return at four this afternoon. I'm having a few friends for dinner, some of them influential at court, so we may as well put your father's insane scheme into motion."

One of the elegant Beaumont coaches carried the two young men to their new London home. Traffic was so heavy that the coachman and his assistant repeatedly shouted and cursed in an attempt to clear a path for the cumbersome vehicle, and occasionally, when several coaches and carts came together, a constable had to be summoned to unsnarl them.

Renno shook his head. "I could run faster than this house on wheels moves," he said.

Jeffrey laughed. "Of course you could. But in this town no gentleman ever walks when he can ride, and he never runs."

"We do not hunt, we do not run. Our bodies will become as soft as the body of a woman."

"No, because tomorrow I'll make arrangements for you to take daily lessons from a fencing master. I taught you all I know of swordsmanship on board the brig. We'll see to it that you get enough exercise here."

The house was tiny by English aristocratic standards but there was more than enough room for the visitors. Renno liked his second-floor bedchamber because it overlooked a small garden, beyond which he could watch ships sailing up and down the Thames.

He particularly liked the goose-down comforter that rested at the foot of his bed. He had already decided that he would sleep on the floor with the windows wide open, but he would enjoy wrapping himself in the comforter.

He accompanied Jeffrey to the dining room, where members of the staff served them with a "light" meal of roasted meat, overcooked vegetables, and something called a pudding that couldn't compare with the dishes of ground cornmeal flavored with maple syrup that Ena and Sah-nee-wa concocted.

After the meal the two separated to unpack their belongings. When Renno learned they would be attending what he interpreted as a feast at Lord Beaumont's house, he dressed in a loincloth, then oiled his skin and daubed on war paint, also fastening into the pigtail of his scalp lock the feathers that denoted his rank as a senior warrior.

For a moment Jeffrey wanted to urge Renno to wear one of his doeskin shirts. But, on second thought, it was better to allow him to create the greatest possible impact on the Beaumont guests. The faster they grasped the difference between the English and the North American Indians, the sooner it might become possible to arrange an audience with King William.

About two dozen guests were gathered in Lord Beaumont's drawing room, and Renno's arrival created precisely the spectacular impression that Jeffrey had hoped. Soon, however, unexpected complications developed. Several of the women, including Beaumont's current mistress, a dazzling blond actress, couldn't resist flirting outrageously with the young Seneca. But Renno quickly demonstrated that he was no fool. Refusing all alcoholic drinks, he looked at the ladies with clear-eyed candor, in no way thrown off balance by their pretty posturings. Gradually they desisted.

One guest, above all others, showed a deep, consistent interest in the white Indian. Renno was drawn to the man, aware that his feelings were genuine. He had no idea that this long-faced, balding man in his late fifties whose spectacles repeatedly slid down his long nose was John Dryden, universally regarded as Britain's leading playwright, poet, and literary critic.

With great skill Dryden persuaded Renno to discuss his impressions of London, then encouraged him to talk about his own, far different life in the land of the Seneca. What impressed the great author most was Renno's total honesty and candor as well as his ability to see through the unnecessary trappings of a highly developed civilization.

Before the evening ended, Dryden invited Renno and Jeffrey to dinner at his home. He also made arrangements for them to see two of his plays currently being revived in the city.

Renno also made an exceptionally favorable impression on the commander of the royal household guards. Tall, husky, and moon-faced, Colonel John Churchill would win renown in the next decade and a half as the greatest commander of the era and, after defeating the armies of Louis XIV, would become the first Duke of Marlborough. Quick to recognize the merits of a soldier, he studied Renno quietly and, liking what he saw, he, too, extended a dinner invitation.

There were a few present who snickered at the half-naked white Indian, but even Lord Beaumont was taken by Renno's calm, dignified manner. Colonel Wilson and Governor Shirley had chosen their emissary well.

"I believe we're off to a good start," Jeffrey told his friend when they returned to their little house.

Renno shrugged. He couldn't understand why it should be necessary for him to meet with other people before he could sit down with the Great Sachem of the English. But everything in London was strange, and he had to bow to the wishes of those who were attending to the day-to-day details.

Within the next few days he became so accustomed to the crowds following him in the streets that he learned to ignore the attention. And he was unable to share Jeffrey's pleasure when, one morning, a journalist appeared at the little house. Young, with breath that reeked of whisky, he called himself Daniel Defoe and announced that he wanted to write a pamphlet about the white Indian.

Jeffrey readily agreed, so Renno forced himself to submit to close questioning for several hours. The interview bored him, although he was interested to note that Defoe scribbled words on paper whiter and more pure than the finest birch bark.

Dinner with Dryden and his family, however, proved to be delightful, and the simple food was delicious. Jeffrey was elated when Dryden, arranging yet another meeting, said he was inspired and intended to write about "a savage whose nobility puts Englishmen to shame." He hadn't yet decided, he declared, whether to write a play or long poem.

A few days later Renno attended the theater for the first time and enjoyed himself thoroughly. The words made little sense to him, but he knew the actors were engaging in make-believe. Some day he hoped to return to London and bring Ba-lin-ta with him. His sister would love the theater.

Renno's favorite pastime was the daily session arranged by Jeffrey with a fencing master. Alexander Califer, whose small salon was within walking distance of the house, was a scarred, middle-aged man who wore a patch over one eye. Lean and sour-faced, he was noted for his insulting manner toward his pupils.

But Renno's natural aptitude soon won Califer's respect, and the swordsman sometimes doubled and tripled the lesson time. Renno, in turn, was awed by the master's prowess with a a a blade. Jeffrey was a clumsy oaf by comparison, and Renno was thrilled when he saw a sword come alive in Califer's hand. The man's thrusts were so rapid that it was almost impossible even for someone with Renno's extraordinary eyesight to follow them. It was also equally impossible to touch Califer with the padded tip of a sword. His instinct on defense was superb.

"I will not be happy," Renno told him one day, "until I can use the long knife as you use it."

"Well, I've worked with swords for more than thirty

years," the tutor said. "So I should be good. It won't take you as long to learn, Indian. You have the feel and you have the eye. All you really need to develop is the instinct to react immediately, without stopping to think."

One afternoon Jeffrey received a note inviting him and Renno to Colonel Churchill's home in the country the following day. There was a scribbled postscript: *Tell our friend to bring his weapons so we can have a day of sport.*

Renno was never without his tomahawk and knife, but he dutifully carried a bow and a quiver of arrows, too.

Lord Beaumont provided a carriage for the journey, much to the relief of Jeffrey, who had not relished the prospect of having a fully armed Indian seen riding horseback through the streets of London.

Churchill's small estate was located on the fringe of Richmond Park, not far from Hampton Court Palace, about a two-hour ride from the center of London. It was rumored, as Jeffrey knew, that he had been given the property as a young officer when he was intimate with Barbara Villiers, Duchess of Cleveland and long the official mistress of Charles II. Until recent years, when he started to prove himself a worthy officer, Churchill's enemies had delighted in attributing his rise in the military to the influence of the powerful duchess.

The colonel met his guests at the entrance to the house, casually attired in leather trousers and boots, the first open-throated shirt Renno had seen on an English gentlemen, and a knit vest of heavy wool.

His wife, Sarah, greeted the guests in the drawing room. She was vivacious, energetic, and pretty, and what impressed Renno was that she made no mention of his unique appearance. No other lady he had met in England had been as diplomatic.

Cold meats and bread were served, and Churchill, saw to it that Renno was given a large mug of sweet tea.

Soon the men were alone, and Churchill ate quickly. "We'll have a rather splendid supper later," he said. "Right now I'm eager to get out of doors."

Renno needed no urging, and in a short time they wandered into a garden behind the house. The branches of several fruit trees were bare, although the grass was green, an English phenomenon that astonished Renno.

"If you don't mind my curiosity," Churchill said, "I'd like to inspect that hatchet you carry."

"Tomahawk," Renno said, and handed it to him.

The colonel weighed it in his hand and realized it was perfectly balanced. "I assumed this was an ornamental weapon, but obviously it's meant for use. How do you employ it?"

"There are many ways," Renno replied. "The best is to throw it."

Churchill looked at the branch of an apple tree, a stalk about two inches in diameter. The tree stood about fifteen or twenty paces from the place where the trio stood. "Could you lop off that branch by throwing this —ah—tomahawk?"

Jeffrey laughed aloud.

It was apparent that the household guard commander failed to understand the delicacy and accuracy with which a tomahawk could be wielded by one who knew how to use it. Renno remained solemn, and now he pointed to a dead leaf that had clung to the outer edge of the branch. "Leaf," was all he said.

Then, taking the tomahawk from the colonel, he squinted for an instant at the target, then threw the weapon, almost effortlessly.

The tomahawk soared as it flew toward the tree, and the finely honed stone blade nipped off a small fraction of an inch of the limb's end. The dead leaf fluttered to the ground.

Colonel Churchill stared at Renno, shaking his head in wonder.

To Renno, the feat was ordinary. "There are many warriors in the nation of the Seneca who can throw it that way," he said.

"What he says is true," Jeffrey added, "although he's too modest. He happens to be the champion of the whole Iroquois League."

Renno took no credit for his standing. A hawk had circled overhead on the day of the contest, so he knew that the manitous had been guiding him, willing him to win.

"Are you as expert with a knife?" Churchill asked.

Renno handed him the knife he had received from Colonel Wilson.

"This is English," the colonel said as he examined it. "I didn't realize it came from Sheffield. It wasn't made for throwing."

Renno and Jeffrey grinned at each other. "Show him," the latter said.

Renno looked around slowly, then saw grapevines growing on a trellis at the far end of the garden. He beckoned the others to follow, and walked to the vines, where he made a nick in a stalk with his blade.

He was showing off now, but he didn't care. This war chief of the English wanted him to demonstrate his skills, and he felt a sense of kinship with the officer. Turning away from the trellis, he began to walk. "Tell me when stop," he said.

Churchill halted him after about ten feet. Renno shook his head. "More far." He walked an additional ten feet. With great deliberation he stood with his back to the grapevine and seemed lost in thought. Then, suddenly he whirled, and without appearing to take time to aim, he hurled the knife.

The colonel was the first to race forward. He bent down, picked up a small section of vine, and stared at it in total disbelief. The knife had severed the stalk less than half an inch from the spot Renno had nicked.

"This is incredible," Churchill said, shaking his head.

"The aim of my father with a knife is better than mine," Renno said. "And there is no Seneca who is better than El-i-chi, my brother."

"I'd like to have some of your warriors in my regiment," the colonel said.

Jeffrey saw an opportunity. "Almost two thousand Seneca are now our allies in the colonies," he said. "And

83

so are another three thousand Iroquois warriors of various tribes. But they can't fight the French and the tribes armed by them, not with primitive weapons. They need firearms, just as our militia need them."

Churchill nodded thoughtfully. "I see what you mean," he said.

Renno and Jeffrey exchanged a glance. Perhaps they had won a supporter who could make his voice heard at court.

The colonel brightened. "I've been planning a treat for you," he said. "How long has it been since you shot a deer, Renno?"

The young Seneca looked wistful. "More moons than I wish to count," he replied.

Churchill summoned an orderly, who brought them each a horse.

Renno was unaccustomed to riding, but managed to retain his seat with a measure of grace as they cantered across the fields.

After a short ride they came to a high gate, guarded by a sentry wearing the green uniform of a royal warder. The man saluted, and as the party dismounted, leaving their horses behind, he opened the heavy wooden gate.

The three men proceeded on foot, Churchill and Jeffrey armed with muskets, Renno carrying his bow and arrows. The woods were thick, a carpet of pine needles covered the ground, and Renno felt more at home than he had at any time since coming to England. This forest was not like the wilderness he knew in the land of the Seneca. For a short time he couldn't pinpoint why, but he soon realized that these woods had been cultivated and pruned. There were evergreens, oaks, and elm trees in profusion, but he saw no wild bramble bushes or other shrubbery that should have been growing naturally. They were in the royal preserve known as Richmond Park.

Although Churchill was the host, he allowed the young Seneca to take the lead.

Renno advanced cautiously, all of his senses alert. His highly trained senses could feel the presence of game nearby. Bending down and looking at the grass underfoot, Renno nodded in satisfaction. He had found a deer trail.

Slowing his pace, he advanced several hundred yards. Then he halted abruptly and raised a hand to warn his companions. They stopped, too.

A moment later Renno caught a glimpse of a deer some distance ahead. Automatically, he notched an arrow into his bow. The buck made no move.

Next, to Renno's astonishment, two does also came into view, complacently grazing on the blue-green grass.

Something was amiss. The deer should have realized by now that there were men in the vicinity, but they neither fled nor indicated alarm in any way.

The young Seneca lowered his bow and turned to Churchill. "How does it happen," he asked in a low voice, "that the animals do not run away?"

"Oh, they'll move fast enough when we draw still closer to them," the colonel replied complacently.

Renno was still puzzled. "Often they see men here?"

"Well, yes. The warders put food here and there for them so they'll stay healthy and fat. King William says he has no time for hunting, so the herd is increasing rather rapidly, and there wouldn't be enough fodder for the deer if they were left to their own devices."

Now the situation was becoming clear. "Where do they go when they run?" Renno persisted.

"Deeper into the park." Churchill didn't understand Renno's question. "I don't know the exact size of the preserve, but there are hundreds of acres."

"The park," Renno said, "comes to an end where we have seen the high fence."

"Certainly. The fence marks the limits of the preserve."

Renno had learned all he wanted to know, and to the surprise of Churchill he removed his arrow from the bow and dropped it back into the quiver. "If you and Jeff-rey wish to shoot deer, that is your right. I will wait here for you."

"But why—"

"In the land of the Seneca," Renno said slowly, speaking with great dignity, "warriors hunt game because they need food to eat and skins to cover their bodies. Here the animals have no chance to escape. Here the deer are fed by men, so they are tame. The English have much food to eat and many clothes to cover their bodies. A warrior of the Seneca cannot shoot an animal that is a friend of men." He didn't mention that the manitous who guided a brave during a hunt would be so disgusted with him that they would withdraw their support from him for all time if he brought down a buck or doe that had no real chance to break free.

Renno's few words made a deep impression on John Churchill, who lowered his musket, rested the butt on the ground, and stared at the so-called savage. "You know," he said, "I've been taking the Richmond Park preserve and other royal game sanctuaries throughout the country for granted all of my life. We English are supposed to be a people who believe in sportsmanship, but you've just taught me a lesson I don't intend to forget, Renno of the Seneca. Obviously you enjoy the woods, so we'll walk here for a time, if you like."

"That will be good," Renno said.

Colonel Churchill turned to Jeffrey. "I've sympathized with your situation ever since I learned of it, but now I'm gaining a far deeper understanding of the New World than I've ever had. Are others in the colonies like this Indian?"

"What Renno feels," Jeffrey Wilson said, "other Seneca and the rest of the Iroquois tribes also feel."

Churchill's jaw set. "By God, I'm going to help you," he declared. "You can count on me to do everything in my power to win Renno his audience with His Majesty—and at the earliest date it can be arranged."

The day spent with Colonel Churchill would linger as one of Renno's more pleasant experiences in England. Other occasions were far less enjoyable, however, and one in particular was thoroughly disagreeable.

He and Jeffrey were bored as they waited to be received at court, even though they were entertained frequently. So, when Jeffrey suggested a night "on the town," Renno was agreeable, not quite knowing what his friend had in mind.

Jeffrey was in high spirits as they first made their way to a small tavern just off the Strand. "We owe ourselves a little relaxation," he said. "I know you don't like English drink, but you really should try a mug or two of ale. It will do you no harm, and you might change your mind."

Renno allowed him to buy two pints of frothing ale, and they carried their drinks to the one empty table they saw in the crowded, oak-paneled room.

Dressed for the outing in a doeskin shirt and leggings, Renno nevertheless drew the usual stares, but he had been so inured to the attention he received that he paid no heed to it.

Suddenly, however, he felt someone or something tugging gently at the wampum, a strip of leather decorated with clam shells, that Sah-nee-wa had given him just before he left home. The wampum was precious to him because his aunt said it was a powerful token endowed with properties to repel evil manitous that might assail him in this strange land.

Not moving his head, Renno glanced in the direction of the tug and saw a man, small and ferretlike, with several days' growth of beard on his face. With great stealth the young Seneca drew his knife and slashed at the offending hand.

The pickpocket's scream silenced everyone in the tavern, and a moment later the man fled, bleeding profusely as he ran. Portions of two of his fingers rested on the hardwood floor.

No one in the tavern seemed too disturbed by the incident. Only a few looked at the severed fingers, then hastily turned away again. The proprietor removed the grisly souvenirs with a broom, and offered Renno his thanks for ridding the tavern of a petty criminal. He then brought over two enormous, foaming tankards of ale which he placed before the white Indian and his friend. "This 'ere be my way o' sayin' thank 'ee."

Jeffrey grinned. "Whether you like ale or not you'll have to drink it all," he said. "You'd offend our host if you didn't."

With Seneca stoicism Renno had put the pickpocket out of his mind, but he looked askance at the tankard. He had been taught that the customs of others were sacred, so he was obliged to drink.

He had to admit, as time passed, that the taste of the ale became less repugnant. However, a sixth sense warned him that he and Jeffrey should leave the tavern as soon as they finished. The atmosphere disturbed him. The air, thick with the smoke of pipe tobacco, made it difficult to breathe. But Jeffrey was beginning to enjoy himself, and the young Seneca was reluctant to interrupt his pleasure. Jeffrey had been faithful to his obligations and deserved a reward.

Gradually Renno became aware of a man sitting with two male companions at the adjoining table. In his late twenties, the newcomer was tall and thick-chested and richly attired. He wore huge, jeweled rings on several fingers, and a barmaid, hovering nearby, addressed him as "milord."

"That's the Earl of Lincoln," Jeffrey whispered. "It's said he seeks the King's favor and wants to win a high place at court for himself, but he's reputed to have a vicious temper. King William is so sensible that people like my uncle are wagering that Lincoln won't win the appointment he covets."

Renno looked at the nobleman for a long moment, not realizing he was being rude. He had to agree with Lord Beaumont's estimate. The way he judged people in England was to picture them as Seneca, and he couldn't see this florid-faced, arrogant man as either a war chief or a member of the Great Sachem's council.

To Renno's dismay Jeffrey ordered two more tankards of the potent ale.

A roar sounded from the next table. "Join me, wenches, and tell the barmaid what you'll drink."

Again Renno turned, and saw two young women, one blond and one dark-haired. Both were exceptionally pretty, their faces were painted, and they wore dresses with low-cut necklines.

The blond was aware of his interest and, fascinated by his appearance, she smiled at him. But the earl promptly hauled her to a seat beside him.

Again Renno turned away and went to work on his third drink of ale.

"Eventually," Jeffrey told him, "we'll try a drop or two of whisky. It can be dangerous to a man's health when you buy it in the wrong places, but this tavern has a splendid reputation, and I'm quite sure they serve it directly out of the casks that come from Scotland."

As the two friends sipped their ale in silence, Renno again became aware of the party at the next table. It was apparent that the brunette disliked the men she was with. Instead she flirted with Jeffrey, her approach subtle, and he was returning her interest.

But it was the blond who attracted Renno's attention, principally because she was trying to ward off the advances of the Earl of Lincoln. He kept ordering more drinks for her, and she drank them, but they made her no more friendly to him. Renno saw that the nobleman was becoming irritated.

In the land of the Seneca no woman was forced to accept the lovemaking of a man she didn't like. If he were home, he would intervene at once, his privilege as a senior warrior. Here, although tempted, he hesitated.

"Damn your eyes," the girl said suddenly in a shrill soprano, "leave me be, Your Lordship."

The earl laughed unpleasantly. "Don't tell me I'm not good enough for you."

"No." The girl sounded desperate. "But I prefer *him*." She jumped to her feet, and seated herself beside the startled Renno, taking hold of his arm.

89

The young Seneca was so stunned he didn't know what to do.

Before he could move, however, Lincoln loomed above him. "This fellow," he boomed, "is an impostor, an actor, or a madman, perhaps all three."

The girl clung all the harder to Renno.

"If you were a gentleman, sir, I'd run you through," Lincoln said as his companions joined him. "As it is, I'd rather not sully my blade."

Renno didn't understand the words, but the insulting tone was clear enough. Sinewy fingers crept toward the handle of the tomahawk.

The alarmed Jeffrey, momentarily paralyzed, came to life and spoke to Renno in the Seneca tongue. "Don't move. Do not harm him. He is a powerful chief. And he has many friends who sit on the council of the Great Sachem of the English."

Lincoln continued to goad, hoping to provoke a duel. "Your liver, sir, is as white as your skin is stained brown."

Jeffrey shruddered. If Renno began to comprehend, even faintly, what was being said to him, he would smash the earl's skull with his tomahawk and scalp the man before he died. Their mission was in jeopardy. King William would never see anyone involved in a scandal that would be certain to become the talk of the entire city.

"In the name of all that is sacred to your people," Jeffrey said, still speaking in Seneca, "I beg you not to move!"

Renno exerted supreme self-control, although the girl was leaning against him and the tall English lord was still glaring down at him. All he knew was that Jeffrey was badly upset, and common sense told him to obey his friend's words.

An expression of disgust and contempt appeared on the Earl's florid face. He spat on the floor at Renno's feet, then stalked out of the tavern, closely followed by his two companions.

Everyone in the place relaxed.

The innkeeper reappeared at the table. "He's a mean one," he confided. "I thank 'ee again. I don't want no troubles 'ere, and you done just right."

The blond cooed her appreciation, too, as she continued to lean against Renno.

Jeffrey laughed aloud in relief. "All's well, or so it seems, and we've found ourselves a pair of charming ladies who will help us put these recent embarrassments out of our minds."

The proprietor returned with a round of free drinks.

That was the beginning. The blond girl, whose name was Liz, was fascinated by him, and she became wide-eyed when she discovered he was an authentic North American Indian, in spite of his hair color and pale eyes. Even more tantalizing, he had a superb, hard-muscled physique. She repeatedly stroked his arm, the back of his neck, and his thigh.

Renno, almost choking on the whisky that followed the ale, looked at Jeffrey in an appeal for help. But Jeffrey was totally absorbed in the brunette.

Gradually, as the liquor took hold, Renno became less rigid. It had been a long time since he had taken a woman, and Liz became increasingly appealing. The dignity of the Seneca prohibited public lovemaking, but no one in the tavern seemed to be paying any attention to the two couples seated at the far corner table, so, little by little, Renno began to return the girl's advances.

All at once Jeffrey slapped some silver coins on the table. "We've spent long enough here," he announced. "Come with us, ladies, and you'll find you haven't been wasting your time."

The blond clung fiercely to Renno's arm as they left.

The cold air struck Renno like a blow, and his mind became even foggier. Later he only remembered walking the short distance home and tumbling into bed with Liz. The rest was just a blur. He was sure it was late at night when Jeffrey handed both girls some silver coins and they departed.

When Renno awakened, he was sprawled on his bed instead of being curled up in the comforter on the floor. And the window was closed. Perhaps that was the reason he was suffering from a splitting headache. He staggered to his feet, looked out of the window, and was astonished to see that the sun stood almost directly overhead. Never had he slept so late.

Soon thereafter he and an equally haggard Jeffrey met at the breakfast table. The sympathetic, amused cook served them raw oysters with a peppery sauce and Renno almost gagged on them, but he did manage to eat what he was served. He refused a pint of bitter ale, the mere sight of which made him feel ill, and instead drank lots of cold water.

"Now you've had your introduction to the real London," Jeffrey said. "Welcome to the city of natural dissipation."

"A tomahawk," Renno replied, "has cracked my head."

"Thank God you didn't crack the Earl of Lincoln's head. He's a mean one, and I'm glad our mission doesn't depend on his favors."

They did not speak again as, increasingly hungry, they devoured steak and kidney pie.

At last Jeffrey broke the silence. "How did you like the girl?"

Renno shrugged. "My mind is empty. I do not like an empty mind."

"Neither do I." Jeffrey pulled himself together with an effort. "Well, we've had our fling, and when I think of all the things that could have gone wrong, all the unpleasant things that could have happened to us, my blood runs cold. Never again! For the rest of our stay here—and may it be short—we'll walk the narrow path of virtue. I'm afraid my father is right when he says sobriety is its own reward."

Renno knew only that he longed for the clear air and

the straightforward way of life he knew and loved in the land of the Seneca.

The Connecticut River ran red with the blood of English settlers as the band of Huron commanded by Colonel Alain de Gramont murdered, pillaged, and burned. Several small settlements were almost totally destroyed, but Alain deliberately allowed a few victims to escape so they could spread the word that the Algonquian were conducting a reign of terror.

Word of the attacks reached Fort Springfield, and Colonel Wilson immediately placed the entire western Massachusetts Bay regiment of militia on the alert.

Tom Hibbard, recently promoted to lieutenant, volunteered his services, and the men of his unit unanimously voted to accompany him. Even Rene Gautier, the most recent recruit, insisted he would march with his new comrades. His new house was not yet completed, and Tom tried to dissuade him, but he insisted.

"This is my country now," he said, "and when one person dies, all suffer."

The militia had learned from the Seneca and other Iroquois who had marched and fought beside them in the Canadian campaign. Each man carried his own ammunition and powder, his own rations of parched corn and smoked meat, enough food for a full week on the trail. The weather was bitterly cold and in places the snowdrifts were deep, but most members of the platoon were accustomed to outdoor labor and had become hardened to the elements.

The reports that had reached Fort Springfield indicated that all of the raids had taken place north of the town, so Lieutenant Hibbard marched his men in that direction. Most of the time they followed the river, but several times each day they fanned out and moved eastward in their search for the elusive savages. In three days they found nothing, so the commander reluctantly turned south again, but continued to be on guard.

No man was more eager than Tom Hibbard to find

the enemy, and his desire would have been even greater had he realized that the band was Huron rather than Algonquian. Huron had murdered his wife, and he believed he would never be able to even his score with them, no matter how many he killed.

Little by little the militiamen worked their way back to Fort Springfield. On the sixth morning of their march, as they were about to break camp deep in the forest, one of the sentries hurried to the bivouac. "Lieutenant," he said breathlessly, "I've found 'em! They've been traveling on the west bank of the river, which is why we haven't found any traces of 'em. And they're just now making a crossing on the ice."

Within moments the entire platoon, thirty-eight strong, was on the move. When the men drew near to the edge of the forest, Lieutenant Hibbard called a halt and went ahead to scout.

Warriors wearing the distinctive red paint of the Algonquian were crossing the ice silently and in single file. They carried bows and arrows. He had no way of knowing that the crafty de Gramont wanted to be sure the English colonists were assaulted by Indians who were not armed with French muskets, as were the Huron.

Making a quick count, Tom knew his men were outnumbered almost two to one, but their muskets gave them the advantage. Returning to the waiting platoon, he ordered the men to spread out. "Go as close to the river bank as you can while staying under cover, and at no time leave the shelter of the trees until I give the word. Don't open fire until I tell you, and then pour it into the bastards as fast as you can reload."

The men trotted through the forest. Most were veterans of the Canadian campaign, so they were nearly as silent as Indians.

A dead branch cracked beneath Rene Gautier's boot, to his great chagrin, and he swore to himself that he would lose no time learning the techniques of wilderness warfare.

Lieutenant Hibbard halted behind the trunk of a maple, and peering toward the river he saw that the

Indian column had almost completed the crossing. In a minute or two the warriors would spread out as they resumed their own march, and his advantage would be lost.

Tom waited impatiently for his men to join him and form a line behind the screen of trees. Then he raised his musket to his shoulder and called, "Fire at will!" He squeezed the trigger, and his own shot opened the battle.

The braves were clustered together on the east bank, so they were a perfect target. Several were killed by the initial volley.

As the militiamen reloaded and fired again, the Indians rallied swiftly under the leadership of an older warrior who looked like a white man. He remained calm under fire, and his subordinates, momentarily bewildered, responded to his commands instantly.

Tom vaguely recalled talk on the march home from Quebec about a leader of the Huron and Ottawa who was actually a Frenchman He told himself to remember this bit of information when he returned home.

The warriors spread out immediately, and as there was no cover near the river they crouched low and sent a hail of arrows into the forest.

"You have the edge, lads," Tom Hibbard called during a momentary lull. "Keep up your fire and we've got them!"

Rene Gautier, taking part in active combat for the first time, remained remarkably clear-headed. Ignoring the arrows that passed close to him on both sides, he maintained a steady, methodical fire, reloading his musket quickly, taking aim, and squeezing the trigger. Later he felt certain he had killed at least one warrior and wounded another.

Alain de Gramont knew that his men would have given a good account of themselves if they had been permitted to use firearms, but they had lost the initiative at the very start of the fight, and it was impossible for them to gain control of the situation when they could use only bows and arrows. He felt it unfortunate that he was being deprived of a raid on Fort Springfield, the largest town on the river, but he had already accomplished his principal aim. He hated to suffer casualties needlessly and, knowing his dead carried no weapons or clothing that would identify them as Huron rather than Algonquian, he gave the order to withdraw.

The Indian wounded able to walk were aided by their brothers. The injured lying on the ground with the dead were left behind.

The warriors started northward along the east bank of the river, gradually inching toward the trees that would shield them. For a moment Tom Hibbard debated with himself whether to follow them, but he quickly decided that the risks would outweigh the potential gains. In the short battle, he had achieved a clear-cut victory. The enemy's strength had been severely sapped, and the Indians would be forced to return to their home base. The raids on the Connecticut River settlements were ended, and the platoon had suffered only one minor injury. It was best to be satisfied with that.

"Let them go, lads!" he called.

The militiamen cheered, and several raced down the slope toward the riverbank. Eight of the warriors had been killed and eleven others had been wounded badly enough that they could not escape. The militia veterans had learned another lesson from their Iroquois comrades, and no prisoners were taken. The wounded were shot, one by one, their executioners showing no feeling. Then, to Rene Gautier's astonishment, the dead warriors were scalped and their weapons were taken as souvenirs.

"You've done well, Rene," Tom said as the unit formed in line for the march back. "You've come through your baptism of fire with honor."

Not waiting for a reply, the commander moved to the head of the column. Shortly before noon the platoon reached Fort Springfield, and the militiamen turned in their captured weapons for examination; ultimately the bows and arrows, tomahawks, and knives would be returned to them. The inspection was a recent practice used to try to determine which Indian tribe made the weapons.

Tom went to Colonel Wilson's office in the Fort and gave a full report.

Andrew Wilson frowned. "Are you sure the warriors were Algonquian, Tom?"

"Well, sir, only fools are positive. All I can say is that they were wearing Algonquian war paint. What troubles me is their leader, a man of about forty. From a distance, at least, he looked white to me and to several of the men."

"There is a Colonel Alain de Gramont of the French infantry who often dresses as an Indian and leads the Huron in battle. But they weren't Huron."

"As near as I could judge they were Algonquian, sir, but I'm no expert," Tom said. "The bodies of their dead are still littering the riverbank a few miles upstream, if you want to send somebody to check."

"Nobody else here would know for certain, either, but I don't suppose it matters. For all we know this Gramont could be leading the Algonquian now. What's important is that the Algonquian are attacking us without cause, which means our worst fears have been realized. There's no longer the slightest doubt in my mind that they've formed an alliance with the French."

"What can we do about it, Colonel?"

Andrew Wilson's smile was thin. "Damn little. I'll notify Governor Shirley and the governors of the other colonies, of course. I'll send a messenger to inform Ghonka of the Seneca and leave it to him to get in touch with the other Iroquois nations. I'll do everything I can to increase the recruiting of volunteers. But—most of all—I'll pray that Renno and Jeffrey are successful in London. More than ever, what they accomplish will determine whether we survive as free Englishmen or become subjects of that bigot who sits on the throne of France. We need all the help that King William will give us!"

Tom sighed deeply.

"We can't solve our problems in a day," the colonel said. "You're tired. We'll ride out to the house, and you'll feel better after a good dinner."

"Thank you sir," Tom said, shaking his head, "but

I'm afraid I'm not fit company for Mildred today. I'm more discouraged than tired, and I don't want to infect her with my gloom. I think I'll just stay in town for a spell until my spirits improve a bit."

Andrew Wilson did not insist.

After bathing and changing into civilian clothes Tom wandered aimlessly around Fort Springfield. Various people greeted him, but he merely returned their hellos and continued walking. Eventually he realized he had eaten nothing since his breakfast of parched corn and smoked meat, so he went to the inn. He retreated to a table in the dark, far corner of the dining room, nodding to the few occupants of other tables.

Thoroughly chilled, he ordered a drink of hot buttered rum. He tried to analyze his feelings as he sipped his rum, but could not. All he knew was that he was enveloped by a bleak despair. Life in Massachusetts Bay was hard as well as lonely, and it promised to become even more difficult in the months ahead. He could move to Boston, of course, but he discarded the idea. That would be running away. Fort Springfield was his home, and here he would stay, regardless of the consequences.

"A penny for your thoughts," a feminine voice said.

Tom looked up and saw Nettie standing beside him. Her cheeks and lips were rouged, her eyelids were daubed with blue, and she was flashily dressed.

He rose at once and offered her a chair.

"I don't want to intrude," she said.

"You're not intruding. Please sit down and have a drink with me."

Nettie hesitated briefly, then accepted. Ordinarily she would have kept her distance from him in a public place, but he looked so forlorn.

"I hear your platoon's mission was successful," she said.

He grimaced. "Well, there's a pile of Algonquian corpses up the river. And it's certain that particular band of marauders won't be troubling folks hereabouts anymore."

She nodded, understanding that he was upset by the killings. Despite his toughness, he was a gentle, sensitive person. No wonder he was depressed.

Nettie did her best to cheer Tom up. He responded very slowly, but he was enjoying her company, so he asked her to dine with him.

"That—that isn't why I spoke to you," she said.

Tom ignored her protest and ordered a hearty dinner for two. When their food came they ate slowly, and it was obvious to Nettie that Tom was enjoying the meal. Certainly the meager rations on which he had lived for almost a week had contributed to his black mood.

Little by little his spirits improved. He was grateful to Nettie for her cheering company. More than grateful. He felt himself being drawn closer to her. Forced to admit it, he knew he wanted her.

Nettie was aware of the slow, subtle change in him. Always alert to the nuances of a man's feelings, she knew before Tom that he was gradually being overcome by desire for her. But she knew too, that he was reluctant to embarrass her by asking.

Nettie took a deep breath, then gently placed her hand on his arm as she looked at him, her eyes wide and unwavering. "Come with me," she said. "Right now."

Tom flushed. He was afraid she thought he expected it from her. He shook his head fiercely.

Nettie refused to be put off. "Please," she said softly. "I want you as much as you want me." Strangely, she realized, she was speaking the truth.

Tom's defenses crumbled. He paid for their meal and drinks, then walked the short distance to Nettie's room. Even on this walk of only a few hundred feet Nettie noted the difference between Tom Hibbard and other men she took home with her. Some were furtive, many seemed ashamed, and a few behaved brazenly. But Tom was completely natural, pleased to be beside her and indifferent to the reactions of anyone who might see them together.

Nettie's room was dominated by a huge four-poster bed, and Tom suddenly felt nervous. Nettie took the initiative and went to him. His kiss was remarkably tender.

His gentleness and consideration for her increased as the pace of their lovemaking intensified. Never had Nettie been with anyone like him. For the first time, she was swept away by real passion.

They lay wrapped in each other's arms, finding solace in this time together.

At last they dressed in silence, and then Tom cleared his throat in embarrassment. "I don't want to insult you," he said, "but all the same . . ." His voice dwindled away and he fumbled with his purse.

Color burned brightly in Nettie's cheeks, and she shook her head vigorously. "No," she said. "And we won't talk about it, now or ever. That subject is closed forever."

He stood still and stared at her for a long moment, his expression unfathomable. Then he spoke huskily. "If you have an hour or so to spare, maybe you'd come with me. There's something I'd like to show you."

She nodded.

He took pains to hold her coat for her, something else that no other man had done.

They went to the stables behind the inn. There, he rented two horses. Gently lifting the girl onto one animal, he led her to the river, then followed the trail that led to the south.

Nettie couldn't imagine what Tom had in mind. They rode past Ida Alwin's place and the almost completed house of the Gautiers, but he did not pause.

Finally they came to a large tract of rolling land. The tablelike crest of a high hill that overlooked a bend on the Connecticut River had been cleared. Tom dismounted and lifted Nettie to the ground.

She looked around slowly, then studied the river. "The view here is lovely," she said at last.

"This is my land," he told her. "Three hundred and twenty acres of it. I cleared this hill a long time ago, intending to build a house of my own here, but I haven't done anything about it. Some of the lads in the militia have offered to help me, so I think that this spring, after the weather turns warmer, I'll build my house. And prepare the land for planting."

"It will be a wonderful place to live," Nettie said. She still didn't understand why he had brought her here.

"I—I wanted you to see it," Tom said lamely, not quite understanding his motives himself.

Andrew Wilson went to Boston to report to Governor Shirley the succession of raids by a band of Algonquian warriors. They conferred at length, and then Shirley granted the officer his new commission as a brigadier, making him second in rank only to Major General William Pepperrell, who was commander in chief of the entire Massachusetts Bay militia. Brigadier Wilson would become his deputy and would take command of the colony's infantry.

Wilson's first task was to go to New Haven, where he would meet with the military representatives of the other colonies in the hope they could work out a joint plan of defense in the new crisis. Covering about forty miles each day, he reached his destination in seventy-two hours.

New Haven was one of the largest, most bustling towns in all of New England. Its harbor was crowded with merchant ships; two churches and an inn faced the green, where cattle and sheep grazed. There was even talk among the substantial citizens about founding a new college that might rival Massachusetts Bay's Harvard, the only institution of higher learning in the English colonies.

Rooms had been engaged at the inn for the military men, and soon after his arrival the newly promoted brigadier sat down to a late supper with his colleagues from Connecticut, Rhode Island, New Hampshire, and New York. After the meal was served the doors were closed, and the discussion began. Wilson was the senior officer present so he presided, and he lost no time coming to the point.

First he described the Algonquian raids, of which

the New Hampshire commander was already aware. Then he said, "Our situation soon could become desperate, as I think all of you know. We have reason to believe that General de Martine soon will have in excess of three thousand French troops at Louisburg, with more than a thousand still on duty at the Citadel in Quebec. Two thousand Huron and Ottawa warriors are definitely in the French camp, and it now appears inevitable that they'll be joined by at least three thousand Algonquian."

Colonel Edward Schuyler of New York ran a hand through his gray hair. "We can't put more than twenty-five hundred of our militia into the field," he said, "and even if all of the Iroquois join on our side, we'll still be overwhelmed."

Colonel Theodore Brownell from Connecticut was a short, peppery man who always spoke decisively. "Our need for modern weapons is even more pressing than our need for men. Blunderbusses would be about as effective as the ancient muskets that some of our battalions have been issued."

"We're hoping that situation will be rectified when the special commissioners we've sent to England gain the ear of King William," Brigadier Wilson said. "In the meantime we've got to organize as best we can with as many troops as we can muster."

Colonel Francis Grey of Rhode Island, who was tall and heavyset, looked apologetic. "I don't want you to think that what I have to say is my personal position. Our legislature, by an almost unanimous vote, has determined that our militia will take no part in any joint ventures in which our men will be placed under the command of an officer from any other colony. No offense meant, Brigadier."

Andrew Wilson found it difficult to reply civilly. The refusal of any colony to accept the authority of men from other colonies, in a spirit of cooperation, was a handicap that would cripple all of them and lead to certain defeat, no matter what Renno and Jeffrey accomplished. He clenched a fist. "We've got to work, plan, and fight *together*. And frankly, gentlemen, I don't give a damn who takes the overall command."

The red-faced Colonel Paul Thomason of New Hampshire laughed sourly. "That's easy enough for you to say, Brigadier!" he retorted. "You and General Pepperrell outrank all of us."

"Not only that," Colonel Schuyler of New York added, "but Massachusetts Bay is the most populous colony. Naturally you and Pepperrell will assume you have the right to gain the command."

Andrew Wilson almost lost his temper. "Tell your damned legislatures to promote all of you to the rank of lieutenant-general, and then you can toss coins for the privilege of commanding our army.

"Fort Louisburg is so strong that, in our feeble condition, it would be madness to think of sending an expedition to capture it. That means we'll have to let the French take the initiative and attack us. When French regiments march through our cities using bayonets on innocent civilians, and our frontier villages are put to the torch by the Huron, Ottawa, and hordes of Algonquian, I dare say we'll still be squabbling about the establishment of a single, unified command."

Colonel Brownell looked apologetic. "Until this evening I wasn't aware of the gravity of the crisis that confronts us. I believe I can assure you, Brigadier, that after I've reported to our governor and legislature, Connecticut will readily accept the leadership of Massachusetts Bay."

"Thank you, Colonel," Andrew Wilson said, "but I suggest, for the present, that we concentrate on building up our regiments. We must double our strength, at the very least."

"We lack the funds," Colonel Thomason replied quickly. "New Hampshire is a poor colony. We don't grow fat on trade and manufacture, as Boston does."

"Rhode Island," Colonel Grey declared, "remains unconvinced that she is in danger of any kind. Our own Indians have given us no trouble. It's true that a few of our merchant ships have been attacked by French privateers, but we can't necessarily blame France herself for that. There are pirates who raise the flags of many nations on their raids."

"New York recognizes the dangers and will take steps to increase our militia," Colonel Schuyler said. "But we want it understood that we'll be given a voice as large as that of any other colony in making final decisions. And if we don't like what's being done, we reserve the right to act independently, on our own initiative."

"All I can do, gentlemen, is to tell you the situation as we in Massachusetts Bay see it," Brigadier Wilson said. "And let me make it very clear to you that when war comes—as it will—we'll fight alone—if necessary —to preserve our freedom. We'll be little better than slaves if the French beat us."

Chapter V

Convinced that the special envoys from Massachusetts Bay needed the help of the Crown and that the colonies faced a real crisis, Colonel John Churchill made repeated attempts to speak to the King about the conflict that was gathering force in North America. But the distant colonies were far from King William's mind. He was learning to work in tandem with a Parliament suspicious of royal prerogatives, there were new taxes to be weighed, and the build-up of the French fleet and army was a constant worry.

So the monarch brushed aside the attempts of his household guard commander to discuss the plight of the colonies. "Later, Churchill," he said on several occasions. "There aren't enough hours in the day to deal with the problems I already face, and my head is bursting."

But Colonel Churchill refused to abandon his quest. Not only had he given his word that he would help, but he was impressed by the integrity and unique dignity of Renno. The white Indian deserved a hearing.

Churchill devised a new scheme and had the opportunity to put it into effect one morning when Queen Mary made a surprise visit to the garrison that stood behind Whitehall Palace for a ritual inspection.

Of all the Stuarts, Churchill reflected, she was possibly the wisest and most competent. Born a princess and reared to become a consort rather than a ruler, she had a strong sense of duty to her people. When she was asked to take the throne with her husband, she had not accepted the obligation lightly. The Queen was unique in a family notorious for its profligacy. She loved her husband, was devoted to his welfare, and her unwavering faith in him set a new standard for a nation long accustomed to Stuart licentiousness.

Unfortunately for the Queen, she was dowdy, dressing only when occasions of state demanded it. In addition she was homely. But Queen Mary had qualities that many of her ancestors had lacked. She was honest and direct, never indulging in subterfuge. She had a quick, retentive mind, and she was sensitive to the feelings of others.

As her inspection of the household guards regiment came to an end, Colonel Churchill, who had been accompanying her, saw his chance and seized it. "Ma'am," he said, "I wonder if I might have a half hour of your time."

Mary sensed that the officer's request was serious and important.

She turned to the young lady-in-waiting who was following them. "What's on my schedule this morning, Daphne?"

"The wife of the Austrian minister is expected to call, and the Countess of Southampton is joining you for tiffin."

Mary made a quick, firm decision. "Let them have tiffin together," she said. "I'll join them when I can. Come along, Colonel."

Churchill matched his long stride to her shorter steps as they made their way to her private apartment. Whitehall was a cavernous, gloomy place, but the Queen had supervised the furnishing of her quarters herself, and the results were surprisingly pleasant.

She seated herself on a divan, smoothing her full skirt, and waved her visitor to a cushioned chair opposite her. "You have a problem, Colonel?"

"No, ma'am. England has a problem, but I'll come to that. First I'd like to tell you about an extraordinary person."

The Queen listened, her interest sparking as he described Renno. "If he's white, he must be the offspring of colonists," she said.

"I assume he is, Your Majesty, but I haven't questioned him about his personal background." Churchill bore down hard as he told her about Renno's refusal to shoot a deer in Richmond Park.

"How wonderful!" she exclaimed, her interest really sparked. "What is this Indian doing in London?"

"I'd prefer he tell you that himself, ma'am. Let me say only that John Dryden is writing either a play or poem about him, and several painters want to do his portrait."

Mary nodded. "Mr. Dryden doesn't suffer fools gladly. Colonel, when will you bring this Indian to me?"

"When you wish, Your Majesty."

The Queen rang for her lady-in-waiting. "Daphne, am I having tea with anyone tomorrow?"

"Yes, ma'am. The Duchess of Norfolk, the Duchess of Grafton and—"

"Reschedule them, please. Colonel, I'll expect you and your noble savage at four."

John Churchill rode straight to the little house overlooking the Thames, arriving just as Renno and Jeffrey were about to go out. He told them of the invitation.

"We'll be on our best behavior," Jeffrey said.

Churchill shook his head and smiled. "You aren't included in the invitation, I fear. Queen Mary has asked to meet Renno, no one else."

"That means he'll stand alone."

"All he needs to be is himself," the colonel replied. "Don't put words in his mouth, and don't rehearse what he should or shouldn't say to Her Majesty."

The nervous Jeffrey disagreed but had to defer to someone familiar with the court.

"It's far more important that he wear enough clothes. There would be a scandal if he appeared in a loincloth and paint."

The following afternoon he dressed for his visit under Jeffrey's strict supervision, and finally consented to wear a buckskin shirt and trousers. But he insisted on oiling his face and the shaved portions of his head on either side of his scalp lock, and daubing his face with paint. It would be disrespectful to the woman of the Great Sachem of the English to do otherwise, he declared, and Jeffrey had to give in.

There was a sudden crisis when they discovered that neither of the young men had brought a gift suitable for the Queen. At Andrew Wilson's request Ghonka had sent a number of gifts to King William, but none was appropriate for presentation to a lady.

Renno rummaged through his own belongings and finally found a small doll Ba-lin-ta had made for him to bring him good fortune. It was a figure of an Indian girl, carved of wood, and was dressed in a miniature version of what Ba-lin-ta herself wore. Every girl in the land of the Seneca made and owned similar toys. It had no particular value, but he took it with him, holding it beneath his ceremonial buffalo robe, because he had nothing else to give to the Queen.

Jeffrey fervently wished his friend good luck.

A cavalry escort arrived, and Renno was accompanied down the Strand to Whitehall. Passersby gathered to stare, but Renno paid no attention.

Sentries at the palace gate saluted, and Colonel Churchill waited for Renno in an anteroom.

He was satisfied with Renno's attire, but was disturbed by the knife and tomahawk he carried. "It's bad manners to carry arms when you visit the private apartment of Her Majesty," he said.

Renno shook his head. "I would not be a warrior if I left my tomahawk and knife behind. I would disgrace the Bear Clan and all my people."

Colonel Churchill heard the note of finality in his voice and decided not to press the matter.

Most visitors to Whitehall disliked the place because the long, broad corridors were bare, with no decorations hanging on the walls. The precedent had been established by Charles II, who had said it would be difficult for assassins to hide weapons if there was no place to hide them. Renno, unlike other guests, was impressed by the lack of clutter. In his opinion this was the most attractive place he had seen in London.

A lady-in-waiting escorted the pair into the Queen's sitting room, and although the young woman long had been accustomed to receiving foreign visitors, Renno was so different, she couldn't help gaping.

Queen Mary was more composed, and nothing in her warm smile indicated that Renno's appearance astonished her.

"Your Majesty," Colonel Churchill said, and bowed deeply.

Renno guessed he should follow the colonel's example, but he had never bowed his head to anyone except his father. Instead, he raised his right hand in formal salute. "I greet you, Queen," he said.

Mary continued to smile as she offered her visitors chairs.

Colonel Churchill moved to a chair, but Renno stood still. The Queen seemed to understand his hesitation. "Sit wherever you please," she said.

He nodded and, thrusting the wooden doll at her, lowered himself effortlessly to the floor, where he sat cross-legged and folded his arms.

Mary was so delighted by the doll that she either didn't notice where he sat or didn't care. "How charming. Did you make this yourself?"

Her ignorance of the Seneca made Renno laugh. "Small girls make toys, not senior warriors. This is made by Ba-lin-ta, my sister. It look like her."

"Then she must be very pretty. Thank her for me. Your name is Renno?"

He nodded, then said, "Your name Mary."

Colonel Churchill caught his breath. He doubted if anyone but King William ever addressed Her Majesty by name. But the Queen laughed cheerfully.

Renno had been taught since earliest boyhood to compliment people when his feelings were sincere. He not only liked the longhouse, but he admired this plain woman who wore no paint on her face and whose dark dress of solid-colored wool reminded him of Mildred Wilson's clothes. Her earrings were small, as was a ring she wore on a finger, but he had no way of knowing that the matched emeralds in her jewelry were priceless.

"A Seneca would be happy to live in this longhouse, Mary," he said. "Where is room where you cook?"

The mortified Churchill sat frozen to his chair.

But the Queen remained unruffled. "Other people cook for me because I'm too busy," she said. "They do it in special rooms." She rang a small, ivory-handled bell, and a major domo stood at the door. "Will you have some sack, gentlemen?"

The colonel nodded his acceptance.

Renno refrained from expressing his disgust at the idea by spitting only because he didn't want to soil the English woman's thick, handsome rug. "No," he said firmly. "Sack make me sick. Tea is better."

Queen Mary nodded approvingly. "I quite agree with you. I'll have tea, too." She had noted Renno's interest in the little bell, and offered it to him.

He started to reach for it, then drew back. "I cannot take," he said. "A warrior must earn gifts of great value."

"But you gave me the doll, Renno."

"Doll has no value," he said, then searched for the

110

right English phrase in his growing vocabulary. "The shell that rings is too expensive."

The Queen began to understand what Colonel Churchill had meant about this young "savage's" extraordinary nature. "The bell has value," she said softly, "only if you will accept it as a gift."

He pondered, then had an idea. "I will take as gift for Ba-lin-ta. I will say Mary send because Mary like doll."

The Queen was more deeply impressed. As refreshments were served she encouraged him to talk about his home. Renno was soon chatting amiably with her.

He was completely relaxed and opened up more than he had since he arrived in London.

There was an uncomfortable moment when Her Majesty asked to see his tomahawk.

"No," Renno said.

Even the Queen was startled by the blunt vehemence with which he denied her request.

Renno saw that she looked surprised, so he hastened to explain. "Tomahawk not good for woman," he said. "Blade very sharp. Woman not hold right. Cut hand." He rose and went to her, then drew his tomahawk.

The sight of a warrior standing over the Queen with a deadly weapon in his hand sent a chill up the spine of the commander of the household guard.

"I hold for you," Renno said and, taking her hand, ran her fingers up and down the handle carved with manitous, taking care not to let her touch the cutting edge.

Churchill winced. No breach of etiquette was as grave as that of touching the person of either the King or the Queen.

Mary, however, was enjoying herself thoroughly and thanked Renno for his help. As he seated himself again she wanted to ask how he had become an Indian but her good manners made it impossible for her to raise such a delicate subject. Instead she asked, "Why are you in England?"

Renno's entire manner changed. As he scowled, the savage element in his nature seemed more pronounced, and when he folded his arms across his chest his solemn dignity was as great as that of this woman whose ancestors had been kings and queens for centuries.

"The warriors of the Huron and the Ottawa are bad. The warriors of the Algonquian are cowards, but they number as many as the pebbles of sand on the beach. The soldiers of the French are wicked, and their firesticks kill women and children, not just warriors. All have joined in a great band to kill my people and the settlers of the English. Those who are not killed will become slaves. The towns and the farms of the English colonists will be no more. The French will be their masters and will rule in the name of their Great Sachem. But these terrible things must not be."

The Queen was shaken. "They must not be," she agreed gravely.

"Soon there will be a war," Renno continued. "The evil ones will lose only if the Great Sachem of the English gives his colonists and the warriors of the Iroquois many firesticks and much help."

Queen Mary sat in silence for a moment, then turned to Colonel Churchill. "Is this an accurate description of conditions in the New World?"

"As I understand the situation, Your Majesty, Renno of the Seneca does not exaggerate," he replied.

"And is the King aware of all this?"

Churchill shook his head. "His Majesty is so concerned about the threat that Louis of France poses close to home that he's paid no attention to affairs in the colonies."

"Surely he's kept informed."

The colonel hesitated, seeking the right words so he wouldn't appear critical of King William. "The reports from the governors of the colonies pass through many hands before they reach His Majesty," he said.

Mary appreciated his delicacy, but was worried. The balance of power between major nations was never far from her mind. "It seems to me," she said, "that if France gains control of our North American colonies, she'll become so powerful there will be no way we can defeat her on this side of the Atlantic."

"You're not the only one who holds that opinion, Your Majesty," Colonel Churchill replied.

Mary understood now why Renno had been sent to London and approved of the strategy. She also realized that this was a situation in which she would be required to intervene herself.

"Renno of the Seneca," she said, "I am very pleased that you came to visit me today. We shall meet again."

After the visitors had gone she resumed her normal routines, but members of her staff noted that she was unusually quiet and reflective. What no one yet realized was that the American colonists had won the support of the most powerful of allies.

King William failed to join his wife for dinner, which did not surprise her. His meetings frequently lasted longer than scheduled, and, as usual, he was almost too thorough, too conscientious in the performance of his duties. His mind functioned slowly, and he had to examine all sides of a problem before making a decision.

Mary made her plans for the evening with care. It was late when William finally joined her in her private sitting room. With a deep sigh he unbuttoned his waistcoat and removed his boots. Stretching his stockinged feet in front of the fire blazing in the hearth, he accepted a silver cup of light Dutch beer.

"After a day like this," he said, "I tell myself we were foolish ever to have left The Hague. Governing this country is a thankless task."

"You had another meeting with a committee from the House of Commons."

"I tried to work out a compromise with them on half a dozen bills. Routine legislation. But they'll argue about anything and everything. I always thought *Dutchmen* were stubborn—until we came here."

Mary refrained from remarking that his own nature

was so perverse he invariably caused members of Parliament to become equally stubborn. "I've dismissed my ladies-in-waiting and your equerries," she said. "I thought it would be more relaxing if you have a meal right here in front of the fire."

"I'm not hungry," William said.

Mary ignored his comment. She tugged at a bellpull.

Several footmen in livery promptly appeared. One placed a small table in front of the King, another set it with dishes and silverware, and a third ceremoniously handed the monarch a square of linen. Then a fourth appeared, carrying a silver bowl with a lid on it.

The Queen waved the servants out of the room, ladled the steaming contents of the bowl into a bowl of exquisite chinaware.

King William sniffed, beamed at his wife, and rubbed his pudgy hands together. "Ah, perfect! I guess I'm hungrier than I thought," he said, and ate heartily.

The Queen ladled the rest of the soup into his dish.

He consumed all of it, then belched happily. His mood was much improved and he rambled for a time, discussing the shortcomings of various members of Parliament. Never again would any monarch have total power, and although William was devoted to the principle of sharing power with Parliament, he found it vexing in practice.

The Queen made no attempt to interrupt, knowing his spirits would continue to rise as he unburdened himself.

"That's quite enough of the stupidities I've had to endure," he said at last. "I trust you had a quiet day."

"I had an extraordinary experience," Mary said. "I entertained a North American Indian at tea. A complete savage—who happens to have pale eyes and sandy hair."

William raised a thick eyebrow. "He's come here to appear on the stage, I presume." He was ready to let the subject drop.

"Indeed not. He's the son of the chief of the Seneca

tribe, who is also the leader of the entire Iroquois League. And I gather that in the colonies he's acquired a rather formidable reputation in his own right."

William wasn't interested. "You may be sure some theatrical manager will get hold of him and make a profit by showing him off to the curious."

Mary poured him another mug of light Dutch beer. "You may be very certain that nothing of the kind will happen. Renno of the Seneca has come to London for a specific purpose. He's come here to see you."

William was startled and faintly annoyed. "These days I simply don't have time—"

"I've given my word," she interrupted firmly, "that you'll grant him an audience in the immediate future. And I always keep a promise."

The King became uncomfortable. "Well, if you're going to create an issue of this—"

"I am, my dear," Mary said. "For your own sake— and for England's. See him, hear him—and I know you'll feel as I do."

"What does he want?"

The Queen smiled. "I believe it best," she said, "to let Renno of the Seneca tell you himself."

Disagreements were a rarity in the household of the Great Sachem. Ghonka's word was law in his sphere and Ena was the sole ruler in her domain. Only when their authority overlapped did questions arise, and even on those occasions they usually respected each other's opinions and common sense prevailed. Now, however, the atmosphere was tense.

Sah-nee-wa discreetly absented herself from the house of her brother and sister-in-law and instead ate with friends in the lodge of the Bear Clan. El-i-chi remained in the longhouse of the bachelor warriors, Walter stayed in the lodge for the boys, while Ba-lin-ta, who had no means of easy escape, bolted her food and then hurried off.

Ghonka and Ena faced each other across the small

fire that burned in the stone-lined pit in the center of their hut, the Great Sachem sitting with his arms folded across his chest, his expression forbidding. Ena, seemingly complacent, dipped porcupine quills in gourds containing liquids of various colors, then held them up to the firelight one by one in order to satisfy herself that the dyes had taken. Others might be afraid of her husband, but she was not.

"In six moons' time, in no more than twelve moons' time," she said calmly, "Wal-ter must return to his own people."

She was reopening their argument, and Ghonka had to exert much self-discipline to prevent himself from showing anger. He replied in a low tone, but the ring of authority in his voice was clear. "A Seneca does not break his pledge," he said. "I gave my promise to Wil-son and to Deb-o-rah that the boy would be welcome for all time in the land of the Seneca. If I break my promise, the manitous will turn against me and bring troubles to our nation."

Ena remained seemingly imperturbable. "Then let Wal-ter go to one of the smaller Seneca towns and let him live there."

"Each day the boy is better. Each day he relies more on himself. And if we send him to another town, he will not have Ba-lin-ta beside him to help him."

"That is why he must go," she said. "Not yet, but soon."

Ghonka concealed his astonishment, but nevertheless stared at her. Surely she could see for herself that Ba-lin-ta played a key role in the white boy's improvement!

"Soon," Ena said, "Wal-ter will be a boy no more. He will become a man."

"That is true. And when the day comes, he will take the tests of manhood that will make him a junior warrior."

There was a delicate hint of impatience in his wife's manner. "Soon Ba-lin-ta will no longer be a girl. She will spend her nights in the longhouse of the maidens."

"That is also true." He didn't understand her point.

Ena sighed. "Always Ba-lin-ta and Wal-ter are together. She is his ears. She is his voice."

"This was done by the spirits who rule the living, and it makes them happy."

"Sometimes Ba-lin-ta and Wal-ter are as one person," she declared. "That is what bothers my mind. They are too young to be married, but soon, if they stay together all of the time, they will want to sleep with each other. Ba-lin-ta will have a baby before she goes to the longhouse of the maidens. Wal-ter will become a father before he can wear the feathers of a junior warrior."

At last Ghonka understood what his wife had been trying to say to him, and he was dumbfounded. Her common sense was greater than his, a fact he acknowledged by bowing his head.

The tribute gave Ena no sense of satisfaction. She had no desire to humble her husband, even in private. "I worry for Ba-lin-ta and I worry for Wal-ter," she said. "Today they are still children. Tomorrow they will be children no longer."

Ghonka pondered. "It is wrong to send Wal-ter away," he said at last.

"It is not good," Ena agreed. "But it may be worse if he stays."

"When Renno comes home he will take charge of Wal-ter, and the boy will spend much time with him."

"We do not yet know when Renno will return."

"Until that day comes, Wal-ter will be in the charge of El-i-chi. Only when we eat our meals will he and Ba-lin-ta see each other."

The idea had complications. "A warrior takes one who is younger in his charge only when the younger has performed a deed that pleases the manitou of the hunt or the manitou of war. Wal-ter has learned to hunt and fish with the other boys. He has learned to make a path for himself in the forest, and he does not lose himself there. But he has done no great deed to win the favor of the manitous."

Her point was well taken. The rules of Seneca society were rigid, and not even the head of the nation could change them. There was no way that Walter could be placed in El-i-chi's charge until the boy demonstrated to the satisfaction of the entire community that he stood on the threshold of manhood. On the other hand, Ghonka could not allow the present situation to continue indefinitely. His wife, far more practical in day-to-day matters, had issued a warning that could not be ignored.

Again Ghonka thought long and hard. "We will sleep now," he said at last. "And when the sun returns we will know what must be done."

Ena was satisfied and reached out to touch her husband's wrist with her forefinger and thumb, a sign that she felt confident he would solve the problem.

In the morning he looked serene again, and Ena was tranquil, too, so Ba-lin-ta guessed everything was calm again. El-i-chi did not reappear, preferring to stay for breakfast at the longhouse of the bachelor warriors, so Ghonka sent Ba-lin-ta to summon his younger son.

When El-i-chi appeared, the Great Sachem donned his cloak of buffalo hide, and the pair went off across the barren fields to the forest, a sure sign to El-i-chi that something of vital importance had been decided.

They walked in silence, with Ghonka leading the way, and at last he halted. "For ten days," he said without preamble, "you were the hunting teacher of the young boys. Is Wal-ter ready to become a warrior?"

"He uses a light bow and arrow as a warrior should," El-i-chi replied. "He uses a knife like a man. But he does not yet use a tomahawk or a spear as a warrior uses them."

Ghonka nodded as he weighed his son's words. There was a considerable risk involved in the course of action he had determined, but that couldn't be helped. Often is was necessary to take chances and rely on the protection and assistance of the spirits.

"You will hunt with Wal-ter," he said. "You will

shoot no deer or small game. You will seek a beast that is dangerous to man. When you find it, my son, you will stand aside. Wal-ter must kill the beast. You will not interfere. You will shoot the beast yourself only if your life or the life of Wal-ter is threatened."

It was apparent to El-i-chi that Walter was being required to take one of the harsh tests that faced every boy as he began to approach manhood. In his own opinion Walter wasn't yet sufficiently accomplished as a hunter to face such a severe trial, but it was not the place of a warrior to argue with the nation's chieftain, especially when that leader was one's own father.

They returned to the town, and soon thereafter El-i-chi and Walter started out on their hunting expedition. Both had oiled their bodies as a protection against the unseasonably cold autumn weather, and both carried several days' supply of emergency rations. Game was growing scarce at this season, but El-i-chi knew he and the boy would be expected to remain in the wilderness until the Great Sachem's commands had been obeyed to the letter.

Walter managed to maintain the pace set by his companion as they roamed through the forest. Actually Walter was elated. Ba-lin-ta had told him in their private sign language that her father was testing him, and he welcomed the challenge. For too long, back in Fort Springfield, he had been "poor Walter," the object of either pity or derision. Here he was being taught to stand on his own feet, and he relished the opportunity. He intended to prove himself worthy.

El-i-chi set a blistering pace, pausing only when one or the other picked up the trail of game. Twice they found deer tracks, and occasionally they saw traces that might lead them to raccoons, porcupines, or rabbits, but El-i-chi ignored such animals, and even a fox did not tempt him. With luck he might find a bobcat, but if all else failed he might track a wolf.

By sundown they had found nothing and called a halt for the night. Their rations of jerked venison and parched corn were adequate, but Walter was so hungry that he went fishing in a pond, and after hauling up two large fish he also found some edible roots that they roasted in the coals of their small fire.

Early the next morning they started out again. El-i-chi was pleased when he found the trail of a bobcat, but soon lost it.

Hour after hour the pair scoured the forest, and early in the afternoon El-i-chi called a halt. Walter had doggedly kept up with him, but it was plain that the boy was tired, and it was unfair to expect him to keep up with a grown man who had spent his entire life in the woods.

They stopped at the base of a small hollow where the cover provided by spruce and hickory trees had kept the ground sufficiently smooth that they could sit on it without discomfort. There they chewed slowly on strips of jerked venison, occasionally grinning at each other.

El-i-chi had to admit to himself that he enjoyed Walter's company and no longer thought of the boy as a white settler. If he continued to learn and to toughen up, he might eventually acquire the prowess of a Mohawk or Oneida. It was too much to hope that he would ever become as skilled as a Seneca.

No sooner had the slightly demeaning thought passed through El-i-chi's mind than Walter leaped to his feet and reached for his bow and arrow. The young warrior, slightly ashamed of himself, could hear nothing but realized that Walter, handicapped in some ways, was more sensitive in others than even the most accomplished warriors.

Then El-i-chi heard a rustling sound in the thick brambles and reached for his own bow and arrow.

A few moments later they made out the shape of a wild boar approaching them cautiously but firmly. Apparently the pair had chosen a resting place near the boar's lair.

The boar was ugly and large, weighing close to three hundred pounds, and the expression in its beady red eyes was malevolent.

El-i-chi fitted an arrow into his bow, then paused.

Here was a test that would try Walter's skill, strength, and courage to the breaking point, a trial even more severe than had been in Ghonka's mind when he sent the pair on their mission.

However, so be it. El-i-chi believed in the presence and power of the manitous with all his heart, and he could not think it was a coincidence that the boar had appeared at just this time. The spirits had established their own conditions for the trial, and he could not interfere. Walter would face this fiery, outraged creature alone.

The boy was concentrating all of his attention on the approaching boar and had no idea he would face the animal without help from the infinitely more experienced warrior. As a matter of fact, he had almost forgotten about El-i-chi. Here was an opportunity to kill a wild beast, and it didn't bother him that he had never before faced a boar. It was enough to know that the creature was stubborn and, considering its size, was surprisingly quick and agile.

Walter's throat felt dry, and in spite of the cold a feeling of warmth flooded him. He was testing himself, and he had acquired enough of the Seneca outlook on life not to worry about what might happen to him if he failed. He accepted the God of his own people, but he had come to believe in the manitous who guarded the Seneca, too. One way or another he would be adequately protected.

The boar halted about twenty-five feet from the boy and pawed the ground before charging.

El-i-chi caught his breath and, as a precaution, fitted an arrow into his bow again. Only his memory of the firm orders his father had given him prevented him from killing the beast instantly.

Walter, grinning to himself, pulled his light bow taut, took careful aim, and waited. Months of hunting with the Seneca had taught him never to fire prematurely.

He continued to wait, alert and confident, until the great beast suddenly sprang forward. Then he released the arrow.

The arrow lodged itself in the boar's shoulder.

The wound further enraged the boar, which snorted with pain, then redoubled its fury.

For an instant, Walter stood frozen.

"Use your tomahawk," El-i-chi called frantically, remembering too late that the deaf boy could not hear him.

But Walter recovered on his own, snatched his tomahawk from his belt, and hurled it at the oncoming boar. He missed the animal's head by a fraction of an inch.

El-i-chi drew his bow taut and waited until the last possible moment before letting fly.

As the beast drew closer, Walter knew his life depended on his own skill, cunning, and strength. He drew his knife from his belt, braced himself, and waited, presenting an inviting target. The huge boar was almost on top of him, so close that the boy could feel the almost hypnotic power of its tiny eyes.

At the last instant Walter twisted his body to one side, just enough to avoid the full impact of the charge. The brush was so close that the foul odor of the beast's fur filled his nostrils. Using all of his might, Walter plunged his knife into the back of the boar's neck and severed the animal's spinal cord. The huge creature collapsed at his feet and died.

The relieved El-i-chi raced forward and enveloped the boy in a hug. Even by Ghonka's exacting standards Walter had performed superbly.

The danger ended, Walter began to tremble. But such a reaction did not become a warrior and somehow he managed to regain control. Gradually a feeling of great pride overwhelmed him.

El-i-chi took charge, and together they butchered the carcass, salvaging the edible portions. El-i-chi took care, too, to save the beast's tusk and hoofs. When the grisly task was done, they started back at a trot.

The pair entered the town in triumph and went straight to the house of the Great Sachem. There El-i-chi told his family what had happened, and Walter grinned self-consciously. Ba-lin-ta insisted on hugging her friend even before he could clean off the boar's blood and make himself presentable.

Then Ghonka beckoned, and Walter stood before him. The glow in the Great Sachem's eyes told Walter all he needed to know. Then Ghonka's sinewy hand gripped his shoulder, and the boy stood straighter.

Ena smiled quietly, sharing her husband's pride in Walter. Now all was well. Thanks to Walter's skill, he would be placed under El-i-chi's tutelage until Renno returned from his mission to England. Walter and Ba-lin-ta would continue to see each other every day, but the time they spent together would be limited.

A large fire was built in the pit outside the hut, and Ba-lin-ta was dispatched to the lodge of the Bear Clan to invite all members to a feast.

Then, while Ena and Sah-nee-wa roasted the wild boar meat, El-i-chi and Walter went off to the lake to bathe and change into clean clothing.

At the feast Sah-nee-wa composed a song extolling Walter's triumph. Everyone in the Clan chanted it, and Ba-lin-ta conveyed its meaning to the proud, happy boy. Then Walter presented the boar's hoofs to Ghonka and Ena as tokens of his fealty and love. The women and children stamped their feet, and the warriors filled the air with cries.

Suddenly Walter became shy. After returning from the lake he had barely found time to attach a length of rawhide to the boar's tusk, which he had cleaned by scrubbing it with sand. It was his most precious possession. Glancing at Ba-lin-ta for an instant, then staring off into space beyond her, he thrust the tusk in her general direction.

Her manner changed, too. Overwhelmed by Walter's generosity, she stood indecisively; then she straightened, turned, and accepted the gift, her face wreathed in a dazzling smile. Afraid she would be regarded as bold, she clutched the tusk with both hands and stared down at the ground.

The women of the Bear Clan exchanged significant

glances. When an unmarried warrior presented a girl with the prize trophy of a hunt and she accepted it, they were considered betrothed. Ba-lin-ta and Walter were still quite young, but it was not unusual for a couple to wait many years before they married.

On the other hand, Walter was an outsider who was still unfamiliar with many Seneca customs, so it was possible that he didn't know the meaning of his gift. It would have been bad manners to pry, so the warriors as well as the women looked at Ghonka and Ena for an explanation.

They learned nothing from the Great Sachem, whose face revealed no emotion. Ena looked untroubled, even secretly pleased with herself. She had been right about the changing nature of the friendship of Ba-lin-ta and Walter. For a long time to come the young ones would not see more of each other than was good for them. As for the future, Ena viewed it with Seneca fatalism: the manitous would decide whether Ba-lin-ta and Walter should marry or go their separate ways in different worlds.

Although Ghonka gave no visible signs, he was relieved. A family problem had been solved, and now he could devote himself to a crisis of primary importance to the entire Seneca nation.

The following morning the sachems of the other Iroquois tribes began to arrive in the town. Ordinarily, a meeting between the leaders of the league would be marked by elaborate feasts, ceremonial dances, and evenings of songs and speeches.

This, however was a special conclave, the sachems leaving their own lands as winter approached only because an emergency threatened the security of all. Each leader was accompanied only by a small escort of warriors.

As soon as the last tribal delegation arrived, Ghonka convened the meeting, and the five sachems, each wearing the elaborate, feathered headdress of his rank, went to the Council Lodge. No subordinates were allowed in attendance, and senior warriors of all five nations formed a protective ring around the building. These same men would remain on sentry duty as long as the conclave lasted and would permit no one but authorized food bearers to go inside.

Ceremonies were held to a minimum. The five chieftains sat cross-legged around a fire in the middle of the lodge, and a long clay pipe was passed from hand to hand. They smoked in silence, and not until the last of the tobacco had been consumed did Ghonka set the pipe aside. Now the meeting could begin.

The sachem of the powerful Mohawk, the largest of the Iroquois tribes, was the first to speak. Within the past half-moon, he said, some of his senior warriors, posing as members of the Pequot tribe, had gone to the land of the Algonquian on a supposed trading mission. There they had confirmed what all of the Iroquois had feared.

"It is true," he said, "that the Algonquian have made a treaty with the men of France. Many French firesticks have been sent to them. Many more will arrive in their towns soon. Now the Algonquian wear the blankets of the French on their shoulders. They have put aside the skins of animals they themselves have shot. They cook their food in the pots of black metal the French have given them. Soon many hundreds of Algonquian warriors will go to the new fort the French call Louisburg, where they will make an alliance with the French that will certainly lead to war against the Iroquois and English."

The leader of the Oneida, the youngest of the Iroquois chieftains, now spoke. "That which we feared has come to pass. The Algonquian have joined our enemies. The Huron and Ottawa seek our blood. The French seek our blood. And Algonquian by the thousands seek our blood."

"We must act," the sachem of the Onondaga declared. "We gave wampum to the English settlers and they gave wampum to us. But they have not kept their word. They have not attacked the French or destroyed the Algonquian with their firesticks. The Iroquois must make war before our warriors are killed, our towns are burned, and our women and children become the slaves of the enemy!"

One by one the others agreed, and the most vociferous was the chieftain of the Cayuga, the smallest of the tribes.

Ghonka remained silent, taking no part in the discussion. The others were so excited and angry they failed to notice. He remained withdrawn, even after Ena and Sah-nee-wa brought the evening meal.

The talk became less vehement while the leaders ate, and then the tension rose again. A massive attack on the Algonquian was proposed. The Mohawk preferred an immediate assault on the Huron and Ottawa, arguing that they should be eliminated before the Algonquian were confronted. And the Oneida suggested an assault on the Citadel at Quebec, where the French still maintained a large, strong garrison.

Not until all of the others had presented their arguments did Ghonka speak. "My brothers," he said, "you are wrong. All of your plans will lead to certain defeat."

They stared, aware of him for the first time.

"You forget too quickly that the English settlers are our allies. It may be that we could win a war only with the Algonquian, the Huron, and the Ottawa, but you forget that the French will come to the aid of their friends. You forget that we need the firesticks and the big thunder machines of the English settlers to win a war with the French. We need the help of the English settlers or we will lose!"

The others now spoke in turn, and their arguments were much the same as before. The English settlers had promised many firesticks, but only a few had been delivered. The English settlers had sworn they would go to war again with the French, but they were still at peace, even though the Algonquian had raided towns of the English on the Connecticut River. Therefore, the sachems concluded, the English settlers were not reliable allies.

Ghonka waited patiently until his tribal brothers had expressed their views. Then he spoke again with deliberate, quiet vehemence. "The English settlers have not lied to us. They have not cheated us. They fought beside us at Quebec and there we won a great victory. We *must* trust them. *I* trust them. Not only have I sent my best senior warrior to meet with the Great Sachem of the English, but I remind you that Renno is my son."

His colleagues were impressed and they listened to every word.

"The Great Sachem of the English lives far from our lands. I am told he has many warriors, many firesticks and thunder machines. He has not sent them to us because he does not understand that the English settlers will die with us. Renno will have a conclave with him. Then he will know. He will honor the treaty made with us by the English settlers."

The others hoped he was right, but they remained dubious.

"We have no choice," Ghonka said emphatically. "We need the warriors and firesticks of the English. Without them we will be crushed. So we must wait for Renno to return. We will post many sentries in our lands so the Algonquian, the Huron, and the Ottawa cannot surprise us with many warriors. But I think we are safe. There will be no attack against us at this time."

The other chieftains knew Ghonka's wife was a medicine woman, that it was probable she communed with the spirits and advised the Great Sachem. But the leader of a nation, particularly the Great Sachem of all the Iroquois, should know better than to base his military strategy on advice from the spirit world.

Ghonka knew what was going through their minds, and a hint of humor appeared in his eyes. "I have received no messages from the manitous," he said. "The English and the French are soft. The English will not make war when the air is cold and snow lies upon the ground. Neither will the French. That is why I believe we are safe until the weather becomes warm and grass appears. By that time Renno will return, and all will be well with us."

The sachems were forced to agree that, as Ghonka had said, they had no choice. They could not take the initiative in this war and would have to wait, hoping that Renno's mission would prove successful.

Chapter VI

Renno came to resent being treated as a freak at London dinner parties, although he appreciated the friendship extended to him by Colonel Churchill, John Dryden, and a few others. Jeffrey Wilson sympathized with him and, while they awaited the summons to Whitehall for an audience with King William, he turned down far more invitations than he accepted.

Eager to escape the confines of their little house, the pair sometimes went to a small tavern just off the Strand for a quiet supper. Most of the patrons were ships' captains or merchants engaged in international trade, men of sufficient sophistication to take the presence of the white Indian for granted once they became accustomed to seeing him regularly, so Renno felt as much at home in the Crown and Star as he did anywhere in this alien land.

After Renno's meeting with Queen Mary the two young men were too restless to remain at home, so they began going to the Crown and Star every evening. There they occupied a table at the rear of the dining room, and

Renno ordered a steak and kidney pie, the one English dish he had learned to enjoy. Regular patrons greeted him with brief nods, which he returned, and then paid no further attention to him, much to his relief. Only here and during his daily fencing lessons did he feel comfortable.

One evening the pair left their house, strolled the short distance to the Crown and Star, and took their regular table. As they waited for their food, Jeffrey sipped ale and Renno contented himself with tea, wishing it was the bitter herb tea that Sah-nee-wa brewed.

Neither speculated on the possibility of being called to Whitehall in the near future. They had exhausted the subject and were heartily sick of it. Lord Beaumont had been encouraged by the Queen's friendly reception of Renno and thought it likely that King William would send for him soon. Until then they would have to exercise patience.

Having nothing better to do, Renno observed an exceptionally pretty young woman who was dining alone at the far side of the room. She had flowing red hair that tumbled down her back, chiseled features, and enormous, liquid green eyes. She seemed to be wearing no paint on her face and was modestly attired. She held herself with grace and a sense of dignity.

Jeffrey grinned at his friend. "You'll have to admit that London living has certain advantages."

"I like girl," Renno admitted.

"I must agree with you," Jeffrey said. "She's uncommonly attractive."

Renno continued to watch her covertly. Her demure manners, lack of cosmetics, and understated clothing marked her as a lady.

Two men entered the Crown and Star, looked around the room, and went straight to the woman's table.

Apparently she didn't know them, and did not look up until one of them spoke. Then she looked alarmed and jumped to her feet. It was obvious to Renno that she was badly frightened.

One of the men caught hold of her arm and the

other crowded close to her. She made a desperate but futile effort to free herself. Leaping to his feet, Renno raced across the dining room.

The surprised Jeffrey followed him, taking the precaution of loosening his sword in its sheath. He was as willing as Renno to act as the lady's champion.

By the time Renno reached the struggling trio he held his tomahawk in his hand. "Leave woman alone!" he said sharply. The woman gaped at him, her eyes even larger.

The two men were stunned. Not only were they being challenged by a savage in barbarian dress, but he held an evil-looking, if primitive, weapon in his hand. Judging by the expression is his eyes he was prepared to use. it.

Jeffrey came up beside his friend. "You're in the wrong part of London, lads," he said. "No one assaults a lady who can't protect herself, not here."

The taller of the men was the more aggressive. "Mind your own business," he said.

Renno moved between him and the woman.

"We're on the King's duty," the shorter of the pair said.

Others were on their feet now, and one of them called, "Prove it! Show us your warrant!"

"We carry no warrant," the man said. "We don't require it. We do special work."

"I urge you to leave before you're scalped," Jeffrey said. "My friend is very direct in his dealings, and he can't tolerate liars and bullies."

The woman was looking at Renno in openmouthed admiration. Unaware of her gratitude, he continued to glare at the two intruders. All he knew or cared was that the young woman required protection, and he was doing all he could for her. And if these two men refused to leave her in peace he would make it impossible for them to annoy her further. He raised his tomahawk, intending to bring it down on the head of the taller of the pair.

The man shrank from him. "I order you to halt in the name of the Crown!" he shouted.

"If you're on legitimate Crown business," Jeffrey said, "tell us who you are and what this young lady has done."

"That's a confidential matter," the shorter man said in a surly voice, and after looking hard at Renno he decided not to draw his own short sword.

"You're interfering with an arrest," the taller man said.

Renno backed them to the entrance. "You go!" he directed, and again raised the tomahawk.

The patrons demonstrated their feelings by applauding him. The two men looked at Renno, then at Jeffrey, who held his sword in his hand. Realizing that they would be fortunate if they escaped with cracked heads, they withdrew in great haste.

Renno turned to the young woman, and to his astonishment she was nowhere to be seen. She had obviously slipped away during the commotion, but no one had seen her go.

Renno and Jeffrey returned to their own table, and a few moments later the innkeeper himself brought their meal to them. "You're not paying for your supper tonight," he said. "Thanks for ridding the place of those two. I won't tolerate brawls here."

"What happened to the girl?" Jeffrey asked him.

The proprietor shrugged. "One minute she was here and the next she wasn't. When the argument started, my helpers and I came out into the dining room, so she must have run off through the kitchen. There was no other way she could go." Shrugging and thanking them again, he returned to his work.

Renno was unruffled and ate his steak and kidney pie with relish. Jeffrey took his time with his meal, and was still intrigued by the incident. "It isn't likely that those two men were Crown agents," he said. "But I won't deny it was possible. My father has said that some branches of government work are so delicate that the representatives of the Crown carry no warrants or other identification."

Some phases of English civilizaton were too complex for Renno to grasp, so he concentrated on his meal.

"What's more," Jeffrey went on, "I can't imagine what the girl could have done that would cause Crown agents to arrest her."

"Woman is good," Renno said firmly. "Not bad."

Jeffrey chuckled. "Oh, she's beautiful. There's no denying that. And from a quick glimpse of her expression I'd say you made quite an impression on her. But you know how my father would react to all this, or do you? He'd tell us we had no right to interfere, that for all we know that very pretty girl could have committed all kinds of crimes."

"Woman is good," Renno repeated stubbornly, then fell silent.

Jeffrey let the matter drop, knowing it was impossible to change the mind of the young Seneca. The incident had been strange, but it was unlikely they would learn more of the story. So he, too, dropped the discussion.

After they finished their meal, Renno was ready to leave. He had been unable to break a lifetime habit, and no matter when he went to sleep he always awakened at dawn. He started his day so early in fact that he lighted the kitchen fire for the cook.

The wind had shifted to the southwest, so the air was warmer than it had been earlier in the evening, and London was shrouded in fog. Few people were still out, and the sound of an occasional rider's horse on the cobblestones of the Strand was muffled.

This was the London that Renno liked best, and he was in no hurry. Suddenly he halted.

Jeffrey was faintly annoyed. "Come along," he said. "It isn't all that warm tonight."

Renno raised a warning hand, listened intently, then started forward again. After moving only a few more paces he halted for a second time.

Jeffrey said nothing as he waited impatiently.

Not until they reached the house did Renno explain. "Somebody follow us," he said.

"That's unlikely," Jeffrey replied with a laugh. "Any robber would take one look at those vicious weapons you carry and change his mind in a hurry, I can tell you."

But Renno knew better. "Somebody follow us," he repeated.

"Well, I can imagine who would bother. Or why." Jeffrey said good night and left him.

Renno mounted the stairs to his own room. Ever since he had come to England this had been the most difficult hour of the day for him, the time he felt the most lonely. He was beginning to doubt that the Great Sachem of the English would receive him, and he was so homesick for his own land that he could almost smell the clean, sharp odor of the evergreens in the forest, the scent of venison stew bubbling in Ena's cooking pot.

He moved to the window, lost in thought, and stood there for some time. The fog was so thick he could not see the Thames. For that matter, even the garden below was a fuzzy blur.

Nevertheless, he opened the window wide, removed the quilt from the bed, and rolled himself in it on the floor. When morning came he knew his feeling of depression would lessen.

He began to drift off to sleep, but suddenly he was wide awake, all of his senses alert. Someone was climbing up the garden trellis and through his open window. He grasped the hilt of his knife and, pretending he was asleep, peered in the direction of the window.

He was astonished when he recognized the red-haired woman he had saved from the two men. Perhaps, as Jeffrey had said, she really was a criminal.

Renno waited until she stood inside the room and then sprang to his feet, his knife in his hand. She did not flinch as she looked at the blade. "Oh, dear," she said in strangely accented English. "I hope you won't kill me after going to all the bother of helping me."

Renno felt slightly foolish and lowered the knife. As nearly as he could judge she carried no weapons beneath her cloak, but even if she did, it would be easy enough for him to disarm her.

"Thank you for opening the window for me," she said, shivering, "but please close it. I've been out-of-doors for hours, and I'm frozen."

"You follow me," Renno said.

"Yes. I waited for you and your friend in the alleyway outside the Crown and Star, and I followed you back here. It was the only way I could find out where you lived. Please, the window."

Renno closed the window, then lighted a large candle.

The girl stared hard at him in the flickering candlelight. "You really are an Indian," she said. "While I was standing out in that alleyway I wondered if I had been dreaming."

"I am Renno of the Seneca."

She nodded eagerly. "Oh, I know all about you. I read Daniel Defoe's pamphlet about you. And even if most of it can't possibly be true I think it's wonderful you've come here to get help for the fight against the French in the New World."

Ah, now he recognized her accent! It was similar to what he had heard at Quebec.

"I am Adrienne Bartel," the girl said. "I have no right to ask this of you, but you were kind and generous to me earlier tonight, and I beg you to help me now. I can turn to no one else."

Renno didn't know what to reply, but he was certain she was not a bad person and that she had not come here to rob him.

She hesitated, then seated herself at the foot of the bed, smoothing her skirt. "I am French, as you may be able to tell, and a Huguenot. After my parents died and I sold their property, I made no secret of my opinion of King Louis. No one in France is allowed to criticize him, and when I learned that his secret police planned to send me to jail, I—I ran away. I hired a fishing boat that brought me across the English Channel. But I've had more troubles here. I have no papers, you see."

Renno knew nothing of such documents.

"Those men you stopped from arresting me tonight

really are agents of the British Crown. Technically England and France are still at peace. If they had caught me they would have deported me. They'd have sent me back to France—where I face certain imprisonment. I've been running and hiding for weeks, but they have always found me. And now I have no place else to turn. Will you help me? Will you let me stay here until I can figure out what to do next?"

Her talk of Englishmen sending her back to France and imprisonment confused Renno. Jeffrey would have to hear her story and decide if it made sense. All the young Seneca knew was that a beautiful woman on the verge of tears was asking for his help. He recognized the desperation in her eyes, the terror in her voice.

"I—I'll do anything if you'll let me stay," Adrienne said, her voice breaking.

Renno tried to make sense of what little he could grasp. "Louis, the Great Sachem of the French, is your enemy?"

"He's the enemy of all Huguenots—and of me in particular," she replied.

He felt great contempt for a ruler who made war on women, and his own hatred for the French flared anew. Equally important, he found it impossible to resist the appeal in the woman's liquid eyes. "I will help," he said. "You stay."

His words transformed Adrienne Bartel. Her smile of joy and relief was dazzling, and she impulsively hugged him. "I was right!" she cried. "I knew you would be kind!"

Renno was dazed and stood unmoving. "When the sun returns," he said, "you will tell Jeff-rey what you tell me. He will know what to do."

"Thank you, Renno," she murmured.

The matter settled, Renno reopened the window and pointed to the bed. "You sleep," he said, and returned to the quilt on the floor, turning his back to her.

There were rustling sounds, but Renno tried to ignore them. Ordinarily he fell asleep instantly, but the proximity of this attractive young woman bothered him.

Suddenly Adrienne was standing above him, extending her hand to him.

"There's no need to give up your bed for me," she said softly. "All I can give you in return for your generosity, for the risks you're taking—is myself."

Renno was on the verge of explaining that he never used the bed. Then, even though the candle had been extinguished, he was able to see that the girl was standing before him in the nude. Her figure was breathtaking, and the sight of her inflamed him.

Scarcely aware of what he was doing, he leaped to his feet, swept her into his arms, and carried her to the bed.

Adrienne had needed all of her courage to give herself to him, but now, suddenly, the intensity of his own desire aroused her, too.

Her experience with men was limited, but she recognized Renno's tenderness and skill as a lover. He was gentle and considerate, concerned about her pleasure as well as his own. His strong, muscular body excited her and she was swept away by feelings she had never experienced before. Renno savored her response to him, overcome by her beauty. They found immense pleasure in each other until the final moment of release.

Then they became drowsy, and for once Renno did not mind sleeping in the bed. To his surprise he slept later than usual the next morning. Adrienne was still asleep as he closed the window, bathed in a pail of cold water, dressed, and went downstairs.

The kitchen fire had already been lighted, and the cook was busily preparing the morning meal.

Renno was ravenous. "Three eat breakfast today," he told the cook.

The woman glanced at him slyly, then spoke to the butler, who set another place at the dining-room table.

A few moments later Adrienne Bartel came down the stairs. She had dressed hurriedly and there was anxiety in her face, but her eyes cleared when she saw Renno.

He did not speak because he felt no need for words.

The English, including the colonists, often talked unnecessarily.

When Jeffrey reached the dining room he stopped short and his jaw dropped. "Well," he said, swallowing hard. "I'm damned if I know how you've done it, but I see you two have become acquainted. Well acquainted," he added as he noted Renno's protective attitude toward the woman.

As they ate their meal Adrienne repeated the story she had told Renno the previous night.

Jeffrey leaned back in his chair reflectively, looking remarkably like his father as he listened. When Adrienne was finished he nodded. "Now I can see why the Crown agents refused to identify themselves or create a fuss. Whitehall is buying time, returning Huguenot refugees without papers to France in order to give King William more time to prepare for a major war. The French realize what the English are doing, of course, but they like the arrangement. Not only can they clap recovered Huguenots into jail, but they have more time to get ready for war, too."

Adrienne agreed with him. "For the present both countries like to pretend their relations are normal, even though both are preparing for the biggest war they have ever fought. You cannot believe how happy I was when the fishing boat that brought me here set sail out of Calais. I told myself that now, at last, I would be free. No longer would I be persecuted for my beliefs or threatened with prison. But when I landed at Dover everything was changed. Because I had no papers the English authorities there wanted to send me straight back to France. I was lucky. I escaped. And ever since then I have been hiding, running away from them, and using up my money."

Renno began to understand her story. "The sachem of the French is your enemy. But the English—who are his worst enemies—wish to send you back to him!"

Adrienne nodded solemnly, then brushed back a lock of her long red hair. "I could not believe what was happening to me, but it happened."

Renno was angered anew on her behalf. When Indian nations were enemies they put up no pretenses, no false fronts. They went to war, and the stronger prevailed. But these countries apparently were far different, and it shamed him that his skin was the color of theirs.

"I am afraid," Adrienne said, "that I am helpless. Renno has been good to me, but sooner or later I will be caught and sent back to France!"

"No!" Renno said vehemently, and clenched a fist.

"We'll do what we can to prevent you from being caught," Jeffrey said. "For the present, as long as we're living in this house of my uncle's, you have a sanctuary."

"I thank both of you," Adrienne said. "But there is still dread in my heart. Eventually I must leave, and then I will be trapped."

"We'll see about that." At last he and Renno had something to do while awaiting the summons to Whitehall. "The Crown agents must move very cautiously because public opinion here would be aroused if people learned what's being done to you and people like you. So that gives us an opportunity to play for time."

Renno thought briefly. When Indian warriors went on scouting expeditions they frequently disguised themselves by wearing the war paint of the nation on whose territory they were encroaching. "Adrienne must change," he said. "Look like somebody else."

"That's it!" a delighted Jeffrey declared. "I should have thought of it!"

Adrienne smiled slowly, indicating her willingness.

Jeffrey wasted no time and went off to the shop of a wigmaker, returning a short time later with a wig of long, blond hair. He had also purchased a variety of cosmetics.

Adrienne immediately retired to Renno's bedchamber to don the wig and experiment with the cosmetics.

Soon thereafter a dressmaker and a bootmaker summoned by Jeffrey arrived at the house and spent a considerable time with the girl, taking her measurements.

Several gowns, the dressmaker said, were available at once, having been made for a young actress who had lost her protector and consequently had been unable to pay for the clothes. Only minor adjustments were needed, she said, and promised that the gowns would be ready that same day.

The bootmaker was equally optimistic. He had several pairs of shoes in stock that would fit Adrienne. He, too, said he would return shortly.

Jeffrey was filled with the spirit of adventure. He grinned at Renno. "We're using substantial sums of my father's money and the funds given us by Massachusetts Bay," he said. "But we've spent very little on ourselves here, and I'm sure my father and Governor Shirley would agree that the money isn't being wasted."

Renno agreed. If the scheme proved to be effective, Adrienne would be safe, and he was not concerned with what it cost.

"I don't know and don't care to know how you and Adrienne managed to get together last night or how you achieved such a quick conquest," Jeffrey said. "But it's plain you've learned the ways of our civilization more rapidly than I gave you credit for. And I envy you. She's as beautiful as any girl I've ever seen."

Renno sought for the right English words to express his admiration for the young woman who had entered his life so dramatically. "Adrienne is lady," he said.

"Indeed she is," Jeffrey agreed.

In due time the dressmaker and the bootmaker returned with their deliveries and were paid. Both promised to return in a few days with additional items for the girl's new wardrobe.

The young woman who came down the stairs later to join Renno and Jeffrey in the sitting room in no way resembled a lady. The ringlets of her blond hair were brassy, picking up the light that came in the windows. Her cheeks and mouth were heavily rouged, her eyebrows were bold, kohl was thick on her lashes, and a green substance on her lids emphasized the color of her eyes, which looked even larger. Her snug-fitting silk gown brought out every line of her superb figure, and the neckline was daringly low cut. She had added final, provocative touches by applying a beauty patch of black velvet to one cheekbone and another just above a breast.

Her hips swayed as she walked in her high-heeled shoes and tight skirt. For good measure she carried an ivory fan, and she halted on the landing long enough to peer over it, then snap it shut as she descended.

The cook felt certain that Renno was taking up with doxies, and other members of the household staff agreed. The white Indian had been quick to acquire the habits of the English gentry.

Renno and Jeffrey stared in silence as Adrienne came into the sitting room.

"I didn't recognize myself," she said, "when I looked into the pier glass."

"Nobody know you," Renno said.

"I feel like a woman at Louis's court," she said. "Either a courtesan or a noblewoman. Not that there's much difference between them anymore."

"The transformation is remarkable," Jeffrey said. "Only your voice is unchanged. It will be impossible for the Crown agents to recognize you. We're going out to celebrate."

Adrienne became alarmed. "I don't dare!"

"But you must," he said. "It could be that we're suspected of harboring you because we had a hand in your escape last night, and Crown agents may be watching this house. But once they've seen you they'll go elsewhere. There's no way they'll connect you with the genteel, red-haired young lady they were pursuing."

His logic made sense to Renno. "We go," he said, and touched the tomahawk at his belt in a silent promise to Adrienne that no harm would befall her.

The trio went off in one of Lord Beaumont's carriages to the theater, where they saw a performance of Shakespeare's *King Lear*, and then, at Jeffrey's insistence, they went on to the Crown and Star for supper. For the first time the attention of the crowd which Renno usually stirred was diverted to his glamorous, spectacularly attired female companion.

As Adrienne became accustomed to her new role, she gained confidence. She was flamboyant, sure of her appeal, and she carried off the deception with a flair.

When they left the tavern they walked back to the little house overlooking the Thames, and Renno made certain they were not being followed. It seemed reasonable to assume that the Crown agents had not recognized her.

Adrienne took it for granted that she would sleep with Renno again. They made love, and when Adrienne drifted off to sleep Renno remained awake and pondered the strange turns of fate that had brought him and Adrienne together. With a shock he recalled his dream that had convinced him he must make the long voyage to this alien land. The young woman who had appeared before him in that dream, beckoning and insisting that he come to England, had red hair and green eyes!

He couldn't recall her features clearly, hard though he tried, but he was convinced it had been Adrienne. How that could have happened was beyond his comprehension, but no warrior wasted time trying to solve the puzzles of the manitous. One accepted the wisdom of the spirits and obeyed.

He had no idea what might happen to him and Adrienne, but he accepted as a fact that they were bound together by forces stronger than their own feelings. So be it.

On the other hand, the manitous never denied a devout warrior the freedom of choice. This woman was lovely and was endowed with courage and an inner strength. Remembering how she looked after her transformation, however, he could not picture her being at home in the land of the Seneca. Could she cook his meals in his hut, as Deborah had done? Could she work in the fields with Ena and the other women?

No. Adrienne was not only white, she was unlike the women of the colonies. She was unused to the hardships of the wilderness, and Renno couldn't imagine her finding even temporary contentment with him in the land of the Seneca. But he was not closing the door to the possibility that she might change. If that happened, he would then think about making her his wife.

At present he was certain only that he would not change. His weeks in London had convinced him of the superiority of the Seneca way of life to any other, and his inner doubts about being tempted by the more advanced civilization had vanished. The values of the Seneca were based on the earth, the sky and water, the forests, and the changing seasons. Those things were real. Here in England, men indulged their whims of the moment, living without principles and obeying no laws other than those sparked by their own desires.

So for the time being he would continue to live with Adrienne, enjoying her company and relishing their lovemaking. The manitous would guide and guard him, and they alone knew what the future held in store.

The summons to Whitehall was delivered early in the morning by a royal equerry. His Majesty was pleased to grant an audience at noon the following day to "Prince" Renno of the Seneca.

Jeffrey immediately went to his uncle, and Lord Beaumont acted with dispatch. Not only would he be present at court for the occasion, armed with the letters from Andrew Wilson and Governor Shirley, but he promised that a number of noblemen and several members of the House of Commons, all friendly to the cause of the colonists and sympathetic to their present plight, would be in attendance, too. Whatever might develop, they would support him.

Before leaving Boston Jeffrey had received specific instructions from his father. "When Renno goes to court," Andrew Wilson had said, "let him handle the audience in his own way. Don't try to lead him, and put no words in his mouth. He'll be effective only if he behaves in his usual manner."

Jeffrey had taken his father's words to heart and

made no attempt to coach his friend. He did, however, decide to take the disguised Adrienne with them. At first she was frightened, but her desire to witness the historic event overcame her fears. Jeffrey explained to his uncle only that the young woman was currently having an affair with Renno, and the amused Lord Beaumont could see no harm in allowing her to be present.

Renno shaved his head on either side of his scalp lock and, wearing only a loincloth and moccasins, daubed his face and torso liberally with the paint of the Seneca. He decided to carry a bow and a quiver of arrows in addition to his tomahawk and knife, and Jeffrey wisely made no attempt to dissuade him. The more striking his friend's appearance, he thought, the more of an impression on King William he was likely to make.

An hour before the appointed time Jeffrey, the bewigged and spectacularly gowned Adrienne, and Renno, a cloak of buffalo skin thrown over his shoulders, were driven in a Beaumont carriage to Whitehall.

The sentries saluted, and Colonel Churchill appeared in order to conduct the special guest. An equerry led Jeffrey and Adrienne away unobtrusively to join Lord Beaumont's party.

The commander of the household guard walked beside Renno down the drafty, high-ceilinged halls of the palace. "There are more people—many more—than usual in the reception hall today," he said. "Word has leaked out that there is going to be an unusual presentation, and Queen Mary is on hand. She rarely attends one of the King's audiences, so you must have made quite an impression on her."

Renno nodded, but was not awed. Mary was his friend, and he was pleased he would see her again.

The audience chamber indeed was crowded. Lords and ladies by the score were in attendance, all in their most glittering attire. High-ranking officers, including several generals and admirals, wore uniforms studded with decorations. The mistresses of the mighty were on hand in their most stunning finery, so Adrienne certainly would not be out of place, and red-coated troops of the household guard, armed with muskets and bayonets, stood at attention around the room.

The audience chamber itself was a cavernous hall, its most attractive feature a huge crystal chandelier; but thanks to William's parsimony the cheap candles burning in it gave off an acrid smoke.

The small fires burning in two hearths did almost nothing to remove the chill from the room, and the underdressed ladies shivered. They were there only because it had been whispered that they would witness a rare spectacle, and most were already hoping the audience would be short. Most of the men were wearing plumed hats, the King generously having granted his permission for them to cover their heads because of the cold.

A narrow purple rug ran the entire length of the chamber, and at the far end King William and Queen Mary were seated in armchairs on a dais raised about a foot above the hardwood floor. The Queen, knowing the hall would be chilly, was sensibly attired in a simple dress of brown wool. William was also, as usual, simply dressed, with only the blue ribbon of the Order of the Garter extending from one shoulder across his paunch to relieve the drabness of his appearance. Only the members of the House of Commons who clustered behind Lord Beaumont were as inconspiciously dressed.

The King looked old and tired. There were smudges beneath his eyes, and he drummed restlessly with big-boned fingers on one arm of his chair. He was granting this audience only to please his wife, and his mind was already on a meeting of the Privy Council that he had called. As soon as he could get rid of his guest he would retire with the members of the council to a small room where they could put in several hours of hard work.

Renno stood beside Colonel Churchill at the entrance to the chamber. He could see Jeffrey and Adrienne standing beside Lord Beaumont. And on the opposite side of the hall he saw someone else he recognized: the Earl of Lincoln, who had quarreled with him.

He felt no nervousness, no apprehension. This visit

was his right, as the son of Ghonka, and he had waited a long time to be heard.

A chamberlain approached, his aplomb shattered when he gaped at the white Indian, and there was a tremor in his voice when he called, "Prince Renno of the Seneca."

Renno advanced into the chamber and, with Colonel Churchill beside him, began to walk the length of the purple carpet. He removed his buffalo cloak from his shoulders, impervious to the gasps of the ladies and gentlemen. Colonel Churchill took the cloak and halted.

Renno advanced to the dais alone.

The Queen apparently felt the need to put the visitor at his ease. "It's good to see you again, Renno," she said, speaking slowly and distinctly.

"Is good to see you, Mary," he replied amiably.

The members of the court were astonished by the appearance of the warrior, but his conduct was even more shocking.

He halted at the base of the dais and raised his right arm. "Hail, Great Sachem of the English," he said. Then, before the soldiers had a chance to stop him, he sprang effortlessly onto the dais and grasped the King by the forearm.

The startled William was no longer bored. For an instant he thought this half-naked savage was attacking him, but then he realized he was merely being subjected to an Indian form of greeting. "Hail, Renno of the Seneca," he replied.

The laughter that had started to well up in the audience chamber died away abruptly. The King was displaying a dignity and courtesy as great as that of his guest.

Renno was pleased. His first impression of William had not been good. He had noticed that the man was flabby, unlike the chieftains of the Iroquois League, all of whom were capable of leading their men into strenuous combat. But William conducted himself like a leader, and that was equally important, so Renno relaxed. This room was the only place he had found in England that was cool enough for him, and he concluded that the monarch was sensible.

The King was intrigued and inquired about the meaning of the feathers that the young Seneca wore in his scalp lock. Renno explained they were the insignia of a senior warrior, and that each signified the performance of deeds of valor in battle. As he spoke it occurred to him that he had neglected to bring a gift for the Great Sachem of the English, and he was horrified because he had forgotten such an important act of kinship. Impulsively he took one of the many scalps hanging from his belt and presented it to William.

Many of the ladies gasped, some covered their faces with their hands, and a number of gentlemen looked as though they would become ill.

Again William was equal to the situation. He accepted the strip of dried human skin, examined it with care, and thanked his guest graciously for it. Then he beckoned to an equerry and whispered something to him.

The official hurried from the audience chamber.

"I assume you use the various weapons you're carrying," William said. "Would you show us what you do with that knife?"

Renno nodded and looked around the chamber. The gleam in his eyes caused several of the timid to shrink.

"Colonel Churchill," William called, "be good enough to arrange a target."

The commander of the household guard was at a loss for a moment, but his face lightened when he saw that the mistress of a duke was wearing a short cape of beaver skins. He borrowed the cloak from her, then draped it over a chair, which he placed on the purple carpet just inside the entrance at the far end of the chamber.

"If that target is too far for you," the King said, "it can be moved closer."

Renno shook his head and smiled. Drawing his knife, he turned his back to the target and faced the King.

One of the younger officers of the household guard

instinctively reached for his sword. The savage stood within arm's reach of the monarch and could assassinate him with a single slash of his knife. Colonel Churchill caught his subordinate's eye and shook his head.

Suddenly Renno whirled and, without appearing to take aim, threw the knife.

The point of the blade cut through the center of the cloak and pinned it to the back of the chair. There was a moment of stunned silence, and then King William led the applause.

Colonel Churchill retrieved the knife, which he returned to Renno, and then gave the young woman her slightly damaged fur.

William was fascinated. "If it isn't asking too much," he said, "could you show us how you use that— ah—hatchet?"

"Tomahawk," Renno said, and as he drew it from his belt he looked around the chamber. A man's broad-brimmed hat of scarlet velvet stood out against a wall about forty feet from the dais, and attached to it was a white plume, perfect for his needs. It was no matter to him that the hat was being worn by the sour-faced Earl of Lincoln.

Drawing the tomahawk, Renno first handed it to the King as a courtesy. William examined the weapon with great interest. "It's heavier than I realized," he murmured.

Renno took it from him and grasped it firmly. Then he startled all by leaping from the dais and emitting an ear-shattering Seneca war cry. He flipped over in a forward somersault, and as he regained his feet the tomahawk left his hand. A moment later the white plume on the Earl of Lincoln's hat was severed no more than an inch from its base.

The applause was deafening. Queen Mary forgot her dignity and cheered aloud, and many of her subjects heartily followed her example.

A junior officer retrieved the tomahawk and, holding it as though he was afraid it was a living thing that would assault him, he returned it to Renno.

Only the glowering Earl of Lincoln looked displeased.

King William sat grasping the arms of his chair and shaking his head from side to side.

Renno returned to the dais, marveling that these people found his simple feats extraordinary. He needed no urging to demonstrate his skill with a bow and arrow, and decided to create a more difficult task for himself. He sat informally on the dais, at the feet of the King, drew an arrow from his quiver, and fitted it into the bow.

Everyone in the chamber was silent, motionless. King William was so excited that he rose to his feet. Renno wanted more room and motioned him aside. The monarch obediently moved closer to the Queen's gilded chair.

Renno jumped onto the dais and spun himself around and around, like a top. While in motion he raised the bow and, still spinning, let fly with the arrow. There was no sound in the huge hall but the twang of the bow.

Those who stood nearest to the Earl of Lincoln were the first to realize what had happened. The arrow had cut through the crown of the red velvet hat, removed it from the nobleman's head, and skewered it to the wall behind him. There was complete pandemonium as members of the court realized what had happened. Ladies screamed happily and sedate gentlemen stamped their feet and pounded each other on the back.

Only when the King tried to make himself heard did the crowd become quiet. "Renno," he said, "you've given us the most marvelous exhibition of marksmanship I have ever seen."

Renno had not forgotten that he had made the long journey to England for a purpose other than showing off. "In the land of the Seneca," he said, "there are nearly two thousand warriors. In the lands of the other Iroquois nations there are more than three thousand warriors. All use knives and tomahawks and bows and arrows. All are the friends of the English settlers."

"I'm delighted to hear it," William said.

Renno folded his arms across his chest. "Soon," he

said, "the warriors of the Iroquois will die. The soldiers of the settlers will die. They will be killed by the soldiers of the French and their friends. The Algonquian. The Huron. The Ottawa."

The King tried to grasp the significance of what was being said to him.

Renno had acquired no reputation as an orator in the land of the Seneca, and certainly he was not the equal of Ghonka as a speaker. But at this moment he felt as though manitous were inhabiting his body, loosening his tongue, and inspiring him.

"The warriors of the Iroquois and the soldiers of the English settlers will surely die!" he intoned. "The women of the Iroquois and the women of the English settlers will die. Their children also will die. Those who die will enjoy good fortune. Because those who live will become slaves. The slaves of the French!"

Color drained from William's face and he sat frozen in his chair.

Lord Beaumont stepped forward quickly and approached the dais. "Your Majesty," he said, "permit me to clarify what Renno has said to you and to expand on it. With your permission I'd like to read two letters addressed to you, one by the Governor of Massachusetts Bay and the other by my brother, who commands the colony's militia."

The dazed King nodded.

Beaumont read the two letters, which explained the plight of the English colonies in North America in full detail.

"Why was I never told these things before?" the monarch demanded.

No one had the courage to tell him that the originals of the letters had been held up by bureaucrats in various government ministries.

"If France overruns our New World possessions she'll be twice as powerful! That must not be allowed to happen." The King paused. "Tell me more about this new fortress called Louisburg. How many troops and how many French warships are stationed there? What is the size of the fortress and how many cannon does she mount?"

There was an uncomfortable silence.

"It's my understanding, Your Majesty," Lord Beaumont said at last, "that none of our colonials have set foot on Cape Breton Island. The French maintain a highly developed sentry protection system both on land and at sea."

William turned back to the white Indian. "Do you know the answers to my questions, Renno?"

"No. Only the friends of the French go to island."

"Obviously we'll require information," the King said. "I'll discuss that at length with the Privy Council and the War Council. Is Sir Harold Phipps here?"

The white-haired lieutenant-general who commanded the Royal Army stepped to the foot of the dais and saluted. "Your Majesty?"

"The colonies will need regiments of troops, arms and munitions, and all kinds of supplies. We'll discuss the matter at length in the War Council, but I want you to begin organizing the delivery of arms and supplies at once. Renno cannot be allowed to return to America empty-handed."

The general saluted.

The thoroughly aroused monarch was not done. "Lord Catton?"

The First Lord of the Admiralty, trim and erect, came forward. "Yes, Your Majesty?"

"A meeting of the War Council will be the appropriate place to discuss the size of the naval expedition we'll need to send to America. But we've already lost enough time, so be good enough to arrange for a convoy of ships to take the initial arms and supplies to the New World."

Lord Catton saluted and retired.

The King beckoned his equerry, who brought him an oblong box of inlaid wood, and then the monarch turned back to the grave, silent white Indian. "Renno of the Seneca," he said, "my people and I are in your debt. Thanks to you we have become more aware of the dangers to all of us in the New World. I apologize to you for the delays that prevented this audience from taking place when you first reached our shores, and I assure you the negligent will be punished. A convoy will sail to America as soon as arms and supplies can be gathered. I offer you and your party a place in that convoy."

Renno inclined his head in a gesture of thanks, a gesture he would make to no one but a Great Sachem.

"You have given me gifts today, including the precious gift of opening my eyes to problems I never knew existed. The least I can do on behalf of my people and myself is to present you with a token in return." He paused for an instant. "Are you familiar with pistols?"

Renno nodded. "I learn many moons ago to shoot with small firestick," he said.

The King smiled and proved he wasn't totally devoid of a sense of humor. "There's no need to demonstrate your skills. I'll take it for granted you have them." He handed his guest the box.

Renno opened the container and found a brace of dueling pistols inside. Even though his experience with firearms was limited he knew at a glance that these were exceptional weapons. Their barrels were short, the handles were made of mother-of-pearl, and, as he would discover when Jeffrey later examined the pistols, they had hair triggers that responded instantly to the slightest pressure.

"I want to give you a small gift, too, Renno," Queen Mary said. Making a gesture that everyone present would long remember, she removed a medallion of gold, the size of a woman's fist, from her neck, and handed it to him.

The courtiers applauded spontaneously.

The audience was at an end, and when the King and Queen walked down the length of the carpet together the women curtsied to the floor and the men bowed low. Only Renno continued to stand erect as befitted the son of a Great Sachem.

An elated Jeffrey raced to Renno's side and soon was joined by Lord Beaumont, Colonel Churchill, and a number of others long concerned about the colonies.

"That was magnificent," Jeffrey said. "You not only captured the King's complete interest, but you appear to have won us all the help that we and the Iroquois need!"

"Your skill with Indian weapons made it impossible for His Majesty to ignore you, and no one could have delivered a more effective speech," Lord Beaumont said. "No one has contributed more to the survival of the colonies or the Indians who are our allies. All of them are permanently in your debt."

Colonel Churchill added his warm congratulations, as did a number of others.

The disguised Adrienne, looking no more flamboyant than many ladies of the court, stood somewhat apart. She was smiling, pleased because Renno had succeeded.

He himself was calmer than any of those who surrounded him. In his opinion the skill he had demonstrated was nothing out of the ordinary. As for the few words he had spoken, he had told the truth, so he had expected no other response from the Great Sachem of the English. The real credit, he thought, should be given to the manitous who had shown him the vision of Adrienne that had impelled him to come to this strange land.

The one thought that excited him was the prospect of returning to his beloved forests in the immediate future. He had no idea how long it might take to load several ships with arms or supplies, but William had spoken firmly, so he assumed it would be soon.

He and his companions left the palace and crossed the courtyard to their waiting carriage.

Three men approached, walking rapidly, and in the center was the still red-faced Earl of Lincoln, who was hatless. He blocked Renno's path and spoke angrily. "You went out of your way to humiliate me in the presence of the King, the Queen, and the whole court!"

Beaumont and Churchill tried to intervene, but the enraged earl brushed them aside. "My quarrel is with this damned savage, not with you," he said. "This is the second time he has mocked me, and I won't tolerate it!" With great deliberation he removed a glove and slapped the young Seneca across the face with it. Then he turned on his heel and stalked off.

Renno didn't yet know it, but he had been challenged to a duel.

Chapter VII

Massachusetts Bay was the wealthiest, best organized, and most heavily populated English colony. It therefore became the key to the survival of the English in the New World. If Massachusetts Bay became heavily engaged in defending itself, it could leave the other English colonies stripped of their central leadership.

Alain de Gramont evaluated the success of his mission after his return to Quebec. His raids with his Huron warriors, disguised as Algonquian, had been partly successful. The English colonies had added the Algonquian to the list of their enemies. But the counterattack by the militia on his raiders near Fort Springfield had forced him to withdraw. As a result he had not achieved a major goal, that of inciting an all-out campaign by Massachusetts Bay against the Algonquian.

He discussed the matter with General de Martine just prior to the latter's return to Louisburg. "The present situation makes me uneasy, sir," he said. "Your new fortress is a natural target for the English, and Paris is so slow in sending you reinforcements that—one of these days—London may be impelled to take the initiative."

"I think it unlikely," de Martine replied. "Even without the additional troops and warships that I've been promised, I can give the English a terrible drubbing."

"True, sir, provided their colonies—with a population several times that of New France—don't become actively engaged in the fight. Will your new troops and ships arrive by spring?"

The general smiled wryly. "They've been promised for spring, Gramont, but the joys of life at Versailles tend to make officials of the war and navy ministries lose count of the calendar. I must admit I don't share your worries, but it would make my task simpler if the English colonies were kept busy."

"They're first-rate soldiers, sir, and that's why I'm apprehensive. I've faced them in battle, and they understand the principles of wilderness warfare. I succeeded in convincing them that the Algonquian launched unprovoked attacks on them, but I didn't goad them enough to retaliate. I was hoping they'd become totally involved in a full-scale war with the Algonquian. If that had happened the tardiness of Paris wouldn't matter, and you'd have all the time you need to prepare your own invasion of Boston and New York."

"I never waste time regretting what might have been," the general said crisply.

"Neither do I." Colonel de Gramont bristled. "Just as I was about to carry out the most important part of my mission I stumbled onto a superior force of Massachusetts Bay militia and was forced to withdraw. But that doesn't mean I've got to sit on my hands for the rest of the winter."

Obviously he had something in mind, and General de Martine, who had become fond of this hard-bitten officer, raised an eyebrow and looked at him quizzically.

"When strategy is sound," Alain said, "a temporary defeat shouldn't influence a change in basic thinking."

"I see what you mean."

"I still believe Massachusetts Bay can be lured into

becoming so occupied fighting the Algonquian they'll have no time to think about a more important enemy."

"I want to hear no details, please," the general declared. "If atrocities are committed by people over whom I have no control, I don't want to hear about it."

"Go back to your Louisburg headquarters with a clear conscience, General. I hope to have good news for you when I join you there in the spring."

Alain de Gramont made his new plans with great care. He took only twenty-five of his most trusted veterans with him, and they marched south from Canada in the dead of winter. Reaching the English colonies, they kept themselves concealed in the wilderness on the west bank of the Connecticut River until they reached a point a short distance to the north of Fort Springfield. There they crossed to the east bank and, disguised as Algonquian, they launched a series of lightning, brutal raids on isolated farmhouses. Only highly disciplined warriors could have followed Gramont's instructions to the letter. No booty was taken and no prisoners were captured. In the event resistance was encountered, the band was under strict orders to retreat rather than fight. The whole purpose of these raids was to create as much havoc in as short a time as possible. Gramont wanted to arouse the authorities of Massachusetts Bay so thoroughly that they would go to war against the Algonquian without delay.

Houses and barns were set on fire, and all crops stored for the winter were destroyed. Men, women, and children alike were murdered and scalped. All livestock was slaughtered.

Gramont struck swiftly and mercilessly, venturing as close to Fort Springfield itself as he dared, then crossing the river, disappearing into the forest again, and returning to Canada under forced march.

No one in the Fort Springfield area could doubt the effectiveness of the brutal raids, and several witnesses, who saw the attackers from a distance but managed to escape their wrath, identified them as Algonquian.

A farmer named Fred Browne, who lived near the

Connecticut border, was murdered in his barn, and his wife, Emma, and all four Browne children were killed in their house.

Abel Adamson, the town's leading blacksmith, had gone home for dinner with his wife, and both died.

Ida Alwin escaped death only because she had gone into Fort Springfield, but her home was once more burned to the ground, and she lost most of her belongings. There was no way her house could be rebuilt for several months, so she was obliged to move into the parsonage with Deborah and her husband.

None of the murders created greater indignation than that of Louise Gautier. She had brought her husband his noon meal, and, finding that he had apparently gone down to the river for water, she had waited for him on the small porch of their almost-completed house.

When Rene returned a few minutes later, he found Louise dead of stab wounds and scalped. Something had frightened the raiders away before they could put the torch to the house.

Rene was in a state of near-collapse, and Mildred Wilson ministered to him and looked after the two small children, who were bewildered by the tragic, sudden loss of their mother.

Brigadier Andrew Wilson immediately mustered all available militiamen in the area, and two units were sent out to look for the marauders, one led by Captain Donald Doremus and the other by Lieutenant Tom Hibbard. Both groups spent a full week scouring the countryside, but they found no trace of the savages. Alain de Gramont had been totally successful in carrying out the initial phase of his plan, and he and his warriors escaped unscathed.

The Reverend Jenkins conducted a communal funeral service for the victims, which was attended by almost everyone in town, and the burials followed at once. Rene Gautier was so dazed that he scarcely seemed to know what was happening.

The people of Fort Springfield were outraged by the massacre, and a petition demanding that an expedition be sent to punish the Algonquian was signed by more than six hundred persons.

Brigadier Wilson almost fell into the trap that Colonel de Gramont had set and baited for him. But his own sense of strategy was so keen and far-sighted that he refrained. As he told Captain Doremus, "God knows the Algonquian deserve to have their noses bloodied, but I don't want us to become mired in a secondary campaign."

Doremus was puzzled.

"The Algonquian are the largest tribe in these parts, and can send several thousand warriors into the field. If we go after them, we'll have to muster every regiment and separate company in the Massachusetts Bay militia."

"And we'll beat the daylights out of them, sir!" Doremus said. "We'll teach them a lesson they won't forget for years to come."

"Oh, there's no doubt in my mind that we can trounce the Algonquian handily," Andrew Wilson replied. "But we'll be squandering our ammunition and other resources and wasting our manpower. The Algonquian are already the allies of the French, are they not?"

"Yes, Brigadier, but—"

"And the French—from the bits and pieces of information that we've been able to glean—are still working on Fort Louisburg, building it larger and adding to their forces there. There's the real threat to us, Don. If we weaken ourselves by sending a punitive expedition against the Algonquian, we'll have almost nothing left in our arsenal when the time comes to hold off the French. We've been waiting for Renno to enlist the aid of the Crown, and we'll have to continue to wait until he returns with Jeffrey from London. If he's successful, we can re-examine our situation. If he's failed, we'll have to bite the bullet and wait for a more opportune time."

"Feelings of folks hereabouts are running mighty high after this raid, Brigadier."

"I'm well aware of it, and no one is more indignant than I am. But our supplies of ammunition and powder are limited, and so is our manpower. We'll just have to be patient a little longer. We'll have our chance to even the score with the Algonquian, never fear. But we won't clash with them until we are in a position to meet the French in battle, too—and at least have a chance of not being inundated. I suspect this raid was conducted simply in order to provoke us into taking action prematurely, and that's something I refuse to do. The future of Massachusetts Bay and all of the other English colonies depends on our ability to keep our heads and not react rashly. We've got to hold tight, Don—and pray that our time will soon come!"

Colonel Churchill paced up and down the length of the small sitting room in the house overlooking the Thames. Although he spoke ostensibly to Renno, he was actually talking to Jeffrey Wilson and a badly worried Adrienne, who sat with her hands clenched in her lap. "Pardon my language in the presence of a lady, but Lincoln is a two-faced, conniving bastard. A man with his experience has no right challenging a novice to a duel. It will be murder, not a fair fight!"

Renno was unperturbed by his friend's concern for him. He didn't understand what took place in a duel, but he had complete confidence in his own abilities as a warrior.

Jeffrey laughed unhappily. "As the challenged party, Renno has his choice of weapons. I'd love to see the faces of Lincoln and his seconds if we tell them that our principal has elected to fight with tomahawks."

Renno grinned. He would enjoy decapitating the red-faced Englishman with a single, well-aimed blow.

"Like you, Mr. Wilson, I'm tempted," Churchill said. "But the rules of civilization must apply to affairs of honor here, unfortunately. The duel will have to be fought either with pistols or swords."

"Why must there be such a duel?" Adrienne cried. "It is not only unfair, it is uncivilized! Surely your King and Queen would not approve!"

"Indeed they wouldn't, young lady," the commander of the household guard replied gravely. "They're opposed to the whole concept of dueling. But when a custom has been ingrained in a society for centuries, not even monarchs can uproot it overnight. Renno won a great victory for the English colonists and his own people today. But that doesn't mean that help for America will begin to flow automatically. Men who were impressed by Renno's performance and skills at Whitehall will be needed in every step of what lies ahead. Gathering munitions and supplies of all kinds, assigning troops and sending warships across the Atlantic all take time. A great many people must cooperate and work together. And if word gets out—as it most assuredly would—that Renno refused to accept the challenge of the Earl of Lincoln, he'd lose the respect and esteem of men who now admire him. They'd start dragging their heels. A mere trickle of aid, rather than a stream of it, would find its way to the New World."

"The English gentry," the girl said with contempt, "are as obsessed with their supposed sacred honor as their enemies, the French. May the Lord preserve us from gentlemen."

"I'm afraid I must agree with Colonel Churchill, Adrienne," Jeffrey said. "No one here would openly defy King William's direct orders, but the delays would be interminable and the problems that would arise would be endless. The colonies need help, and they need it immediately. That means Renno must fight the Earl of Lincoln."

Renno nodded, and couldn't understand why Adrienne was so badly upset.

"Suppose he's killed," she said. "Will the duel still be worthwhile?"

"We're doing our best to see to it that he isn't killed," Churchill said. He halted and opened the box containing the magnificent pistols the King had presented to Renno. "I wonder," he said.

Jeffrey shook his head. "The same idea crossed my mind, Colonel, but I think not. Renno has a marvelous eye, and he's already learned to handle a musket better than most veteran soldiers. But he isn't all that familiar with pistols."

"And dueling pistols are a special breed, thanks to

their balanced weight and their hair triggers," Churchill said. "I'm afraid Renno would need a great many hours of special practice before he would become proficient with pistols such as these. And you can be quite sure that Lincoln has been practicing with them ever since he was a boy."

"That leaves swords," Jeffrey said.

Adrienne covered her face with her hands.

"It isn't as hopeless as you think," Jeffrey went on. "I taught him the rudiments of swordplay on board the brig that brought us to England, and he's been taking daily fencing lessons since we've been here."

"How do you rate him?" the colonel asked.

Jeffrey weighed the question. "He can give a fair enough account of himself with anyone except a master," he said. "His eye is remarkable, he has great strength, and he's quick, very quick. What he lacks most is the polish that comes with experience. And I dare say that the Earl of Lincoln has been handling swords all of his life."

"He's won several duels," Churchill said. "But swords seem to be our better wager. The greatest advantage is that the danger of being killed is vastly reduced."

"Of course," Jeffrey said. "Once a duelist is wounded, his opponent's honor is regarded as satisfied and the fight is ended. I'll cast my vote for swords, too. What do you think, Renno?"

The white Seneca smiled. "I fight with swords."

"Splendid," Churchill said. "I'll call on the earl's principal second and notify him of our decision."

Adrienne looked at each of the men in turn. She had grown increasingly attached to Renno, and now she would lose him in a sword fight with a bully because of the absurd value of honor. "I think," she said distinctly, "that all of you are mad."

When Tom Hibbard's militia unit returned to Fort Springfield, he requested permission to go off into the wilderness alone in order to continue his search. Brigadier

Wilson tried to dissuade him, but Tom's demand was so urgent, so persistent, that his superior finally gave in.

Wilson was quick to realize that Tom had his own reasons for taking the raid to heart. He seldom mentioned his wife, Agnes, who had been murdered and scalped by Huron four years earlier. But it was obvious that he was thinking of her in these trying times. With the additional death of the wife of his close friend Rene Gautier, he was even more committed to obtaining vengeance.

His search was thorough, and he spent more than two grueling weeks in the wilderness, a feat that, at this time of year, few other colonists could have matched. When he finally returned to Fort Springfield, he reported to the brigadier, told Rene he had failed, and then went to Doremus's Inn to sit alone and brood.

Those who saw the expression on his face gave him plenty of room. Jack Davies, who dropped in with a couple of his cronies for a pint of ale, hastily changed his mind and left the place. Tom sat alone, drinking for hours.

Late in the day Nettie wandered in and immediately went to Tom's side. He smiled at her, brightening for the first time since the massacre.

It was obvious that Tom had consumed more liquor than usual; he rarely drank, so she knew he was sorely troubled. He was in no condition to ride or walk all the way to his quarters at the Wilson estate, so she asked him back to her room. Tom agreed without a murmur and went off with her at once, his step unsteady.

Lovemaking was out of the question. Nettie had heard of his search for the raiders but took care not to say anything about it. Instead she soothed him with a few quiet words and helped him undress.

He dropped off to sleep the moment his head touched the pillow.

Nettie covered him with a blanket and, as night fell, lighted a small oil lamp. She watched him for a long time in its flickering glare, wishing there were something she could do to ease this good, kind man's lonely suffering.

Like everyone else in Springfield she knew about his wife's murder and why he was grieving over Rene Gautier's loss.

When Tom awakened in the morning, Nettie was preparing breakfast on her tiny stove and had already heated a pail of water for him. Somehow she had got a razor for him, and she also gave him a small dish of soft, yellow soap so he could shave.

Tom accepted her kindness in silence and did not speak until they had eaten and were seated opposite each other, sipping steaming tea.

"I reckon," he said, "that I made a bigger jackass than usual out of myself yesterday."

"You did no such thing," Nettie replied. "You were awful tired, so I brought you back here with me, and you went right off to sleep like a little baby."

"Damned if I know why you bothered," he muttered.

"It was the least I could do after all the kindness you've shown me," she said.

Tom stared at her over the chipped rim of his mug. "I want to say something to you, and I hope you won't be offended."

Nettie shook her head.

"For more than two weeks I've been off in the forest alone, searching for those cutthroat savages. Well, I didn't find them, but I will in good time."

Nettie heard the hard note of determination in his voice.

"You don't know those forests, and there's no reason you should. Back when I was a boy in London I wouldn't have believed I'd ever be at home in the wilderness, but I am. Provided my mind keeps busy. It's so blamed quiet that a man would go mad if he didn't do a heap of thinking."

His tone had changed subtly, but Nettie wasn't sure why. All she knew was that he sounded less brittle.

"I spent most of those two weeks thinking about three people," Tom said. "Two of them are dead. My wife and poor Rene's wife. And all the thinking in the world will never bring them back. That's why I told myself I had to think most of all about the living, so I did." He paused for a moment. "Did I talk about this when I was in my cups yesterday?"

"No, Tom."

"The person I thought about most was you," he said bluntly. "Day and night."

She was so startled she didn't know what to say.

"Life on the frontier is risky," he said. "You never know when there's going to be a fresh catastrophe. So it seems to me folks have to do what's right and good when it ought to be done. You swear you won't laugh at me?"

"Why on earth would I do that?"

Tom Hibbard placed his mug of tea on the floor beside him and, swallowing hard, rubbed the palms of his sinewy hands back and forth on the sides of his linsey-woolsey breeches. "Nettie," he said solemnly, "I'd be muchly honored if you'd consent to be my wife."

For a moment she was stunned, almost convinced he was still intoxicated. But she knew he was both sober and in dead earnest, so she shook her head.

"Why not?"

"There are a lot of reasons," Nettie said, "and one of them is as plain to you as it is to everybody else in Fort Springfield. I'm a whore."

"It's wrong for a girl like you to be living like you do," Tom said. "Oh, I know that one day your seamstress work will earn you enough. But there's no reason in this world you have to bed every man who comes along. You can stop it today. Right now."

Tears came into her eyes, and she brushed them away with the back of her hand. "I never thought I'd hear anybody propose to me, Tom. And I won't forget this morning, not ever. But I respect you too much to marry you. Everybody in town would be laughing at you and saying mean things behind your back."

"Not everybody, you can bet. As for those who do,

let them whisper all they please. Talk is cheap, and it never hurt anyone yet."

"I—I just can't, that's all. But—thank you."

"Let me tell you a few reasons you should," he said with great vigor. "First off, there's you and me. We've gotten fond of each other, and you can't deny it. I help you and you help me. That's what marriage is all about. I know in my bones that we're right for each other, and you know it, too. I can see it in your eyes."

"I won't listen to you!" Nettie cried, and clapped her hands over her ears.

Tom rose slowly to his feet and, grinning at her, gently forced her arms down. "I don't like being made to act like this," he said. "So behave yourself and talk sensibly." He turned and resumed his seat.

"I'm being sensible," she replied heatedly. "I think too much of you to let you marry the town trollop."

"You think I'm better than you. Is that it?"

She nodded.

"We come from the same part of London, you and me," Tom said. "So I don't need to be too explicit in what I'm going to tell you. My pa had a weakness for cards. He died leaving me with his gambling debts. I guess it won't surprise you much to learn that when I was young, my ma had to take in men visitors to put a roof over our heads and food in our bellies so we could go to school instead of work. Well, you're no more a trollop than my ma was. I've lived long enough to know a decent, honest woman when I see one. So I'm telling you plain that—regardless of whether you marry me or not —your days of bringing men back to this room are finished." No one who knew him had ever heard him make that long a speech.

Nettie fought hard to prevent herself from weeping, but silent tears streamed down her cheeks.

He pretended not to notice. "Now, there's plenty of other good reasons for you and me to be married. There's Rene Gautier, living in Mildred and Andy's house, grieving his heart out for Louise. There's his young ones, feeling lost and lonely. They ought to be in their own house, settling in, putting the finishing touches on the place. Keeping busy so they don't think and think about the past."

"What do the Gautiers have to do with my marrying you?"

"Folks hereabouts help their friends, the way Louise tried to help you. Well, Rene can't just move into that house with his children. He needs somebody to cook the meals and look after the young ones until he's better organized. He needs a friend to give him a hand finishing his barn. If we were married, we could live with them for a spell. We could help him and the children get settled. In his spare time Rene could help me work on our own house and property nearby. We're going to be neighbors, so we would work together. I could keep him so busy he wouldn't have time to brood about Louise. Meanwhile, you'd be a substitute for the mother the young ones miss. Mildred does what she can to comfort them, but she's more like a grandmother to them. With the loving and attention you could give them, their loss of Louise wouldn't be as sharp."

He had touched a vulnerable spot, and Nettie hesitated.

Realizing he had scored, Tom became more casual. "That's just a notion that came to mind, of course. I see it as a chance to lend a hand to good folks who need the help. But it has nothing to do with you and me, really. We'd be moving into our own house in a few months, no matter what."

The tears dried on Nettie's cheeks. He was tricking her, as she well knew, by using the motherless Gautier children, but that was only a part of the problem. She wasn't sure she loved Tom because she didn't really know the meaning of love. But she admired and respected him, and he was the only man other than Renno who had ever made her feel truly alive in bed.

"Why do you want to marry me?" she asked, managing to sound far calmer than she felt.

Tom exploded. "Hellfire and damnation, what kind of fool question is that? Why does any man want to marry a woman?"

"I don't know. That's what I'm trying to find out."

"Because I can't get you out of my head. I keep thinking about you. I keep worrying about you. I want to protect you. I want to get you out of the life you're leading. Forever. Before you get into bad troubles. Oh, I know you can look after yourself. You couldn't have survived this long if you were weak. But I can look after you better than you can by yourself. It's rough on the frontier, and a woman needs a man."

His reply more than satisfied her. In fact, she was shocked when she realized that Tom Hibbard actually loved her, even if he didn't know it himself. A feeling of great warmth spread through her, and she couldn't help smiling.

Tom was on his feet again. "I've talked myself hoarse," he said. "As soon as I make myself presentable we're going out on a little errand."

"What kind of errand?"

"You'll see." He had said enough, and the discussion was closed. A few minutes later he took Nettie's cloak from its wall peg and held it for her. She put it on, then turned impulsively and kissed him. "Thank you for proposing to me," she said. "It's something I'll never forget."

"You'll have no chance to forget it," he replied as they started down the steps.

Tom appeared to be in a hurry, determined to reach his destination as soon as possible, and Nettie made a vain attempt to match her pace to his as they splashed through the icy quagmire of the dirt road. "I can't keep up with you," she gasped.

He muttered an apology, slowed down, and took her arm. Her heart pounded when she realized he was taking her to the parsonage. She tried to free herself from his grasp, but his grip was too strong.

Deborah Jenkins, wearing a mobcap and apron,

came to the door, a straw broom in one hand. "Oh, dear," she said. "I didn't expect visitors this early in the day."

Tom cut her short. "We'd be obliged if the Reverend could spare us a few minutes," he said.

Obadiah came out of the parlor, which he also used as his study. He had been preparing his Sunday sermon and held a quill pen in one hand.

Tom got right to the point. "Obadiah," he demanded, "will you oblige us by performing a wedding? We want to get married as soon as we can send somebody to fetch the Wilsons, Rene Gautier, and his children."

The clergyman was startled but readily agreed and sent a neighbor's son to the Wilsons' house to fetch the witnesses. Deborah was so pleased that she hugged them both.

Everything was happening so quickly that Nettie felt she had lost control of her life, but she was given no opportunity to do otherwise. Even her request to go back home and change into more suitable wedding clothes was ignored.

The Wilsons soon arrived, accompanied by Rene and his excited children, and for the first time since the murder of his wife, the Huguenot refugee was smiling. The entire party adjourned to the church, and Brigadier Wilson insisted on escorting the bride down the aisle.

The dazed Nettie was so numb that she felt nothing, merely going through the motions throughout the ceremony.

Rene accepted Tom's suggestion that the newlyweds move into his new house with him and his children. The two men were so eager to be off that Deborah barely had time to prepare a hasty meal.

Then, with the two Gautier children supposedly "helping" her, Nettie moved all that she owned to the new farmhouse. Members of the Wilson staff pitched in, the Brigadier made a few wagons available, and by mid-afternoon Tom, Rene, and his children were also moved into the new house.

The men built roaring fires in both hearths, taking the chill out of the air. For the rest of the day Nettie was frantically busy putting away kitchenware, linens, her own clothing, and the belongings of the children. Occasionally she paused long enough to tell Tom and Rene where to place the various items of simple furniture that belonged to both of them.

The chaos was almost over by sundown. Mildred sent a coach laden with provisions and Deborah had baked a cake for the occasion. Nettie, still whirling, put everyone to work cleaning vegetables and peeling potatoes while she cut chunks of beef and started cooking a stew. The meal was ready an hour and a half after night fell.

But her work for the day was not done. She accepted the offer of Rene and Tom to wash the dishes, but she insisted on cleaning the iron pot herself. And she took time to tuck the children into bed. Remembering that Louise had always told them a story before they drifted off to sleep, she made a gallant attempt at her own story. She thought her efforts feeble, but the youngsters seemed more than satisfied, and both were smiling as they dropped off.

The full impact of her new situation dawned on Nettie as she accompanied Tom to the little room that her bed seemed to fill. She was married, and would sleep only with Tom Hibbard from now on. Glancing down at the fourth finger of her left hand, she was overwhelmed. Tom had given her his late wife's gold ring, and nothing could have been more important to her, no gift more precious.

Within a few hours her entire life had changed. She felt insecure and unworthy, but she was determined to live up to the promise of that gold ring. Only now did it occur to her that she had never actually agreed to marry Tom. He had simply made the arrangements on his own.

Well, it was too late now for worries or regrets. For better or worse she had become Tom Hibbard's wife.

The fire burning in the main room of the new house barely reached the small chamber, so Nettie didn't linger.

After undressing quickly, she climbed into bed. A sober-faced Tom joined her. He did not speak but took her in his arms, kissed her, and held her close.

Comforted by his strength, his compassion, his essential goodness, Nettie felt her doubts disappear. Tom had become her champion, protecting her from the evils of the world. Somehow, with him beside her, life would be worth living at last.

Members of the Bear Clan built a small, special hut in a tiny clearing deep in the forest, on the far side of the cornfields. Everyone contributed something: the men fashioned stakes and crossbars, then fastened them with rawhide thongs; the women plaited mats of reeds that were used as walls, and the children covered them with layer after layer of clay.

The house would stand for only a short time, but it was constructed with the same care that was devoted to a permanent lodge. Skins were stretched over the entrance and windows to keep out the cold, and a bright fire burned in the stone pit dug in the center of the hut, the smoke escaping through a hole in the ceiling. The only furniture was a shelf, slightly more than six feet long and about four feet wide on which were piled tender boughs, covered with a sheet of doeskins. This was the bed.

Next to the hut, a platform was built with the same care and effort. The top was several feet above the ground.

Representatives from every Seneca community came to the main town, and each included a Bear Clan delegation. The other nations of the Iroquois League sent special envoys, and they, too, were members of the Bear Clan.

Leading the procession, in which every Seneca participated, was El-i-chi, acting in the place of his absent, older brother. He was wearing the head and skin of the bear that had been Renno's lifelong friend.

Then came nine drummers, playing in unison, and their throbbing, steady beat echoed across the wilderness.

Next in line were a score of medicine men, all wearing the intricately carved masks of the Great Faces. Each carried a bag of dried herbs that had been consecrated in the name of the Great Spirit, spoken of only on special occasions.

Ghonka, pale and strained beneath his war paint, clad only in a loincloth and moccasins, walked alone. Ena, her face expressionless, walked directly behind him, her face, cheeks, and hands smeared with ashes. Ba-lin-ta and Walter Alwin, both simply attired, walked directly behind Ena.

The eight powerful war chiefs of the nation, Ghonka's direct subordinates, formed the core of the procession. No warriors in all of America were more ferocious than these men who had won their places by their exploits, cunning, and skill in battle. Yet they were remarkably gentle and glided rather than walked so they would not jar or otherwise disturb the precious burden on the litter they carried.

Stretched out on the pallet was Sah-nee-wa. Her arms were folded across her breasts, and her aged, veined hands were still. But her eyes were open and she was aware of everything happening around her. If she was in pain, no one knew it: her face was relaxed and the expression in her eyes indicated that she was at peace.

On either side of the bearers were two medicine women wearing Great Face masks. They occasionally sprinkled Sah-nee-wa with ashes or herbs as they chanted an ancient prayer to the manitous. The ashes touched only her clothes and body.

Behind them came the representatives of the other nations of the Iroquois League, and one member of each tribe was draped in a bearskin. They, too, were chanting.

Then came the Seneca, with the senior warriors in the lead, all fully armed, clad only in loincloths and smeared with ceremonial war paint. They marched in solid ranks, all staring straight ahead, their expressions stern. They were followed by the junior warriors, who tried to emulate them but were less successful in concealing their emotions. The Seneca women made no attempt to walk in formation, and mothers were accompanied by their small children. But they were solemn and silent, and it was plain that they, more than any of the others, were aware of the loss the Seneca were suffering.

Sah-nee-wa was deposited on the bed in the hut, and the war chiefs stood in a phalanx as the people filed through to pay their final respects. The medicine women did not sprinkle her with ashes or herbs now, and the rattles they carried were silent. They were being careful to follow her instructions for the occasion. "I know that I am dying," she had said. "Make no attempt to save my life. The time has come for me to join the spirits of my ancestors. It is right that I leave you and go to them."

After the last of the procession had moved through the hut, the war chiefs withdrew so that members of the old woman's immediate family could say their last farewells to her in privacy.

The first to go into the hut were Ba-lin-ta and Walter. They were ill at ease, frightened by the solemnness of the moment, and they hesitated just inside the entrance.

Sah-nee-wa smiled at them. "Come closer, children, so I may see you more clearly," she said.

They advanced toward the pallet and stood silently, looking down at her.

Again she smiled, and her voice seemed to grow stronger. "Before I leave you," she said, "I will tell you of a vision that came to me on my last night on this earth. The future of this land lies in your hands."

As the dying woman spoke, Ba-lin-ta communicated her words to Walter in their private sign language.

"Together," Sah-nee-wa said, "you will make a new people. Your sons and your daughters will be Seneca. But they will also be the English who will spread across the wilderness. The sons and daughters of Ba-lin-ta and Walter will show them how the people of two nations can live together in peace. It is your mission to teach your sons and daughters to be true to all the good that is in you.

They must learn all that you believe. Evil spirits will tempt you. Do not heed them. Listen only to the good in your own hearts."

The children nodded solemnly.

"Long ago," Sah-nee-wa said, "the Seneca took this land. Now the English will come in numbers greater than the geese that fly to the north when the weather becomes warm. Some Seneca and some English are greedy. Many will fight with each other for the land. They must not fight. Let your children and their children set an example for all. Let them teach the Indian and the white man to live together in peace."

"It will be as you say," Ba-lin-ta replied.

Walter nodded vigorously.

"Go now, before I grow too weak."

Seneca custom demanded that they lower their heads for a moment, then depart. But Ba-lin-ta, giving in to a sudden impulse, bent down and kissed the withered cheek of her aunt.

Walter hesitated for an instant, then followed the little girl's example. Sah-nee-wa's warm smile followed them as they silently left the hut.

El-i-chi was the next to appear. He stood beside the bed, his body rigid, his face immobile, and then he slowly raised his tomahawk in salute.

"Son of my brother," Sah-nee-wa said, "you walk on a trail that is filled with many snares. It is not easy for a man to walk in the shadow of another. But you are the brother of Renno. When you show courage, the courage of Renno is greater. When you perform great deeds, the deeds of Renno are greater."

"It is so, sister of my father," El-i-chi replied. "But there is no hate in my heart for Renno. I feel only love for him. Gladly I walk in his shadow."

"That is good," the old woman said. "There is none in all the land like Renno. But his trail is strewn with thorns. They tear his flesh and cause the blood to flow. Renno needs El-i-chi. In the many moons to come, El-i-chi must stand beside Renno. He must become the strong arm that helps Renno."

174

"This I will do," the young warrior promised.

"Then you will become a great war chief in your own right. If you are loyal to Renno, the spirits will reward you and give you all that you wish."

"I swear I will be loyal to Renno," El-i-chi said.

Sah-nee-wa dismissed him with a feeble wave of her hand. He stood for a long moment, silently gazing down at her. Then he turned away abruptly and stalked out of the hut.

The last to appear were Ena and Ghonka, who entered together and stood beside the bed. Sah-nee-wa looked up at them, and for a long moment no one spoke. There was no need for words. They had spent most of their lives together, and each understood the thoughts and feelings of the others.

"Good-bye, my sister," Ena said at last.

"We will meet again in the land of our ancestors," Sah-nee-wa replied.

"It shall be so," Ena agreed.

Now it was Ghonka's turn, and he stood erect, his body like the trunk of a great oak tree, his brawny arms folded across his thick, bare chest. Only a muscle that twitched slightly at one side of his mouth betrayed his pain. "Soon," he said, "you will see our father and our mother. You will sit with them and eat the cakes of corn filled with dried grapes that only our mother knows how to make. You will feast with them. You will rejoice with them. Say to them that I think of them every day I walk this earth."

"I will say it to them," Sah-nee-wa replied. "Even though there is no need for me to speak. They know of your thoughts."

The Great Sachem nodded. "Say to them also that Ena and I will come to them when our work here is done."

"I will say it," his sister declared. "But you still have much to do. You must lead our people for many summers."

"I will do the work the spirits have given me to do," Ghonka said firmly. "I will be faithful to my trust."

The ceremonial farewell was finished, but Sah-nee-wa still had something to say. She looked first at Ena, then at Ghonka, and said, "Soon Renno will return to the land of the Seneca. Tell him for me that he must not suffer a heavy heart because he was not here to bid me farewell."

"I will tell him," Ena said.

"Tell him also that my spirit will watch over him and help him. Tell him to remember, always, that in his mind and his body are the future of our people. Always he must grow in wisdom and in strength. Through him the Seneca and the English will remain friends. Through him they will flourish together."

"I will tell him," the Great Sachem said in a ringing voice.

Sah-nee-wa closed her eyes. "Farewell, my sister. Farewell, my brother. I will greet you again in the land of our ancestors."

"May your journey be swift," Ghonka said, and only his iron will made it possible for him to keep his voice from breaking. "Go in peace."

Sah-nee-wa's breathing became shallow, and then she lay still. She had done her duty, and now her departure was quiet and gentle.

Ghonka and Ena left the hut together, nothing in their faces or bearing revealing their deep feelings. The Great Sachem raised a hand, and the drums began to throb again, softly at first, their volume gradually increasing.

The war chiefs who had carried her to the hut now went in, gently lifted her frail form, and placed it on top of the platform. Then everyone left the hut and the entrance was closed. It would remain so until Sah-nee-wa's spirit had departed to join her ancestors. Then her bones would be buried.

All of the Seneca began to chant in unison, and the envoys of the other Iroquois raised their voices in the chorus. The beat of the drums rolled through the forest.

Then the procession formed again and everyone returned to the town, leaving only the warriors on sentry duty in the forest.

The members of the Bear Clan ate a feast together in their longhouse and were joined by the Great Sachem and his family. Ghonka and Ena sat slightly apart, leaving an empty place between them, and a bowl was placed on the ground there, filled with food. Sah-nee-wa no longer required the food of the living, but her family and her clan were offering a symbol to speed her on her journey to the land of their ancestors. Perhaps she was already there, perhaps she would not arrive until the following day. No man knew how much time the journey took.

Ghonka broke the silence with an ear-shattering war cry. Then everyone relaxed and ate with good appetite. Mature warriors and their wives chatted quietly, young men and maidens flirted with each other, and when the children finished their meal they were permitted to go outside and play. Sah-nee-wa had wanted no one to mourn her, and those who had been closest to her were abiding by her wishes.

Dawn would not break for more than an hour. Adrienne Bartel sat in bed, wrapped in a padded robe. Shivering slightly she watched Renno by the light of two oil lamps. Clad only in a loincloth and moccasins, he dressed his scalp lock and carefully adjusted the feathers in it, oiled his body, and then smeared on war paint. He was calm and seemed totally absorbed in what he was doing.

"I don't see why you're required to obey the rules of honor that apply to the English gentry. You're neither English nor a gentleman. If I were you, I'd tell the Earl of Lincoln to go to the devil. No one of intelligence will blame you for refusing to fight a duel with him."

Common sense told Renno that her arguments were true, but his own pride was at stake. It was unthinkable that anyone might question his courage, even in this strange place so far from the land of the Seneca. But it was difficult for him to explain his feelings, and he had learned enough about white women to know that nothing he might say would soothe her.

So, when he was ready to leave, he smiled at her reassuringly. Adrienne jumped out of bed, threw herself into his arms, and clung to him. "I'm afraid for you," she murmured.

"No be afraid," he said. "Renno not afraid." He turned and left the bedroom.

Jeffrey was waiting for him in the dining room, and they stood together in silence, drinking mugs of hot Dutch chocolate.

Jeffrey was deeply troubled. He would be blamed— by his own father, Governor Shirley, and the Seneca—if something happened to Renno this morning, but he was forced to agree with Colonel Churchill that the duel could not be avoided.

Jeffrey was the first to speak. "When we reach the dueling ground," he said, "you'll have to give me your tomahawk and knife. The code of honor permits you to carry no weapon other than the sword you'll be using."

A few weeks earlier Renno would have refused. As every Indian knew, a man carried as many weapons as possible into a fight. But his stay in London had convinced him that the English were a far from sensible people. So, on this one occasion, he would accept their ways. Never had he lost a fighting contest, and he had no intention of losing today.

His shrug indicated his reluctant agreement.

A coach halted outside the house. Jeffrey donned his greatcoat, Renno threw his buffalo robe over his shoulders, and they went out to join Colonel Churchill. He greeted them briefly.

The coachman drove across London Bridge to Southwark, then headed toward the woods of oak and elm that lay beyond the populated area.

Dawn broke as they entered the woods, and the carriage headed down a broad path. Colonel Churchill sighed and broke the heavy silence. "Renno," he said, "I want you to remember what I've told you several times. In a duel here a man does not try to kill his opponent. A flesh wound, even a tiny scratch that draws blood is enough to satisfy honor. King William hates dueling and would be badly upset if you killed Lincoln, so you must be doubly careful."

"I remember," Renno said.

"Good. And above all, protect yourself as best you can. The earl is an exceptionally clever swordsman. He's quick, his footwork is sound, and his hand is steady. If you think you're going to be wounded, try to take the thrust on your arm rather than your body."

"I remember." Renno remained stolid.

The coach drew to a halt, and the trio walked toward a nearby clearing.

These woods, like others Renno had seen in England, were manicured. All the same, the familiar smells of earth and trees and leaves rotting on the ground comforted him. He knew Jeffrey and the colonel were nervous, but he was not. A senior warrior of the Seneca could face any foe without fear.

They were the last to arrive. The Earl of Lincoln, dressed in black, stood at the opposite side of the clearing and deliberately turned his back as he chatted with his own two seconds. A physician was in attendance, and Colonel Churchill presented Renno to the referee, whom all the seconds had chosen together.

Major Sir Philip Rand, the youngest son of the Earl of Worcester and himself a baronet, was about thirty, tall and powerful, with clean-cut features. Like Churchill he was a professional soldier, and he was both competent and dispassionate. But the expression in his eyes hinted that he was not lacking in compassion. He had seen Renno's remarkable performance at Whitehall and had been impressed by it, and now he looked curiously at the young warrior.

"Are you quite sure you want to go through with this?" he asked. "I know what you can do with your own weapons, but swordplay is altogether different."

Renno's lips parted in a faint smile, but he said nothing.

"Very well," Sir Philip said with a sigh, and went to

the center of the clearing, a long, wooden box under his arm. Then he summoned the seconds, and they went through the ritual of choosing the weapons their principals would use.

Jeffrey relieved Renno of his knife and tomahawk, and Colonel Churchill extended the sword, hilt first.

Renno took it and made several experimental slashes with it. A small bar separated the handle from the supple blade, and the weapon was lighter than any he had used in his fencing lessons. But he liked its balance and was satisfied.

"Milord, Master Renno, be good enough to join me, please," the major called.

The two principals walked to the center of the clearing.

"In order to prevent the unnecessary shedding of blood, it is my duty to inquire if you are willing to abandon your mutual grievances. Will you be reconciled?"

Lincoln replied instantly. "Under no circumstances will I be reconciled," he said. "This person is a lout and a boor as well as a savage."

His words made it unnecessary for Renno to speak, and he contented himself with baring his teeth in a grin of contempt.

Sir Philip drew his own sword. "Stand ready, gentlemen," he said.

Renno had been drilled in the ritual that preceded a duel and went through the motions of raising his blade to the referee, then saluting his enemy.

"On guard!" the major cried.

Renno assumed the appropriate stance, one foot in front of the other, his weight evenly distributed as he balanced on the balls of his feet, his sword arm slightly crooked.

"You may begin," Sir Philip said and, withdrawing his own sword, retreated at once to the side of the clearing.

The Earl of Lincoln lost no time attacking, obviously hoping to catch his opponent flat-footed and end the 'duel quickly. He feinted, then thrust for the white Indian's body.

Renno was prepared and parried neatly, his foe's blade sliding harmlessly up the length of his own.

Lincoln was astonished. It had not occurred to him that this savage knew how to handle a sword. Very well, he would change his entire approach. He feinted repeatedly in a dazzling display of swordsmanship.

Renno mechanically parried blow after blow as he studied his foe. The earl was as competent as his instructor had been, he decided, but this was no mere fencing lesson. The expression in Lincoln's eyes told him that the earl wanted to humiliate him as well as wound him severely, perhaps even kill him.

The earl pressed his attack, and the sound of steel clashing against steel echoed through the woods.

Renno retreated slowly, step by careful step, and weighed his situation. Now he knew why Adrienne, Jeffrey, and Colonel Churchill had been so concerned for him. He had gravely underestimated the gravity of this duel. There was no doubt in his mind that he was in mortal danger.

He knew, too, that Lincoln had the upper hand. His thrusts were sure, well-timed, and he knew how to conceal the direction of a thrust until the last instant. Renno had only two advantages: his eyesight was superb, and he had an instinct for reacting without hesitation.

Sooner or later, however, his own lack of experience would betray him, and his opponent would penetrate his tight defense. He continued to parry unceasingly, looking for some tiny chink in this man's armor.

Lincoln was becoming frustrated. Plainly the savage had received competent coaching, and he had grace and speed. It was not going to be easy to humiliate him, and Lincoln's temper soared as he found it more and more difficult to achieve a clean thrust.

Renno saw the rage in his foe's eyes, and for the first time he felt a flicker of hope. A Seneca warrior was taught never to lose his temper in battle. He remembered Ghonka telling him that the brave who remained calm, no matter what, always left the field with fresh scalps hanging from his belt.

However, nothing could be achieved without taking risks. Renno laid out a simple plan. Without warning he took the offensive for the first time, feinting and then thrusting wickedly.

The earl parried without difficulty but was outraged. This damned barbarian had not only mocked him at court, but was aggravating the insult now. Wildly angry, he made an attempt to regain the initiative.

For a moment Lincoln was careless, leaving himself open, and Renno unhesitatingly took advantage of his break. Mindful of the instructions he had been given, he took care to inflict only a slight wound on his opponent's arm.

Blood was drawn, and the duel should have ended at that moment.

Sir Philip Rand called in a loud voice, "Stand apart at once and lower your blades, gentlemen!"

But Lincoln did not hear him. The fact that he had been defeated in a fair duel by this near-naked savage so infuriated him that he lost his head and launched a series of vicious thrusts. Had just one reached its target, Renno would have died.

Both principals' seconds added their shouts to those of Sir Philip, but the earl had gone mad, and they were afraid to come close to his sword.

Parrying desperately, Renno knew he had to end the fight as quickly as he could. Stifling a sudden feeling of panic, he realized that his foe was leaving himself wide open. So, after parrying a thrust of such force that it almost knocked his sword from his hand, the young Seneca drove his blade deep into Lincoln's shoulder.

The earl staggered backward and collapsed onto the ground.

Now Renno reacted strongly. His enemy had broken the rules of dueling, so he no longer felt obliged to obey them.

Horror mingled with pain in the helpless Lincoln's

eyes as he became aware of Renno's intentions. No one else had as yet guessed.

Renno threw down his sword and snatched his tomahawk from Jeffrey. He started toward his fallen foe.

Colonel Churchill was the first to react, and Jeffrey and Sir Philip were not far behind. One caught hold of Renno's arm while the other two did their best to stop him. Renno shook them off.

Jeffrey was desperate and called in Seneca, "Stop, son of Ghonka!"

Renno's mind cleared. He had lost his calm, and he felt deeply ashamed. He stood still, his arm dropping to his side, and then he absently placed his tomahawk in his belt.

It was safe now for the physician to attend the wounded nobleman, and he began at once to try to stop the bleeding.

Sir Philip Rand looked at Renno in admiration. "I don't blame you for wanting to bash in his head and scalp him," he said, "but that sort of thing simply isn't done here. My only regret is that this duel didn't take place in the New World, where the rules must be more—ah—elastic."

The relieved Jeffrey and Colonel Churchill offered Renno their congratulations. The major approached the fallen earl. "Doctor," he asked, "is your patient conscious?"

"Indeed, Sir Philip, although he'll become drowsy after I've given him a dose of laudanum."

"Then you can hear me, Lincoln?"

The earl grunted and nodded.

Sir Philip's tone was scathing. "You've disgraced yourself, your name, and England today. I urge you not to return to London and to go instead to your estate in the country and stay there. No gentleman at Whitehall will shake your hand when your conduct becomes public knowledge, and I assure you it shall!"

The earl's seconds, deeply embarrassed by his unscrupulous behavior, nodded their assent. Clearly they wanted to make it plain that they would have no more to do with him.

Sir Philip turned to Renno and extended his hand. "You fit into Whitehall's plans even better than you know," he said, but made no attempt to explain the mysterious statement. "We shall meet again—and sooner than you think."

Chapter VIII

Two days after Renno's duel a carriage arrived for him and Jeffrey, and a young officer conducted them to the Royal Navy docks. There they were greeted by Commodore Charles Markham, a senior officer with white hair but a youthful, ruddy face.

"How soon can you be ready to sail for Boston?" he asked as he escorted them in the direction of several ships tied up at adjoining piers.

"We'll sail today," Jeffrey said.

"Not quite that soon," the commodore replied with a smile. "But I'm hoping to make the late morning tide the day after tomorrow. These are the ships that will sail in convoy."

Renno stared in awe at the vessels, all of them larger than the brig that had carried him to England. One was enormous.

"Four are merchantmen," the commodore explained. "Their holds are already filled to bursting with cannon, muskets, munitions, and other supplies for Massachusetts Bay, the other colonies, and your Indian allies. We're still loading all sorts of items, including the cooking pots you wanted for the Indians, and we have no place to store them except the open decks. The fifth ship, yonder, is a Royal Navy frigate, the *Princess Anne*. It's my flagship and will escort the brigs. You've been assigned cabins on board. Will you join me now for a visit?"

Jeffrey and Renno exchanged gleeful smiles as they walked toward the warship. King William had been lavish in keeping his promise, and the cargo would be a god-send.

"A sloop-of-war was sent to Boston last week with advance word of our coming, and she'll require far less time crossing the Atlantic than we need," the commodore said. "She'll become part of my squadron after we reach Boston."

"Your squadron, sir?" Jeffrey was startled.

The officer grinned. "I neglected to mention that I've been given New World duty. I'll be joined shortly by three other ships. We don't intend to let the French control those waters, you know." He spoke casually, but with the authority of a sailor who knew his business.

A bo's'n's mate piped the commodore aboard, and Renno was impressed when scores of sailors at work on the deck of the warship jumped to rigid attention when they heard the high-pitched squeal of the strange musical instrument.

"We work far faster than the army, you know," Commodore Markham said smugly. "I carry forty-eight guns and a crew of five hundred, but I could have sailed a few days after the Admiralty handed me my orders. But the army! They're sending several regiments of troops to America—I don't know the details—but I'll wager it will be summer before they arrive."

Jeffrey didn't care how long it took for the Royal Army to organize its expedition. He knew his father and Governor Shirley would be overjoyed. The full power of English might was being placed in support of the colonies at last, and Renno's mission had succeeded beyond any-one's hopes.

Renno was stunned by the strength of the *Princess Anne.* Her cannon were mammoth twelve-pounders, twice the size of the thunder machines he had seen at Fort Springfield, with twenty-four of them mounted on each side of the frigate. He was intrigued when a gunport was lowered for his benefit, and the cannon was moved forward until its muzzle protruded into the open. Still other surprises were in store: a half-dozen smaller cannon were situated on the main deck of the frigate. And the crow's nest was mounted on a mast as high as the tallest trees in the wilderness.

If there was any doubt that Renno enjoyed the special favor of King William, it was dispelled when he saw his cabin, a chamber easily as large as the bedroom in which he had been sleeping. It was twice the size of the quarters given to Jeffrey, and Renno thought that an entire Seneca family could live there in comfort.

The commodore took the pair to the wardroom, where his officers would eat and relax on the voyage. He tapped at the door, then said brusquely, "I'll leave you here." Without another word, he left.

The door was unlocked, then opened, and Renno and Jeffrey saw Major Sir Philip Rand, resplendent in his scarlet uniform. He greeted them with a chuckle, then waved them to chairs. "Forgive the drama," he said, "but I couldn't resist surprising you. We shall be seeing a great deal of each other in the weeks ahead. I'm sailing to the New World with you."

Renno liked Rand and was pleased.

"You're going in advance of the main army body that Commodore Markham says is en route to Boston fairly soon?" Jeffrey asked.

Sir Philip shook his head. "I understand my old regiment will be stationed in America, but I'm on special assignment. I'm not at liberty to discuss it at present. But I will tell you one thing." He turned to Renno. "It wasn't accidental that I acted as the referee when you fought your duel with the Earl of Lincoln. John Churchill suggested me—at my request—and luckily Lincoln's seconds agreed. It was terribly important that I see you under fire, so to speak."

Renno didn't understand.

"You'll learn more after we reach Boston, and I've had the opportunity to confer with the authorities there." Sir Philip grinned. "All I'll say for the present, Master Renno, is that I like your style. I can't imagine anyone I'd rather have fighting beside me in battle."

"Soon we fight French together," Renno replied.

The smile faded from the major's face. "We shall indeed fight them," he said quietly, "and there are more ways than one to do it." He clapped Renno on the shoulder. "We'll become better acquainted on the voyage, and I hope you'll give me lessons in your language. I want to learn as much as I can about the New World before we get there."

Jeffrey realized there was more to the situation than met the eye, but being the son of a military man, he knew better than to ask questions. It was enough, for the moment, that the Crown was amply aiding the hard-pressed colonials.

A short time later the commodore saw the two young men ashore, and they went directly to the house of Lord Beaumont. Their good news pleased him, too.

"The colonies will have some teeth now," he said, "and the French will feel their bite."

"We go to William and Mary," Renno said. "Give them thanks."

Lord Beaumont shook his head. "Their Majesties are in the Netherlands for at least a week," he said. "I'm afraid they won't return before you sail. Besides, King William isn't the sort of man who would want thanks. He realized he was being derelict in his duty, and now he's simply making up for lost time. The only thanks he'll want will be to see the colonies give a good account of themselves in the struggle with the French."

Not until Renno and Jeffrey were returning to their own house did their euphoria begin to fade. "We face a nasty problem," Jeffrey said.

"I know." Renno nodded somberly. "Adrienne."

They decided it was Renno's place to break the news to her, and when they found her in the sitting room, reading, Jeffrey immediately disappeared.

Adrienne looked up from her book, saw the expression in Renno's eyes, and knew something was wrong.

Renno was unable to break the news gently. "In two days," he said, "Jeff-rey and Renno go home. King send many ships with firesticks for Iroquois and English colonists."

Adrienne accepted the statement with surprising calm. "I've known all along that this arrangement couldn't last. Thanks to you I've had a breathing spell, with time to make plans."

He was deeply concerned for her. "What you do?"

Her smile was bright but enigmatic. "I'll manage," she said confidently.

Renno stared at her for a moment, then turned and went upstairs, returning with the gold medallion and chain that Queen Mary had given him. He had learned during his stay in London that gold was valuable. He found it pretty, but it meant nothing to him. He liked his dueling pistols and intended to take blankets of wool, cooking pots, and small mirrors to members of his family, but he was indifferent to the jewelry and the furnishings that meant so much to the English.

Holding the medallion in the palm of his hand, he extended his arm.

Adrienne's eyes widened. "—I can't take that from you, Renno!" she said. "It was a gift to you from the Queen!"

"You take," he said. "Gold buy much. Then bad Englishmen not send you back to France."

Tears came to her eyes, and she brushed them away. "Your generosity overwhelms me, but I really can't—"

"You take!" It was obvious to him that she needed the bauble which he had no use for. White women were even less sensible than Seneca. Adrienne should know by

189

now that when a senior warrior made a decision, he expected it to be obeyed without question. He cut the argument short by draping the chain around her neck.

Adrienne stared at him for a moment. Then her luminous eyes filled with tears again and she fled from the room.

Watching her as she raced up the stairs, he could only shrug. It was impossible for him to figure out what took place in a woman's mind.

Jeffrey joined him a few minutes later, and Renno told him what had happened.

"You were wonderful to give her the medallion. Adrienne can live for a year on what that and the chain will bring her. But I've been doing some thinking myself, and perhaps my uncle will give her sanctuary, if she's willing. I'll speak to her about it later, after she's had time to pull herself together. Come on, we have to do some errands."

Jeffrey wanted to buy gifts for his parents, and he also gave Renno money for the few presents he wanted to take with him. The young Seneca indulged in only one extravagance: he found a large doll, dressed in a courtly gown, and he immediately purchased it for Ba-lin-ta.

Then he and Jeffrey went to the nearby open-air food markets, and there they bought sacks of apples, pears, and peaches, some plum puddings and several fruitcakes. Like all sensible and experienced travelers, they were supplementing the fare they would be served on board ship. Presumably the food would be better on board a Royal Navy frigate than it had been on the brig that had brought them to England, but there was always a need for fruit and sweets.

Heavily laden with their purchases they returned home. Not until more than a quarter of an hour had passed did they realize that Adrienne was nowhere to be seen. Renno assumed she had also gone out to do some errands, but a thought struck Jeffrey, and he led the way to Renno's bedroom.

All of Adrienne's things were gone. Jeffrey questioned the members of the household staff, but no one had spoken to her or seen her leave.

A thorough search revealed that she left no note, either. Adrienne Bartel had simply vanished without leaving a trace.

"I feel badly about all this," Jeffrey said. "She must have been planning this for a long time. All the same, she owed it to us, especially you, to take us into her confidence. Or to say good-bye at the very least."

"Where she go?" Renno asked.

"Only she and the Lord know," Jeffrey replied. "It isn't very difficult to hide out in a city of a million people. Or, for all we know, she may have changed her disguise and gone off somewhere else. Since she's a fugitive, we can't ask the authorities to search for her. We've got to assume she knows what she's doing—and hope she's safe."

"Adrienne is safe," Renno said firmly. Even though he didn't know her every thought he had come to know her well, and he admired her courage and resolution. She was determined not to be caught by the French, and in one way or another she would manage to survive.

He was sorry she had gone without saying farewell to him, but he refused to dwell on what could not be changed. Certainly he was very fond of her and had enjoyed their intimacy. But he was not truly in love with her. The meaning of love sometimes confused him, and he could only look to his parents for an example. Ghonka and Ena found deep, mutual satisfaction in their lives together, and he sometimes marveled at their ability to understand each other, even when no words were spoken.

Certainly he didn't intend to marry until he found a woman with whom he could have the same kind of rapport his parents had. He felt close to Adrienne and wished there were something more he could do to help her. He was sorry that she'd be alone now. But she had elected to go her own way, and he had to respect her decision.

At least she had solved one major problem for him.

He had lived for long periods with only two women, Adrienne and Deborah, both white. So he had sometimes wondered, because his own skin was the same as theirs, whether it was his destiny to marry a white woman.

Adrienne had taught him not to care and to stop worrying. When he found the right woman, regardless of her race, he would know it. He was now completely confident that the manitous would guide him, so he was leaving the question in their all-seeing, all-powerful hands.

He had succeeded in his mission to this strange and bewildering country. Although he couldn't quite understand why he won the enthusiastic favor of King William and Queen Mary, it was enough that the Iroquois and the English colonists would be amply supplied with arms and powerful ships, and that English soldiers would cross the great lake to fight against the French.

Now he was eager to take his place on the war trail with his Seneca brothers. He had no desire to visit England again and yearned more than ever for the wilderness of his home.

The *Princess Anne* was the first of the flotilla to hoist anchor and raise her sails, and she moved slowly out into the Thames, marking time as the four merchantmen fell into line behind her. Then all five ships sailed down the river, and by nightfall they reached the choppy waters of the English Channel.

Renno was relieved he was able to quickly get used to the erratic motion of the frigate. Sir Philip promised to give him daily lessons in the use of the dueling pistols that had been the gift of King William. Commodore Markham, fascinated by the white Indian, lingered at the table after meals in order to talk with him.

A day and a half after reaching the channel, the flotilla arrived off Land's End, and Renno joined Jeffrey and Sir Philip on the main deck soon after daybreak for their last glimpse of England. When they next saw land it would be the welcome soil of the New World.

By the time they went below for breakfast, the officers had finished their meal and reported for duty.

Commodore Markham left the actual operation of the frigate to his deputy, the ship's captain, and joined them. The cook brought in platters of fried fish and freshly baked bread, Jeffrey and Renno provided some fruit, and Sir Philip contributed a container of roasted, salted nuts. Everyone but Renno drank ale; he contented himself with hot chocolate.

"When do you begin to teach your pupil the mysteries of dueling pistols, Rand?" the commodore wanted to know.

"This afternoon, sir, if the captain will give us the freedom of the aft deck."

"I'm sure he will, provided Renno will oblige me with a demonstraton of his skill with a tomahawk. I'm afraid I missed his performance at Whitehall, but everyone at the Admiralty who saw it has spoken of little else."

Renno nodded. He was still unable to understand why his skill with a tomahawk was considered remarkable, but he was always glad to demonstrate.

The door opened, and the group at the table looked around, then gaped.

Standing in the entrance was a young woman with streaming blond hair, wearing a low-cut gown of ivory satin, a large gold medallion resting on her breasts.

The stunned commodore began to sputter. Jeffrey could not control himself, and his loud laugh filled the wardroom. Renno grinned and was relieved.

"Good morning," Adrienne said calmly. "I hope I'm not disturbing your breakfast."

Sir Philip was so astonished, he could not speak. But the commodore could. "Young woman, how in the devil have you—"

"I bribed two members of the crew. They kept me hidden until we left the British Isles behind us." Adrienne remained remarkably poised. "I've promised them I won't reveal their identities, and I shall keep my word. But I desperately require passage to the New World."

Jeffrey stood and held a chair for her. "I can offer a partial explanation, Commodore. Mistress Bartel is a

French Huguenot refugee who came to England without proper papers. Renno and I helped her so she would not be deported back to France."

"Then you're responsible for this—this outrage?" Commodore Markham glared first at Jeffrey, then at Renno.

The young Seneca refused to be intimidated. "We not know that Adrienne here. But I glad."

"We last saw her two days before we sailed, sir," Jeffrey said. "She disappeared from our house."

"I alone am responsible for what I've done," Adrienne said. "I had thought of asking Renno and Jeffrey to take me, but I didn't want to embarrass them. So I made my own plans. I was smuggled on board the night before we sailed."

"This is contrary to all navy regulations," the fuming commodore said. "But I can't take five ships all the way back to England just to return you !"

The major, trying not to smile, cleared his throat. "I may be able to suggest a solution, Commodore," he said. "According to the orders issued in His Majesty's name, the navy was directed to provide passage to the New World for Prince Renno of the Seneca and members of his party. Master Wilson wasn't specified by name. It also happens that Mademoiselle Bartel is a member of the party."

"I'll gladly move in with Renno," Jeffrey said hastily, "and Adrienne may use my cabin."

The commodore was trapped and knew it. But the problems that an attractive woman could cause on board a warship during a voyage of more than a month's time were enormous. "We'll have to find you suitable clothing," he said. "I'm damned if you can prance around half-naked on one of my ships."

"My clothing boxes are deposited just outside in the gangway," Adrienne said. "I—I wasn't sure how I'd be received, so I dressed as I have recently in London. But I can assure you I don't want hundreds of sailors licking their lips every time they see me."

The commodore was only partly mollified. "Seamen are a superstitious lot, and a blond female on board a navy ship supposedly brings bad luck!"

Renno grinned and Jeffrey laughed aloud.

Adrienne became bolder and, removing her wig, shook out her own red hair.

Even Commodore Markham joined in the group's hearty laughter. "I can't put all this in my report to the Admiralty," he said, "because no one would believe it."

Adrienne sobered, and she became earnest. "I have no wish to be a nuisance or cause problems," she said. "But I was truly desperate. Without the shelter that Renno and Jeffrey provided me, I was certain to be caught and deported to France sooner or later. My family are dead, our property was all but seized by the Crown, and my friends are afraid to help me. I would do anything rather than spend the rest of my life rotting in one of King Louis's foul prisons."

The mention of the hated Louis XIV made up the commodore's mind. "I'll have the lady's belongings moved into your cabin, Wilson. See to it that you move in with Renno at once. Are you hungry, young woman?"

His gruff kindness caused Adrienne to blink away tears and she could only nod.

"Serve her some food," he commanded. "And before she appears on deck, give her a coat so she can cover herself. I don't want a mutiny on board!" He stormed out, slamming the door behind him.

The last of Adrienne's bravado vanished, and she broke down and wept. Renno handed her his plate.

She smiled at him through her tears, then began to eat ravenously. "I knew you and Jeffrey would hate me when I disappeared, Renno, but I had no choice. There was no way you could bring me on board with you."

"I never hate you," Renno declared.

The major looked thoughtful as he ate an apple. "Renno," he said, "I knew you were resourceful when I saw you at Whitehall and again when you fought your duel. But I had no idea how ingenious you could really be!"

As soon as Adrienne had eaten, all three men escorted her to her cabin, and Jeffrey loaned her his greatcoat for the short walk up the passageway. He hastily removed his own belongings, and she closed the door behind her, taking care to bolt it.

Renno went up to the main deck with Jeffrey, and they stood together, staring out at the sea. Adrienne's dramatic reappearance had startled both of them, but they were pleased that she had not stayed behind in England. Her future might be uncertain, but at least she was safe now.

Her raw courage was great, and Renno admired her for it. He realized, however, that he no longer wanted her as a woman. They had needed each other, but now their situation was changed. She would be his friend. He felt no regrets and was satisfied.

By this time the entire crew had heard the whispers that a spectacularly attractive blond was a stowaway on board. So, when Adrienne came on deck, dozens of sailors happened to find chores in the immediate area.

They were doomed to disappointment. The young woman's face was scrubbed clean and free of cosmetics, and her red hair was in a demure bun beneath an old-fashioned bonnet. She was wearing a drab, wool dress with a high neck, long sleeves, and a very full skirt. She was so ordinary, in fact, that no self-respecting Royal Navy sailor would have bothered to glance in her direction.

Jeffrey, aware of her cleverness, knew Commodore Markham would approve of her transformation.

"I'm sorry I tricked both of you," Adrienne said, "but the sailors who hid me swore that the commodore is an unholy terror. So I spent all my time hidden in the hold, praying he wouldn't find some way to send me ashore again. But he's very sweet."

Jeffrey grinned and shook his head. "That's not an accurate description, but I think you can tame any man when you set your mind to it."

Adrienne became demure. "I'll try not to be a burden to either of you."

Renno shook his head. "Not burden," he said. "Adrienne is our good friend. We help her."

His flat, unequivocal declaration comforted her. Her need for him had also changed, and she was relieved to find the feeling mutual. The knowledge that he still intended to stand by her, along with Jeffrey, gave her renewed courage. She knew nothing about the English colonies in North America, and she had no idea how she would make her way there or where she would live. But with Renno and Jeffrey on either side of her she knew she would be all right.

Lieutenant Tom Hibbard had a working knowledge of the languages of the Indians of the northern colonies, so he was assigned as the head of the party dispatched to the land of the Seneca with the news that had just arrived from Boston.

Renno and Jeffrey, he told Ghonka, had succeeded in their mission and would arrive very soon in Massachusetts Bay with arms and supplies. A squadron of Royal Navy ships had been assigned to duty in American waters, and in due time several regiments of regular troops would be sent to form the core of an army capable of beating the French and their allies.

The Great Sachem rejoiced.

Then Tom extended the invitation from Governor Shirley: the leader of the Iroquois and as many people as he cared to bring with him were asked to come to Boston to be on hand to greet Renno when he arrived.

A gleam appeared in Ghonka's eyes.

Ba-lin-ta immediately begged to be allowed to go and Ghonka agreed. He decided to take Walter, too, and leave the boy in Fort Springfield for a visit with his mother. It was taken for granted that El-i-chi would be one of the warriors assigned to the escort.

Then Ena astonished her husband by expressing her desire to go to. She had never traveled farther than two days' duration from the main town of the Seneca, but she was overjoyed by Renno's success and was determined to share in his triumphal welcome.

It was unusual for a Seneca chieftain to be accompanied by his wife on state visits to other lands. But as Ena vehemently pointed out, Ghonka's grandmother, a woman so wise that many songs were still sung about her, had gone everywhere with his grandfather and had even participated in meetings of the Iroquois council.

Ghonka was convinced and then had to make hasty plans accordingly. Ena and Ba-lin-ta would be tempting targets for the Algonquian. So, instead of just taking a token escort with him, he assigned a detail of fifty men, thirty of them senior warriors, and placed them under the command of Sun-ai-yee, his most competent war chief. He insisted, however, that his wife and the two young ones maintain the pace set by the men. Under no circumstances would he miss Renno's arrival.

Ena nodded complacently. She knew her own endurance was equal to that of any warrior. Walter was strong now, and Ba-lin-ta had the energy of youth.

They began their journey the following morning, accompanied by Tom Hibbard and his detail. The late winter weather was raw and foul, but they moved swiftly and after a few days they reached Fort Springfield.

Brigadier Wilson was delighted to see Ghonka, and Mildred immediately ordered sides of beef and venison to be roasted for a feast. Ba-lin-ta and Walter went to spend the night with Ida Alwin at her newly rebuilt house, and Mildred insisted that Ghonka and Ena stay at the Wilson house rather than join the other Seneca on the parade ground at the fort.

Never before had Ena seen a white man's town, much less a grand mansion like the handsomely furnished Wilson house. But no one knew she was awed by her surroundings. She was being honored because she was the wife of Ghonka and the mother of Renno, and she was determined not to let them down. So she watched the way Mildred Wilson sat in a chair, drank tea, and ate, and quietly copied her.

Ida Alwin soon came to visit, with Leverett Carswell

insistently escorting her while Ba-lin-ta and Walter trailed behind.

"Tell your mother," she said to Ba-lin-ta, who was translating, "that I thank her with all my heart for her kindness to Walter."

"He is a good boy and he will be a fine warrior," Ena replied. "I have done for him only what any mother would do."

"You've been a better mother to him than I ever was." Ida surprised herself by bursting into tears and felt ashamed of herself.

Only on the rarest of occasions did a woman of the Seneca allow herself the luxury of tears. But when Ena heard Ba-lin-ta's translation of the white woman's words, she immediately understood how Walter's mother felt. Nothing she herself might say would be adequate for the occasion, Ena knew, but she placed her hands on the white woman's shoulders.

Ida embraced her and wept harder.

Only a lifetime of self-discipline made it possible for Ena to hold back her own tears.

"Here, now," Leverett muttered, and blew his nose vigorously.

Scores of local residents accepted Mildred's invitation to the unexpected feast and, in spite of the nasty weather, ate out-of-doors without complaint. The Seneca, eating roasted potatoes for the first time, had to admit they liked them, and they devoured large quantities of cornbread. Beef was new to all but those who had participated in the march to Quebec, and the warriors took huge chunks, which they tore apart and ate with their fingers.

A subdued Nettie Hibbard, sitting beside Tom, was thunderstruck by the ferocious appearance of the Seneca. It was hard for her to believe that these people were the relatives and close friends of Renno, who had treated her so gently. "They look so wild," she murmured to Tom. "It's amazing, but Renno isn't like them at all."

"If you ever saw him in battle," Tom replied with a chuckle, "you'd know he's the wildest of all."

Perhaps the least comfortable person present was

Rene Gautier. Indians had murdered and scalped his beloved Louise. He had to tell himself repeatedly that these Indians were friends and allies, who would help them defeat the French.

Most of the Fort Springfield men followed the brigadier's example and sat cross-legged on the ground with the Seneca. Andrew Wilson, who had given Ghonka the place of honor to his right, was completely at ease and lavished praise on Renno.

Ghonka, not to be outdone in politeness, insisted that, even though they didn't yet know details, much of the credit had to be given to Jeffrey.

"One thing I know," the brigadier said, speaking the Seneca language, which he had learned during the Quebec campaign, "your son and mine are making it possible for us to defend ourselves. You and I have a right to be proud of our sons."

A Seneca never boasted about his family, so Ghonka did not reply directly. He became thoughtful, then said, "It may be that we can attack the great new fort of the French."

"Louisburg!" The same thought had occurred to Wilson. Such a scheme was preposterous because the English colonies were too disorganized. Governor Shirley and General Pepperrell would never allow it. But Ghonka was a kindred spirit, and Wilson grinned at him. "There's nothing I'd like more," he said, "than to reduce Louisburg to rubble."

Nearby, but eating separately, were a number of ladies, most of whom were following Mildred Wilson's example and sitting on benches at long tables. Ena sat between Mildred and Ida, and no one would have guessed that this was the first time in her life she had ever eaten at a table. She even managed to use a knife and fork, and her natural grace made her appear less clumsy than she felt.

Ba-lin-ta, a mischievous gleam in her eyes, followed her mother's example, and having spent some time in the Alwin house in the past, she handled her eating utensils deftly. Walter, however, preferred to tear his food apart with his fingers Seneca-style. To his astonishment his mother made no objection. It was possible, he thought, that she had also changed.

The party ended early in the evening because of the busy days ahead.

Early the next morning the Seneca and Donald Doremus's company of militia formed a joint escort for the journey to Boston. A carriage had been provided for Mildred Wilson, and she insisted that Ena ride with her. Ba-lin-ta happily agreed to accompany them as their interpreter.

Brigadier Wilson was mounted, and offered one of his horses to Ghonka. But the Great Sachem declined. "I am not yet so old and feeble that my own legs and feet will not carry me. My warriors would laugh if I rode."

Andrew Wilson did not insist. He had learned to accept the Indian ways without argument. Certainly he was not surprised to find that Ghonka was tireless on the march and more energetic than many warriors half his age.

The journey was uneventful, and when the party reached Boston, the Seneca and militiamen made adjoining camps on the Common. The Wilsons were guests of Governor Shirley, who also invited the Great Sachem and his family. But he did not insist, as Andrew advised him that Ghonka and Ena would probably feel more comfortable in a tent pitched on the Common.

No one had any idea how soon the convoy from England would arrive, and each day the tension mounted. Governor Shirley supplied food for the Seneca, and the warriors, with no need to hunt or fish, became bored. But, at Ghonka's orders, they stayed on the Common and did not wander freely around the city. The Great Sachem was determined that there be no unpleasantness.

Major General William Pepperrell, the commander in chief of the Massachusetts Bay militia, arrived from his home in the Maine District. He and Ghonka had been comrades in the Quebec campaign and were pleased to see each other. But no one could make concrete military plans for the future. Until they knew how much aid they were getting from King William, they had to wait.

A full week passed, and then the governor received word that a large British warship was leading a convoy into the harbor. A company of Boston militia marched to the docks with the unit from western Massachusetts Bay, and sealed off the area. The colony's civilian and military leaders arrived a short time later, accompanied by the Seneca, and the warriors formed a solid phalanx behind the Great Sachem.

The group watched as the *Princess Anne* dropped anchor and furled her sails. The merchantmen could navigate in shallow waters, so they edged toward the wharves, where they would dock while their valuable military cargo was being unloaded.

The sloop-of-war that had first brought the news to Boston fired a salvo in salute. Then the frigate's gunports were lowered and her large cannon responded. Their roar sent seagulls flying high in the air, and some of the younger Seneca could not conceal their awe. Never had they seen such potent thunder machines.

A gig was lowered into the water from the frigate, and a number of people followed the sailors down a rope ladder into the boat. It was impossible to see them clearly from a distance, but one, who required assistance, appeared to be a woman.

The small craft bobbed as it made its way across the choppy waters of the harbor toward the pier that jutted out into the bay.

The impassive Ghonka, his arms folded across his chest, felt greatly relieved when he saw his son. Renno had shaved his head on either side of his neatly-dressed scalp lock, he had oiled his body, and was wearing full war paint. It was obvious that he was still a Seneca, that he had not been tempted by the white man.

The first to step ashore was Commodore Markham, resplendent in his uniform of blue and gold. He was followed by Major Rand, elegant in full-dress scarlet. Then came Renno and Jeffrey Wilson, and together they reached down and helped Adrienne ashore. She was wearing one of her more revealing gowns.

Governor Shirley moved to the base of the dock to greet the party and was followed by General Pepperrell, Brigadier Wilson, and Ghonka. All were somber, as befitted a great occasion.

For a long moment Ghonka did not speak, and neither did his son. They grasped each other's right forearms, and pride shone in the Great Sachem's eyes. "My son," he said at last.

"My father," Renno replied. Suddenly, a few feet away, he saw Ena. It had not occurred to him that his mother might also be there to greet him, and his poise totally deserted him. She was drab in her doeskins and leggings, with her gray hair falling forward across her shoulders in two tight braids, but Renno had never seen anyone lovelier.

Bolting toward her, he ignored the ancient tradition that required him to exchange formal greetings with her and instead swept her into a fierce embrace.

As El-i-chi came forward to welcome his brother, he caught a glimpse of the tears in their mother's eyes, but he pretended not to see them. On an occasion like this, it was a woman's privilege to weep.

Jeffrey presented the newcomers to the various officials, and when the brief ceremonies were over, the entire party, with the exception of the Indians, climbed into carriages for the short ride to the Governor's House. Somewhat to Adrienne's surprise, she was included and found herself in a coach with Sir Philip.

Jeffrey rode with his proud parents, and Andrew inquired about Adrienne. "I assume she's associated with the commodore or Major Rand," he said.

"No, Papa." Stumbling at first, then gaining courage, Jeffrey explained how he and Renno had helped her.

The brigadier listened in silence, then said incredulously, "Surely you're not telling me she's Renno's mistress!"

"No, sir. She was, in a way, for a time, but that's ended now. She was grateful to him." Jeffrey went on to explain how Adrienne had arranged to be smuggled aboard the *Princess Anne*.

Mildred had only listened, but now she intervened for the first time. "The young woman is what she says, a Huguenot refugee?"

"There's no doubt of that, Mama. If she had been sent back to France, she'd have gone to prison."

"She has friends and relatives here?"

"No, Mama, she knows no one in the New World. She wanted to come here because she felt the English colonies offered her the only chance she would have to lead a good, safe life."

"Surely she's intelligent enough to know this is only a half-civilized country."

"Well," Jeffrey said, "Adrienne is remarkably resourceful, and she has great strength of character."

Mildred shook her head. "An attractive young woman needs a great deal more than that to survive here these days." She turned to her husband. "You realize what will become of this girl if she's allowed to drift on her own. Especially in Boston, filled with sailors and frontiersmen who haven't set eyes on a woman in months."

"What are you suggesting, my dear?" Andrew spoke mildly, knowing his wife had already made a decision of some sort.

"We're taking the girl back to Fort Springfield with us and giving her our protection!" Mildred spoke firmly. "She was fortunate to meet Renno and Jeffrey in London, but it's unlikely she'd be as lucky another time. I shall speak to her as soon as we reach the Governor's House." The matter was settled.

The members of the small group gathered in Governor Shirley's library studied the list of military supplies sent by King William. Brigadier Wilson translated the key items for Ghonka.

The governor finally broke the silence. "If I understand correctly, Commodore Markham," he said, "we should be able to hold our own by spring or summer."

"We'll do better than that, Your Excellency," the

Royal Navy officer said. "We should be able to mount a major offensive against the French sea forces, and we hope to put a real crimp in their operations."

"The dispatch of regular troops to this side of the Atlantic is what intrigues me," General Pepperrell declared. "Obviously they'll bolster our strength accordingly, but they should do a great deal more than that. Their arrival will spur the recruitment of militia in New York and Connecticut, perhaps even in Rhode Island."

The governor nodded. "The knowledge that we have Crown support should encourage every colony to make a greater effort. The steps London is taking are precisely what we need to bring all of us together."

Brigadier Wilson conferred in a low tone with Ghonka, then turned to his colleagues. "The Great Sachem and I have had the same thought. We're wondering if it might not be feasible to strike a major blow at the very heart of the French. If we allow them to take the offensive they'll kill our women and children, destroy our farms, and burn our towns. However, if we can capture Fort Louisburg, the French and their Indian friends will lose the ability to wage war!"

Ghonka nodded vigorously. It was a proud Seneca tradition always to be first to attack, never to give that advantage to an enemy.

General Pepperrell frowned. "I agree with you in principle, Andrew, but we face one insurmountable obstacle. We know nothing about Louisburg. We have no information on the size of the fort, its armaments, or the size of its garrison. We don't even know how large a fleet the French may be stationing on Cape Breton Island. Without adequate information, we'd be striking blind. If an attempt to reduce Louisburg should fail, we'd have exhausted ourselves—and we'd be helpless."

"Gentlemen," Sir Philip said, "I have been authorized to inform you of a decision made in secret by the Privy Council and approved by His Majesty."

As he spoke, the brigadier translated for Ghonka.

"The Council," Rand said, "authorizes you to place Fort Louisburg under full siege. And His Majesty will provide whatever additional assistance may be needed to guarantee that the French and their allies surrender."

The others nodded and smiled in approval.

But Pepperrell was not satisfied. "My objection still stands, Major."

"Your objection is valid, General, and no one is more aware of the problem than the Privy Council. That's why I'm here. I've been sent on a specific mission to overcome that handicap."

The others stared at him, and even Ghonka's eyes widened.

Sir Philip smiled. "For several weeks before I left London I was seen in a number of gaming houses, supposedly playing cards for high stakes. No secret was made of my departure for Boston on board the *Princess Anne*. A day or two after I sailed, a notice was posted in the Royal Military Gazette, dismissing me from the army for squandering the regimental treasury on a wild gambling spree. The news of that disgrace presumably will reach you via the next ship that comes here. In the meantime, you may be certain the French will know it, too. We know for a fact that their agents in London read the Royal Military Gazette.

"I shall go to Quebec and offer my services to the French. In one way or another I shall see to it that they send me to Louisburg. There I'll glean all I can about the place. At an appropriate time I'll slip away and bring all the information I've learned to you."

"You could be hanged by the French as a spy, you know," Governor Shirley murmured.

"I'm prepared to take that risk, Your Excellency." Rand spoke crisply. "I've had a great deal of experience and extensive training. I assure you I shall be quite careful that the French don't guess my true mission."

"Do you really think you can carry it off?" General Pepperrell asked.

"If I didn't think so I wouldn't have accepted the assignment. I volunteered for it. But I do have a weakness that could prove fatal, not only to me, but to all that we hope to accomplish. I've never before been in

North America. I know nothing about your wilderness, how to survive or find my way through your forests, which I understand are vast. I shall need help."

The mood of everyone in the room had become grim.

"It wasn't accidental that I made the voyage here on the *Princess Anne*," Sir Philip said. "I saw Renno demonstrate his marksmanship at Whitehall. I acted as the referee of a duel in which he handled himself with skill, courage and ingenuity. I confirmed my opinion of him on board the frigate. He has now become a superb shot with dueling pistols. I ask you to send him with me—if he gives his consent—as my guide, my companion, and my partner in this enterprise."

The entire group turned to Ghonka.

The Great Sachem's expression did not change. "Renno would pretend to be a traitor to the Seneca," he said at last.

Sir Philip nodded.

"The French would believe him. But the Huron and Algonquian know Renno is a senior warrior. They know he is my son. It may be they also know he went to the land of the English. Why would he become a traitor?"

Sir Philip shrugged. "I know little about your people. That detail, important though it is, I must leave to you."

For a long time Ghonka pondered. Then he said, "It could be that Renno became evil in the land of the English. It could be there is hate in the hearts of the Seneca for Renno now because his skin is white. It could be that we place the brand of the traitor on his hand and drive him from our land."

Brigadier Wilson explained it to his colleagues. "From what I understand of Indians, the Algonquian and the Ottawa would accept such a story almost as readily as would the French. The Huron are wilier, but a brand on Renno's hand surely would convince them."

The major drew in his breath. "Then Ghonka approves?"

The Seneca chieftain looked at each member of the

group in turn. Then he said, "The Great Sachem speaks for all the people of the Iroquois. But now you ask that my son pretend he is a traitor and a renegade. I understand your reasons. They are good reasons. But in this no man can speak for Renno. Ghonka cannot speak for his son. Only Renno can speak for himself."

They discussed the problem briefly, and then an aide was sent to the Common. There Renno, shaken by the news of Sah-nee-wa's death, was visiting with his mother, brother, and sister. He was surprised that his presence was required at the meeting, but he immediately donned his buffalo cloak and accompanied the aide.

The faces of the men in the library were grave. Renno looked only at his father, but, as he had anticipated, Ghonka's features gave him no clue.

Sir Philip explained the situation in detail.

Then Brigadier Wilson told Renno why the future of the English colonies depended on the success of the mission that Sir Philip was planning.

Ghonka's face was still wooden.

Renno turned to him.

The Great Sachem rose and, not saying a word, left the room, with Renno silently following him.

Commodore Markham and the major were startled by their abrupt behavior, but the brigadier explained. "They'll speak privately," he said, "and then we'll be told their decision."

Ghonka led the way to a deserted portion of the Common, as far as he could go from the camp of the Seneca and the bivouac of the militia company from western Massachusetts Bay. There he found a boulder and, settling himself on it, he filled and lighted a clay pipe.

Renno sat beside him, accepted the pipe, and puffed on it, then handed it back to his father.

Not until all the tobacco in the pipe had been burned to ashes did Ghonka stir slightly.

The time had come for Renno to speak. "For many moons," he said, "I have been far from the land of the Seneca. I have dreamed of sleeping in my own house. I have dreamed of the venison, the corn, the squash, and the beans that are cooked by my mother. I have dreamed of telling stories about the foolishness of the English to Ba-lin-ta. My heart has ached for the day that I would hunt with El-i-chi in the wilderness. Now I have another wish. Only now have I learned that the sister of my father lives no more on the earth. It is my wish to visit the place where her spirit rose to the land of our ancestors. My mother has told me that Sah-nee-wa promised to watch over me. If I go to that place, perhaps her spirit will visit me." He fell silent.

"It is good that my son wants to return to the land of his people. It is right. My son won a great victory in the land of the English. The Great Sachem of the English gives us many gifts so we can win a war with the Algonquian, the Huron, and the Ottawa. And the French. I am proud of my son."

"Gladly will I follow my father into battle, even if we are outnumbered ten to one by our enemies," Renno said. "Gladly will I lead a war party on a raid deep into the land of the Huron or the land of the Algonquian. Gladly will I face the arrows and the firesticks of our foes." He paused for a long moment, then added forcibly, "But it is hard to bear the mark of the renegade on one's hand."

"It is very hard," Ghonka agreed.

"The mark that is placed with fire on the hand of a man stays there until he dies. Strangers who meet him will not know he is a true Seneca, not a renegade."

The Great Sachem disagreed but was surprisingly gentle. "The mark that is placed on a man's hand with fire can be changed with fire." The agony of submitting to the trial by fire twice was of little consequence to him.

That didn't bother Renno, either. But he was still troubled. He had already performed a difficult mission, suffering discomfort and loneliness, and now, instead of being rewarded, he was being asked to undertake an even more hazardous and complicated task. "I did much in London for the English colonists. Now they will have many firesticks and bullets. They will have the warriors of the

Great Sachem of the English to fight beside them. They will have many ships filled with thunder machines. It is not right that they ask one warrior to do more for them."

"It is not right," Ghonka replied, then added calmly, "but the Seneca will have many firesticks and bullets, many blankets of wool that our warriors will carry on the trail. Other warriors of the Iroquois will have them also. Without them we would be helpless when the Huron and Algonquian attack us, and the Ottawa follow them like dogs. They would swarm over the land of the Seneca like an army of ants."

"That is true," Renno was forced to concede.

"If we and our brothers attack first and capture the great fort of the French," Ghonka said, "our lands will be safe. No enemies will hurt our people."

"That also is true," his son replied grudgingly.

"It is the wish of Rand that Renno go with him," the Great Sachem declared, speaking more forcibly. "He knows that no other warrior in all the lands of all the tribes has the skills at war of Renno. Only Renno speaks his tongue. It may be," he added thoughtfully, "that the manitous, many summers ago, wished Renno to do this deed. It may be that is why they made Renno my son. His skin is like the skin of the English and French. So the enemy will believe he is truly a renegade."

Renno had exhausted his own arguments.

"No warrior has greater courage than my son," Ghonka said. "His courage is greater than mine. I would falter if the English asked me to do this task for them. But they have not asked me. They ask Renno. Only he, of all the warriors who walk the earth, can do this work for them."

His heart heavy, Renno gazed up at the leaden sky. He was looking for a hawk or some other sign from the manitous that would tell him what to do. But no hawks flew over this large English town. The manitous showed themselves only in the deep recesses of the wilderness.

This was one decision he had to make himself. Despite his reluctance, only he could help insure the safety of the Seneca. As a last resort he prayed to the spirit of Sah-nee-wa for guidance. But there was no response.

So be it. The decision was his alone.

He rose slowly to his feet, folded his arms across his chest, and squared his shoulders. "My father," he said, "I will do as Rand wishes. I will go with him to the land of the French, to the great fortress of Louisburg. In the eyes of all the world I will be a traitor to my people. I will become a renegade."

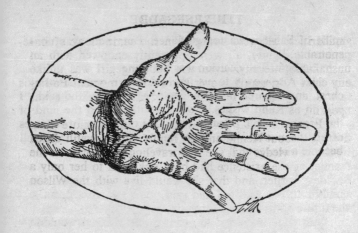

Chapter IX

Captain Doremus's militiamen and the Seneca escort marched together on the road that led westward to Fort Springfield, both parties heartened by the knowledge that in a few months they would be going off to fight their mutual foes. Horses had been provided for Sir Philip Rand and Jeffrey, and they rode with Brigadier Wilson. Renno elected to walk and trudged beside his father, silent and grim. He had accepted the assignment, but he didn't relish what lay ahead.

Adrienne Bartel rode in Mildred Wilson's carriage, along with Ena and Ba-lin-ta. The girl clutched the handsome doll Renno had brought her and talked incessantly, sometimes in English, sometimes in her own tongue. Ena, proudly wrapped in the blanket of wool that had been one of Renno's gifts, insisted on holding a large iron cooking pot, a mirror, and a pair of shears in her lap.

Renno bore no physical resemblance to this woman and child, any more than he did to the barrel-chested chieftain he called his father. But Adrienne could see

212

similiarities: all were wrapped in the same cloak of impenetrable dignity, all were apparently endowed with an unshakable integrity. Even this bubbling girl was unlike any child Adrienne had ever known. One moment Ba-lin-ta was laughing and clapping her hands, the next she was speaking solemnly, like a small adult.

It was difficult for Adrienne to think more than fleetingly about Renno and his family. She was still dazed by the knowledge that she was traveling to a town on the frontier whose existence had been unknown to her only a few days earlier, and that she would live with the Wilson family until, as Mildred had said, "We see what promise the future holds in store for you."

Adrienne had tried to protest, but Mildred wouldn't listen. Jeffrey's mother was slight and feminine, but she allowed nothing to stand in her path when she had made up her mind. Even the brigadier quietly accepted his wife's decisions.

Adrienne had hoped to find work as a governess or French teacher in Boston, but Mildred wouldn't hear of it. "What nonsense!" she had said. "The Lord only knows what might become of you if we leave you behind. You're coming with us, and that's that!"

Grateful for the kindness, Adrienne was also heartened by the knowledge that other French Huguenots were living in the vicinity of Fort Springfield. Perhaps life on the edge of the endless forests of North America wouldn't be as dreadful as she had imagined. At least she would have shelter, food, protection, and the company of her own kind.

The Seneca were eager to return home as soon as possible, so they stayed only one night in Fort Springfield. As soon as they arrived, Ba-lin-ta raced off to Ida Alwin's to tell Walter they would be leaving the next morning.

At dawn Renno said good-bye to his mother and sister, and although they knew they might never see him again, neither shed a tear. Ena's farewell was almost casual, but she betrayed herself by reaching out and touching Renno's arm before turning away abruptly.

Major Rand, who was staying with the Wilsons, had a final word with the Great Sachem. "If anyone can learn what we need to know, Renno and I will do it." he said. "We'll return in no more than three months. If we don't, you'll know we're dead."

There was one last act that had to be performed before the Seneca departed. El-i-chi took a pair of tongs and, removing several burning chunks of wood from the fireplace in the Wilson house, carried them in a metal bucket to an isolated spot behind the barns. He was followed by his silent father and brother. Making certain no one was watching, he exchanged forearm clasps with Renno, then walked off abruptly to await his father at the house.

Ghonka had elected to brand Renno himself, and in secret, so no other Seneca would know that his elder son bore the mark of a traitor and renegade. Grasping the tongs, he picked up a piece of wood that glowed a deep red.

Renno extended the palm of his left hand and held it at arm's length. Ghonka showed no emotion, and his hand was steady as he burned a double cross about three inches long onto the palm of the son of whom he was so proud.

The searing pain was excruciating, but Renno neither flinched nor moved a muscle, and his expression remained unchanged. Even the stench of his own burning flesh did not make him move. He had been trained to endure torture, and he had known far worse than this. But his heart felt like a lump of heavy metal in the pit of his stomach, and, even though he thoroughly understood the need for the mark, he was suffused with shame. His soul cried out against this cruel torment, and he told himself that his unswerving loyalty to the Seneca was being put to the supreme test.

The task completed, Ghonka flung the offending brand from him as though it had been a loathsome reptile.

Renno slowly lowered his throbbing hand to his side and faced his father.

For a moment Ghonka's face became distorted in a rare display of emotion. Then he instantly regained his self-control, although there was a suspicious huskiness in his voice as he said, "My son, when you were a small boy it was my hope that you would become a great warrior. Even more, that you would rise to the rank of war chief. You are already a senior warrior. It will not be long before you earn your next promotion. But now I know what I never dared to hope. The day will come when you will wear my bonnet of many feathers. You will become the sachem of the Seneca, the Great Sachem of all the Iroquois. May you soon learn all we need to know so we can make war on our enemies. And may the manitous bring you home in safety."

Not waiting for a response he turned and walked away quickly so his son would not see that the most powerful of the Seneca was badly shaken.

Renno stood motionless, watching him until he vanished from sight. He was now alone again. A new mission separated him from his people once again, and now he was responsible for another's well-being.

He emptied the bucket of the remains of the burning wood, filled it with snow, and then plunged his hand into it. The pain grew more intense, but even now, with no one to see him, he gave no sign of his distress. Gradually his hand became numb.

The sound of chimes from the house signaled breakfast, so he walked back slowly, leaving the pail outside the dining-room door.

Renno had no appetite, but went through the motions of eating, using only his right hand. For the moment his left was useless.

Adrienne was the first to notice something was wrong. Jumping up from her own place, she caught hold of Renno's wrist. "What happened to your hand?" she demanded.

He made no reply.

Brigadier Wilson and Major Rand, the only others present who were aware of the reasons for the brand, kept silent.

Mildred Wilson was sympathetic and agreed at once when Adrienne insisted that Renno see a doctor.

Renno shook his head. He placed no faith in the healing powers of anyone but the medicine men of the Seneca.

"It might not be a bad idea to see a physician," Sir Philip said quietly. "As soon as your hand improves, you and I can go about our business."

The suggestion was sensible, Renno realized, but even more important to him was the urgent desire to have these women stop making a fuss over him. In the land of the Seneca no woman would insult a warrior by even noticing a minor wound or injury. A visit to a doctor could do him no real harm, he supposed, and then Adrienne and Mildred would leave him in peace. So he reluctantly agreed to go.

Afraid he might change his mind, Adrienne said she would go with him. Mildred agreed, thinking it wise that she begin to familiarize herself with Fort Springfield.

Soon after breakfast one of the Wilson carriages drove up to the front door. Renno would have preferred to walk, but his hand was aching badly, his spirits were low, and he didn't feel like arguing.

Adrienne tried to make conversation on the ride into town. "Are you and Sir Philip going somewhere?" she asked.

Renno nodded, but made no reply.

She had learned that when he withdrew into himself it was useless to question him, so she did not press the point. It was strange, she thought, how well he seemed to blend into this primitive community, and at the same time he had become alien to her. It was difficult to believe, glancing at his expressionless face, that she had once been close to him. In London he had seemed different. Now, having seen him with his family and other warriors of the Seneca, she knew he lived in a far different world. She would always be grateful to him, but there was no future for them together here and she felt no regrets.

A light, cold rain was falling when they reached

town, and they left the carriage in a vacant lot on the High Street. Renno immediately departed, walking several squares to the doctor's office.

Adrienne headed in the opposite direction, and as she walked down the muddy road she knew Mildred had been right to suggest that she buy clothing suitable for living in a frontier community. Her frivolous, high-heeled shoes made walking difficult, and she appreciated the shapeless calf-high boots of rawhide that she saw other women wearing. Her silk, wool-lined cloak was not waterproof, and she knew she should purchase a cape of thick leather. It might not be attractive, but it would keep her dry.

Her first stop was a general store, where she bought thread, a length of cloth, and a container of green tea that Mildred had asked for. When she emerged from the store, Adrienne was amused to note that the town seemed almost deserted. There were no pedestrians on the muddy roads, and a farmer's open, ramshackle cart, filled with hams, was the only vehicle. Fort Springfield was a far cry from Paris or London. Even Boston was busier.

On sudden impulse she decided to visit a shop whose weathered sign, "Leather Goods," had caught her eye on the drive into town. Her funds had been shrinking, but she had no expenses these days, thanks to the generosity of the Wilsons, so she decided to treat herself to a pair of stout boots and a leather cape.

The proprietor carefully took her measurements, promised to have the boots and cloak finished in a few days, and said he would deliver them to the Wilson house. The price was almost absurdly small, and he refused to accept any payment until she received her order and was satisfied. For the first time Adrienne began to appreciate the advantages of frontier living.

The walk back to the coach chilled her, and when she saw from a distance that Renno had not yet returned, she decided to find some place where she could order a cup of hot tea. She turned back, and on a narrow side road she saw a tavern.

The place was dismal, with only a few tables and rickety chairs of unpainted pine. But a fire was burning in the hearth, the place was empty, and the barman, after looking long and hard at her, went off to boil a pot of tea for her. Warming up by the fire, Adrienne had no way of knowing that the tavern had a questionable reputation because it was frequented principally by hard-drinking trappers and others who came in from the wilderness.

A heavyset young man wandered in as she was served her tea, but she ignored him.

Jack Davies ordered a hot rum drink and stood near the fire as he drank it. "You're new here," he said.

Adrienne pretended not to hear him. Perhaps it was the custom here to speak freely to total strangers, but that wasn't her way.

Davies eyed her slowly, taking in every detail of her shoes, her open silk cloak, and her gown with a low, square-cut neckline. "You'll do fine here," he said. "There ain't been anybody in your line of work since Nettie got fancy ideas and found herself a husband."

Adrienne wasn't sure what he was talking about but preferred not to find out. Boors were alike everywhere, and the sheer bulk of this unpleasant man made her nervous, so she drank her tea quickly.

"You're one of them fancy ones, eh?"

She drank the last of her tea, pushed back her chair, and picked up her bundles. Davies opened the door for her, then bowed low, mockingly.

Adrienne walked out into the cold rain with her head held high. The man dashed ahead and blocked her path on the narrow road. He grinned at her without humor.

Rather than push past him, Adrienne halted.

"You're the kind that thinks she's too good for the likes of me," he said. "But you ain't."

She became alarmed when he began to advance toward her, and she instinctively took several backward steps. An alleyway opened off the road and she moved into it, realizing too late that a one-story log building blocked the other end.

Davies continued to pursue her. "Be nice to me," he said, "and you'll get paid. Otherwise you won't get nothin' out of it."

The man was dangerous. Adrienne knew she had to get past him. He guessed her intent and lunged, forcing her back against the building of rough logs. Then a brawny hand shot down the neckline of her dress.

Terrified and frantic, Adrienne tried to fight him off, but he was too strong for her. Cupping a breast in one hand, he pushed her to the muddy ground. Gasping, Adrienne managed to suck in her breath, then screamed.

Renno sat interminably in the waiting room of Dr. Marsh, ignoring the surreptitious stares of other patients. He felt like bolting, but he knew Mildred and Adrienne would give him no peace, so he forced himself to go through with the disgrace of allowing himself to be treated.

At last he was admitted to the inner room.

The physician, who knew of Renno, thought it best not to inquire about the cause of the young savage's burns. Instead he applied a salve and poultice to the injured hand, then added an outer bandage for good measure.

As Renno left the doctor's office, he had to admit that the strange, sticky substance smeared on his palm relieved his pain, and his hand no longer throbbed much. Perhaps there was something to be said in favor of white men's medicine. The bandage made him feel guilty, to be sure, and he was glad there were no Seneca in town to see the depths to which he had gone. He took his time walking back to the coach, oblivious of the rain.

A woman's scream startled him, and he broke into a run. Then she screamed again, more feebly, and he raced still faster.

When he reached the alleyway, Adrienne lay on the ground, struggling in vain to push Davies off her. Her skirts were around her waist.

Without hesitation Renno leaped forward. He

reached out with his right hand, caught hold of the attacker's hair, and tugged hard.

Jack Davies was hauled to his feet, and he whirled to face his attacker. When he saw Renno, he reached for the pistol in his belt.

Renno knew he had to disarm the man instantly and launched a hard, vicious kick. His foot caught Davies's hand before he could shoot. The weapon flew upward, then landed in the mud some feet away. Adrienne scrambled to her feet and watched in horror, one hand pressed to her throat.

Renno drew his knife. At the same moment a knife appeared in Davies's hand. They circled each other, each looking for an opening.

The bruised, badly upset Adrienne could think only that this scene was a crude version of the duel Renno had fought in London. But this time he was in even greater jeopardy. He would have to kill or be killed, and he was hampered by an injured hand.

By now Renno had put his useless hand out of his mind. He was intent on sizing up his opponent. This man was taller, perhaps stronger, and was so burly that his weight gave him an added advantage. He was surprisingly light on his feet, too, so it would be fatal to make even the slightest error.

Renno realized he had to strike first and might have only one chance to disable or kill the man before he felt the point of his foe's knife. Very well, there were fights in which cunning was more important by far than brute strength. Renno raised his knife over his head, then leaped. Before he came within striking distance, however, he twisted his body. At the same moment he lowered his arm to waist height, and, using all his force, he drove the blade deep into his enemy's stomach.

Davies staggered, then collapsed slowly onto the ground. Reno pounced on him and struck again, mercilessly slitting his throat.

Jack Davies died without making a sound. The blood was still pouring from his wounds as Renno swiftly and expertly scalped him. The dead man's features sagged, and he resembled a ghastly caricature of himself.

It was all too much for Adrienne. Sobbing and gagging, she covered her face with her hands.

As Renno rose to his feet, two men appeared. Tom Hibbard and Rene Gautier had come into town to buy some nails. They heard the screams and had arrived just in time to witness the grisly end of the fight.

The hysterical Adrienne began to babble in French without even realizing it. She then changed to English, and told what happened.

Tom nudged the body of the dead man with the toe of his boot. "Renno," he said, "I reckon you've done Fort Springfield a favor by ridding us of Davies."

Renno indicated his own feelings by spitting on the corpse. Adrienne wept quietly.

Tom took charge. "Rene," he said, "maybe you'll do the lady a favor and see her back out to the Wilson house. Renno, we'll have to report this to the constabulary, if you don't mind. Not that you're in any trouble."

Adrienne collected herself enough to start in the direction of the carriage. Rene made it a point to address her in French.

By the time they were settled in the carriage, she had recovered sufficiently, at least for the moment, to ask him about himself.

"Like you," he said, "my family and I are Huguenots. There are a number of us in the area now."

"The barbarism of these people doesn't bother you?"

"My wife was killed by Indian raids," he said simply.

"Oh, I'm sorry." Adrienne was abashed. "I didn't mean to pry."

"At first I was bitter, naturally," he said. "But little by little I have begun to understand. My children may live and worship as they please here. No one will persecute them, confiscate their property, or imprison them because of what they believe. Everything in the world has a price, you know, even freedom."

Adrienne did not speak again on the ride, and when they reached the Wilson house she went to her room. Rene waited only until Renno and Tom returned and then took his leave.

Adrienne did not appear at dinner, and Mildred counseled patience. "She has had a terrible experience. Let her rest, and perhaps later in the day she'll feel better."

Dr. Marsh had given Renno a small phial of laudanum to take when his hand began to bother him again, and when he again felt the throbbing sensation, he poured the contents of the phial into a glass of water and drank it. His hand improved, but he felt surprisingly sleepy, so he went off to his own room.

Jeffrey was alone in the parlor, reading a book he had brought with him from London about the organization of the French Army. He heard approaching footsteps, and a white-faced Adrienne came into the room.

"How do you feel?" he asked.

"I—I still can't believe the things that happened today. Fort Springfield is a jungle, worse than the slums of Paris and London!"

"Not really." He put aside his book and poured her a small glass of sack. She accepted it gratefully.

"I've never before heard of a lady being assaulted on the streets here," he said. "Jack Davies was a vicious brute, especially when he was drinking. A number of people had problems with him, and you can be sure no one will mourn for him. He got what he deserved."

"I don't feel sorry for him," Adrienne said. "I've had unpleasant experiences since I've been in the world, but none was as bad as that."

"This is easier for me to say than for you to do," Jeffrey told her. "But it does no good to dwell on the incident, so try to put it out of your mind."

"I'll do it, I'm sure," Adrienne replied, showing a trace of her old spirit. Then, looking into her glass and seemingly studying the amber-colored wine, she murmured, "That isn't what haunts me."

He waited for her to continue.

Twice she started to speak, then stopped. "I—I don't quite know how to say this to you, Jeffrey. You and Renno were wonderful to me in London. You took great risks for my sake. You made it possible for me to cross the Atlantic on the Royal Navy frigate—"

"No, you impressed Commodore Markham so much that you had him eating out of your hand."

"And today Renno saved me from a vicious assault. I shall be thankful to him as long as I live." She drew in her breath sharply. "Then he killed the man with as little feeling as one would kill an insect."

"From the way I heard the story, he had no choice in the matter, Adrienne. Davies would have shot him, and after Renno got rid of his pistol, the man drew a knife."

"I realize he had no alternative. It was the—the way he killed him. He showed no anger, no feeling of any kind. It was as though he killed in cold blood every day."

"Surely you know by now that Renno never shows his feelings. He's a true Seneca in every way."

"That I learned, too," she said, and shuddered. "I shall live the rest of my days with the nightmare of watching him cut off the top of that man's head and place it in his belt, still running with blood!"

"When an Indian defeats an enemy in battle," Jeffrey said inadequately, "it is his right to take the man's scalp."

"He is a savage," she said flatly. Swallowing hard, she continued, her voice trembling. "I have known from the start that Renno was different, not like you or me or other civilized people. Seeing him with other Seneca made me realize the difference was greater than I had realized. And then today! You've been very circumspect, but surely you know that—in London—Renno and I were more than friends. Now all I can think is that this man—to whom I was so close—first killed in cold blood, then tore off the top of the head—" She could not continue and began to weep.

Jeffrey had no idea how to console her. Impulsively he went to her and placed a hand on her shoulder. Adrienne looked up at him, rose to her feet, and buried her face in his shoulder.

He held her gently, not speaking, offering her what comfort he could. This was no time to think in terms of the future, he told himself, but his mind nevertheless worked furiously.

He had admired Adrienne since the first time he had seen her in London, but she had become Renno's woman so quickly he had had no chance to express his own interest in her. So, even though he had been drawn to her, he had put her out of his mind rather than betray his friendship with Renno.

Now, however, everything was changed. He had hesitated to approach her on board ship because she had been under great tension, and he hadn't wanted to take unfair advantage of her vulnerability. Today a new element had been added. Adrienne had no understanding of the New World. She was unfamiliar with Indian ways, so she was revolted by what had been a natural act on Renno's part. She was being unfair to him, but as she came to know Indians better she might understand why he had scalped Davies.

She seemed so resourceful and full of confidence, Jeffrey reflected, but in this harsh land the rules of conduct she had taken for granted all her life were no longer applicable. He felt a great desire to shield her, to protect her from the primitive wilderness in the same ways that his father had so long protected his mother.

Well, there was no reason to hold back any longer. Adrienne had no ties, and he was free, too. Furthermore, she was a lady, a young woman well qualified to join the Wilson clan. Despite his parents' open-mindedness about class on the frontier, his family was the wealthiest and most prominent in the Fort Springfield area. Anyone he married had to be prepared to cope with responsibilities far greater than those of a woman who lived on a simple farm in a log cabin. Adrienne would be able to cope.

Gradually Adrienne regained control, and when she looked up at Jeffrey it was as though she was really seeing him for the first time. "Thank you for being so patient with me," she said.

"I want to do anything I can to help you." He was tempted to kiss her, his instinct telling him she would not resist, but his own conscience would not permit it. She was still shaken and she trusted him. He had to be faithful to that trust. With great reluctance he released her.

Adrienne returned slowly to her chair, and again she looked at Jeffrey. Her mind was still whirling, but even in her confused state she sensed the change that was taking place in their relationship. It occurred to her that she had taken him for granted. He had always been on hand when she needed him. Somehow she needed to reassert her own sense of values, to determine what she wanted and how she intended to build a solid, secure life for herself. It was a comfort to know she could lean on Jeffrey Wilson, and for the moment that was enough.

Three days after the brand was burned in Renno's palm, he was healed sufficiently to travel. He and Major Sir Philip Rand, who was dressed for the first time in buckskins, held a private farewell meeting with Brigadier Wilson in his study.

"I'm not sure I approve of this mission," Andrew Wilson said. "The risks are enormous."

"There's no other way to get the information we need if we're to lay siege to Fort Louisburg," the major replied. "We have no real choice."

"The weakest point in your story, it seems to me, is that you and Renno should be defecting together."

"Not at all, sir, After all, we spent weeks together on board ship and became friendly. I influenced Renno, who agreed to help me. I think that part of our story is solid."

Renno nodded. "Huron and Ottawa will believe," he said. "Algonquian stupid, so easy to fool."

"It's the French I'm worried about," Andrew Wilson replied with a sigh. "How do you plan to break away—assuming you can carry out your plan—and bring the information back to us?"

Rand grinned. "I have no idea, sir. It depends on our situation. We'll simply have to improvise."

"May God protect you," the brigadier said and shook their hands.

"Expect us before summer, or you'll know we've failed," the major told him.

The pair started that same day, deliberately saying good-bye to no one in Fort Springfield and holding their farewells at the Wilson house to a minimum.

Jeffrey knew only that his friend was going off on a dangerous mission. He asked no questions, and felt confident that Renno would succeed.

At Renno's request he did not see either Mildred or Adrienne before he left. He disliked the emotion exhibited by white women, and it was easier simply to disappear.

Both men carried supplies of jerked beef and parched corn, the usual fare for a trek through the wilderness. Rand also carried a blanket, but the young Seneca refused to be encumbered, arming himself only with his Indian weapons.

For the first two days Renno led them northward along the western bank of the Connecticut River, then took a route that led through the land of the Mohawk. As a traitor who carried a brand on his hand, he could not afford to be seen by the Seneca's brothers in the Iroquois League, so he took care to avoid their towns.

The long winter was coming to an end, the snows were melting, and, during the hours when the sun was shining, there was a hint of spring in the air. At times the ground underfoot was sloppy, but Renno was pleased. "When snow melts," he said, "no leave tracks."

Philip was deeply impressed by the white Indian's expertise. Renno used no compass and was guided only by the sun and stars, yet he seemed to know at all times precisely where they were and in which direction to travel. He marched from dawn to sundown without tiring, and at the end of the day he was just as fresh as he had been that morning. On several occasions in the first few days he heard sounds inaudible to the Englishman, and each time he froze, first taking refuge in a wild tangle of bushes, where he seemed to become invisible.

On the third day of the journey Renno cut a hole in the ice of a small lake, and, using only a length of vine to which he attached a long, barbed thorn, he caught two large fish. That night he permitted a fire to be made for the first time.

One morning, soon after they started their march, Renno listened intently, then placed his ear close to the muddy ground. Gesturing for silence, he climbed a large oak tree, helping Rand up behind him. They climbed to a height of more than twenty feet, and while they perched, motionless, four Indian warriors passed below.

"Mohawk," Renno explained.

Philip acclimated quickly to the wilderness but still had much to learn. On the sixth day Renno was pleased, announcing they were approaching a salt lick. As they drew near it he halted, then pointed. A fair-sized doe was feeding at the lick.

Philip grinned, then raised his musket to his shoulder. Renno gestured sharply, ordering him not to shoot.

The smile faded from the major's face, and in some bewilderment he lowered his weapon.

Renno strung an arrow into his bow, took careful aim, and let fly, killing the doe with a single shot. "Firestick make too much noise," he said.

The chastened Philip watched as Renno slung the deer across his shoulders and resumed the march, obviously not hampered in any way.

Renno maintained his usual rapid pace for hour after hour and did not halt until shortly before sundown. Then, deep in an almost impenetrable part of the forest, he gathered firewood, butchered the carcass, and roasted the meat. While it cooked he took care to bury the inedible portions. "Not good to leave signs," he explained. "Maybe enemies find."

That night they ate their fill of roasted venison, and the following morning they feasted again before Renno carefully obliterated the remains of the fire.

He made a package of the uneaten portions of the

cooked meat, tying his bundle with vines. It dawned on the Englishman that they would not make a fire again, but at least for a while they would be eating fresh meat.

On another occasion they found bear tracks, and Philip assumed they would track the beast and kill it.

But Renno told him otherwise. "Bear my brother," he said.

That night, after they had eaten, Renno told his companion about the bear he had rescued as a tiny cub and kept as a pet until Ja-gonh had grown old enough to return to the forest and look after himself. On one occasion Ja-gonh had saved his life.

Had Sir Philip Rand heard the story in London he would have scoffed, but in the remote interior of the North American wilderness, he could accept every word as the truth. Ever since the beginning of this trek to French Canada, the respect and admiration he felt for Renno had been increasing, and now he realized how badly he and his fellow countrymen misjudged Indians. There was a rich, mystical quality in the character of the Indian that outsiders rarely saw or appreciated. Men like Renno had a morality all their own.

One day on the trail was like another, and the major found it difficult to keep count of time. Renno told him when they reached the land of the Huron, and Rand wondered how it was possible to distinguish this portion of the forest from the land of the Mohawk. Renno just smiled and shrugged.

At last they came to the St. Lawrence River a short distance to the east of the fur trading village that the French called Montreal. Making certain they kept themselves hidden, they marched eastward toward Quebec, and one night Renno announced they would reach their destination in another two days.

Two afternoons later, just as Renno predicted, they looked out through the screen of trees and saw the ramparts of the Citadel, surrounded by a palisade of logs, sitting high on the cliff that crowned Quebec. The initial portion of their journey was coming to an end.

Acting boldly now and seemingly without guile, they

walked to the bank of the broad St. Lawrence and looked across the water at Quebec. Perhaps the sentinels on duty at the fort were being negligent, but no one paid any attention to the pair. Philip raised his musket and discharged it into the air.

All at once the Citadel came to life. An officer and several soldiers in the gold and white uniforms of French infantry hurried down through the town that lay below the fort and ran to a dock. There they climbed onto a barge manned by half a dozen bearded civilians in buckskins. The craft crossed the river, an undertaking made hazardous by ice.

Philip tied a strip of white cloth to the muzzle of his musket and raised it high over his head.

The officer, a young lieutenant, came ashore with a cocked pistol in his hand, and his men leveled their muskets at the two strangers.

"I am Sir Philip Rand, lately a field officer in the Grenadier Guards of His Britannic Majesty," Philip said in French. "This is my good friend, Renno, formerly of the Seneca tribe. We have come here to offer our services to your commander in chief."

The young Frenchman was astonished. "General de Martine is making a short visit to Quebec," he said, "and I have no doubt he will judge your offers on their merits. For the present, however, you are my prisoners. Be kind enough to surrender your weapons."

Renno handed his tomahawk, knife, bow, and arrows to a soldier and felt naked.

He and Philip were separated on the barge, and neither tried to communicate with the other during the time the craft spent in the water. When Renno had participated in the raid on the town, he had seen the place only at night, and as he and Philip were taken up a winding path to the Citadel, he gazed in interest at the small homes and smaller shops. Quebec, he judged, was considerably larger than Fort Springfield but much smaller than Boston. Another difference was that there were many Indians here; he saw the war paint of the Huron, Ottawa, and Algonquian and was puzzled by that of another tribe, which he guessed might be the Abnaki, who lived farther to the north.

The people of Quebec paid scant attention to the new arrivals. Men in buckskins and women swathed in clothes of thick wool barely bothered to glance at the pair being escorted to the fort. A few of the warriors stared briefly at Renno, but he preferred to ignore them. He had a difficult role to play, and he felt handicapped by his own lack of war paint and the familiar feel of his weapons.

A pair of sentries in gold and white opened a huge wooden gate, and Philip was hustled away. The sergeant in charge led the detail that took Renno to a small wooden cabin with a fire burning in the hearth, furnished with a table, chairs, and a bed. The soldiers left him there and slid a heavy bolt into place on the outside.

Renno sat cross-legged near the fire and tried to compose himself.

He did not have long to wait before a war chief of the Huron entered and exchanged a cursory greeting with him. Then the Huron demanded brusquely, "Who are you, why are you here?"

"I am Renno, once of the Seneca." Renno showed the brand on his palm.

The war chief studied it with great care, assuring himself that the mark was genuine and had been burned into the young warrior's flesh. "Why did the Seneca make you into a renegade?"

"I wanted to help my friend. The English did not want him anymore, but I was loyal to him. The Seneca are the friends of the English now, so they sent me away from their nation."

The Huron's eyes bored into Renno, whom he continued to question at length.

Renno had no way of judging whether the Huron believed him. He knew only that if the Huron didn't, he would be handed over to the tribe's warriors for torture and execution. If it was the will of the manitous, he would accept that fate with as much courage as he could muster.

At last the war chief turned away and left without another word.

Night came, and a younger warrior brought Renno a meal of roasted meat, a bowl of beans, squash, and corn, and a slab of cornbread. The food tasted much like that of the Seneca, and he guessed it was true that the Seneca and Huron once had been brothers. They spoke the same language and many of their customs were identical. He still believed that they had separated because the Huron had worshiped the manitous of evil. Sah-nee-wa had told him the story when he was a small boy, and to this moment he hated the Huron more than any other people.

Soon after Renno finished his meal, several soldiers came to the cabin and escorted him across the parade ground to a two-story building that was a part of the Citadel. There he was taken to a large, ground-floor room, handsomely furnished in the style of the whites and illuminated by several oil lamps and a log fire burning in a huge hearth. Seated behind a large desk was a steely-eyed officer in the gold-encrusted uniform of a French colonel, the hair of his powdered wig spilling across his shoulders. Silently he waved the young warrior to a chair.

Renno had spent enough time in England to sit in the chair comfortably. The man looked familiar to him, but he couldn't have imagined where they might have met.

The officer astonished him by speaking to him in his own tongue. "Renno of the Seneca has come a second time to Quebec. He has the heart of a lion, the courage of a bear. Surely he knows that if he lies, the warriors of the Huron will make sport with him in the torment of one hundred nights."

"I am no more a Seneca," Renno said, showing his brand. "And I do not lie."

The colonel removed his wig, revealing his Indian scalp lock.

Now Renno knew him! This was his great enemy Golden Eagle, who had escaped from him during the attack on this very place! Never before had the young warrior been forced to exercise such self-control, but he managed to sit very still.

Alain de Gramont knew how much the effort cost him and was amused. "You are a white Indian. I am a white Indian. I have always known the manitous would arange for us to meet again."

"The manitous have arranged it," Renno replied, and managed to speak calmly.

"I have heard the story of why you carry the mark on your hand and why you are here," Alain said. "But something is missing. There must be another reason why a senior warrior of the Seneca would desert his people and be disgraced by them."

At last Renno was compelled to use the final piece of his cover story, and this man, of any of the French, had the insight to recognize a false note.

"You and I are alike," Renno said, "so you will understand. I fought in many battles for the Seneca. I won many scalps. But some of my brothers grew to hate me because my skin was not the color of their skin."

It was just possible, Alain thought, that he was telling the truth.

"Philip is my friend. We came together on the ship of the English to Boston. On the ship I learned that the English will no longer let him lead their warriors into battle. I wished to help him. But my enemies in the Seneca are the allies of the English. They scrubbed away my war paint. They burned the mark of shame on my hand. Now I am here. I will fight at the side of the French against the Seneca and the English."

It was difficult to believe that any warrior could be this convincing a liar, but doubts lingered in Alain's mind. However, time was pressing. He had already spoken at length with Sir Philip, and now General de Martine was waiting for a report. Damn the general for coming unexpectedly to Quebec from Fort Louisburg! Left to his own devices, Alain would have solved the problem quickly by having both prisoners executed.

He dismissed Renno, sending him back to the cabin. Then, after donning his wig again, Colonel de Gramont walked down the corridor to the suite of his waiting commander in chief.

General de Martine, sipping wine as he played a game of solitaire, looked up from his cards. "You've taken long enough," he said peevishly.

"The prisoners were questioned by others, sir, and then I interrogated them myself. Also, I had the adjutant check recent English military publications. All of these efforts required time."

The general drummed impatiently on the table. "And what are your recommendations?"

"Major Rand is a member of a prominent English family and had a distinguished military record. But it is true he has been dismissed from the British army for using regimental funds to pay his very large gaming debts. I can find no flaws or discrepancies in his story. He might be reluctant to tell us much about the organization of the British army or their plans for defending their New World colonies, at least until he feels secure with us. I recommend that we accept his services. I also recommend that he be given a staff position rather than a combat command."

De Martine grunted. "Precisely my intention. I'll take him with me when I go back to Louisburg next Thursday. I'll interview Major Rand myself this evening. Be good enough to have appropriate quarters prepared and uniforms made for him."

"Yes, sir. What rank will he hold?"

"His present rank, naturally." The general began to drum again. "What about the Indian who came with him?"

"Renno was a senior warrior of the Seneca. Not only did he fight well against us when the English colonials and the Iroquois launched their surprise attack on Quebec, but a man of his position normally would remain fanatically loyal to the Seneca. He tells me he had enemies in the tribe because he's white-skinned, and it's possible, sir. But I personally have my reservations about him."

"It strikes me he could be of value to us, too."

"There no doubt of it, sir, if his defection in legitimate."

"The issue is simple. The white Indian has fought well against us. Obviously he is courageous, resourceful, and skilled in the arts of war. Now he has been disowned by the Seneca and has become a renegade. We can use a man of that caliber in the campaign that will determine whether all of North America will belong to France or Great Britain."

"I know, sir." Gramont hesitated.

"Then be direct, Gramont!" The general's temper rose. "What is your specific recommendation regarding this Renno?"

"With your permission, sir, I would like to delay giving my reply for another twenty-four hours. I want to put Renno to one more conclusive test."

Renno was given his breakfast at dawn, and shortly after the sun appeared briefly above layers of thick clouds three heavily armed warriors of the Huron came to the cabin. They raised their left arms in perfunctory greeting, then beckoned.

They escorted him out of the Citadel, took him through the lower town of civilians, then walked with him up the bank of the St. Lawrence. The signs of civilization disappeared, the forest stretched endlessly toward the north. Plunging into the woods, they trotted in single file.

Renno wasn't sure whether or not he was being led to torture. If that should be his fate he hoped the spirits of Sah-nee-wa and Ja-gonh would appear to sustain him and let him show the dignity of a senior warrior of the Seneca.

Soon he and his escorts came to a large clearing, and Renno was surprised to see several longhouses inside a palisade. Apparently a watch had been kept for his arrival. As he was led inside the palisade, scores of Huron warriors appeared, all in full war paint, and went to an open area in the center of the compound. There they sat in a circle, with the senior warriors in the front rank, the juniors forming in solid ranks behind them.

Renno was left standing in the center.

The war chief who had been the first to question him the previous evening appeared and exchanged greetings with the captive. Renno steeled himself for what he regarded as the inevitable.

"The words spoken by Renno may be true," the war chief said. "They may be false. Only in one way will the Huron know. Will Renno fight a trial of strength with the champion of the Huron? If his words are lies, he will lose. Then he will die."

The faint flicker of hope became a roaring flame. "I will fight in a trial of strength with the champion of the Huron," he said in a ringing voice.

The warriors stirred, and there was a sense of mounting excitement. Everyone knew this outsider had been a senior warrior of the hated but respected Seneca, and they were in for a rare treat.

Suddenly the entire group stood, and the sound of the Huron war cry filled the air.

Golden Eagle, clad only in a loincloth, walked into the circle.

Raising his arm in salute, Renno was puzzled as well as stunned. He could not imagine why this leader of the Huron would choose to engage in unarmed combat. At least twenty of his senior warriors could have substituted for him, yet he was willing to risk losing a measure of his own prestige.

Certainly he was a magnificent physical specimen. At least fifteen years Renno's senior, he had a thick chest and husky frame, muscles rippled in his arms and legs, and there was no fat on his superbly conditioned body.

The two fighters retreated to opposite sides of the open area, both raising their hands high above their heads to show that they carried no weapons.

Renno kicked off his moccasins and was glad his hand had healed. Golden Eagle obviously had chosen to represent the Huron because he was their best fighter.

There was another reason, too. Renno saw the hatred pouring out of the man's blue eyes and felt a chill as he realized that Golden Eagle fully intended to kill him. Perhaps he had been unable to decide whether his young foe was truly a traitor. He could solve the problem by killing the supposed renegade.

But Renno's options were limited. If he killed the leader of this band, he would be torn apart by three hundred merciless Huron warriors, every one of whom would want to participate in the act of vengeance. This placed him at a disadvantage, but his pride and his sense of dignity made it impossible for him to back out. Besides, if he refused to fight he would surely die. At least he was being given a chance to defend himself.

No one gave a signal for the fight to begin. Both men lowered their arms and at the same instant sprinted toward each other across the still-frozen ground.

Ordinarily Renno would have ducked or feinted, moving aside at the last moment. But the situation demanded that he not shrink from hard contact, just as Gramont had no intention of being evasive.

The pair collided with a sickening thud, then fell to the ground together, both pummeling with their fists and kicking viciously. No holds were barred in a trial of strength, and combatants were forbidden only to bite or to catch an opponent's scalp lock.

The spectators were silent, scarcely breathing. The Seneca had surprised them by his willingness to collide with their powerful leader, and they already knew they were witnessing no ordinary combat.

Renno landed several solid punches, his fists smashing his enemy's head and body, but for each blow he landed he received at least two in return. Golden Eagle had earned his high place in the ranks of the Huron and was endowed with such brute strength, stamina, and skill that the great Ghonka himself would have been a fitting opponent. Never had Renno fought with anyone of this caliber in a trial.

Gramont's knee caught Renno in the groin, and the

pain was excruciating. But Renno did not so much as grunt. Knowing that a blow to his face would follow, he managed to slip to one side, avoiding the lunge, and at the same time he landed a staggering punch that split the skin on Gramont's cheekbone.

Gramont retaliated furiously, and blows rained on Renno's face and body.

It dawned on the young Seneca that he was making an error that could prove fatal unless he immediately changed his tactics. He had allowed himself to be drawn into the kind of fight that this powerful man preferred, a combat in which strength alone would determine the issue.

Ja-gonh would have known better. A bear had cunning as well as strength, and Renno could imagine the way Ja-gonh would have fought an enemy. In fact, the spirit of the bear who was his brother seemed to enter his body, giving him fresh energy and enabling him to think with the mind of a bear.

Renno kicked hard at his opponent but deliberately missed. Seemingly losing his balance, he rolled over and over. Gramont was on his feet instantly and threw himself at his foe.

This time, however, Renno was not there. He rolled over yet again, then bounded forward in a somersault that brought him crashing down onto Gramont's back with such force that the air was knocked from his lungs as he struck the hard earth.

Here was Renno's opportunity. Kneeling on Gramont's back, his weight keeping the man's arms pinned to his sides, Renno caught hold of his head and banged his forehead repeatedly against the ground. A lesser man would have succumbed quickly, but Gramont continued to struggle.

Almost imperceptibly he grew a trifle weaker.

Renno wasn't sure if the man was tricking him. Alert to the chance that Gramont might spring to life, he withdrew his weight, at the same time flipping the man onto his back, then kneeled on him again.

Although Gramont had been badly battered, he was not ready to give up, and he kicked hard with what remained of his strength and lashed out repeatedly with his powerful arms.

But Renno had the advantage now. He was still relatively fresh, his energy was unimpaired, and his fists smashed again and again into the older man's face.

No longer able to defend himself effectively, Gramont knew the end was near. He looked up at his foe, and there was hate as well as pain in his eyes.

A final blow knocked him unconscious.

Renno knew that he had gained a reprieve, and that the Huron would be compelled to accept him as one of them. But he realized, too, that the French white Indian would never forgive him for the humiliation he had suffered. Gramont was certain to keep a sharp watch on the renegade in the future.

Rising slowly to his feet, Renno stood and caught his breath, ignoring the blood seeping from several cuts on his face and body. It was his right, as the victor, to stomp on his fallen opponent, but he knew enough not to further irritate the Huron. He raised both arms high above his head briefly, giving the obligatory signal that he had won, but then he turned away and modestly allowed his arms to drop to his sides again.

No one cheered, but the spectators talked to each other in low tones. None had thought it possible that their leader could be defeated in a trial of strength, and the senior warriors accorded Renno their grudging respect. Some of the younger men openly admired him.

Buckets of cold water were thrown on Gramont to revive him, and he regained consciousness, then slowly recovered his equilibrium. His lips were swollen, he found it difficult to open one eye, and his face was a mass of puffy, discolored welts, but somehow his dignity was still intact. Renno knew that Ghonka would behave in the same way if he were defeated in a similar fight, and he had to give his enemy credit for behaving with the decorum that every Indian nation had the right to expect from its chief.

"Renno has beaten me in a fair fight," Golden Eagle said, speaking as best he could. "Now he is a Huron."

The ceremonies were brief and informal because it was taken for granted that the new member of the tribe was aware of his responsibilities and knew what was expected of him. Five owl's feathers were affixed to Renno's scalp lock in place of the feathers of the hawk that he had always worn with such pride. Then his face and torso were smeared with the war paint of the Huron, which he found almost unbearable, although his features remained immobile.

Only Ghonka and El-i-chi knew he was still a Seneca and that his loyalty to his own nation was unchanged. If any of his former brothers encountered him in the forest, it would be their duty to kill and scalp him. In the eyes of the world—his own world—he was a traitor and deserved to die.

Chapter X

Ida Alwin suffered a badly sprained ankle when, drawing water from her well, she slipped on a patch of ice that had not quite melted in the early spring thaw. Deborah insisted that her aunt move into the parsonage until she recovered. No one was surprised when Aunt Ida refused, but the Reverend Obadiah Jenkins arrived unexpectedly at her house later that day and, paying no attention to her vehement protests, carried her to a coach and took her home.

Duly ensconced in a rocking chair in front of a blazing parlor fire, Aunt Ida was in such a foul mood that the young couple left her alone. Obadiah went to the church to supervise a rehearsal for a wedding ceremony, and Deborah retired with discreet haste to her kitchen outbuilding to prepare supper, not bothering to inform her fuming aunt that she had invited several friends to share the meal in order to reduce the evening's tensions.

The first to arrive was Leverett Carswell, who

greeted Aunt Ida with a bow. "I'm sorry to hear about your accident," he said. "I hope you're not suffering too much."

"Deborah had the doctor come here to bind up my ankle, even though she knows I hate having a fuss made over me," Ida replied curtly. "She's gone off to the kitchen because she's afraid to face me, but the minute she comes in here I'm going to give her a piece of my mind!"

"Your accident did no damage to your tongue, I can tell," Leverett said, and grinned at her.

"Now you're making fun of me. You know I hate to be mocked, Leverett."

His smile faded and he stood in front of the fire, his hands locked behind his back as he regarded her solemnly. "I'm not mocking you, Ida. I'm just thinking about your future. What a mean, crabbed old woman you're going to be."

The blunt comment was so startling that she had no reply.

"It's what comes of living alone," he said.

Ida sniffed. "What's *that* supposed to mean?"

"You spend most of your time by yourself. You try to do a man's work on your property, and it's too much for you."

She was tight-lipped. "The work is there to be done, and there's nobody else to do it."

"You needn't lead that kind of a life, you know." His confidence faltered for a moment, and he moistened his lips. "You need a husband who will take care of you while you look after him."

Ida found it difficult to breathe, and she spoke in a strangely muted tone. "I'm an ugly, old scarecrow."

"You're a right handsome woman. What's more, you have a backbone and a mind of your own. Anyone you choose to marry would be a very fortunate man."

She reddened and was tongue-tied.

It was Leverett's turn to show irritation. "Damnation, woman," he said, "I proposed marriage only once in my life, and that was many years ago, so I'm out of practice. The least you can do is help me!"

Ida averted her gaze. "I had only one proposal in *my* life, and it was so long ago that I can't remember the details, except that I did agree. So I don't know what to say now."

He rocked back and forth on his heels, his hands clasped so tightly that his knuckles turned white. "We're both too old for games and such-like! Will you or won't you?"

To her astonishment a tear trickled down one cheek. Leverett went to her, bent down, and kissed her gently.

"You should be locked up in Bedlam Prison for the Insane," she murmured.

"If need be, we'll go there together," he said, and his laugh was shaky.

They looked at each other for a long moment, and Ida felt comforted, at peace within herself. She couldn't remember when she had felt so good. But her mood changed quickly and all at once she bristled. "We'll not say one word of this to the young people, Leverett!"

He raised an eyebrow.

"Deborah thinks she's fooling me, but from all she's doing in the kitchen I know she has a number of people coming to supper tonight. And I don't want a big commotion."

Leverett patted her shoulder. "Don't you fret, Ida," he said. "We won't say a word until we can tell Deborah and Obadiah in private."

She smiled for the first time. "You know," she said in wonder, "you and I are going to get along just fine."

The issue was settled barely in time, because a few moments later Nettie and Tom Hibbard arrived, accompanied by Rene Gautier. The Gautier children were spending the night with Mildred Wilson. The two men stayed in the parlor, and Nettie hurried out to the kitchen to join Deborah, quickly pitching in to help with dinner.

"Jeffrey Wilson stopped in to see Obadiah this noon," Deborah said, her tone conspiratorial, "so I invited him for this evening, and I told him to be sure to bring Adrienne."

Nettie couldn't help giggling.

"Does Rene suspect?"

"Well, he's hoping," Nettie said. "On the ride into town he asked Tom and me twice if we thought Adrienne would be here. I'm not sure he realizes it, but he's smitten with her."

"I'm convinced Jeffrey has fallen in love with her, too," Deborah said. "His face lights up whenever her name is mentioned."

Nettie sighed happily. "Adrienne will have a choice, and they're both good men. I think it's nice when a girl can take her pick."

"So it is. Provided the one she rejects isn't too badly hurt. But I'm glad for Adrienne. Life hasn't been easy for her, and she deserves happiness."

Nettie became thoughtful. "I wouldn't ask her because I'd hate her to think I was prying, but I don't think she's anywhere near making up her mind. Tom and I were sitting right behind her in church on Sunday. She had Rene on one side of her and Jeffrey on the other. Every time she'd whisper something to one of them and smile at him, she'd balance it by whispering to the other and giving him the same smile."

"Then she's enjoying herself, and that's good," Deborah said. "I wouldn't dream of trying to influence her. No one could make up her mind for her."

"Oh, she'll make her own decision when she's ready, never fear. A problem like this has a way of working itself out."

Adrienne arrived with Jeffrey a few minutes later, and Rene Gautier, who had been silent, suddenly came to life. Both men devoted themselves almost exclusively to Adrienne, to the amusement of the others, and they were so much the center of attention that no one noticed that a smiling, subdued Ida Alwin was in a rare good humor. When supper was served she leaned on Leverett's arm rather than use a walking stick, and not even Deborah and Obadiah understood the significance of her gesture.

Adrienne was seated between her two suitors. She handled them with aplomb, chatting first with one and then the other, and it was apparent, as Deborah had remarked, that she was enjoying herself.

They began the meal with a chowder of freshly caught fish, and then Deborah served a steaming beef stew. "It's too bad Renno isn't here. This dish is an adaptation of a recipe I learned from his mother."

"I wonder what's become of Renno," Adrienne said. "I thought it odd that he and Sir Philip disappeared without saying anything to anyone."

The men exchanged glances, but remained silent.

But Ida was forthright. "Young lady," she said, "after you've lived on the frontier for a spell you learn not to ask too many questions. Especially when we know it's certain that we'll soon be at war with France and her Indian allies."

Adrienne nodded. "I've suspected their trip has some military purpose. They're both competent, and Renno is so sure of himself that it would be wrong to worry about him."

"A waste of time," Deborah said, and smiled at her husband, who sat at the other end of the table. "No man is immortal, to be sure, but I saw Renno in action when he rescued me from the Huron, and he's a—a hurricane in battle."

"We're hoping there will be many Seneca hurricanes," Jeffrey said. "And I guess this is as good a time as any for me to tell you my news. This is the last night I'll be seeing any of you for several months." He was including the whole company, but he spoke directly to Adrienne. "My father gave me a militia assignment just this afternoon, and I'm leaving Fort Springfield early tomorrow morning."

"Are we allowed to know where you're going?" Obadiah asked.

"There's no secret," Jeffrey said. "Five hundred muskets have been delivered to the Seneca, and another consignment that has just arrived in Boston on a new convoy will be going out to them within a few days. Now they need to be taught how to use firearms, so we're sending ten instructors to their main town. I've been given command of the unit."

Jeffrey's news gave Adrienne an unsettled feeling. She had relished being courted by two attractive men, but that situation was changing abruptly. She honestly had been unable to decide which man she preferred, and now she would have to postpone making a decision.

Rene Gautier was disturbed, too. He had been enjoying his competition with Jeffrey, but he realized at once that he would need to take a more careful approach to Adrienne in the future. Under no circumstances could he allow himself to be accused of taking advantage of Jeffrey's absence from town.

Immediately after supper, Leverett helped Ida back to her rocking chair, then brought her paper, a quill pen, and a jar of ink so that she could write a letter for Jeffrey to take to Walter. She wrote at length, then showed what she had written to Leverett before he scribbled his own communication.

Only then did it dawn on Deborah that Leverett Carswell was on the verge of becoming something more than a friend of the family. She felt sure of it when, after writing briefly to Walter herself, she was not shown either Aunt Ida's letter or Leverett's.

People who lived in the countryside beyond the town disliked traveling too late in the evening, especially when there were women in the party, so the guests soon departed. Rene rode beside the Wilson carriage until it was time to go his own way.

Neither the young woman or man in the coach felt like making small talk, and the tension between them grew. Jeffrey remained silent until they turned a bend in the river road and the Wilson house came in view. "I suppose I'll see you at breakfast before I go," he said, "but I'd appreciate a few words with you tonight, if you don't mind."

Adrienne merely nodded.

They turned the coach over to a groom, and Adrienne led the way into the sitting room. The elder Wilsons had already retired, but a bright fire was still blazing in the hearth, and the girl stood near it, warming herself.

Jeffrey watched the firelight play on her red hair and swallowed hard. He had prepared a speech, but he couldn't remember a word of it. "My departure tomorrow morning is very sudden," he said. "I was tempted to ask my father for a delay of a few days, but that wouldn't have been right. We don't know how soon we'll be at war with the French, so every day is important."

"I understand," Adrienne said.

"If I'd been staying here for the next few months, I'd have taken my time saying what I must," he declared, searching her face as he spoke. "Adrienne, I can't be subtle about this. I love you and want to marry you. I fell in love with you in London, but I held back because of Renno."

The girl nodded. "I knew it all along," she said, "long before you knew it yourself."

"And you didn't object?" He took a step closer to her.

"Hardly. I was flattered, and I still am. You're a member of one of New England's leading families, and you hold a military commission in your own right, a commission you earned. I'm nobody, a penniless refugee."

"You're very dear to me," Jeffrey said, and took another step toward her.

"Please, no more," she said.

He stopped short, his arms falling to his sides. "You prefer Rene."

"No," Adrienne said. "But I don't prefer you to him, either. I've loved the attention of both of you, but now the pleasure is gone. Your mission makes everything far more serious."

"I—"

"Let me finish what I want to say. It isn't easy for me, but there are things I've wanted you to know for a long time. The night I came to your house in London I was truly desperate, at the end of my rope. I—I gave myself to Renno because I thought that was the only way I could be sure of being helped. I'm not that kind of woman. I hated myself for it, but I felt I had no choice."

"I know the kind of woman you are," Jeffrey said. "That's why I want to be married to you for the rest of our lives."

"You don't know, really, because I don't know myself," Adrienne said. "Frontier life has been a shock to me, and I'm just beginning to understand myself. Perhaps for the first time in my life. I couldn't marry you unless I knew in my heart that I was the right wife for you. Just as I couldn't marry Rene for the same reason. So I—well, I'm asking you to be patient with me, Jeffrey. I need more time to sort out my feelings."

"I see."

"I hope you do. I'm not rejecting your proposal, but I can't accept it, either. Not yet." Adrienne hesitated for a moment. "I'm sure I'll continue to see Rene while you're gone. It would be strange and unnatural if I didn't. But I'll make you a solemn promise. If he should propose to me while you're away, I'll give him the same answer I've given you. I won't make up my mind until you've returned. I must learn to live with myself on the frontier before I can think of spending the rest of my life with a man here."

There had been a time when Jeffrey Wilson would have tried harder to destroy her resistance. But he had matured and somehow managed to keep himself under control. "I'll abide by your conditions," he said.

"And you have my word that I'll be here when you come home, that I'll be as free then as I am now."

"You're worth any wait, no matter how long it takes."

"I won't see you at breakfast," Adrienne said. "Your parents deserve the right to see you off in privacy. May the Almighty guard you in that land of barbarians and bring you back here safely. You'll be in my thoughts always." Adrienne reached up and kissed him, then turned away and quickly left the room.

Jeffrey remained in the sitting room and stood unmoving long after she vanished from sight.

General de Martine rode on the trail to the northeast that led through thick forests to the mouth of the St. Lawrence River. Then he and his party of officers, which included Colonel Alain de Gramont and Major Sir Philip Rand, headed south again toward the region called Nova Scotia. There they would board a ferry that would carry them the short distance to Cape Breton Island.

The general was escorted by four hundred French regulars whose gold and white uniforms soon were soiled and torn. The three hundred Huron from the compound near Quebec were in the party, too, and Renno marched with them, holding his place in one of the front files as befitted a senior warrior.

The French were stupid, he thought, not to provide their troops with attire more suitable to the forest. And he was surprised that the Huron shared his opinion, quietly joking among themselves about the lack of sense displayed by their European allies.

The attitudes of the Huron, in fact, were a revelation to him. Their jerked venison and parched corn were identical to the wilderness fare of the Seneca, and they, too, could subsist on a few handfuls a day. They were still fresh at the end of a day's march, when the French troops collapsed in exhaustion at their campfires. Long familiar with firesticks, the warriors carried these European weapons in addition to their own, and several of Renno's new colleagues told him in confidence that their marksmanship was far superior to that of the white soldiers.

What astonished him most was that the Huron prayed to the same spirits and manitous the Seneca worshiped, and many of them, it appeared, had seen visions similar to those Renno had known. He could not allow himself to forget that these people were the sworn enemies of the Seneca, and he remembered, too, that Sah-nee-wa had told him they worshiped evil spirits. It was inconceivable to him that the sister of his father, the wisest woman he had ever known, could have been mistaken. So he could only conclude that they prayed in secret to the wicked ones and were being careful to conceal the truth from him.

He and Philip saw little of each other on the ten-day journey. Philip had not concealed his pleasure when he had first seen Renno wearing the war paint of the Huron, but they had taken care to exchange only a few words on infrequent occasions. Both thought it likely that the French might make an attempt to keep them apart if they displayed too strong a bond of friendship before they performed tasks that convinced their new "allies" that their transformations were sincere. There would be opportunities to communicate after they reached Fort Louisburg.

A score of ferries and numerous small ships were anchored at what appeared to be a French naval base on the Nova Scotia mainland, and the task of carrying the new arrivals to Cape Breton Island began as soon as the expedition reached the shore. The general and his staff were taken first and were followed by the French troops.

The Huron had to wait until some of the ferries could unload and return for them. They squatted near the shore, their weapons resting on the ground beside them. Many of them were bitter and freely expressed the hatred they felt for the French, who always treated them as inferiors.

Their attitude startled Renno, who had automatically assumed that the relations between the French and their allies were as solid as those of the English settlers and the Iroquois. He kept silent as he listened to the scathing comments of those around him, but he would not forget what they said.

One remark in particular gave him cause for long, deep thought. "The French treat the Huron as though they were lowly Algonquian," a senior warrior said, and spat on the ground.

After pondering for a time, Renno decided the most

important information he could take back to his father and Brigadier Wilson was the attitude of the Huron. He could not imagine the day when the Seneca and the Huron could be allies, yet he could see that older, wiser men might find some way to wean the Huron from the French and persuade them at least to remain neutral in the coming war.

Thunder machines roared in the distance, the sound coming from Cape Breton Island, and Renno raised his head.

The senior warrior sitting beside him spoke contemptuously. "The French always make a great noise with their thunder machines when their chief returns to his camp. They waste much gunpowder."

Renno couldn't help asking, "Why do they do this?"

The Huron's shrug indicated that the ways of the French were incomprehensible to him.

At last the cumbersome ferries returned to carry the Indians across the narrow, fast-flowing strip of water known as the Strait of Casno.

As he and Philip would learn, Cape Breton Island, which the French now were beginning to call Île Royale, was a U-shaped island, slightly more than one hundred miles long and, at the base of the "U" perhaps seventy-five miles wide. The interior of the "U" surrounded a huge salt-water bay, and at both outer points, jutting out into the Atlantic Ocean, were strong forts armed with artillery to discourage the entrance of enemy warships into the bay. One of these points, located at the eastern-most tip of the island, was called Cape Breton.

The island was hilly, and at the inner lip of the U-shape was a plateau that rose to a height of one thousand feet. This was where the French had constructed Fort Louisburg. The new arrivals landed in a town that lay beyond the great bastion, at the portion closest to the Nova Scotia mainland. Copying what they had done at Quebec, the French had built a community whose principal purpose was to provide the everyday services needed by the military and naval garrisons.

There were a surprising number of women on the island. Many were flashily dressed and reminded Renno of the prostitutes he had seen in London. Scores of them had been sent from France and lived in the town's bordellos.

Girls of another class also were prominent. They were respectable young women known as "basket brides" because they came to the New World carrying most of their possessions in baskets. They lived under the strict supervision of priests and nuns in dormitorylike buildings in the town, but most stayed in these buildings for only a short time. They married noncommissioned officers and civilians and moved to the area in Nova Scotia known as Acadia when their husbands were relieved of their obligations and could become farmers. A very few married commissioned officers and ultimately returned to France.

The forests on the island were unlike those on the mainland. Trees were relatively small, rarely rising higher than fifteen or twenty feet, and bushes, which also failed to thrive in the salt air, were sparse.

The Huron marched on the main road that led to east of town, and Renno was overwhelmed when he caught his first glimpse of Fort Louisburg. It was far larger than any other fort he had ever seen. A high stone wall surrounded the entire compound, and cannon were emplaced in turrets spaced only twenty feet apart. The defenses appeared to be as impregnable as the French boasted they were.

A series of huge ancillary forts had been constructed at intervals along the walls. Renno later learned from Philip that there were twenty-seven such structures, all connected by underground passageways. The largest of them stood on the plateau facing the bay and rose five stories high. Made of thick stone, it bristled with more than a hundred cannon, and the crews that served these guns were quartered in that same section.

There were scores of buildings inside the compound, including barracks for the troops, handsome quarters for the officers, and private homes for the commanders. Special quarters were available for officers of the French navy when they came ashore. Five warships, three of them frigates and two sloops-of-war, were riding at anchor in the bay. There were numerous parade grounds inside the compound, too, but most were occupied by various Indian tribes, who had erected tents and dug cooking pits. As Renno quickly discovered, the Huron did not associate much with the other tribes. Occasionally a war chief or senior warrior of the Ottawa made a brief visit to the Huron camps, but there was no talking of any kind to the Algonquian, whom no one respected. They were dangerous because there were so many of them, but as individual fighting men they were quite inferior.

Large herds of cows, constantly being replenished from France, were maintained west of Louisburg, and beyond the barns were coops for thousands of chickens. Eggs and dairy products were plentiful, but the Huron—like the Seneca—did not care for such food. The French supplied them with corn, beans, and beef, which they found less to their liking than the venison and other game they were used to. The Indians also fished and in the spring and autumn they brought down geese, ducks, and other wild fowl. Renno learned that, although it was forbidden to leave Cape Breton Island without permission, parties of Huron frequently slipped off to the mainland to hunt. It seemed likely that Alain de Gramont knew what his Indians were doing, but deliberately closed his eyes to it.

Renno was housed in a tent with two Huron senior warriors, and the day after his arrival they took him on a tour. No restrictions were placed on the movements of Indians as long as they stayed on the island, and they frequently went off alone or in small groups to fish.

This gave Renno the opportunity he needed, and he was able to explore the better part of the island, although the forts located at the outer top of the U-shape were too far from Louisburg for him to go to and return on the same day. The warriors had no duties and no obligations, unlike the soldiers, who were required to mount guard duty every day and to spend several hours at drills. In order to prevent them from becoming bored they were given musket target practice every few days. Renno was relieved that he didn't have any duties but he soon grew restless, and he knew that many of the Huron were also.

There was a break in his lazy routine when he was summoned to the house occupied by Alain de Gramont, who sat in his comfortable living room. He was wearing his wig and French uniform and bore little surface resemblance to a Huron chieftain.

"I wish to speak with Renno about the Seneca," he said. "How many warriors can the Seneca send into battle?"

As a renegade there was no reason for Renno to hesitate before replying, and he was relieved that his father had discussed the subject with him in detail before he had been branded. "The number is not what it was," he said. "It is not what it will be."

Gramont persisted. "If the Seneca go to war when the weather becomes warm and there are leaves on the trees, how many will they send?"

Renno pretended to ponder for a moment. "Ten times one hundred," he said, answering as Ghonka told him.

Gramont was surprised, and his eyes narrowed suspiciously. "No more than that?"

"Many warriors lay on their pallets with the bad sickness when the snow was thick on the ground," he said.

The colonel knew that smallpox sometimes struck tribes suddenly and with great force. He had not heard of an epidemic in the land of the Seneca, but they would have gone to great trouble to keep it a secret.

"When another summer comes," Renno added, "many who were sick will be strong again. Then the Seneca will send two thousand warriors into battle."

That figure more nearly coincided with Gramont's own estimate, and he was more than satisfied. It was good to learn that the strength of the Seneca had been cut in half for the coming season's campaign. "How many warriors will the other nations of the Iroquois send?"

Renno had an answer to that queston, too, and although he actually knew how many warriors the Iroquois nations were able to send into the field, he simulated scorn, his tone contemptuous. "In the land of the Seneca," he said, "a senior warrior does not sit in the councils of the sachems."

Veteran warriors knew nothing of long-range Huron plans, either, so Gramont had to accept his evasion. The colonel made several more attempts to pull more information from Renno but got nothing of substance and finally dismissed him.

Renno was wary of the expression in his enemy's eyes. It was difficult to determine whether Golden Eagle believed him, but he felt certain the man was still suspicious of him.

Now, with nothing better to do, Renno made an effort to locate Sir Philip Rand. He had seen his friend only from a distance soon after his arrival at Louisburg, and since that time nine days had passed.

Renno wandered nonchalantly around the compound. Common sense told him that the major would not have been given quarters alone, and it took only a short time to locate the buildings in which French officers were housed. By now the young Seneca had learned to distinguish French insignia, and he wasted no time loitering in the area where he saw the small epaulettes of young lieutenants and captains. But he slowed his pace when he saw two majors entering a stone building, and then he halted beside a flagpole that could be seen from the windows of the two-story structure, pretending he was trying to remove a speck from his eye.

A window on the ground floor opened, and Major Rand appeared, beckoning briefly before he vanished again.

Renno entered boldly through the main door, then walked a short distance down a stone-lined corridor.

A door opened and closed behind him, then was bolted, and he found himself in the living room of a small suite furnished with tables, chairs, and bric-a-brac from France. Obviously the government of King Louis had spared no expense in establishing this great fortress.

Wasting no words, Renno told his friend about his session with Gramont.

Philip nodded. "I've been interrogated at least a dozen times about the Royal Army by everyone from General de Martine down. But I've found out far more than I've told them. I've already made a tour of the whole island, and now I'm making maps of gun installations. The French are planning to attack Boston in midsummer, it seems, and they're building a force of great strength. They intend to conduct their campaign with at least four, perhaps five, thousand of their regular troops, augmented by several thousand Indian warriors."

The numbers were overwhelming, but Renno had other matters to discuss and told the major about his own observations, including the dissatisfaction of the Huron.

"So the alliance isn't as strong as it appears, Renno. Good! Are you free to go where you please in the town?"

"Go anyplace, anytime."

"Then go there a couple of times. Remember what you see and where it is located. Pay special attention to the wharves and other docking areas on the Strait of Canso. We should be ready to escape in about two weeks. Do you have any idea how we can do it?"

Renno nodded. "Huron go mainland for hunting. Golden Eagle know, I think, but close eyes. Huron keep canoes in small cove near waters of Canso. We take canoe at night. Go mainland and make trail for English."

"Perfect! Better than any schemes I've been able to develop. We'll plan to leave the tenth night after tonight. By then we should know everything of value about this place. When you hear the bells of the big church ring nine times, come here. I'll be waiting, and we'll leave. But between now and then don't come here again unless there's an emergency."

Renno understood and nodded.

"I should have all of the fortifications mapped by then, and I'll rely on you for information on the town and the countryside around Louisburg. Between us we should be able to make a complete report."

Renno went into the town that same day and wandered around for several hours. Obeying his instructions to the letter, he particularly noted the location of the small wharves where the barges and boats were tied.

The next day spring weather came unexpectedly to Cape Breton Island. The sun was warm, and Renno could smell the earth. He spent the entire day scouting the fields to the north and south of Louisburg, paying special attention to the hills and patches of woods that might provide concealment for an attacking force.

The days grew warmer, although the nights were still rather chilly, and the coming of spring made Renno increasingly impatient. He hated living a lie, and he counted the days until he and Philip would make their departure.

On the seventh day after his brief meeting with his friend, Renno sauntered through town again at sundown, and then made his way to the cove where the Huron concealed the boats they used for their clandestine mainland hunting trips. A group of warriors was sneaking away under cover of dusk, and one raised an arm.

Renno calmly returned the greeting. Then he inspected the thick bullrushes at the water's edge and was delighted to find a number of canoes of various sizes, each with its own paddles. Transportation to the mainland would be the least of his problems.

He retraced his steps, taking a last tour of town before returning to the Huron camp at Louisburg. He walked slowly, as though he had nothing better to occupy his time. Then he heard someone behind, keeping pace with him. Twice he halted, and the footsteps stopped, too.

Moving soundlessly, Renno doubled back, one hand gripping his tomahawk. Soon he made out someone standing still in the road, and when he drew closer he was surprised to see a young woman. She had coal black hair and dark eyes, and wore European attire. As he got closer, he noted that she wore heavy makeup and, even though the night was cool, she had opened her cloak to disclose a snug-fitting satin gown with a neckline so low it revealed her breasts.

Renno halted when he realized she was a prostitute. What made her different, however, was that she was apparently part Indian.

The girl addressed him in the language of the Algonquian, which all Indian nations understand. "I saw you in the town, Seneca," she said. "I thought you were looking for me. Or someone like me." She came toward him boldly.

Renno had learned in London how to discourage whores. "I have no wampum," he said, "and no money of the French."

The young woman came close and looked him up and down slowly. "I have heard of you," she said. "You are the white Indian who has joined the Huron."

He nodded and was not surprised there had been talk about him. Every Seneca knew the Huron were notorious gossips. "I am Renno."

"I am called Marie," she replied as she continued to study him. "You are tall. You are strong. You have the face of a true warrior." A slender hand touched his biceps, then slid across his chest.

He had not known a woman for a long time and knew he should stop her while he still could. Apparently she had ignored his protest. "I have no money of the French," he said again.

Marie shrugged prettily. "Sometimes I take money. Sometimes I seek my own pleasure. Come."

She gestured down the road, then fell in beside him, and he thought it odd that they were walking toward Fort Louisburg rather than the town, where the bordellos were located.

"You have heard of the Comte de Chambertin?"

He shook his head.

"He was the Great Sachem of the French soldiers before General de Martine came. I was his woman." The girl spoke in a matter-of-fact tone, without apparent bitterness. "When the comte went back to France, he left me with only the clothes and jewels he had given me."

The walls of the fortress loomed ahead in the dark.

"I had other friends," she said. "They have given me a home here."

He had observed that several favored courtesans appeared to live inside the fort.

"Stay here until I have entered the gate," Marie said. "I will wait for you inside."

Obviously she was offering herself to him at no charge, which puzzled him; however, he saw no reason to reject her. The night was dark, and he halted for a few moments in the shadow of the wall, then sauntered forward again.

The French infantrymen on sentry duty studied him briefly, saw the color of his war paint, and waved him through the gate.

Marie materialized beside him and pointed. He accompanied her to her door. Then she took a large key from a silk purse and undid the lock.

"Wait here for a moment," she said. He could hear the flint scratching against a tinderbox, and then several candles were lighted.

Renno entered, closing the door behind him, and found himself in the tiny sitting room of a suite. Beyond it stood a larger chamber in which he saw a four-poster bed, and the girl was already there. Looking around the sitting room, he saw several dolls, all beautifully gowned, and thought that Ba-lin-ta would like them. But this was no time to think of his young sister. He went into the bedchamber.

Marie had removed her clothes and stood naked before him, her straight black hair tumbling down her back. She was slender, with the firm figure that distinguished young Indian women, and she welcomed him with a slow, tantalizing smile.

Renno went to her, and a moment later they were locked in an embrace on the four-poster bed. The girl was not coy. She clearly wanted him, and he obliged her, causing her to squirm and squeal in delight beneath him.

Then, as they rested side by side, the girl took hold of his left hand and her fingertips lightly brushed the brand on his palm.

"If you could," she said softly, "would you join the Seneca again?"

Renno was instantly alert. Although this girl might have learned about him from one of the Huron, she seemed unusually well informed. "I am a Huron now," he said.

"Why did you leave them?"

"They said I was a traitor and a renegade. Because my skin is white and my eyes are pale, I had many enemies." Increasingly certain she was trying to obtain information from him, he repeated the story he had told the Huron and the French.

Then she snuggled close to him. "In your heart you are still a Seneca," she said.

"I have put the Seneca out of my heart." He spoke quietly and, he hoped, convincingly, almost positive that she was a spy.

"Your father must grieve."

Marie had touched the most sensitive of nerves. At no time had Renno mentioned to anyone that he was the son of Ghonka, and he had every intention of keeping that quiet. "My father has joined his ancestors in the land of the spirits," he said.

She seemed satisfied and let the subject drop. But, when she began to dress again later, she returned to it. "There must be many days when you wish you were back in the land of the Seneca."

"I do not think about the Seneca except with hate. Now I am a senior warrior of the Huron, and I will meet the Seneca only in battle. Then I will take many scalps."

She accompanied him to the door and embraced him

briefly. "We will meet again," she said. "You will come to me whenever you feel lonely."

The door closed behind him, and Renno moved a short distance down the inner wall of the fortress, pressing himself against it. He was troubled and suddenly he realized why. Marie had taken care to dress again, which meant she was going some where. Disturbed by her questioning, he made up his mind to follow her.

Only a short time passed before the girl appeared and locked her door behind her. Then, instead of going toward the iron gate and returning to town, she began to walk across the compound.

Renno followed her, and although no Seneca was more proficient in the art of tracking, the task was difficult. He couldn't let Marie discover him, and certainly he could not allow the many officers, soldiers, and Indians who were around to guess what he was doing. So he had to combine stealth with an air of bland unconcern. He crept without seeming to creep, he stayed in the shadows of various buildings whenever he could, and when forced to cross a parade ground or other open area he was obliged to stroll casually.

Paying no attention to the stares of various men she passed, Marie took a roundabout route, sometimes doubling back on herself, but at last she approached a small stone building that Renno knew. This was the house of Golden Eagle.

He watched as Colonel de Gramont opened the door and admitted the girl. The last of Renno's doubts were dispelled. Marie was acting as Golden Eagle's agent.

Renno forced himself to walk slowly as he went straight to the building where the French majors resided. The manitous were watching over him, he reflected, because a heavy fog was rolling in from the sea, making it difficult for ordinary men to see more than a few yards. With luck no one would notice him.

A light was burning in the window of Sir Philip Rand's sitting room, and the young Seneca tapped almost inaudibly on the glass. Even at this tense moment he couldn't help thinking that, of all the wonders of European civilization, glass was the most remarkable.

There was no response so he tapped again, a trifle louder. If his friend was entertaining visitors, he would have to disappear.

The window opened and Philip peered out into the gloom cautiously. Then he caught sight of the young warrior and beckoned.

Renno slid through the window, his body marvelously supple. "We go tonight," he said as soon as the window was closed.

"What's happened?"

Leaving out no essential detail, Renno told of his encounter with Marie and the questioning to which she had subjected him.

Philip listened carefully, and then a wry smile appeared on his face. "Only two nights ago," he said, "the same girl spent the evening here with me. She questioned me, too—but I was less sharp than you. I thought she was just curious about a former British officer." He sighed. "There can be no doubt whatever that Gramont is still testing us, snooping until he finds some way to have us executed as spies."

"We go tonight," Renno repeated.

"I wish we could, but I have some preparations to make that are essential. I'll have to do them tomorrow. Do you know the little stone church about a mile down the main road to the town?"

Renno nodded.

"It is locked at sundown, and the priest lives in the town, so the place is deserted after dark. Do what you need to do tomorrow, and we'll meet in back of the little church at nine o'clock."

There was no more to be said, and Renno departed the way he had come. Making his way back to the Huron camp he knew that, although he and Philip had succeeded so far, their escape back to the English colonies and the land of the Seneca would be the most difficult and hazardous task.

He refused to dwell on the problems, however, and with Indian practicality told himself he would face them one by one. That night he slept soundly.

In the morning he returned to the cooking area after breakfast, and it was a simple matter for him to fill one of his pouches with parched corn, then cram as much jerked beef as he could carry into the other. Later in the day he helped himself to a horn of gunpowder and a handful of bullets for the musket he had been issued, which he felt it would be wise to carry. His Indian weapons were more reliable, but he reasoned that the firestick might be useful, too.

At sundown he sat around the fire with the senior warriors of the Huron and ate a somewhat larger meal than usual. He needed no excuse to slip away, and, stealing a chunk of beef fat, he carefully greased his body with it to keep himself warm in the cold night. Of necessity he applied Huron war paint, then donned his buckskin shirt.

Afraid that one of the Huron might interfere with his plans by suggesting a visit to the town, he left Louisburg. The only moment of acute danger came when he went through the gate, where the sentries might wonder why a Huron would be carrying his bow and arrows as well as a musket just to visit town. But the sentinels, as usual, paid scant attention to an Indian. They were deep in conversation and continued to talk as one of them waved the savage into the open.

Renno breathed more easily but was taking unnecessary risks. Waiting until he passed a turn in the road that obscured him from the view of the sentries, he left the road and plunged into the scrub underbrush beside it. He knew too many people here and didn't want to meet one of them.

He took the additional precaution of making a detour, then approached the little church from the rear. The much larger church in town came to life, its bell chiming eight times.

There was only an hour to wait. The cloud cover

was thick, Renno noted with approval as he sat with his back to the rear wall of the church. His escape was under way, and he prayed to the manitous, asking them to help Philip and enable him to leave Fort Louisburg without incident.

Chapter XI

Commodore Markham's flotilla was being expanded gradually and now numbered nine vessels. The Admiralty notified him that soon he would be joined by the first of two ships of the line, the largest vessels in the Royal Navy. He looked forward with great anticipation to the transfer of his flag to the seventy-four-gun *Duke of York*. He told the pleased and relieved Governor Shirley that his fleet was already strong enough to cause severe damage in the event of a French invasion.

Army transports were arriving on a regular schedule from London. Every five or six days another half battalion of red-coated Royal Army regulars came ashore. Two and a half regiments of infantry had arrived, along with a battalion of cavalry, and the first artillery units were expected at any time. Nine hundred Redcoats were already on hand, and housing facilities for them in Boston were inadequate, so they were sent across the Charles River and made their bivouac in the open fields of Cambridge, not far from Harvard College.

The colonies were buoyed by this strong Crown support, and the task of Governor Shirley and his immediate subordinates became much easier. Unfortunately, another problem needed attention. French privateers were taking a heavy toll of English colonial shipping, and merchants in the major towns on the Atlantic coast were clamoring for help.

Massachusetts Bay rose to the challenge, and new recruits swelled the ranks of the militia. General Pepperrell predicted that at least twelve hundred of his own men would take to the field by the middle of spring.

Connecticut pledged its full cooperation and promised to send a contingent of seven hundred and fifty men to the new army. Rhode Island agreed to send five hundred but added the condition that its troops would be responsible only to their own commanders. New Hampshire hedged officially, but two hundred and fifty volunteers arranged on their own initiative to come to Boston. The Maine District of Massachusetts Bay was thinly populated, but her people were loyal to their first citizen, General Pepperrell, and two companies, each comprising seventy-five militiamen, were formed.

New York argued that one of its leaders should be given the overall command. But London was depending on Governor Shirley for advice, and the War Office settled the issue by giving the command to General Pepperrell. The order specified, however, that he had the right to appoint a New Yorker as one of his deputies. Mollified, New York pledged a minimum of seven hundred and fifty militia.

The leaders of the growing force were encouraged by a totally unexpected development. Virginia, which had not been asked for a contribution because of its distance from New England, petitioned for the right to participate. The offer was gladly accepted, and word came to Boston that the owners of merchantmen would provide twenty ships as transports and another eight, all of them sloops, as ships of war. Virginia also promised to send two hundred of her superb frontier militiamen under the command of Colonel Austin Ridley, a man who had made a name for himself by winning three hard-fought Indian campaigns against overwhelming odds.

The Seneca responded in typical fashion. Ghonka was as good as his word, and a letter sent by Captain Jeffrey Wilson confirmed that two thousand of the Great Sachem's own warriors would join the march.

The other Iroquois were disappointing, however. Only the Mohawk, who themselves had faced the French, Huron, and Ottawa before, were willing to send a large contingent of warriors. The other Iroquois nations felt they were in no immediate danger and promised only that they would dispatch "a number" of warriors.

The high command decided it was essential that a full-scale attack be launched against Fort Louisburg before the French had a chance to attack first. The date depended on the speed with which the army could be assembled, supplied, and transported. Equally necessary, although few knew this, were the reports that Major Sir Philip Rand and Renno would bring back to Boston. No one had heard from them, and even the English colonial agents in Quebec had no idea what had become of them.

"What's happening these days is extraordinary," Brigadier Wilson told Governor Shirley on one of his regular trips to Boston. "This coming campaign will mark the first time that our colonies will have joined in a major, common effort. It's too bad it takes the threat of annihilation to force us to unite, but unified we are, at last."

"I'm encouraged," Shirley replied thoughtfully, "because no one colony will ever be isolated again. After the war ends we'll be able to trade more with each other and start dealing with our common problems jointly. Instead of each of us being tied only to England, we'll be bound together."

Andrew Wilson allowed himself the luxury of a rare smile. "The one great advantage the French have held is that they've always stood together, even though there are fewer of them than of us. If our union doesn't fall apart after the war ends, every English colony will prosper."

The momentum of the increase in military strength was so great that relatively few people were aware of another significant development. King Louis of France had made a major change in his policies, and instead of sending the Huguenots to already crowded jails, he was exiling them. Most of these refugees crossed the channel to England, but many could not find jobs. So every convoy of troop transports that came to Boston also included at least one merchant ship crowded with Huguenots. There were too many of these newcomers for the local economy to absorb, so they headed for the frontier. Some went to western Connecticut, others to New Hampshire, and a large number made their way to the Fort Springfield area.

At least two hundred Huguenots claimed land and began to clear it for homesteading. A few of the residents were resentful, but most people were sympathetic. They themselves—or in some instances their fathers and mothers—had come to the New World in order to escape the grinding poverty of their existence in the British Isles. Here they had found the opportunity to live freely and build a home for their children. They could not deny to others the same advantages.

Most of the new arrivals were bewildered and had no idea how to begin their new lives. Rene Gautier promptly offered to help out. Leverett Carswell gave him office space in a building on High Street, and the former refugee began to spend as much time as he could spare to guide the newcomers and answer their many questions.

His time was strictly limited because of the demands of his own property, so Adrienne Bartel volunteered to help. Here, at last, was something constructive she could do. She went into town early every morning, and she stayed in the office until almost sundown. What she didn't already know about Fort Springfield life, she learned from the Wilsons, the Hibbards, and Donald Doremus. Obadiah Jenkins gave her all the assistance he could, and Deborah, with whom she was becoming friendly, began to spend a portion of her own days in the office.

Adrienne was perfect for the task. She was one of the

few people who could speak French and she well understood the Huguenots' confusion in the new land. She was also able to empathize with their feelings of loss and anger as a result of their persecution.

After spending countless hours working with the refugees, Adrienne began to become aware of a change in her own attitude about the wilderness. The primitive living conditions, the cruelties and dangers of the frontier were far less important than the benefits. People lived in complete freedom here, and not only could they worship as they pleased but had every chance to start anew. They were limited only by their capacity for hard work and their ingenuity or lack of it. There were few of the luxuries the Huguenots had known in France, but the land on which they settled cost them nothing, and they had no need to fear arrest and imprisonment by agents of the Crown. Skilled carpenters, masons, tanners, and other artisans quickly found work and rented quarters in the town until they could save enough to build their own homes.

"There are no limits to what a man can do for himself and his family here," she said one day to Rene.

"That is why I love this country in spite of what I have suffered," he replied. "My children—and their children—will never know the tortures that we have undergone."

As the weather continued to grow warmer, Tom Hibbard put a number of Huguenots to work building his own house and clearing the land for his new farm. Nettie came to like them and their families, and she decided to give a party, to welcome them. Adrienne and Deborah agreed to help.

All of the newly arrived refugees were invited to the uncompleted Hibbard house after church one Sunday in early April. For a week prior, Deborah and Nettie had baked cakes, put crocks of beans in their ovens, and prepared other dishes. Adrienne, who had been reared as a lady, was unfamiliar with kitchens, but the Wilson cook taught her to make bread, and by the end of the week she was turning out loaf after loaf. The Wilsons, Leverett Carswell, and Captain Doremus insisted on making substantial contributions of their own to the meal.

Early on the morning of the affair, Tom Hibbard and Rene Gautier dug a large pit behind the new house, lined it with stones, and built a roaring fire. By the time they returned from church the fire had died down sufficiently for them to put a side of beef and two sides of venison on spits to roast.

Ida Alwin took charge in the kitchen. A dozen of the younger women helped her, but the refugees were regarded as guests and were not allowed to work.

Rene's young son and daughter took the lead in the games the children were playing on the lawn, and the newly arrived Huguenot youngsters, in no way hampered by the language barrier, ran, shouted, and laughed as loudly as the sons and daughters of the English.

When the feast was ready the Reverend Jenkins asked for a moment of silence. People bowed their heads, and he asked the Almighty to bless the company and provide health, security, and prosperity for all.

Then Rene Gautier moved to a place where he could be seen and heard by all, with Adrienne beside him to translate into French for the benefit of those who were still having trouble with English.

"I am speaking to you in English," Rene said, "because you have chosen to make your homes and spend your lives in an English colony. King William is now your sovereign, and by swearing your fealty to him you have become citizens of Massachusetts Bay. Be proud of your new citizenship. Live up to its responsibilities. In order to survive and prosper here, all must work together. You will work not only with your fellow Huguenots but with your fellow English colonists. I urge all men among you to join the militia. I urge all women to become active in the work of the church and in helping those who are worse off than you. I urge you to send your children to the Fort Springfield school without delay. The sooner they learn their new language the easier life will become for them, as it will for you. We welcome you to our midst!"

The established colonists applauded.

The newcomers listened intently, husbands and wives nodding in agreement. Several unattached young women studied Rene as he spoke. They had learned he was a widower, it was obvious that he was good-looking, and they had walked past his new house in order to reach the Hibbard property. He would be a splendid husband for any woman fortunate enough to win his proposal of marriage.

What these young women didn't know was that Rene had eyes only for Adrienne. He was so busy carving the meat and she was so busy serving that they barely had an opportunity to exchange a few words. But Rene was conscious of her at all times.

The party lasted until mid-afternoon, when most people departed. Rene and Adrienne and Obadiah and Deborah remained behind to help clean up, and on the spur of the moment Rene invited all of them to supper at his house.

They walked across the cleared fields of the adjoining farms, with everyone carrying leftovers from the feast. The children scampered ahead, apparently tireless, and Rene deliberately lagged behind with Adrienne.

"You worked hard today," he said. "You never stopped."

"It was the least I could do for people who are still frightened and upset," Adrienne said.

"But *you* are no longer frightened. You have accepted the life here."

"I suppose I have, Rene. I changed without quite knowing it was happening to me. Talking to all of those poor people these past weeks has made me realize that the conditions here aren't as bad as I thought. I can tolerate the difficulties, even the dangers, because liberty is so precious. And because people are so sincere in wanting to help each other."

"What are your plans?" Rene asked.

She shrugged. "I have none yet. And I'm in no

hurry. Mildred and Andrew Wilson are being wonderful to me. They truly want me to continue living with them, and I know I'm no burden on them."

"One of these days you'll marry." He sounded positive.

"Perhaps." She wished there were some way to avoid what she knew was coming, but she didn't know how.

"My children are fond of you," Rene said.

"I like them, too. Very much. They're adorable."

"I have grown even fonder of you myself," Rene said, speaking softly.

"Thank you." She knew her reply was inadequate and wished he would drop the subject.

But he was compelled to go on. "I am much more than fond of you, Adrienne. When Louise was murdered I believed I would never love again, and she will always have a part of me. She was the love of my youth, the mother of my children. What I feel for you is different, but it is real."

"Before you say too much, Rene," she interrupted, "I wonder if you don't care about me because you need someone. You need a wife. You need a mother for the children. With Nettie and Tom soon moving to their own farm, you need a woman to take care of your house, perhaps help you with the planting and the weeding and all the other things that must be done."

He didn't agree. "The point you make is unfair, I think. I can't separate my feelings from my situation."

"There were several pretty girls watching you very carefully today," Adrienne said. "If I didn't exist, you'd probably be drawn to one of them."

"Oh, I saw them," Rene said with a laugh. "Especially that little brunette, Michele Bovier, who seems to be bright and sensitive as well as pretty. But you *do* exist, and it would give me great happiness if you would become my wife."

"I wish you wouldn't," Adrienne said.

"Then you reached an understanding with Jeffrey Wilson before he left?"

"No, Rene, I did not. I told him exactly what I am

telling you. I don't know if I want to be married to either of you."

"I see."

"Oh, I hope you do," she cried. "I'm no longer whirling madly inside myself. I've found peace, and I think I'm becoming more sensible. And now that I know I shall spend my life here, I must consider carefully how to spend it."

He recognized her dilemma, perhaps understanding it even better than she did herself, and he was remarkably gentle and patient. "In which direction does your heart lean?"

"It doesn't," Adrienne said. "When my heart speaks, then I will know what is right for me to do."

"Then I shall wait," he said.

On sudden impulse she raised her face and kissed him. "Thank you, Rene. I shall try not to keep you waiting too long."

There was a quality in the members of Ghonka's family that set them apart from all others, Jeffrey Wilson thought. Within a surprisingly short time El-i-chi had become a sharpshooter and had gained such an understanding of muskets that he was now an instructor. In fact, he acted as Jeffrey's assistant, and they walked together through the fields, halting as they came to each group of thirty warriors firing at targets.

Because the warriors responded more readily to one of their own, Jeffrey gave El-i-chi his head.

"Hold the butt firmly against your shoulder," El-i-chi directed as he moved down the line. "Do not pull the trigger. Squeeze it. . . . Never lower your sights. . . . When you find your target, do not hesitate. Wait long enough to blink your eyes and your target will be gone."

The militiaman in charge of the group, who spoke only a few words of the Seneca language, was grateful for the help.

Jeffrey and his companion moved on. "I have Renno very much on my mind today," El-i-chi said. "Last night

my mother dreamed about Renno. He is in great danger."
El-i-chi spoke with the monumental calm that only a
Seneca warrior could achieve.

Jeffrey didn't believe in dreams, but he was concerned because he knew Indians had sensitivities the
white man didn't.

"The sister of my father came to my mother in the
dream and told her. Sah-nee-wa said that Renno is in
grave peril." El-i-chi spoke again, displaying no emotion.

"Surely you are worried about him." The words
were out before Jeffrey could stop himself.

The young warrior shook his head. "Sah-nee-wa will
keep watch over Renno, so he will not die. She will guard
him, and even if she does not reveal herself to him, she
will tell him what he must do."

Never, Jeffrey reflected, would he fully understand
the Seneca. It might or might not be true that Renno was
in serious danger, but it was impossible to imagine how
the spirit of his late aunt could protect him.

They slowed their pace as they approached the next
group of Seneca riflemen. Many of the warriors had
already completed their instruction, and now some of the
young boys approaching candidacy for their manhood
tests were being permitted to participate. Jeffrey stopped
short when he saw Walter Alwin in the line.

Nowhere in the English colonies, including the Fort
Springfield area, would a boy as young as Walter—
especially one who suffered from his disabilities—be permitted to take part in active militia training. Here no one
seemed to object.

Jeffrey halted behind Walter and watched him.

The boy loaded his musket quickly and took aim at
his target, the head and torso of a warrior drawn with
charcoal on a sheet of birch bark pinned to the trunk
of an elm tree. He squeezed the trigger, and the bullet
made a hole in the chest.

Immediately and without prompting, Walter swabbed
out his musket and reloaded, moving with the speed and
efficiency of a veteran militiaman. Then he realized some-

one was standing behind him. Seeing Jeffrey, he smiled shyly.

It was not possible to discourage the boy when he displayed expert marksmanship, so Jeffrey grinned at him, clapped him on the shoulder, and moved on.

He could not put Walter out of his mind, however. Ida Alwin was right to be concerned about her son, and Jeffrey felt compelled to speak to Ghonka. It was the right of the Seneca to train their own sons at an early age, but Walter was a citizen of Massachusetts Bay, even though he was living here.

Late in the afternoon, after the day's instruction was finished and the muskets were cleaned, then stacked for the night, Jeffrey went to see the Great Sachem.

Ghonka had just returned to his house from a meeting of his council, and he sat in front of the supper fire. He was smoking a pipe, deep in thought, and looked up absently. Immediately alert when he recognized the visitor, he raised his arm in greeting.

Jeffrey returned the salute, sat beside him, and accepting the pipe, cheerfully took a puff, despite his dislike of the Indian tobacco.

Neither man spoke until the tobacco in the bowl of the pipe had been reduced to ashes. Had Jeffrey been visiting any other Seneca, he would have opened the conversation by discussing the weather and the day's hunting, then would have progressed to more important matters, including Ena's dream about Renno and the current state of musket training in the towns of the other Iroquois nations. He knew, however, that one did not waste words when addressing the Great Sachem.

"Walter," he said, "learns to shoot a firestick."

Ghonka nodded. "He learns well. Already he is better than many junior warriors."

Jeffrey came to the point. "The heart of his mother would be heavy if she knew her son is learning the arts of war."

"She does not know." Ghonka was practical, as always.

Jeffrey had to try again. "There are many in the

town of the English colonists who would be unhappy. They would say it is too soon for a young boy to shoot a firestick."

The Great Sachem was unmoved. "Wal-ter lives now with the Seneca," he said, gently but firmly. "He learns to use the knife, the tomahawk, and the bow. Now he learns also to use the firestick."

Jeffrey knew he couldn't argue. Walter had been placed in the care of the Seneca, and his improvement spoke for itself. "It is so, as the Great Sachem says."

Now that the subject had been opened, Ghonka seized the opportunity to express his own mind. "After another winter, Wal-ter will take tests of manhood. Then he will become a junior warrior. He will go on the trail and fight the enemies of the Seneca."

Jeffrey was startled and worded his reply with great care. "The mother of Walter expects that he will return to her home."

"Wal-ter will not go there to stay. He will visit. But he will make his home always with the Seneca. It will be his own wish. He will take a wife here. His children will be Seneca, also."

Jeffrey knew that Ghonka spoke the truth. Walter was far happier here, where his disabilities became advantages, than he had ever been in Fort Springfield. Here he would lead a life that was useful and productive. But someone else would have to eventually break the news to Aunt Ida.

"Wal-ter will win honor in the land of the Seneca," Ghonka said, and although he did not raise his voice he spoke with great emphasis. "When his mother knows this, her heart will not be heavy."

It occurred to Jeffrey that, for all practical purposes, Walter Alwin had been taken under Ghonka's personal protection and was being treated like one of his own sons. If he grew to emulate Renno and El-i-chi, no more could be asked of him. Jeffrey closed the conversation in the only way possible. "Walter," he said, "will become a great warrior of the Seneca."

Ghonka merely grunted. He wasn't being told anything he didn't already know.

The Reverend Obadiah Jenkins quietly performed the simple ceremony that united his wife's aunt and Leverett Carswell in marriage. Ida was adamant in her refusal to invite large numbers of friends, so only Deborah and the Wilsons were in attendance. It was a pity, Leverett said, that more people didn't see his wife in the new dress of tan wool that Nettie Hibbard had made for her. Certainly the radiant Ida actually looked pretty when her gaunt features softened.

The little group went to the parsonage for dinner, and that ended the celebration. Tom and Rene brought Ida's personal belongings from her house to the new home in town that Leverett had built, and she settled in at once.

Forty-eight hours later the honeymooners went off to Boston, where Leverett had business to attend to. He confided to Andrew Wilson that he also wanted to buy various items of imported English furniture, unavailable in Fort Springfield. "She's worked hard all her life, and now she's going to start enjoying the life of a lady!" Leverett said.

The couple traveled at a leisurely pace, stopping at small inns on the road, and when they reached Boston they took rooms at the Hancock House. There Ida was initiated into the role of acting as her husband's hostess when he entertained business acquaintances. She was customarily opinionated about them and Leverett, who respected her views, listened carefully.

On their last night in Boston the couple ate supper in the taproom of the Hancock House. Ida enjoyed her meal, but she felt uneasy.

"The prices here are terrible," she said. "Eight people could eat at Doremus's Inn for what it costs here for two."

"Someday we'll go to London," her amused husband replied, "and then you'll really have cause to complain about prices."

"My appetite would be spoiled!"

"Just remember," he said quietly, "that you can afford expensive meals now."

Ida refused to budge. "Just because I can afford them don't mean I have to spend the money!"

After dessert they returned to their own sitting room, and there a barmaid brought Ida a pot of tea and Leverett a goblet of mulled wine. The night air was still cool, so they sat across from each other, relishing the warmth of a small fire.

"There's something I've been wanting to ask you," Leverett said. "What thoughts have you had about disposing of your property?"

"I suppose I should give some thought to that, much as I don't want to. The land doesn't amount to much, but it's plain I can't keep up those few acres as I used to, and hiring somebody wouldn't pay because folks don't work as hard for others as they do for themselves. I had thought of giving the place to Walter, but I fear I have lost him to the Seneca. Perhaps I'll give half the property to the Hibbards and half to Rene Gautier, although I don't know what to do about the house."

"Tom will be kept busy farming the property he now owns, and the same is true of Rene. Don't forget that when the circuit judge came to Fort Springfield last month he let each of them pay a token for a part of Jack Davies's farm. Both of them will have their hands full."

"Deborah and Obadiah have no use for the land," Ida said with a frown. "But I want to give it to somebody who will make good use of it."

"Sell it," Leverett said emphatically.

She looked scornful. "Who would want to buy property when there's free land for the taking, as much as a body would want?"

"Forest land. Not good, cleared land that's been worked for years and has a house as well. There should be plenty of buyers, including some of the Huguenots who managed to come over here amply supplied with funds."

Ida was stunned.

"You'll have no need for money for yourself as long

as you live. So I suggest you put aside whatever we can get for your place. Save part of it for Walter and give the rest to Deborah, dividing it as you please."

"Well, Deborah and Obadiah could use some spare funds. And the Lord only knows what Walter's needs will be in the years ahead. How do I go about finding a buyer, Leverett?"

"You don't do anything. Just leave the whole matter to me, and I'll take care of it." He spoke with finality.

It occurred to Ida Carswell that her second marriage had changed her life in more ways than she had imagined it might.

The approaching footsteps were soft, but Renno heard them from a distance. He rose to his feet, flattened himself against the wall of the little church, and waited, tomahawk in hand, ready for use.

Sir Philip approached, resplendent in his French uniform. "I had to wear this to get past the sentries at the gate," he said as he drew near. "But I brought my buckskins with me."

He changed, and they buried the uniform in the scrub woods behind the church.

"Here, take this," the Englishman said, handing his companion a pouch. "I've made copies of my maps and all the other information I've gathered. If only one of us gets through, pass it along to our own people in Boston. But I won't blame you if you don't want to carry it. You're certain to be hanged or shot if you're caught with them."

Renno shrugged. "If Golden Eagle catch me," he said, "he not wait to find papers before he kill me."

They made their way toward the Strait of Canso, taking care to avoid the town. Renno led the way and took a roundabout route to the little inlet where the Huron canoes had been hidden. As they approached the place he halted, raising a hand in warning.

Philip could hear nothing, but he trusted Renno completely.

Renno remained motionless for the better part of a quarter of an hour, then started forward again. "Four Huron take canoe," he said. "Not good if they see us."

It was extraordinary that he had been aware of them, and it seemed miraculous that he had somehow divined their number.

His advance scouting paid off, and he knew where to look in the high rushes for the hidden Huron craft. He rejected one canoe as too large, then found another that was more to his liking.

"Tell me what to do," Philip said as they climbed into the boat.

"You never paddle before? Then you sit. Do nothing." Renno propelled the craft with sure, powerful strokes, sending it hurtling out of the inlet into the swift-moving waters of the Strait of Canso. He deliberately allowed the current to carry him toward the south, but at the same time he edged closer and closer to the shore of the mainland of Nova Scotia.

Philip understood his tactics. He not only wanted to avoid the Huron hunting party, but he was allowing the canoe to carry them as far as he could in order to shorten their long march through French Acadia to the Maine District of Massachusetts Bay. Thick layers of clouds filled the sky overhead, obscuring the moon and stars, and soon a slight drizzle began to fall. Under other circumstances the combination of wind and rain would have made the evening miserable, but the English officer was delighted. He couldn't have ordered weather more perfect for their escape.

On the mainland they saw lights near the shore, and Philip realized a farmhouse was located there.

Renno, already aware of it, kept the canoe far out into the water as they passed. Then, still paddling steadily, he lifted his head for a few moments. Aware that sound carried clearly across water, he spoke very softly. "Somebody follow," he said.

Philip strained hard but could hear nothing except the singing of the wind. The mainland forest was dark, and he could make out no sign of movement on the water behind them, but he took no chances and removed the catch from his musket.

Renno paddled still more rapidly, and suddenly he turned toward the Nova Scotia shore. Beaching the canoe, he leaped up onto the land, with Philip following close behind him, then drew his knife and slashed at the canoe. Philip did the same.

When the craft had been hacked into smaller pieces Renno and Philip picked up some of the portions, and a short distance inland they threw the pieces into a clump of dense bushes, then broke the paddles and hurled them into the brush, too.

"Not stop Huron for very long," Renno said. "But give us a little extra time."

Without further ado he started off at a trot. The wilderness here seemed impenetrable, but he made his way through it unerringly, never slowing his pace as he avoided fallen trees and other obstacles.

Philip trotted behind him, conserving his strength as best he could. He was in excellent condition, yet he knew from experience that his stamina was not equal to that of his companion. As nearly as he could determine, Renno was trying to shake off their pursuers.

They trotted for a long time, increasing their speed to a full run whenever they came to fairly open areas, and rarely reducing their gait to a walk.

When Renno finally called a halt, Philip leaned against the trunk of a tree, unwilling to admit even to himself that he was growing weary. But he knew the night was still young and that a grueling march lay ahead.

Stretching out on the ground, Renno pressed an ear against the earth, at the same time spreading out his hands and placing them palms downward on the bare soil. As nearly as the Englishman could judge, he was "listening" with his hands as well as his ear. Renno made no move for some moments, then leaped to his feet. "Huron come. Eight warriors, maybe more."

"How do you know they're Huron?" Philip hated to

waste precious breath but, as they began to trot again, his curiosity overcame his caution.

"Not French," Renno replied. "Too smart and quick for Ottawa or Algonquian."

His logic was unquestionable, Philip thought, and realized it was highly probable that he had been followed by Huron warriors when he had left Fort Louisburg. Colonel de Gramont had probably kept him under observation, and Philip had failed to escape unnoticed. Well, regardless of any errors he might have made, the damage was done, and now they would have to pay accordingly.

All through the long night Renno kept an unvarying pace. His body responded to his will like a machine, and when the first streaks of dawn could be seen through the tops of the budding trees he appeared as strong and fresh as he had been at the beginning of the flight.

Philip, however, did not know how much longer he could go on without rest. He was afraid his legs would buckle beneath him. Sensing that his friend was reaching the limits of his endurance, Renno pointed toward a partly concealed hollow behind a boulder. "Wait," he said. "Sit and rest."

Philip gratefully complied, but to his surprise Renno trotted off, heading toward the west. He moved at a deliberate, slow pace, and Philip assumed that he was scouting the area.

In any case, Philip was thankful for the rest. He removed his moccasins, then massaged his feet and calves. His mouth felt parched, but there was no water nearby. At least he was sitting.

At last Renno returned, beckoning urgently, and when Philip rejoined him he started off again, this time moving toward the east. "I leave false trail," he said. "Give us extra time."

They trotted for no more than an hour before they came to a small stream. Renno leaped across it with Philip following, and for some time they made their way parallel to the brook.

"Drink now," Renno said, and kneeling beside the

stream, he cupped his hands. Never had any beverage tasted as good as that cold water, Philip reflected.

Then they were on their way again, leaving the brook behind them and moving due south. The sun had risen, the sky was clear, and when they reached the top of a hill Renno paused to study the terrain ahead. He seemed to find whatever he was seeking, and with quiet confidence he led his companion to a still higher hill. There, on the far side of the crest, he pushed into a thick tangle of evergreens. "Eat now," he said as he squatted on the ground. "Then rest."

Philip took a handful of corn and several strips of jerked beef that he, too, had managed to steal before their departure. "Can we get away from the Huron?"

"We try," Renno said.

"Gramont must have kept watch on me, if not on you."

The young Seneca nodded. "Huron always watch."

"But you think we've given the slip for the moment?"

"Follow false trail," Renno said. "Discover mistake, then find right trail again. You sleep now, Philip. I wake you up when time to go again."

Somewhat to his own surprise Sir Philip dropped off to sleep the moment he stretched out on the ground. His faith in his companion was absolute, and there was no doubt that he was safe.

He had no idea how long he had slept when Renno gripped his shoulder. "We go now."

"Did you sleep, too?" Philip asked as he struggled to his feet.

The white Indian grinned and shook his head. "Make another false trail," he admitted.

The grueling march began again, and only twice during the long day did the pair pause briefly to drink. Only when night offered them cover did they stop to eat once more.

Philip was dismayed when Renno indicated that they would resume their flight without further delay. But he made no protest. The success of his mission and his life itself depended on Renno's judgment.

Renno did not stop again until long after midnight. Had he been alone he would not have paused even then, but he realized his companion was in desperate need of another rest. The last false trail he had left gave them a lead of several hours, and now the time had come to use a part of that cushion. They drank water from another little river, and Renno gave the signal to rest.

It was still dark when Philip was awakened, and he still felt exhausted. "Renno," he said, "I want you to go on without me. I simply can't keep your pace."

"We go together," was the firm reply.

"Listen to me and be sensible. I can't stay ahead of the Huron indefinitely, and sooner or later they'll catch up with us. One of us must take what we've learned about Fort Louisburg to Boston. If both of us die, all we've tried to do will be wasted."

"We go now," Renno said. "Together."

It was some time after the sun rose again that Sir Philip began to lose all count of time. His mind became almost blank, but his body continued to move and he trotted for hour after endless hour. Pauses for water and food became blurred in his memory, and whenever Renno ordered him to rest he obeyed instantly. On most of these occasions, he realized dimly, the young Seneca took no rest himself but went off on his own, creating new false trails. His stamina was almost unbelievable, but so was that of the pursuing Huron. By now it had to be obvious to the Huron that they were spies and Gramont would want them killed on sight.

Day and night blended in Philip's mind, his blistered feet were bleeding, and he knew that, even though his friend was offering him every possible opportunity to regain his strength, he could not go on much longer.

Renno was more concerned than he would admit. Twice they avoided parties of Algonquian warriors who were hunting in the forest, but he said nothing. There was no point in alarming a man who was struggling to keep up. Common sense told Renno it would be wise if he went on alone and left Philip to fend for himself, but he could not. No Seneca deserted a fellow warrior, and even if they were caught his honor was more important than any mission, more precious than life itself.

He, too, was weary. By refusing to rest, in order to have time to create false trails, he had denied himself much sleep, and he realized his own stamina was ebbing. Perhaps he and Philip would have to stop and do battle with their pursuers, even though they were badly outnumbered.

His one consolation was the knowledge that the Huron had to be very tired, too. But knowing they had followed any number of false trails undoubtedly had made them more cautious so it was unlikely that the trick would be effective again.

By now, Renno estimated, they had reached the Maine District, but that would not deter the enemy, who would not stop until they saw the stockade of an English colonial town ahead of them. They might also add a number of Algonquian to their party, and the dangers would increase for this land was Algonquian territory and they knew it well.

Little by little Philip grew weaker and could no longer maintain the blistering pace set by his partner. Renno tried to accommodate him by slowing down, but he became increasingly worried. One afternoon, at the crest of a hill, he stood for a long time looking back over the route they had taken. Had he been alone he might have left no trail, particularly in places where the ground was hard. But the Englishman was too clumsy, so Renno knew they were leaving tracks that the Huron would have no difficulty following.

After he had remained motionless for a long time, his worse fears were confirmed. Very slight movements in the woods told him that the Huron were only three or four miles behind them, working their way forward at a steady clip.

Aware that a crisis was at hand, Renno pushed his

companion to the limit of his endurance. But Philip had drawn on the last reserves of stamina, and by now he stumbled frequently, sometimes dropping to one knee and occasionally sprawling on the ground. Only his stubborn willpower made it possible for him to continue.

At dawn they paused, and Renno helped his bone-weary friend climb over the huge, rotting trunk of a fallen oak to a place of momentary security behind a boulder. Then he bent close to the ground, listening, and spoke quietly.

"We will fight," he said. "Soon the Huron will be here. They are very close."

Phillip moistened his cracked lips. A battle, he knew, would end in certain death for both of them, and he had already formulated a different plan. "Maybe they won't find us here," he said. "That tree and this boulder will hide us nicely."

"At first the Huron will not find," Renno agreed. "They will go on. Then they will lose trail. So they will come back—and find."

"I think we can outwit them," Philip said. "I'll be safe here for a time. That gives you the opportunity to create another false trail. By the time you come back here for me, I'll be rested enough to start again."

The scheme was outrageous, Renno knew. He would never willingly leave his comrade behind. Still, he realized, it might be the only way to buy some time.

"A campaign to capture Louisburg," Philip continued, "depends on at least one of us getting back with our reports. You take these." He handed the Seneca his satchel and kept a few useless papers for himself.

That settled the matter. "I come back for you," Renno said, and promptly disappeared into the forest.

Major Sir Philip Rand knew his duty. Under no circumstances could he march any farther, but his own fate did not concern him. When he had first accepted this assignment he knew the dangers. All that mattered now was that Renno be given sufficient time to make good his own escape.

Calmly and methodically he made certain his musket was ready, then smiled slightly to himself as he checked his pistols. With any luck he would take three of the pursuers with him.

No more than a quarter of an hour passed before the Huron came into sight. They were walking at a rapid pace, led by a husky warrior whose full attention was on studying the trail. The man made a perfect target.

Raising one of his pistols and taking careful aim, Philip squeezed the trigger, and the Huron dropped to the ground. The other members of the party immediately reached for arrows and strung their bows. A second pistol shot brought down another warrior.

The surviving members of the group fanned out, using the trees as cover. By now they knew the general direction of the shots that had been fired, and they formed a rough semicircle around it.

Philip waited as long as he could. When he saw one of the warriors only partly hidden from view, he knew this was his last chance to strike another blow. He stood, allowing the enemy to see him, and then he fired at the third Huron. The man dropped, and Philip laughed aloud.

He was still laughing when several arrows pierced his body, and his smile was frozen permanently on his lips as he slumped onto the boulder.

Renno heard the two shots and halted. Then he heard the louder musket shot, which was soon followed by a triumphant Huron war whoop. Philip had been found. The papers Philip carried meant nothing to the warriors, but they would take the documents back to Gramont, who would know for certain that the English officer had been a spy.

Surely there was no way that the Huron could have found Philip's hiding place in so short a time. That meant he had deliberately called attention to himself. Why? He could have had only one reason: he was giving Renno the chance to go on alone.

Even as Renno grieved for his courageous friend, he

knew he could not allow Philip to have died in vain. He turned and started off toward the south at a full run. The Huron would follow him, of course, but having disposed of the man Golden Eagle undoubtedly had told them was more important, they might grow careless.

Besides, now the Seneca warrior had the opportunity to prove that he was stronger and more cunning than a whole band of Huron. That thought spurred Renno on. He ran for a long time, and when he came to a broad but shallow river he crossed the better part of it, then made his way with great care in ankle-deep water near the farther bank. The Huron would have to search at length before they could pick up his trail again. The icy water chilled him, but he ignored it, and soon his efforts warmed him.

He ran as he had been taught from early boyhood, wasting no motions, avoiding obstacles, and breathing deeply. Now the Huron would learn why their ancient rivals regarded them as inferior. Not until nightfall did Renno slow his pace, but even then he continued at a trot.

It was very late that night before he caught sight of a hollowed, fallen tree, partly covered by underbrush. He knew he had a good lead on the Huron and could afford the luxury of a brief rest. His wilderness instincts would warn him if there was danger.

He crawled into the hollow log, relishing its warmth, then pulled dead leaves and vines over the end to conceal him further. Long training prompted him to draw his tomahawk, and he held it as he dropped off to sleep.

A dream came to him quickly and was so real, so vivid that for a long time afterward he could not distinguish it from reality. The top of the hollow tree seemed to open wide, and although Renno was hemmed in at both sides, he could look up into the open with ease.

A bulky figure took shape above him, and gradually he made out the shaggy body, then the face of his brother Ja-gonh, the bear. They looked at each other in silence, as they had done so many times in the past, when the bear was alive. They exchanged greetings, and then Renno's spine tingled. Ja-gonh was warning him that great danger lay ahead.

Gradually Ja-gonh vanished, his body becoming increasingly transparent until he could be seen no more.

Renno stirred in his sleep and was on the verge of awakening when another figure began to materialize. Alert now, he recognized Sah-nee-wa even before she made herself fully known to him.

"You sleep, son of my brother," she said.

He tried to reply but could not.

"Would you join me here in the land of your ancestors, before your time has come? You sleep too soon, son of my brother," Sah-nee-wa said.

She, too, was warning him!

"A warrior of the Seneca," she said, "does not rest or sleep until he has finished with those things which he must do." There was a note of reproof in her voice. "You are warm. You are comfortable. But you will not live unless you arouse yourself."

The threat was urgent!

"Three trials await you, son of my brother. Meet them as you must, and you will triumph. Fail and you will die!" The apparition faded quickly.

As soon as Sah-nee-wa had vanished, Renno awakened and was instantly alert.

His guardians from the world of the spirits had instructed him and he obeyed immediately. He resumed his journey even though the night was still very dark and he could not be sure how soon daylight would come.

The dream had been so vivid that he lived it again, but all at once he halted and froze. He had been careless, and the warrior who was slipshod in the wilderness often was not given a second chance. There were men in the immediate vicinity, a large number of men.

Renno focused on the farthest tree he could make out in the gloom, and gradually other figures began to take form before him. He had nearly blundered into a large camp of Algonquian warriors.

There were fifty warriors in the party, all of them sleeping, wrapped in blankets of fine wool. No, there were more, perhaps twice fifty. If they caught him they would skin him alive for his stupidity before they killed him.

He moved away from the camp with infinite care, aware now of all that was to be seen, heard, or felt in the forest. A group of this size would be guarded by many sentries, and one or more had to be in the immediate vicinity.

Ah! An Algonquian sentinel was standing directly ahead of Renno, no more than ten feet away, facing in the opposite direction. It was fortunate that the man was not a Seneca—or even a Huron—because he already would have been aware of Renno and would have given an alarm.

Renno crept closer, then closer still. Reluctant to throw his tomahawk because it might bounce off the warrior and strike a tree, clatter to the ground, or make some other noise, he gripped it. The man was almost within reach.

All at once the Algonquian sensed the menacing presence behind him. He turned, his stone knife raised.

Before he could cry out Renno struck with all his might, bringing his tomahawk down onto the warrior's forehead. The Algonquian crumpled to the ground, dead.

With great self-control Renno refrained from taking the man's scalp. His own life was still in danger, and he fled silently.

Renno managed to avoid two other sentries, neither of them close, and as he resumed his journey, he was able to breathe more easily. Shaking off his weariness, he began to trot again, and when daybreak came he broke into a full run. Trying to make up for lost time, he ate as he ran.

The spring sun stood directly overhead when he finally halted to drink water from a small lake, surrounded on three sides by cliffs so steep they were almost perpendicular. Splashing water on his face and body to refresh himself, Renno drank again.

Suddenly he sensed danger. He whirled around, snatching an arrow from his quiver and fitting it into his bow.

A wildcat was poised at the top of the cliff behind him, its fangs bared, its lithe, tawny body tensed. The creature was menacing—it had selected a victim, and all of its wild, lean fury was concentrated on destruction.

Before Renno could shoot, the wild cat leaped. Unable to take careful aim, Renno let loose his arrow at the blurred figure that hurtled toward him.

An instant later the wildcat landed in a heap only a few feet from him, the arrow protruding from its body. The animal was still alive, ready for a fight to the death in spite of its injury.

Quickly, Renno reached for another arrow and fitted it into his bow as the wildcat gathered itself for a last, desperate lunge. In that brief moment the young warrior had just enough time to take careful aim, and he let fly. The arrow traveled only a short distance, but it had been fired with such force that most of the shaft penetrated the beast's body.

The dying wildcat collapsed only inches from the spot where Renno was standing. Rather than allow it to die slowly, he took his tomahawk from his belt and mercifully delivered a final blow.

Another time, Renno would have taken the head as a trophy, but he could not afford such a luxury now. He cleaned the blood from his tomahawk, then immediately resumed his flight.

Twice he had almost lost his life because of carelessness, he thought as he trotted through the forest toward the southwest. Twice he had failed to observe the precautions that every warrior knew were essential to his survival. His mind was not functioning properly. He was too tired to think clearly. He needed a hearty meal and a full night of sleep to restore him.

But that was out of the question. He had no doubt that the Huron were pushing themselves to the limits of their endurance, and he had to do the same. No matter how great his exhaustion, he could not pause for more than brief periods.

As he continued his endless journey he caught occasional glimpses of the sea off to his left. The sight of waves crashing over rocks fascinated him. He had to cross several large, swift-flowing rivers that were emptying into the ocean, which was a problem. He could swim across smaller streams, but he realized that in his weakened condition he would risk being carried away by a strong current. So he halted long enough to make small, crude rafts that helped him to stay safely afloat.

An additional advantage of these crossings was the obliteration of his trail, but the Huron undoubtedly knew he was trying to reach the town in the Maine District that the English colonists called Kittery. It would not be difficult for them to pick up his trail again each time they, too, managed to cross one of the great rivers.

Renno kept on the move day and night, halting only when his body refused to move anymore. He could not allow himself to fall into a deep sleep for fear that if he did, he would not awaken for a long time, and he had to ration his supplies of parched corn and jerked beef even though he was tempted to eat it all at once. Occasionally he stumbled, but he reminded himself that he was a Seneca, and somewhere within he found the strength to go on and on and on.

One thought was uppermost in his mind and was far more important to him than the fact that the Huron were still in pursuit. In his vivid dream Sah-nee-wa had warned him that he would face three severe trials, that in each his life would be in grave jeopardy. He had blundered into the camp of the Algonquian and had almost paid for the error with his life. He had failed to take basic precautions when he had paused to drink water at the base of the cliff and had come within a hair's breadth of being killed by the wildcat.

So two of his trials were behind him, but a third remained. There was no question in his mind that he would be required to face yet another test. Never had Sah-nee-wa lied to him when she had lived in this world, and her spirit would never mislead him now.

He did his best to remain alert, to observe all of the fundamental rules for survival in the wilderness. One day he avoided a party of Abnaki fishermen, and the following day he had to hide for a time when several Algonquian passed by. At no time was he afraid, which would have been a sign of weakness, but neither did he relax his vigil.

Late one morning, no longer able to keep count of the days in flight, Renno again approached the sea. Far out in the water he caught sight of a small vessel with sails, a white man's boat. His legs aching, he climbed to the top of a high sand dune to survey the territory ahead. To his astonishment and joy he saw a high palisade, with many houses inside it, and flying from twin flagpoles were the Union Jack of Great Britain and ensign of Massachusetts Bay. Kittery lay directly ahead, and his long trek had come to a sudden, unexpected end.

Summoning the strength to walk the last few hundred yards, Renno made his way down the sand dune and approached the high fence. A shot rang out, and the young warrior heard a bullet whistle past him. A militia sentry, seeing the ragged, heavily armed warrior approach, was taking no chances.

Renno was outraged. This violent greeting, after all he had suffered, was more than he could endure. He reached for an arrow, knowing he had ample time to dispatch the sentry, who was trying frantically to reload his musket.

But a sudden thought sobered the young warrior. This was the third and greatest hazard. If he killed a militiaman, his trouble would be just starting, not ending. This was a situation that called for restraint, not retaliation. In the world of the English colonists, it was necessary to abide by their rules and laws.

THE RENEGADE

Dropping the arrow back into its quiver, he raised his arm in greeting. "I come to see Pepperrell!" he cried hoarsely, then walked forward with as much dignity as he could muster.

Chapter XII

General William Pepperrell's gracious country house,
built a decade earlier outside Kittery at a place
called the Point, was a perfect, isolated spot for Renno to
rest from his ordeal. He spent a full week here, eating
heartily, sleeping long hours, and, when he was awake,
answering the countless questions of the general, who
also absorbed every detail of Major Sir Philip Rand's maps
and notes.

"What you've told me," the commander of the Massachusetts Bay militia said, "combined with Rand's information, is just what we need. Now we know we can
attack Louisburg instead of waiting for the French to
bring the war to us!"

Renno accompanied General Pepperrell to Boston.
A messenger had carried advance word of the success of
the spy operation, and Brigadier Wilson was already on
hand when the pair arrived, with the commanders of the
militia from other colonies on their way.

Renno was given a room in the splendid house adjoining the Governor's House, and the place immediately became the headquarters of the expeditionary force. Commodore Markham, soon to be promoted to rear admiral, took up residence there, too, as did Brigadier Lord Dunmore, the commander of the Royal Army regulars, who were still arriving from England. King William had made the daring personal decision that the war in the New World should be under the overall command of a colonial, and William Pepperrell was given the assignment. It was the first time that a native of the colonies had been given authority over personnel of the Royal Navy and Army.

The long sessions at Kittery proved to be only a taste of what was to follow. Renno attended every session of the high command, and in each step of the planning he was questioned sharply about Fort Louisburg and Cape Breton Island. His memory for details was remarkable, and when a model of Louisburg was constructed as a guide to the operation, he was required to supervise the task, correcting errors and making changes.

The young warrior found the task boring. His health and energy fully restored, he was eager to return home, which he had not seen since going off to London so many months earlier. But he alone could advise the men who intended to conquer Louisburg. Therefore he had to remain in Boston while the tedious conferences were held.

His duty was clear, and something else made it equally impossible for him to return to his own people. He still carried the brand of a renegade on the palm of his hand, and he would not be welcome in the land of the Seneca until it was obliterated.

Brigadier Wilson understood the young Seneca's feelings and was sympathetic. "Renno," he said, "we haven't given you the thanks you deserve because there's no way we—or the generations that will come after us—can repay our debt to you. What you've done, first in England and now at Louisburg, will make America secure for us. Governor Shirley is signing a decree making you a full citizen of Massachusetts Bay, but that's only a token. Be patient with us a little longer, and you'll soon have your reward."

The militia leaders of other colonies arrived, and they, too, held long meetings with Renno, questioning him about the Louisburg defenses. No one appreciated him more than Colonel Austin Ridley, the Virginia commander. Tall, lean, and prematurely gray, the Virginian had been dealing with Indians for more than a quarter of a century, friendly with some tribes and fighting with others.

"It's no wonder that Renno has been able to do so much," he said one evening in private to Andrew Wilson. "He's a complete Indian, but he's one of us, too. Do you have any idea who his real parents may have been?"

"Some people used to say that his parents died in the Great Massacre at Fort Springfield years ago, but that is merely speculation. I've finally realized it doesn't matter. Regardless of whether he's dealing with Indians or whites, he has the instincts of a true leader. I don't mind telling you I thank the Almighty that he's on our side."

"Amen to that," Austin Ridley said.

Late one morning, when the military leaders had finished inspecting the newest addition to the scale model of Louisburg, they began to discuss the problems of transporting men, weapons, horses, and supplies to Cape Breton Island. The subject was beyond Renno, but he had not been dismissed, so he wandered to the nearest window and stared out at the Common.

The window was open, and the air that blew in was balmy, full of the promise of spring. The grass was becoming green, turning into a thick carpet, and pale leaves were appearing on the branches of the trees. Renno was so homesick for his own land that his insides ached.

An aide tapped at the door, and a newcomer came into the room. Ghonka, the Great Sachem of the Iroquois League, attired in his full, feathered headdress and ornamented buffalo cape, had come to join the conference.

Andrew Wilson grinned, enjoying Renno's surprise.

Father and son had eyes only for each other. Their faces immobile, they stood motionless, looking hard at each other. Then they advanced several paces and, still not speaking, gripped each other's forearms. Renno knew by his father's tight clasp how pleased Ghonka was to see him.

The military leaders whom the Great Sachem had not yet met were presented to him, and then he went off into a corner and spoke quietly with Andrew Wilson for a few moments. The brigadier gave some orders to an aide, who hurried away.

A short time later Andrew Wilson made an announcement. "Ghonka and his son have not seen each other since Renno's return from Cape Breton Island. As all of us can understand, they have private matters to discuss. The Great Sachem will rejoin us this afternoon."

Renno took his father to his own bedroom because there was no other place they could go. To the young warrior's surprise a fire was burning in his hearth, even though the day was warm, but all at once he understood. A rite of utmost importance had to be performed before he and his father could talk.

Ghonka wasted no time. He went straight to the fire, picked up a pair of the metal tongs that the English colonials used, and plucked a burning stick from it.

Renno unhesitatingly extended his hand. Father and son watched together as the new burn obscured the renegade's mark of shame on the young warrior's palm.

The pain was so great that it withered Renno, but he stood very still, his face revealing none of the agony he felt. The worst of the torment was momentary and did not really bother him. He was becoming whole again, his heart sang, and his spirits soared. He thought of the hawks that had watched over him in battle and knew they were helping him right now as he struggled to prevent himself from snatching his hand away or screaming.

At last Ghonka threw the burning chunk of wood back into the fire. Then he addressed his son for the first time. "It is done. I welcome you, Renno."

"I greet you, my father."

A few minutes later the governor's personal physician, sent by Brigadier Wilson, walked into the room. Ghonka and Renno were sitting cross-legged on the floor, both of them ignoring the severe burn on the younger man's hand as they talked calmly to each other.

With great difficulty the doctor was able to persuade Renno to allow his hand to be treated. Indians were remarkable: neither father nor son indicated that anything out of the ordinary had taken place.

Later, when Renno accompanied Ghonka out of the building and onto the Common, the young warrior's step was lighter than in all the time that had passed since he was branded as a traitor.

Additional surprises awaited Renno on the Common. A number of tents had been erected there by the Seneca who had escorted the Great Sachem to Boston.

The first to step forward was Sun-ai-yee, the portly, grizzled war chief, and then the senior warriors came forward one by one to greet Renno. They were followed by the full warriors, and El-i-chi alone could not conceal his pleasure.

Renno's joy was so great it numbed him. His brother gave him the war paint of his nation that he had not worn for many weeks, and after he daubed it on his face and torso he felt like himself again. Then he sat down with the others around a cooking fire, and the Seneca food tasted better than any he had had in a long time. Those of his fellows who had gone off on solitary missions could well understand why he ate far more than anyone else.

For the next week Ghonka and Sun-ai-yee attended the meetings of the colonial and English leaders, with Renno in attendance to act as an interpreter and to complete the task of insuring there were no errors in the making of the Fort Louisburg model.

At long last the Seneca were free to return to their own home, with Ghonka promising to lead the warriors of the Iroquois to Boston in three months, when the invading force would embark for Cape Breton Island. Renno was so eager to see his own land again that the Great

Sachem decided to waste no time on the trail. A visit to Fort Springfield would have caused a delay, so the party bypassed the town and plunged into the wilderness. Renno was the first to awaken, the last to abandon the trail at night.

His sense of excitement mounted as they passed through the land of the Mohawk and came to an area where every hill, every river, and every hollow were familiar. Then, ultimately, came the day of which he had dreamed, when he saw the cornfields in which he had played as a small boy and, beyond the open area, the high stockade of the main Seneca town.

The drums of the sentries had given advance word of his arrival and the entire community turned out to give Renno a hero's welcome. The returning party marched in single file, as was customary, and he was given the place of honor, directly behind Ghonka and Sun-ai-yee. Small children raced forward to touch him, accompanied by barking dogs. Women raised their arms in silent greeting, and the inhabitants of the longhouses of the maidens flirted openly with the hero, hoping to catch his eye.

The warriors showed off their new prowess by firing their muskets into the air, and the roar of the firesticks momentarily drowned the sounds of beating drums and shouting children.

When Renno saw Ba-lin-ta, he expected her to throw herself at him, as she had always done in the past. Instead she stood shyly, awkwardly, her head lowered as she peered at him. It was a shock to realize that she was becoming a young woman. When he hugged her, however, her shyness vanished and she returned the gesture with her customary, almost overwhelming enthusiasm.

Walter was changing, too. He stood with the other boys who would soon take their manhood tests. He held a musket in one hand, and his face was as wooden as those of the boys on either side of him. He, too, broke down when Renno paused long enough to greet him, and a slow grin spread across his face.

Members of the Massachusetts Bay militia who were

acting as firearms instructors took part in the greeting, too. Renno halted for a moment to shake the hand of Jeffrey Wilson, according to the English custom, and they exchanged quick, pleased smiles. There would be ample opportunity for them to talk later.

Renno saw no sign of his mother anywhere and became apprehensive. Surely Ghonka would have told him if she had died or fallen ill. His step became heavier as the procession came to an end. Ghonka went off at once to a meeting of his council, and Renno walked alone to the little house.

Ena awaited him inside the entrance. She had chosen, as was her right, not to greet her son in public. Here, in private, they could express their feelings freely.

The relieved Renno embraced his mother tenderly. A lump formed in his throat and would not dissolve.

Ena wept without shame and made no attempt to wipe away her tears. Then she led her son into the open, where the light was stronger, and taking his face in her hands, studied him critically.

"You look older, my son. You have suffered."

"I did what I was bidden to do, my mother," he replied with quiet pride. "Now we will fight the French and their allies in their land, not in our land."

"You have grown too thin."

"I will eat the food prepared by my mother," he said with obvious relish.

Ena smiled because, for a brief moment, he looked and sounded like a small boy again. Then her smile vanished. "The warrior of the English who went with you is dead."

"His spirit will be happy. He was a man of courage."

"How did it happen," Ena asked, "that you did not die, too?"

Renno was willing to tell his mother what he would reveal to no one else. "When I was in great danger, the spirit of Sah-nee-wa and the spirit of Ja-gonh came to me in a dream and gave me warning."

Ena was not surprised. "I prayed to them to help

you." She led him back into the house, and they sat opposite each other on rush mats. "When does the war begin?"

"In less than three moons' time."

Ena sighed gently. "Your father will lead the Iroquois into battle. You will fight, too, as will El-i-chi. Only Wal-ter will remain here. He would go, too, but your father will not permit it."

Renno remained silent. It was a man's duty and privilege to fight for his people, but he could understand how difficult the time of waiting had to be for the women who stayed at home.

His mother brightened. "You will win a great victory," she said. "With your father in command and you to help him the Seneca cannot fail."

His role would be far more modest than her description of it, but a man did not correct his mother.

Ena knew what was going through his mind but made no comment. This was one occasion when she knew more about his future than he did. Abruptly she changed the subject. "Jeff-rey will eat with us this night. Soon he will return to his own people. His work here is done. Now all the warriors of the Seneca can use firesticks."

He knew she wouldn't understand that bows and arrows were still valuable, so he made no attempt to explain. So he, too, spoke of something else. "Ba-lin-ta soon will become a woman."

His mother nodded. "Yes, and Wal-ter will be a man."

Renno chuckled. "One day they will want to marry."

"That day will come sooner than you think." Ena's tone became somber. "Soon you must take a wife, Renno. You are the oldest son of your father. You have traveled to many far places and you have seen many wonders. But you must take a wife! It is your duty to give grandchildren to Ghonka and Ena."

Feeling uncomfortable, he thought briefly of Adrienne, then of Deborah. "There is no woman I want to marry," he said.

"That is not right. When a warrior reaches high places it is his duty to the Seneca to marry." Ena pondered for a time. "I have long thought about this, my son. There are many young women in the land of the Seneca who wish to marry you. But it may be they would not satisfy you. You have seen more than they will see. You know more than they will know."

Renno was astonished. "Do you tell me to take a wife from the land of the English colonists, my mother?"

"I do not choose your wife for you," she replied, a sharp edge appearing in her voice. "The spirits will guide you, as they guided your father and me. Your father lived always in this town. I came from a small town of the Seneca. He went there when he was a young warrior. We saw each other. At the same moment we knew we would marry. The spirits led us to each other."

Never before had he heard how his parents had met, and he listened with interest.

But Ena chose to say no more. "Trust your spirits, my son, and they will lead you to the woman who will become your wife."

Renno was relieved when he saw El-i-chi standing in the entrance.

"The council has sent for you, Renno," he said.

When a warrior was summoned to appear before the council he did not delay. Renno went immediately to the small council lodge.

As usual, everyone sat in a circle around a small fire that burned in a stone-lined pit. A long pipe was passed from member to member, and when it burned out another was lighted because tradition decreed that all were required to smoke while a session was in progress.

Ghonka beckoned, and his son sat at his left. "Speak, Renno, of the nations of our enemies," he said.

It was far more pleasant to talk of such matters with his own people than to be subjected to the endless questions of the military leaders in Boston. "There are many Algonquian in the land of the French," he said. "But they are weak. Our junior warriors could win a battle with them. The Ottawa are fewer, but they are as cunning as the Erie. They have no friends. If they are cut off from all others in battle they can be beaten. They will fight hard, but when they know they stand alone they will stop and give up their tomahawks."

So far he had said nothing unexpected, and the members of the council nodded.

Renno paused and puffed on the pipe that was handed to him. Then he surprised himself. "The Huron are a great nation," he said. "They have courage. They have strength. They have a cunning almost like that of the Seneca."

The war chiefs, who knew their ancient enemies well, were not surprised, but the medicine men, who did not take an active part in war, were stunned. No one had ever praised the Huron in this lodge.

"Many warriors of the Huron followed me through the wilderness," Renno said. "I did all I could to fool them, but still they followed."

One of the elders, a retired war chief, looked at the young warrior with hard eyes. "Do you tell us the Huron can beat the Seneca in battle?"

"No nation can beat the Seneca in battle," Renno replied flatly. "But I came to know the Huron well in the land of the French. They will fight very hard, and many Seneca will die." He glanced at his father, silently asking for permission to say what he had revealed in their private discussions.

The Great Sachem inclined his head slightly.

"It may be," Renno said, "that the Huron will not always be the allies of the French."

His words had a profound effect. The war chief who was raising the pipe to his mouth froze, several members of the council were incredulous, and some looked as though they thought the young warrior had gone mad.

"The French do not treat the Huron as friends. They have contempt in their hearts for the Huron. The Huron hate them for this. When there are no others who can hear, they spit at the French."

"How can the Seneca use this?" a husky war chief demanded.

"I have thought long," Renno replied. "No one knows what the Huron may do."

"Tell us," Ghonka prompted, "what you would do if you were a war chief fighting against the Huron at the place called Louisburg."

"First I would fight them," Renno said. "I would win a battle. Then I would ask them to join us and become our brothers. Brothers for a short time. There is too much hatred in the hearts of the Seneca for the Huron, and in the hearts of the Huron for the Seneca, for them to become our true brothers. But I believe many would accept our offer. They would leave the side of the French and join our side. It might be they would join us only until the war ends. I believe they would become our enemies again after the war. But if they stopped fighting against us for even a short time it would be easier to win the war."

His suggestion was so daring it was received in total silence. Sun-ai-yee was the first to speak. "Would you trust the Huron?"

"Never!" Renno was emphatic. "If they join us, even for a few days, I would give them harmless work to do. They might turn against us without warning. But, if we are prepared to deal with treachery, they can do us little harm. The French are very strong, but without the help of the Huron they would be weaker."

Again there was silence.

Ghonka folded his arms across his chest. "When we meet the French and their allies in battle, we will remember the words of Renno," he said.

Renno knew he would be required to say nothing more at present, and he rose to his feet, waiting to be dismissed.

The Great Sachem gestured curtly, ordering him to sit again. Then Ghonka made a short speech, embarrassed because he was praising his own son. "Renno won the help of the Great Sachem of the English," he said. "Now the Seneca and other Iroquois have many firesticks. We have gifts. We have the friendship of the English colonists. Then Renno went to the land of the French. There he did what no other warrior could do. Now we will make war against the French and their allies in their own land."

One of the war chiefs rose, went to a cover of skins that lay on the ground beyond the circle of warriors, and removed an object, which he handed to the Great Sachem.

Ghonka struggled visibly to control his emotions, and never before had Renno known him to show his feelings so plainly. Then the young warrior saw what his father was holding, and his mind reeled. It was the feathered bonnet of a war chief.

Renno fought hard to regain his composure and sit motionless as his father placed the bonnet on his head.

The silence in the lodge was profound.

Stunned by the promotion, which had been farthest from his thoughts and infinitely beyond his expectations, Renno realized that never before had someone of his age reached such an exalted rank. In all the land of the Seneca there were no more than ten war chiefs. Not even Ghonka himself had received his bonnet until he had been much older.

The responsibilities were enormous. A war chief participated in all councils, and in battle he could command as many as ten times one hundred warriors. He was one of the leaders of the nation, respected by all of the Iroquois.

"May the manitous guide and guard the new war chief of the Seneca." Ghonka's voice was husky as he intoned the ancient words of the simple ceremony.

The entire council began to chant softly, offering a joint prayer to the manitous. Renno joined in, his arms folded across his chest, and looked in turn at each of the powerful men responsible for his promotion. All of them, elders and medicine men and war chiefs, returned his gaze steadily. They had known what they were doing, and none regretted the decision.

At last Renno looked at his father.

The love and pride that shone in Ghonka's eyes were overwhelming. Nothing he had ever done had given him greater joy. His feelings were matched by his son's determination to live up to the trust that had been placed in him.

Renno now realized, too, why his mother had urged him to find a wife. She had known of his pending promotion and obviously believed it unseemly for a man of such high rank to remain unmarried. Ordinarily he would have tried to follow her advice, but in this instance he could not. He knew of no woman with whom he would be willing to spend the rest of his life, and he had too many urgent matters on his mind to spend time finding one. A return to Louisburg was pending in what promised to be the biggest war ever fought by the Seneca, and he was in a position to contribute more to that campaign than any other member of the nation. There would be ample time, after the French and their allies were defeated, to think in terms of marriage.

The senior warriors standing sentry duty outside the lodge heard the chanting and knew what it meant. Soon the word spread, and people came out of their longhouses to await the end of the meeting. Night came before the chanting died away.

The council members filed out in solemn procession, with Ghonka in the lead. The last in line was Renno, the junior member, his feathered bonnet feeling heavy on his head.

There was a murmur that soon grew louder when people saw Renno. Warriors whooped in delight, women shouted, and small children joined in the chorus, even though they had no idea what was causing the commotion.

Renno accepted the rare tribute by acknowledging the ovation with a slight, dignified inclination of his head. His new rank would put new restrictions on his life. Never again would he be able to engage in trials of strength or participate in games with the warriors; instead he would be obliged to act as a judge. On social occasions he could not seek a casual dancing partner for fear that the girl and her family would consider the invitation significant. His hunting and fishing companions necessarily would be the other war chiefs, all of them many years his senior. Only members of his own family were exempt from this rule, which meant at least he could take El-i-chi or even Walter with him when he went hunting.

He walked beside Ghonka as they made their way through the town, and as always the Great Sachem wasted no words. "At another time," he said, "we will speak of the forces you will command at the fort of the French."

Renno knew that his role in the coming campaign had already been determined, but he was content to ask no questions. When it was appropriate for him to learn what was in store for him, he would be told.

The family was already gathered around the cooking fire outside the Great Sachem's house. Ena's eyes sparkled when she saw the eldest of her children, but her pride was so evident there was no need for words. El-i-chi and Walter stood, and after inclining their heads to Ghonka they saluted Renno. He grinned at them in return and was pleased that El-i-chi was not jealous. When the campaign began, he would request that his brother be assigned to his unit.

Ba-lin-ta was so excited she lost her new restraint and all but danced.

Jeffrey Wilson was impressed but not surprised. His friend seemed to lead a charmed life, and he felt confident that someday Renno would succeed his father as the sachem of the Seneca.

Renno's return home and prompt promotion made this a special occasion, and Ena served a festive meal.

Eating two portions of everything, Renno returned his bowl to his mother for a third helping of stew. He was a war chief by virtue of his accomplishments, but tonight, at least, he ate with the gusto of a growing youth.

After the meal Renno went off with Jeffrey to his

own hut, and in a long talk brought his friend up to date. He described Fort Louisburg in detail, and making light of his own role in the escape from Cape Breton Island, told the story of Sir Philip Rand's deliberate sacrifice of his own life. He ended by explaining the military developments in Boston.

Jeffrey, who had been cut off from his own world, listened intently, sometimes interrupting with questions. Finally, when Renno was done, he was able to turn to personal matters. "You stayed at Fort Springfield on your way here, I suppose."

Renno shook his head and explained that he had been too eager to return home to visit there.

The young militia officer's disappointment was obvious. "When you were in Boston, did my father speak of my mother?" He hesitated. "Or Adrienne?"

"No. But your father would have told me if they had been sick." Renno peered at his friend in the soft light of a half-moon. "You ask about Adrienne."

"After you went off to Canada," Jeffrey said, "I came to realize I love her, and I asked her to marry me."

Renno was pleased. "That is good."

"Well, she didn't accept me. Rene Gautier is paying court to her, too. He's been right there, seeing her regularly all these weeks, and he has many advantages. He's a French Huguenot as she is. He has two little children who need a mother, and Adrienne's maternal instincts may be aroused. There must be a dozen good reasons why Adrienne will choose him rather than me."

"No. Adrienne will want you."

"What makes you think so?" Jeffrey asked.

"You help Adrienne in London. You help her on ship. Your family gave her home. But you ask nothing from her. She will want to be your wife." In Renno's opinion the issue was settled, and he wondered why the thinking of Englishmen was so complicated.

Jeffrey was unable to share his friend's optimism. Women were unpredictable, and he had no way of guessing what Adrienne might do.

Recruits were drilling on the parade ground of Fort Springfield when Captain Jeffrey Wilson led his detachment there on their return from the land of the Seneca. The new militiamen stared curiously at the travel-stained veterans, weary after their march through the wilderness and eager to return to their homes.

Jeffrey dismissed his men without ceremony, then started out toward his family's house, taking care not to spur his tired gelding in his anxiety to see Adrienne again. He could only hope she was keeping her word to him, but it was possible that she had already made up her mind and just kept silent. Well, after his long period of waiting he would soon know.

His parents were sitting in the library, where they always sat before dinner. His arrival was unexpected, and they were overjoyed.

He saluted his father, then kissed his mother.

"You look well," Mildred said. "Life with the Seneca agreed with you."

"That it did, but I don't mind telling you I'll enjoy eating a beefsteak!" Jeffrey turned to his father, who poured him a glass of sack. "Sir, my mission is accomplished. Almost two thousand Seneca warriors are now able to handle firearms."

"How expert are they?"

"On a level with most militia units, I think. At least two hundred of them qualify as experts, and the rest are fair enough. There are some, of course, who would do better to keep using bows and arrows."

"They'll do their own classifying, no doubt."

"Yes, sir. Now that Renno is back there he'll organize them. He's been promoted to war chief, so he'll have the authority." Jeffrey seated himself opposite the open door, which gave him a clear view of the entrance and corridor.

"Will they be ready for the campaign in so short a time?"

"Yes, sir. Ghonka requests that we give him about fifteen days' advance notice so he can get in touch with the Mohawk and the other Iroquois who'll be joining us.

We're to tell him when we want him in Boston, and he'll be there with his warriors."

"I'm sure he will." Andrew Wilson smiled. "Ghonka is as reliable as Renno, and that's saying a great deal."

Mildred saw that her son kept looking out into the corridor. "Are you watching for someone?"

Jeffrey flushed beneath his tan. "As a matter of fact, I am, Mama."

She guessed what she should have known earlier. "Adrienne has gone out for the evening," she said.

"Oh." Jeffrey was badly disappointed.

"Nettie and Tom Hibbard have just moved into their own house, and she was invited there for supper," Mildred said.

"I suppose Rene Gautier took her there."

Mildred nodded. "He came for her about an hour ago. I'm surprised you didn't pass them on the road."

"I took the shortcut." Jeffrey squared his shoulders. "No doubt Rene sees Adrienne frequently."

His parents exchanged glances. Obviously their son's interest in the girl was more serious than they had supposed.

"He's often a visitor here," Andrew said.

"Is she—betrothed to him?" The words were out before Jeffrey could stop himself.

"Not to our knowledge. Adrienne doesn't discuss such things with us." Mildred was gentle. "What does she mean to you, Jeffrey?"

"Everything!" His reply was explosive, and he had to calm himself before he continued. "I proposed to her the night before I left, but she was very honest. She said she didn't know if she wanted Rene or me—or neither of us."

"It's just as well we didn't know," Andrew said. "We wouldn't have wanted to exert pressure on Adrienne on your behalf. In matters of the heart a woman must be free to make up her own mind."

"Well," Jeffrey said, "it's unfair to ask you this, I suppose. But have you had any hints about the way she might feel?"

He was so eager that Mildred felt sorry for him. "I know she enjoys Rene's company and she's quite fond of his children. She's been helping a large number of Huguenot refugees settle in here, and so has Rene, so they've necessarily seen quite a bit of each other."

Her son's face fell.

"On the other hand," she went on, "Adrienne speaks of you constantly. You've done your cause no harm by being off in the wilderness, Jeffrey."

"What makes you say that?"

She smiled. "My intuition."

"I see." Jeffrey was more confused than ever.

"Adrienne has changed since you last saw her," his mother told him. "She's beginning to understand our way of life. It's been good for her to see the welcome the Huguenots have been given. Our ways may be primitive, according to her standards, but she's realizing there are many benefits, too."

"Yes," Andrew said. "I believe she'll be willing to spend her life here. She knows, as everyone else does, that within a few years the frontier will be pushed much farther to the west. If we can give the French a good drubbing and take Louisburg, immigrants by the thousands will be coming to the colonies from England, Scotland, and Ireland. The opportunities here will be unlimited."

His father's vision of the future was an exciting one, and Jeffrey tried to put his personal problems out of his mind. Besides, it wasn't fair to burden his parents with them. "Are you planning to acquire more land before there's a big influx, Papa?"

"I think not," Andrew said. "Hired help is plentiful, but it's all we can do to farm the property we have. I'm increasing our herd of cattle, and I intend to buy more sheep after the campaign ends. But I'll need all the help you can give me Jeffrey."

"You shall have it. I've had my fill of London, and

I'm more than willing to settle down right here for the rest of my life."

Mildred couldn't help wondering if he would continue to feel that way if Adrienne rejected him.

"Nothing pleases me more, Jeffrey," Andrew said. "One reason I developed this property was so you'll have a home and a vocation after I've gone. But first we have a war to win. Is there any particular assignment you want?"

"No sir. I'm at your disposal."

"Good. General Pepperrell and I have discussed you. Because of your closeness to Renno and this stay of yours with the Seneca, we think we have the ideal post for you. How do you get along with Ghonka?"

"Very well, sir. To be candid, he reminds me of you, Papa. He's tough and shrewd and fair. His own warriors are in awe of him, and so are the other Iroquois. If he told them to storm a battery of Louisburg twelve-pounder cannon, they'd obey without hesitation."

"We're appointing you as our principal liaison officer with our Indian allies. You'll report to our high command, probably direct to General Pepperrell, and no doubt you'll have free access to Ghonka."

"There's no assignment I'd like better. Thank you, sir!"

"You can have all evening to talk about your campaign," Mildred said. "But I forbid you to say a word at supper, either of you. I'd like to enjoy my dinner in peace!"

Deborah and Obadiah were the last guests to arrive at the housewarming party being given by Tom and Nettie, and they brought the latest news with them. "I was on my way back to the parsonage a short time before we came out here," the clergyman said, "and I saw Jeffrey Wilson leading his detail into the fort. I was that surprised. I didn't expect them until our own troops are joined by the Iroquois."

"Jeffrey's orders gave him the right to return whenever he felt the Seneca had learned as much as he could teach them about firearms," Tom said. "I'll be eager to hear how he made out. I reckon the brigadier will call a meeting of officers so Jeffrey can tell us."

Rene Gautier looked uneasy and stole a glance at Adrienne. But her face was turned and he could not see her expression.

Adrienne was not taking the news calmly.

Deborah and Nettie, who had become her closest friends, well realized she was disturbed, but neither questioned her.

Nettie then revealed that she would continue to look after Rene's son and daughter, even though she had her own house now. And some of the company teased Rene because the pretty Huguenot girl Michele found frequent excuses to visit his house.

Adrienne took little part in the talk during supper and seemed preoccupied, but no one called attention to her silence.

Rene became increasingly apprehensive as the evening wore on, but he avoided the subject that was uppermost in his mind until he was taking Adrienne back to the Wilson's. "Will I see you again?" he asked bluntly.

"Of course, if you wish." Adrienne's reply was calmer than she really felt.

"I do wish it, as you well know." He was silent for a moment. "I haven't been able to help wondering whether Jeffrey Wilson's return will—make a difference to you."

"I shall be very pleased to see him, just as I'd be pleased to see you if you had been away for weeks, Rene."

He decided she was telling him to drop the subject and his own sense of delicacy warned him not to push her into a corner. It was possible she wouldn't know her feelings until she saw Jeffrey again, so he had to give her the opportunity to make up her own mind. He changed the subject and told her that he had planted two acres of wheat and another of vegetables that day.

"You still belong to the militia, Rene?"

"Of course!"

"Who will take care of things for you when you go off to war?"

"*If* it should be necessary," he said, gently stressing the key word, "Nettie will move back into my house with the children. And, in any event, Tom and I have found two Huguenot brothers who aren't joining the militia because they're having difficulties learning to speak English. They owned a farm in Britanny before it was confiscated by King Louis, and as the property they've staked out won't be ready to produce until next year, they'll be delighted to work for Tom and me and to look after our farms for us. It's a splendid arrangement."

"As you're the father of two small children," Adrienne said, "I believe Brigadier Wilson would give you a waiver so you could stay at home, if you wish."

"I wouldn't ask for a waiver, and I wouldn't accept one if it was offered to me!" he declared. "I was loyal to France until I was persecuted and abused, but Louis has become my enemy, and I will not lose the chance to fight him! He must be defeated, or Fort Springfield will not be safe for my children!"

"I know how you feel," Adrienne said, "and I admire you for it. If I were a man I'd want to fight the French, too. Our new homeland must remain free!"

Their thoughts were in harmony, Rene knew, and he was relieved. Perhaps he still had a chance to win her hand.

Adrienne said good night to him and went into the house. She found the brigadier sitting alone in his study, poring over maps and making extensive notes.

He looked up at her with a warm smile, approving heartily of his son's taste. He would be proud to have Adrienne as a daughter-in-law. "Jeffrey came home this evening," he said. "He arrived soon after you went out."

"So I heard. Obadiah Jenkins saw him near the fort. How is he?"

"Very well. He lost a bit of weight eating Seneca food, but he's already making up for that. He was tired after his long march, so he went to bed soon after supper."

"Then I'll see him in the morning."

Andrew Wilson couldn't decide, as he watched her go off toward the staircase, whether Adrienne was relieved or unhappy not to be seeing Jeffrey tonight.

Adrienne's thoughts were jumbled. She was sure Jeffrey had been tired after his journey, but perhaps he hadn't stayed awake to greet her because he had lost interest in her. Or perhaps he chose not to welcome her on an occasion when Rene had been her escort. Tension kept her awake for a long time, but eventually she slept.

In the morning she spent more time than had become usual for her in this frontier community sitting in front of her dressing-table mirror. She carefully arranged her red hair in curls, and although she had used few cosmetics recently, she added a subtle touch of rouge to her cheeks and lips, then brushed her nose and forehead with rice powder. She wore one of the simple new dresses that had been made for her in Fort Springfield.

The Wilsons were finishing their breakfast when she went downstairs. Jeffrey rose to his feet immediately when she entered the dining room.

"Welcome home," Adrienne said, smiling broadly as she extended her hand to him.

Jeffrey's grip was firm and his lips were warm as he bent over her hand and kissed it. She had no way of knowing that his heart was pounding.

Mildred promptly excused herself, and Andrew left the table, too, explaining vaguely that he was needed in the barns.

"You suffered no hardships in your stay with the Seneca, Jeffrey," the girl said, taking care to pour him a cup of hot tea so he wouldn't leave also.

"I enjoyed it, and I think I accomplished what I set out to do."

"I'm so glad."

He wanted to take her in his arms, but sensibly held back.

"You've acquired a tan," she said. "It becomes you."

"I had little choice. I spent all my days in the open, and the sun has been warm there of late." He looked hard at her. "You look just as I remember you. No, that isn't true. You've changed."

"How, for better or for worse?" she said coyly, in an attempt to break the ice.

"You're—different." He failed to realize that her clothes and the absence of makeup were responsible.

"Now I don't know whether to be flattered or annoyed."

Jeffrey refused to play with her. "You look wonderful," he said forcefully.

"Your father says Renno's mission was successful, but that poor Sir Philip is dead. How did it happen?"

"I'm afraid I can't discuss it. I learned the details from Renno just before I left the Seneca town."

Her interest sparked. "How is he?"

"Indestructible. And he's just received a very important promotion." He explained the significance of the rank of war chief.

"Renno," Adrienne said, "is destined to go from one success to another, each of them greater than the last."

Jeffrey felt a sudden stab of jealousy. "He has many talents."

"None of them more vital than his devotion to duty. It fills him, to the exclusion of everything and anything else. It's the key to his success, but it's probably a guarantee that he'll walk alone. It would take an exceptional woman who shared his sense of obligation—whether white or Indian—to be willing and able to marry him."

Well! At least she didn't seem interested in Renno.

"If he had lived in Massachusetts Bay all his life," she said, "he'd command the army someday."

"He'll certainly succeed his father as the leader of the Seneca, perhaps of all the Iroquois." He didn't want to keep talking about Renno, but didn't quite know how to change the subject.

Adrienne had no appetite, so she contented herself with another cup of tea, wishing she could gain control of the conversation.

"My mother brought me more or less up to date on local news last night," Jeffrey said, then asked casually, "How is Rene faring?"

"He's doing well." She held her cup with both hands because it was a convenient way to shield her face. "Nettie has been taking care of his children, as you may know, and he told me just last night that his spring planting is well under way."

Jeffrey had no interest in Rene's planting schedule.

"He's been working with me to help the new French immigrants settle here. I've been using a little office that Leverett has given me, and I spend at least part of every day there. In fact, I've got to go there shortly."

"Allow me to drive you into town," Jeffrey said. "I have military business at the fort. And if you'll give me some idea of when you're coming back here, I'll bring you home."

"That's very kind of you," she said.

His wall of self-control broke. "Adrienne," he said, "I want to be much more than kind to you."

With great deliberation she replaced her cup in its saucer, then faced him. "I know."

Jeffrey sucked in his breath. "I can't play games with you. What's your answer?"

"I—I wish I had one for you," she said. "I felt panicky last night when I heard you had come home, because I haven't yet made up my mind. One day I'm almost sure what I want, and the next I have niggling doubts. I know it isn't right to keep you dangling—or

317

Rene, either. I hate being indecisive, just as I hate hurting people. I guess I'm incurably romantic, but I'm waiting for a sign of some kind that will point the way. Will you forgive me, and be patient with me a little longer?"

"There's nothing to forgive, and you know I'll be patient as long as I must. I told you before I left that I'll wait indefinitely, if necessary. All I know is that I want to marry you, Adrienne, and that feeling will never change."

Chapter XIII

Two huge ships of the line, the *Duke of York* and the *Duke of Norfolk,* each mounting seventy-four guns, formed the core of Admiral Markham's flotilla, which was further strengthened by three powerful frigates. Four sloops-of-war and two squat bomb ketches brought his total Royal Navy strength to eleven, and a dozen privateers supplied by the colonies, most of them brigs or barques, gave him additional striking power. The privateers were assigned the task of convoying the many troop transports, leaving the warships free for combat.

Boston harbor was so crowded that merchantmen had to thread their way in and out. Certainly, as the high command well knew, any French spies would know at a glance that a major invasion effort was imminent. Secrecy was impossible to maintain, but only the leaders of the expedition knew the invasion target.

Perhaps the most curious aspect of the coming confrontation was that Great Britain and France remained at peace with each other in Europe. Both were girding for a conflict in the New World on what they regarded as a relatively minor scale, but neither as yet felt strong enough for the final showdown at home. Men would die in America, where the fate of both nations' colonies was hanging in the balance, but a mutual sense of caution prevailed and more than another decade would pass before the main armies and navies of the ancient rivals would clash.

In Boston, however, the feeling of urgency was great, and the tension was mounting rapidly. Fourteen hundred of Lord Dunmore's scarlet-clad regulars were bivouacked in Cambridge. These units consisted mostly of infantry battalions, but also included several troops of cavalry, and a half-battalion of sappers who were demolition experts and could build bridges, and nine batteries of artillery. The cannon, a few of them twelve-pounders and the majority nine-pounders, were still stored on board the ships that had carried them to the New World.

The English plans suffered a severe blow early in May, when an epidemic of a disease similar to the ague broke out in New York and spread rapidly to the New England colonies. The victims suffered high fevers, and although most survived, they were so debilitated they needed months to recover. The epidemic cut deeply into the numbers of the militia being mustered for the expedition, and the overall force, thanks to the losses in Massachusetts Bay, New York, and Connecticut, was reduced to somewhat fewer than twenty-five hundred men.

The epidemic moved westward, striking Iroquois nations. The Indians were also unable to prevent the spread of the disease, and as a consequence Ghonka could lead only one thousand warriors into the field. Most were his own Seneca, and of the other Iroquois nations, only the Mohawk were able to send a contingent to Boston.

The day before the departure of the Seneca, Ghonka gave Renno his eagerly awaited assignment. "Only you have seen the fort of the French," he said. "Only you know the fields and the hills and the town. So you will be the chief of the scouts. You will lead ten times ten Seneca and two times ten Mohawk. Your eyes will be the eyes of all."

Most of the scouts would be seasoned senior warriors, but Renno's first selection was El-i-chi.

Ena saw her men off with the stoicism of a woman who has spent a lifetime bidding farewell to those she loved as they went to battle. There were no sentimental scenes, and she did not weep; neither did Ba-lin-ta, who was on her best behavior and said good-bye to her father and brothers with an air of adult solemnity.

There was no restraint in Fort Springfield. Mildred Wilson shed tears without shame, as did Nettie Hibbard and many other wives. Brigadier Wilson's detachment led the march, and before Jeffrey mounted his horse and joined his father, a dry-eyed Adrienne kissed him and wished him a safe return. Then, as platoons were called into formation, she did the same with Rene Gautier.

Standing with the other women on the High Street as the militiamen paraded out of town, marching to the fife and drum, Adrienne turned to Nettie and told her what she had done.

For the moment, Nettie forgot her own fears about Tom's departure. "You kissed both of them?" she asked incredulously.

Adrienne nodded. "Just yesterday, realizing they were leaving and might not return, I finally understood what I should have known all along—which of them I want to marry. It's plain to me now that I have loved him for a long time. But I couldn't let the other go off to his possible death with my rejection sounding in his ears. So I said nothing and treated them as I've done all along."

"You've finally made up your mind, then."

"Yes," Adrienne answered, but said no more.

Obviously she didn't want to talk about it, not at this moment when she was struggling to maintain her calm, so Nettie had to keep silent also.

The first colonials to arrive in Boston were Colonel Austin Ridley and his Virginians, all clad in buckskins. These troops were veteran frontiersmen, skilled in the use of their muskets, which had longer barrels than those used by other troops. They were informal, shunning military formations, and were proud of their talents as marksmen. All of them had contributed funds to a pool which would be won by the Virginian who killed the largest number of the enemy.

Colonel Ridley was greeted by General Pepperrell and his staff, then presented his officers to the commander in chief. The general was struck by the bearing and attitudes of the colonel's son, Lieutenant Ned Ridley. Only in his mid-twenties, the tall, resourceful Ned had explored the interior of North America alone, twice crossing the Blue Ridge Mountains and drawing maps of the eastern portions of what later would become Kentucky and Tennessee. He had spent months at a time with various Indian tribes, was familiar with their ways, and spoke a number of their languages. He was of great value to the entire expedition, so he was detached from duty with his regiment, with his father's permission, and was assigned to serve at Ghonka's headquarters as assistant to Jeffrey Wilson.

Early in June the small contingents from New Hampshire and Rhode Island reached Boston. The latter were particularly welcome because they were artillerymen; they, too, came by ship and left their nine-pounders and six-pounders on board. They were followed by the militiamen from western Massachusetts Bay, who were soon joined by those from Boston and the nearby towns, and a vast camp began to spread across the open fields of Cambridge. The last to arrive, in mid-June, were the New Yorkers, who were able to muster only one regiment because of the epidemic.

The waterfront was busy day and night as huge supplies of food, tents, medical supplies, and munitions were loaded on the ships. The high command met daily, and it was plain that additional supplies would be needed for a siege of any length. Governor Shirley promised to provide whatever was needed, and General Pepperrell and Admiral Markham worked out an ingenious plan. After the landing was made and the site was secured, privateers would shuttle back and forth between Boston and Cape Breton Island, bringing the army the additional supplies it would require.

Two days after the arrival of the New Yorkers there was a stir in Boston, and her citizens lined the streets to watch the arrival of the Seneca and Mohawk. The warriors, most of whom had never seen a town built by white men, marched in a double file. Aware of the crowds, they looked straight ahead, and not until later would they satisfy their curiosity and stare at the huge buildings made of stone, the cobbled streets, and the horse-drawn carriages.

Ghonka immediately joined the meetings of the high command, and now that he had arrived, General Pepperrell raised a quesiton of paramount importance. "Gentlemen," he said, "we can't afford to wait here for more replacements. If we're going to sail for Louisburg, we'll have to go as soon as possible."

"*If*, sir?" Colonel Ridley raised an eyebrow.

"If," the commander in chief replied. "Under our original plan we intended to attack with a force much larger than the number we have now. The epidemic here has taken a heavy toll, and London hasn't supplied us with as many regular troops as were promised."

"I'm quite sure the Royal Army will honor its commitments," Brigadier Lord Dunmore said.

"I hope so." General Pepperrell was polite but firm. "If we decide to sail, they can join us on Cape Breton Island."

"But why should the question arise?" the bristling Ridley demanded. "Good Lord, General, we can't call off the expedition now."

"I'm not saying we should, but I want your opinions. According to our latest information, which is now several months old, the French and their Indian allies may outnumber us by as much as two to one. Fort Louisburg is marvelously strong and heavily armed. We don't want to attack if we're certain to fail. What do you think?"

323

Lord Dunmore spoke first. "I've never seen a Redcoat who is afraid of a Frenchman, General. And my men haven't come all the way across the Atlantic because they enjoy the sea air."

Brigadier Andrew Wilson was succinct. "We attack!" he declared. One by one the other colonial commanders echoed his sentiments.

Then the entire group turned to Ghonka, and Brigadier Wilson translated for him. "Numbers mean nothing," he said. "They are like ears of corn. One does not count the kernels. One Seneca or Mohawk can win a fight with five Algonquian. Or two Ottawa. The Huron are good fighters," he admitted, adding, "but there are other ways to handle them. The Seneca and the Mohawk wish to fight!"

General Pepperrell was relieved, and smiled. "Your feelings echo my own, gentlemen. In all fairness to you I had to raise the question." His grin broadened as he looked at Admiral Markham. "We shall sail as soon as your ships are ready to put out to sea, sir."

"We're ready, sir," the admiral replied.

There would be no turning back now.

While the meeting was still in progress, Jeffrey introduced Ned Ridley to Renno, who was surprised when the Virginian greeted him in the Indian manner and spoke to him in a language that, although it wasn't Seneca, he could easily understand. They liked each other. Ned had already heard of the young war chief's exploits, and Renno, developing an instinct for people, knew that here was a man who would be dependable in a crisis.

A day and a half later, at sundown, the troops began to board the transports, an operation that lasted the better part of the night, with the cavalrymen and their mounts the last to leave. Not until the ships weighed anchor were the troops told that their destination was not Quebec, as most had assumed, but Louisburg.

The members of the military high command accompanied the admiral on the *Duke of York,* his flagship, which automatically became the headquarters for the entire expedition. The great ship of the line led the procession out of the harbor, and then the warships aligned themselves on both sides of the transports and the brigs carrying supplies. The privateers moved into a V-shaped formation in the vanguard, forming a shield and ready to give warning if enemy ships were sighted.

One sloop-of-war crowded on full sail and soon left the convoy behind. She had been given a special assignment, that of determining the strength of French sea forces on Cape Breton Island. Aside from her normal complement she carried only two passengers—Renno and Ned Ridley.

The seas were calm, but a fairly strong late spring breeze made it possible for the sloop to reach the island in less than forty-eight hours. Renno and Ned joined the captain on his quarterdeck, and when the young war chief caught his first glimpse of the small but strong fort on the heights of Cape Breton, the vessel loitered at sea until night came. Then, with most of her sails furled and all of her lights extinguished, she slipped past the fort, just out of range of its cannon, and sailed into the U.

Shortly after midnight Renno could see the towers and buttresses of Louisburg ahead. But, to his amazement and that of Ned, whose eyesight was almost as sharp as his own, there were no warships anywhere.

The sloop followed the contours of the opposite shore on her way out of the U, and shortly before dawn she passed the fort opposite the Cape, again staying beyond artillery range. Not one enemy ship had been sighted anywhere!

The sloop moved away from the island, and in mid-morning with the aid of tailwinds she achieved a rendezvous with the slower moving convoy. Signal flags fluttered at her yardarm as she passed her report.

Admiral Markham was elated. Either the powerful French fleet had learned of the invasion and had gone to sea in the hope of intercepting the convoy, or, out of boredom, planned to sink English and colonial merchant ships. Whatever the reason, there would be no major sea battle right now. The admiral took full advantage of this stroke of good fortune. The *Duke of York* sailed toward Cape Breton, and the *Duke of Norfolk* headed toward the opposite point, each accompanied by a frigate, with the other warships remaining behind to guard the convoy. The scouting sloop tagged along in the wake of the flagship.

Renno and Ned were on the quarterdeck when the admiral sailed within his guns' range of the Cape Breton fort. The *Duke of York*'s gunports were lowered and the thirty-seven cannon on her starboard side roared simultaneously as she let loose her first broadside.

Renno was awed. The thunder machines of the Royal Navy were the most potent weapons he had ever seen, and the marksmanship of the flagship's gun crews was as accurate as that of a Seneca warrior using a bow and arrow. The gunnery officers found the range with their second salvo and began to batter the fort.

The French cannon soon replied, but their shots fell far short of their moving target, and the heavy iron balls splashed harmlessly into the water. The *Duke of York* managed to fire five salvos before she passed out of range, tacked, and sailed in the opposite direction in order to renew the attack.

The defenders replied with spirit, but their nine-pounders were no match for the larger guns of the ship of the line, and one by one most of her guns were silenced. Two shots left gaping holes in her stone walls. Then, while the ship of the line continued to pound the shore installation, the frigate sailed in still closer for the kill. Her cannon added to the din, and Renno watched in fascination as the holes in the walls were made larger.

Only two hours after the unequal battle had started, the shore batteries could no longer respond.

The sloop was dispatched to lead the convoy past the point. Meantime, the *Duke of Norfolk* had knocked out the fort at the opposite point, and all of Admiral Markham's ships were free to sail into the U without fear of attack.

Her new mission accomplished, the sloop was sent

ahead at dusk, and Renno was given specific instructions. He was ordered to select a landing site.

The sloop's captain sailed closer and closer to Fort Louisburg.

"I know right place," Renno told Ned Ridley. "I hope I see it in dark. It is not far from Louisburg. Ships can send men ashore on beach, and climb to the hilltop is easy. There is water to drink, and there are many fish in two lakes only a short walk from the sea."

Ridley approved. The Seneca, in spite of his youth, obviously had earned his war chief's bonnet.

High clouds obscured the moon, reducing visibility. Renno strained as he peered at the shore, sometimes blinking when tears came, sometimes using the old Seneca trick of closing his eyes for a few moments so his vision would be clearer when he reopened them. The captain sailed as close to the rocky shore as he dared, creeping under reduced sail. The success or failure of the expedition might well depend on the site chosen for the invaders' camp.

A small beach loomed ahead, and Renno was on the verge of telling the captain this was the place, but he changed his mind. Warning himself to be patient, he waited.

There! Now he was certain he had found the right place, because he had walked there on several occasions. "We stop now," he said.

The sloop dropped anchor and the two passengers were rowed ashore. They had the dubious honor of being the first members of the expedition to land on Cape Breton Island. As the little craft inched slowly toward the beach, Renno could see the long line of the convoy's ships behind the sloop, their shrouded sails making them resemble ghosts. No lights showed on any of the vessels.

The pair jumped into the shallow water, then waded ashore, and Renno stood still on the beach, getting his bearings.

"Are you quite certain this is the right place?" Ned asked him.

The young Seneca nodded solemnly.

Ned lighted a small yellow flare with a tinderbox and flint, then threw it as high as he could into the air. It flickered for a few moments, then was extinguished as it dropped into the sea. But that one, weak signal was enough, and landing boats were lowered into the water.

The first ashore were the Indians and the Virginians; then their commander came with the other leaders in the admiral's gig. These were the only men with experience in night fighting, and it was their task to make the perimeter secure.

As the Seneca landed they immediately began to deploy under Renno's direction, fanning out in a semicircle that roughly, faced Fort Louisburg. Talking was strictly forbidden. Even the oars of the Royal Navy sailors manning the boats were muffled.

Taking El-i-chi and Ned with him, Renno advanced almost half a mile in the direction of Louisburg. So far the enemy gave no sign of being aware that a landing was in progress, but the young war chief did not feel secure until two hundred warriors were in position, with only a few paces separating each of them. Ned, he noted with approval, was as silent as any Seneca.

Then the Virginians moved into place, forming a thin, single line behind the Seneca nearest the fort. If the French sent out a force to drive the invaders into the water, there were enough men on shore now to give a good account of themselves.

Their number grew minute by minute. Admiral Markham had given his seamen rigorous training in landing operations, and his precautions were paying off. The warriors came ashore forty at a time from each boat, and Renno, constantly on the move, continued to enlarge the semicircle.

Sun-ai-yee, who was acting as Ghonka's deputy, came with Jeffrey to inspect the lines, and his quiet grunt indicated that he found everything in order. Then some of the Mohawk moved into the line, and the next to appear were Tom Hibbard's musketmen from western Massachusetts Bay. No one spoke, and loaded muskets were held ready for instant use, but the men were under strict orders not to fire unless ordered by a war chief or an officer of the rank of captain or higher.

General Pepperrell and the other commanders stayed on the beach, and by the early hours of the morning, when Brigadier Wilson's count of those who had come ashore reached fifteen hundred, the high officers began to breathe more easily. Even the apprehensive Lord Dunmore, unaccustomed to the methods of New World warfare, knew that by now the invaders were in considerably less danger of being overwhelmed.

But the risks were still intense. If the French launched an assault in real force, their enemies could still be driven into the sea.

The horses of the cavalrymen, still on board the transports, were hooded so they would not whinny, and their riders stood beside them, occasionally talking to them in low tones to keep them calm. The cavalry would not come ashore before daylight arrived and neither would the sappers. The last would be the artillery. The landing of their cannon would be difficult, even though special barges built for the purpose would be used.

Meanwhile, Admiral Markham moved two of his frigates as close to the shallow water as he dared. Gunports had been lowered, and the navy's cannon crews were prepared to give the land forces temporary artillery cover if it should prove necessary.

There was a brief, tense flurry in one of the Seneca sectors when two Ottawa who had been fishing in one of the lakes passed within a short distance of the invaders' lines. Unaware of what was happening nearby, the two warriors paid for their outing with their lives. A shower of arrows killed them before they could cry out, and Sun-ai-yee forbade his men to go into the open and scalp the pair. No one was permitted to go beyond the advance line that Renno had established.

At dawn an alert Huron sentry became aware of the invasion and gave the alarm. Colonel Alain de Gramont immediately made his own investigation, taking a band of

Huron with him, and an hour later he returned to Louisburg, reporting at once to his commander in chief.

"General," he said, "there are at least forty or fifty English ships in the harbor, discharging men and supplies from more transports than I took time to count. They've established a strong perimeter, and my Huron and I crept close enough to see Seneca and Mohawk war paint on the Indians who are holding the outer lines. This is a major invasion, sir!"

General de Martine was bemused. "I wonder how they managed to pass our outer forts."

"I imagine the enemy battered them into submission. I knew it was wrong for our whole fleet to put out to sea to look for the confounded English. They should have waited and engaged them here!"

"The forts are too far from Louisburg for us to have heard the sound of gunfire. The English have proved more clever than I would have suspected. Ah, well." de Martine sighed gently.

"If you please, General, let us drive them off before they can dig in! Order our regiments to advance on them and cut them to ribbons! I'll lead the attack myself, with my Huron."

"I won't hear of such tactics," the French commander in chief said, his manner icy.

Alain became desperate. "We can't let them land unopposed, sir."

The general shook his head, his lips forming a thin line.

"I beg you—"

"Gramont, you're a courageous man, but your stupidity astonishes me. Why should I risk the lives of my men in the open when Louisburg was built for the express purpose of withstanding an assault? A hundred assaults, or a thousand!" The general stood and pounded his desk. "Let the English land! When they attack, our cannon will cause them countless casualties, and their survivors will batter themselves to death against our walls! Gramont, Louisburg is the finest fort ever built by French architects to withstand a siege. Louisburg is impregnable, as the English will soon discover. They've made it unnecessary for us to carry the war to them. They've done us the great favor of coming here and giving us the opportunity to defeat them on our own soil. So let them attack us—and die!"

By noon the next day, all of the invading troops were ashore. The cavalry units were held in reserve, ready to ride out into the open area in front of Louisburg in the event the French sent out a major force to repel them. The artillery of the Royal Army and the Rhode Island batteries were placed a short distance behind the front lines, and infantrymen were pressed into service to help carry cannonballs.

The laborious process of unloading supplies was under way, and by mid-afternoon a city of tents was rising on the plateau, with foragers going off into the scrub forest to bring back as much firewood as they could carry. Physicians erected their hospital tents far to the rear, near the dunes that led down to the beach, and it was hoped that all of the ammunition, provisions, and other items the army needed would be landed before the night ended. That would enable the privateers to sail to Boston at dawn and start bringing a stream of additional supplies.

Meanwhile, the navy set up a rough blockade of Cape Breton Island. A frigate was stationed at either end of the Strait of Canso, and two sloops patrolled the narrow channel, cutting off the ferries and small boats that sailed to and from the Nova Scotia mainland. As soon as the landing operation was completed, Admiral Markham told the military high command he would go to sea again with the bulk of his flotilla and seek the French fleet. The invaders would not be secure until there was no chance they could be bombarded by the cannon of French warships standing off the shore.

The blockade was not tight, as the admiral and his subordinate commanders well knew, and it was possible for the defenders to sneak small craft back and forth across the straight, especially at night. But it would be difficult, perhaps impossible, to obtain substantial troop reinforcements from Quebec or to send much food and other supplies to the beleaguered garrison.

On the second night of the invasion, Renno led his Seneca and Mohawk scouts into the open beyond the English lines, and one small band, of which El-i-chi was a member, actually reached a point only one hundred yards from Louisburg's forbidding, bristling wall. But General de Martine sent no one out on probing missions. For the moment, at least, he seemed content to let the English set up their lines without harassment, and the night passed without incident.

The privateers finally weighed anchor several hours later than they had intended. But the landing had been made without the loss of a single man, which Brigadier Wilson regarded as a near miracle, and the delay was worthwhile.

Early in the afternoon the fife and drum players from Massachusetts Bay assembled, and General Pepperrell, preceded by an infantryman carrying a flag of truce, walked slowly into the open and headed toward Fort Louisburg. He was accompanied only by his two brigadiers and Ghonka.

At first there was no response from the defenders. Then a gate creaked open, and General de Martine appeared with several of his subordinates. They, too, followed a soldier carrying a white flag of truce. Ordinarily an officer of Colonel Alain de Gramont's rank would not have been included in the group, but he appeared in Indian attire, smeared with Huron war paint.

The two parties came face to face about two hundred yards from the Louisburg walls. The officers on both sides drew their swords so they could exchange elaborate salutes. Ghonka and Gramont simply raised their arms in greeting, then stood with their arms folded across their chests, neither even glancing in the direction of the other.

General Pepperrell did his enemy the honor of addressing them in strongly accented but understandable French. "Gentlemen," he said, "I greet you on behalf of His Britannic Majesty, William the Third."

General de Martine replied in English. "I return your greetings in the name of His Christian Majesty, Louis the Fourteenth."

"General," Pepperrell said, "your troops and their Indian allies have invaded our colonies in New England and have penetrated as far as New York. Your warships have attacked and captured or sunk our innocent merchantmen engaged in peaceful trade. In order to call a halt to these barbaric outrages, I have placed Fort Louisburg under siege. I call upon you now to desist from these practices and to surrender Louisburg to me."

"I deny your charges, General," de Martine said briskly. "Firstly, no French soldiers have participated in raids on New England or New York. And France takes no responsibility for the conduct of Indian nations with whom she is on friendly terms, even assuming they perpetrated these alleged raids. And in the second place, the warships of France have conducted no raids on your shipping. His Christian Majesty's government can take no responsibility for the acts of captains of privately owned ships. As to your demand that I surrender Louisburg to you, I reject your request."

"Very well, sir," Pepperrell said. "We must allow force of arms to settle the issue."

"I accept your challenge to combat," de Martine replied, and bowed.

There was still more. "If it is your desire to evacuate women, children, and men who will not participate in the defense of your garrison, I will be pleased to arrange a truce while they are transported to safety on the mainland," Pepperrell said.

"I shall take advantage of your generous offer." De Martine had anticipated the move and was ready for it. "In one hour's time, I will send noncombatants to the Strait of Canso, along with civilian residents of the town who may wish to leave. They will be taken on board barges, and I shall hold you to your trust to give them safe conduct to Acadia."

Again they exchanged bows. "Until we meet again, General de Martine," William Pepperrell said, and when he raised his sword in salute his brigadiers did the same.

The French commander in chief's smile was tight-lipped. "I look forward to our next meeting, sir, when I shall accept your sword in surrender." He and his subordinates returned the salutes.

Then both parties turned and made their way back to their respective positions. The rules of warfare had been observed.

Later that afternoon a large number of women and children, accompanied by twenty or thirty elderly men in civilian attire, boarded barges in the town and were rowed across the Strait of Canso. The two Royal Navy sloops hovered nearby, making no attempt to interfere with the operation. It was understood on both sides that any noncombatants who remained on Cape Breton Island were staying of their own free will, and there would be no future evacuations.

At dusk the state of siege was formalized when the cannon of Louisburg fired a brief salvo and the invading artillery replied. Both sides fell far short of their targets, the iron balls falling harmlessly onto the open plateau that separated the armies. The exchange was brief to conserve ammunition.

That night Renno and his scouts encountered their enemies for the first time. El-i-chi distinguished himself by killing two Algonquian warriors and taking their scalps. Renno and his main body of warriors saw a number of Huron at a distance, but the two parties respected each other. There was nothing to be gained by a fight, so the two groups went their separate ways. Indians, Renno reflected, had the good sense to do battle only when a victory or defeat would be significant.

Early the next morning Brigadier Wilson sent a detachment of Massachusetts Bay infantrymen forward to provide cover for a squad of sappers, who took advantage of a heavy, early summer fog to plant explosives at the base of the fort's wall. A long fuse was lighted, and the two units retreated before they were discovered. But an alert sentry caught sight of the burning fuse, and two French soldiers extinguished it by pouring water from the ramparts above. The incident served notice, however, that the invaders did not intend to remain idle.

At midday the ships of the Royal Navy flotilla, except for the vessels participating in the blockade of the island, went off to sea to search for the French fleet. The attackers would suffer severely if their supply lines with Boston were severed.

That afternoon a heavy rain began to fall, accompanied by strong gusting winds. The invaders retired to their tents, leaving only their sentries in the open. No French troops could be seen on the walls of Louisburg; it was a stalemate in such weather.

That night, despite the storm, Renno and his scouts scoured the area in the vicinity of the great fort. Enemy patrols were abroad, too, but most managed to stay away from each other. One band of Ottawa suffered the misfortune of encountering a group of Seneca, however. El-i-chi, who was rapidly acquiring a reputation for ferocity, killed one of the Ottawa and added another scalp to the growing number hanging from his belt.

By morning the storm was raging, and it was impossible for either side to send out patrols. The tents leaked, it proved impossible to keep cooking fires lighted, and soon the Redcoats and militiamen were forced to improve their crude shelters for gunpowder, food supplies, and the horses of the cavalry troops. Only the Seneca and Mohawk, who had oiled their bodies, remained relatively comfortable.

The rivers rose dramatically, sending torrents of water rushing into the sea, and ponds overflowed their banks. The rain fell for three days and four nights, and even after the sun finally came out, the ground was too soggy for infantry operations.

The Indians were able to function, however, and the

first night after the gale ended, Ghonka expanded the scouting patrols, sending a total of five hundred warriors into the field. Renno's braves twice engaged in brief but ferocious fights with roving bands of Huron. Ned Ridley, who had the skill of an Indian with a tomahawk, brought down his first enemy, and El-i-chi again won a scalp. Two Seneca and one Mohawk suffered minor wounds.

When the ground dried, the high command decided to keep the French off-balance by conducting a series of night attacks against Louisburg's walls, in an attempt to harass the French. General Pepperrell and Brigadier Wilson wanted to wear them down by giving them no rest.

Renno was summoned to headquarters before the first of these attacks took place.

"We don't want to lose men when it can be helped," Andrew Wilson explained to him. "So we're relying on you to tell us where we'll find the fewest defenders."

Renno pondered for a time. "Send the soldiers with me," he said. "I will show them where to attack."

Tom Hibbard's militiamen were given the first assault assignment, and immediately after night fell, Renno and a dozen of his warriors led the troops toward a portion of the wall that faced the town. So far the civilians who had elected to remain behind had been left in peace, and it was General Pepperrell's intention to leave them alone as long as they stayed out of the fighting. Renno reasoned that the French would think themselves fairly secure in that area.

The night was dark, and he paused when he came to the small country church where he had met Sir Philip Rand when they had made their escape from the island.

Tom Hibbard came forward to join him.

"No man talks now," Renno said. "Soon we come to Louisburg. You will see two small towers. My warriors will kill with arrows French who watch from towers. Other French will come. But your soldiers wait for my signal before they shoot."

"Fair enough," Tom said.

"Fire only once. Then we leave. Too many soldiers come to tower if we stay, and many of us will die."

Tom gave his troops their orders, and his men spread out, six abreast, the Seneca silently leading.

Rene Gautier's heart pounded. He was going into combat for the first time since he had landed on Cape Breton Island, and he was eager to fight. Here was his chance to avenge the persecution he and his family had suffered in France, as well as the senseless murder of his wife in Massachusetts Bay.

Renno advanced cautiously, enjoying himself because El-i-chi was directly to his left. This was their first fight together, and Renno was reminded of their countless hunting trips. Well, they were hunting now, but tonight men were their quarry.

Suddenly he sensed rather than saw that El-i-chi had halted abruptly. The other Seneca were aware of it, too, and needing no orders, they also stopped. Renno raised an arm in warning, Tom Hibbard saw his signal, and the militiamen stopped, too. There was dead silence.

Two Huron warriors approached from the direction of Louisburg. Both were armed, but were off guard.

El-i-chi's tomahawk flew through the air, and one of the Huron crumpled to the ground.

At almost the same instant the Seneca to El-i-chi's left disposed of the other Huron in the same fashion.

The first Huron was still alive, although badly hurt, and El-i-chi sprang forward, then buried his knife in the enemy's body.

Renno was pleased, but did not move forward immediately. Instead he waited for several moments to give El-i-chi and the other Seneca the opportunity to take the scalps. He would not deny them that right, and he was only sorry they could not take the Huron weapons.

A slight movement to Renno's left told him that El-i-chi had taken his place in the line again, ready to advance. The line started forward.

The wall of Louisburg loomed ahead, and again Renno paused. The gate into the town was locked and chained, and although he could not see it, new masonry had been piled behind it to block the entrance. Twin towers overlooked the gate, standing about twenty feet apart, and Renno peered at them. He was able to make out the shapes of two soldiers in each tower. All four seemed somewhat relaxed.

The young war chief moved forward a few paces in order to allow his warriors to see their targets more clearly. Ordinarily he would have fitted an arrow into his own bow and taken aim, but he was learning that a commander had more important responsibilities. He left that task to his warriors.

They did not disappoint him. Showers of arrows were directed at the opening in both towers, and the sentries disappeared from sight.

One of the Frenchmen groaned aloud.

That sound would bring other troops, as Renno well knew. His warriors withdrew to the rear, and Renno motioned the militiamen forward.

The troops formed a double line facing the wall, and those in the front rank dropped to one knee. Rene Gautier, standing in the second line, raised his musket to his shoulder and waited. Within moments he would taste vengeance.

French infantrymen poured into the towers, and a number of others appeared on the wall itself between the two turrets. They strained as they tried to locate the attackers in the dark.

Tom Hibbard was in charge now, and he waited as long as he dared before giving the brief command, "Fire at will!"

A volley of musket fire broke the silence. No one was certain how many of the defenders were struck, and only later did they figure that at least five of the French soldiers had fallen either dead or wounded.

Tom immediately gave the order to disengage, and his men spread out as they ran to the rear, guided by the Seneca.

The French opened fire and sent round after round

of musket fire into the night. But the shadowy, moving targets were difficult to locate and even more difficult to hit, and Tom's entire unit escaped unscathed.

Rene Gautier felt a sense of bitter, grim triumph as he ran. He knew that his bullet had found its target, but that knowledge failed to give him the sense of elation he had anticipated. He realized that he would not be content until Louisburg surrendered and Massachusetts Bay was no longer in jeopardy.

The Seneca warriors took up positions on all sides of the militiamen to prevent any of the troops from straggling. Renno led them back to their own camp by a different route, and he did not slow his rapid pace until he had left Louisburg far behind. Not until they were challenged by their own sentries and passed safely through the lines did he relax.

The Seneca and militiamen went their separate ways, and Renno accompanied Tom to headquarters so they could make a joint report.

"I reckon we didn't do too bad," the militia officer said.

Renno grinned at him. "Two Huron are dead. Four sentries are killed. Five more French soldiers are dead or wounded. Now Golden Eagle will stay awake all night, and that is good!"

The siege developed its own routines, its own rhythms. Sometimes the French tried to bring food across the Strait of Canso at night, but so many boats were sunk by the Royal Navy that the farmers of Acadia soon became reluctant to run the gauntlet. Only a thin trickle of supplies actually reached the French, who needed much more food if they hoped to survive indefinitely. They were not seriously worried, however, and General de Martine's principal quartermaster estimated there was enough flour, beans, cornmeal, and pickled meat on hand to last them until winter.

Every night the invaders selected a different target, and every night Renno's Seneca led another militia unit in an assault on a different portion of the wall. Some of these raids were total failures, others caused a few French casualties, and on several occasions one or more of the attackers was wounded. These pinpricks, however, would not determine the outcome of the siege, and both sides knew it.

General Pepperrell was far more concerned because nothing had been heard from Admiral Markham since his flotilla had left to search for the French fleet just a few hours before the outbreak of the vicious storm. Days passed, but there was no sign of the warships.

The colonials in the high command refused to speculate, but Lord Dunmore expressed his worries freely. "If the navy has been defeated," he said, "our own position will become untenable. We'll be caught in a nutcracker, with Louisburg on one side and the French fleet on the other. We'll be trapped without supplies and lose our only means of evacuation!"

General Pepperrell was well aware of the gravity of the situation. But a man born and reared in the New World was accustomed to waiting long periods for news, and he refused to become agitated.

The first word of what had happened reached the invaders about ten days after the storm, when several privateers dropped anchor offshore with fresh supplies. "We've heard," the commander of the convoy told them, "that the French warships were blown far out to sea and suffered frightful damage. One of our merchantmen crossing the Atlantic from England saw two French ships of the line limping toward the mouth of the St. Lawrence, heading to Quebec for repairs."

Another week passed before a Seneca sentry brought word to the Indian camp that a flotilla flying the British Union Jack had passed the battered forts at the entrance to the Cape Breton Island harbor.

Captain Jeffrey Wilson immediately went to headquarters, where he found his father, General Pepperrell, and Lord Dunmore eating breakfast. The commanders hurried to the peak of the highest dune to keep watch.

More than an hour later their vigil was rewarded when they saw the *Duke of York* leading a line of warships.

Admiral Markham and his staff came ashore without delay, and a war council was called.

"The Almighty," the admiral told his colleagues, "saw fit to put the French fleet out of commission for us. We didn't strike a single blow. We sighted the enemy on the last day of the gale, but the winds were so strong we couldn't engage in battle. The French had vanished by the time the gale blew herself out, and our damage was so great I had to put into the nearest harbor, an uninhabited cove on the coast of the Maine District, for repairs. I thank God for those forests! Our carpenters have been spending all this time making new masts and patching holes in our hulls. All of my ships except one frigate and one sloop were damaged."

"What of the enemy?" Lord Dunmore demanded.

The admiral remained patient. "I'm coming to that," he said. "I sent my two sound ships off on scouting expeditions. The frigate found remains floating at sea that we have positively identified as portions of three separate French warships. All were apparently sunk, and there was no sign of survivors."

General Pepperrell and Brigadier Wilson exchanged glances, and both were impressed.

"My sloop," Admiral Markham continued, "did more than was required of her. She sailed up the mouth of the St. Lawrence, and when she approached Quebec she hoisted the French flag so the batteries of the Citadel wouldn't fire at her. Her captain saw two ships of the line and a frigate docked there, all undergoing very extensive repairs. His report leads me to conclude that none of them will see action again for many months. The storm took a far larger toll than our gunners could have done, and at no real cost to us."

"You're telling us," General Pepperrell said, "that the French New World fleet has been destroyed."

"I am, sir," the admiral replied with spirit. "At least

until word can be sent to King Louis, and his ministers can assemble an entirely new fleet. Estimating conservatively, we'll rule these waters until next spring."

"What happened to the rest of the French fleet, Admiral?" Lord Dunmore wanted to know.

Markham shrugged. "There's no sign of them here. They may have been anchored somewhere up the St. Lawrence, past Quebec, but my sloop didn't push her luck in an attempt to find out. I doubt if any of them were in good enough shape to reach France or the French West Indies. I presume at least some of them were sent to the bottom. And our own strength is sufficient to take care of any survivors after they've been made seaworthy."

"How did your sloop escape from Quebec?" Andrew Wilson asked.

The admiral chuckled. "She loitered offshore until sundown, then beat a retreat to the open sea. The French had no warships sound enough to give chase, you see, so she wasn't actually in much danger."

The news spread quickly, and the entire army was heartened. Privateers from the colonies could come and go as they pleased, and the supply chain would continue without interruption.

Admiral Markham sent all of his ships except the *Duke of York* and the *Duke of Norfolk* to the entrance of the U-shaped island. There they patrolled day and night in order to prevent any French vessel from reaching the besieged fortress.

He had other duties in store for his mammoth ships of the line, as he demonstrated at sundown that same day. To the awe of every soldier, militiamen, and Indian in the invading force, the great seventy-fours weighed anchor, inched closer to Louisburg, and opened fire with their twelve-pounders.

The navy's gunners reloaded without delay, their officers meanwhile adjusting the trajectory and a second round was fired. The roar was so great that alarmed seagulls soared high into the air and flew away from the area. Some of the shots found their mark, and chunks of stone masonry littered the area directly in front of Louisburg. A few shots destroyed the walls in spots.

General de Martine could not ignore the impudent challenge. But his own gun crews had not been ready for battle, and by the time they reached their posts, loaded their cannon, and fired, the seventy-fours had withdrawn far enough to be out of range. The French cannonballs fell harmlessly into the sea.

The English had chosen a dramatic way of informing the enemy that Louisburg was vulnerable to attack by sea as well as by land. Cut off from the outside world, with no idea of what might have become of their own fleet, the defenders knew only that the siege was getting worse.

Chapter XIV

Any military investment was dull, tedious work, and the siege of Louisburg was no exception. The summer days dragged, and the troops became bored. Sickness thinned the invaders' ranks, and by the end of August four hundred men were sent back to Boston to recuperate. Their places were taken, however, by three hundred newly arrived Redcoats who were added to Lord Dunmore's command.

A French frigate ventured to crash through the sea blockade but was driven away by Admiral Markham's flotilla. Then a French sloop-of-war made a gallant attempt to reach Louisburg with messages from Paris telling General de Martine he would receive strong reinforcements late in the autumn and urging him to hold out until that time. Royal Navy gunners sent the sloop to the bottom before she could deliver the letters. Half of her crew of twenty-four men perished when she went down, and the survivors, including her captain, were captured by the Royal Navy and sent to Boston as prisoners of war.

The overall strategy of the English colonial high command was becoming clear to both sides. Louisburg was being strangled and gradually starved into submission. The French tried to bring in still more food supplies from Acadia, but no substantial quantities seeped through the blockade. The townspeople were becoming increasingly demoralized.

Only the Iroquois scouts saw action regularly. The nightly attacks on the fortress continued, and Renno's warriors engaged in numerous brushes with the Huron, Ottawa, and Algonquian. El-i-chi continued to develop rapidly as a fighting man, and by the end of August he had accumulated sixteen scalps.

Renno was delighted by his brother's progress. Ghonka said nothing, which disappointed neither Renno nor El-i-chi; both knew their father expected them to live up to the very high standards he set for them. At the beginning of September, however, El-i-chi and two of his peers were promoted to the rank of senior warrior. The Great Sachem had chosen his own way of demonstrating his satisfaction with work well done.

It was obvious to General de Martine that he had to rely exclusively on his own efforts to break the grip of the enemy, and he realized that the spirits of his own troops were drooping. So, early in September, he made a bold move.

Trumpets sounded inside the Louisburg walls shortly after daybreak one morning. The gates opened, and twenty-five hundred infantrymen, clad in gold and white, marched out onto the plateau, formed in hollow squares, and advanced toward the enemy.

Renno, accompanied only by Ned Ridley, went beyond the English and colonial lines to investigate and quickly reported to the high command.

"The French send many soldiers with firesticks to our camp," Renno said.

"They're carrying their regimental banners," the amazed Ned added. "You'd think they were on parade."

"I demand the honor of meeting them!" Lord Dunmore declared, and raced off to send his Redcoats into action.

Brigadier Wilson shook his head. "It appears to me that de Martine is planning to fight a European-style battle. We have our own ways here, and we'd be foolish to abide by his kind of rules."

General Pepperrell seemingly overruled him. "We've got to let the British regulars fight in the only kind of battle they know. They haven't been trained for wilderness warfare."

"But they're badly outnumbered by the French infantry, and you know the cannon of Louisburg are superior to our own guns. We're running the risk of a severe defeat."

The commander in chief grinned at his subordinate. "Who said anything about obeying de Martine's rules? Alert your troops, gentlemen, but hold them in reserve. No unit will go into action without my consent."

The militia commanders hurried off.

The Iroquois were already eager to join in the fight, and Ghonka had difficulty in restraining his warriors. The authority of his war chiefs prevailed, however, and he placed Sun-ai-yee, his deputy, at the head of the column while he and Jeffrey Wilson joined the members of the high command on the crest of a hill where they could see what was happening.

The Redcoats marched off in hollow squares similar to those of the French, and the militia leaders were open-mouthed. Without exception they believed it was absurd to fight in the European manner in the rugged wilderness of the New World. Troops on both sides found it difficult to maintain their formations as they moved toward each other on the plateau. In places the scrub forest was thick, so entire companies had to make detours, and even in the open areas there were many small trees and patches of impenetrable bramble bushes.

Eventually, however, both sides approached each other. Then the powerful cannon of Louisburg opened the battle, sending heated iron balls toward the Redcoats.

"Be good enough to return that fire," General Pepperrell told the commanders of the Royal Artillery and the Rhode Island batteries.

Within moments the English and colonial guns added to the din. Artillery fire on both sides was inaccurate, however, and the general knew it would take a long time before aim could be improved.

Less than a quarter of an hour later the troops in scarlet and the soldiers in gold and white came within musket range of each other. Regiments on both sides halted and opened fire.

Pepperrell was satisfied when he saw that de Martine was using only his infantry. The rough terrain made it impossible to use cavalry effectively, but the French were making a serious mistake by not sending their Indians into the battle.

"Ghonka," he said decisively, "attack the left flank of the enemy. You need no instructions from me. But be sure you keep a sharp watch for enemy Indians. They're certain to join in quickly."

Ghonka departed, with Jeffrey beside him.

"The militia will attack the enemy right flank," the general said. "Your Virginians will form the vanguard, Colonel Ridley. Massachusetts Bay will lead the main body, followed by New York, Connecticut, and New Hampshire, in that order."

The militia leaders raced off, too, and the commander in chief remained behind on the hill, surrounded by members of his personal staff. After months of waiting the two armies would meet in full force at last.

The Redcoats and the French infantry fired volley after volley at each other, both sides holding their ground. If their tactics were not suitable for New World combat, at least neither side lacked courage. When a soldier was killed or wounded, another stepped forward to take his place.

Renno's scouts led the Iroquois, and Ned Ridley kept pace with the young war chief at the head of the column as they made a wide sweep to the left and approached the rear of the French flank.

"We stay on side," Renno said. "If we go behind French, maybe we get caught between them and the Algonquian, who come soon."

Ned agreed. The scouts halted, and Renno raised his arm, giving the order to open fire. Some warriors used muskets while others preferred their bows and arrows.

The rest of the Seneca and Mohawk were strung out behind the scouts, and they, too, used the weapons they liked best. Some warriors crouched, using trees or bushes as cover, while others flattened themselves on the ground. From the moment they entered the battle the Indians began to teach the French a lesson in wilderness warfare.

Renno calmly picked off a junior French officer with his rifle, as did Ned. The infantry company, deprived of its leaders, became confused as its members were felled by an unseen enemy. The troops maintained their formation, but it was only a matter of time before they buckled.

Within a few minutes the right flank came alive, too. Colonel Ridley's Virginians opened deadly fire, and the militiamen from western Massachusetts Bay, who were commanded by Donald Doremus, now a major, were almost as effective. Here and there a French soldier became panicky, but their officers beat the men with the flats of their swords to prevent them from bolting.

Rene Gautier rested his weight on one knee, took careful aim from the cover of a thick bush, fired, methodically reloaded, and fired again. He had intended to keep count of the enemy he killed or wounded, but he soon realized that he couldn't determine whose shot was responsible when a French soldier fell. It no longer mattered. The persecutors of the Huguenots were paying dearly for their bigotry.

On the far side of the field Captain Jeffrey Wilson was discovering, to his surprise, that he actually relished combat. He had thought of himself as a civilized man, but the fight was bringing out a new side of him. He thought of all that Adrienne had suffered, and he felt a sense of savage, unreasoning release each time he squeezed the trigger of his musket, and he found himself rejoicing when a French soldier dropped to the ground. Never again would he think of his Indian friends as barbarians. His own feelings were as violent as any he had ever seen them display.

El-i-chi was discovering that the dignity of a senior warrior could be inhibiting. He brought down two Frenchmen, one with his musket and the other with bow and arrow. As a full warrior he might have been excused for rashly running out into the open and scalping his fallen enemies before returning to cover. Now, however, he had to restrain himself. Eventually, perhaps, there would be a chance to add to his growing collection of scalps.

General de Martine's first error was that of sending only his French infantry into battle with orders to fight European-style. Then he made another mistake by sending his cavalry charging out of Louisburg to support the foot soldiers.

The combination of trees, bushes, and rough ground made it impossible for the horsemen to maintain their formations. Their lines separated as they galloped, and it was difficult for the troopers to attack together. Swinging their heavy sabers as they rode, they became confused when they could not locate the enemy in the scrub forest and underbrush.

They hesitated, and in those few moments Renno and Ned took action. They fired at the horses rather than the riders. Soon the bewildered animals were screaming in pain as they fell, and the other horses took flight, many of them throwing their riders as they ran madly across the plateau, seeking refuge from bullets and arrows.

On the other flank the Virginians and militiamen from western Massachusetts Bay employed the same techniques with similar results. The cavalry lost one rider in ten, and the survivors limped back to Louisburg, those who made it regarding themselves as fortunate.

Only then did General de Martine commit his Indians to the struggle. The battle was becoming more extensive than he had planned, but he had to extricate his infantry regiments at any cost, so he sent his warriors into combat.

Colonel Alain de Gramont had opposed the battle plan from the outset, so he had been relieved of his command and his lieutenant colonel led his regiment. Now, however, Gramont came into his own as the chieftain of the Huron. Dressed in Indian attire and smeared with Huron war paint, he led his warriors toward the positions occupied by the militia. The Ottawa came close behind his own braves, and he felt confident.

At the same time, the Algonquian moved out against the Seneca and Mohawk, pouring out of the fortress's gate in such large numbers they resembled a human tidal wave.

Ghonka became aware of the approach of the hordes of Algonquian and calmly gave the order, "Hold your fire! Wait!"

His warriors temporarily abandoned the fight with the French and braced themselves for the onslaught of the largest number of Indian warriors ever seen in battle.

Some of the younger braves became impatient when the Algonquian, not spreading out as they might have done had there been fewer of them, began to inch forward through the scrub forest and came within musket range.

The Great Sachem continued to study the approaching force, his eyes narrowed, his mood still outwardly tranquil. Not until the Algonquian came within reach of his warriors' arrows did his arm move upward in a sharp, decisive signal.

The Seneca and Mohawk had laid aside their muskets, instead relying on the traditional weapons of their ancestors. Bows were already strung, and when the Great Sachem gave the sign, his braves were on their own.

The advance halted abruptly. The Algonquian were men of courage, but their skills were inferior to those of the most feared Indian nations in all the land. The assault force fought back, but their numbers proved to be a handicap rather than an advantage. Many of the Algonquian could find no cover, and they died before they could throw themselves to the ground.

Those in the rear continued to press forward, eager to show their prowess in battle, and they, like their vanguard, suffered heavy casualties. Many years had passed since the Algonquian had fought a major war, and their chiefs lacked the experience and instincts of the Seneca and Mohawk. The fight lasted for a very short time, but corpses littered the ground before the Algonquian leaders could give the order to withdraw.

Ordinarily Renno gloried in armed combat. But the carnage was so great it sickened him, and he made no attempt to join the warriors who raced forward to scalp their fallen foes as the main body of Algonquian retreated. He wished he and his scouts had been facing the Huron, which would have been a fair test of their skill and strength. But the manitous had willed otherwise, so he had to be content with the results of the struggle.

On the far side of the battlefield Alain de Gramont lived up to his reputation, and his Huron fought brilliantly. Experts in the art of concealment, they held their own against the militiamen from Virginia and western Massachusetts Bay. Waiting patiently until flashes of fire told them the location of muskets, the Huron actually gave better than they received.

Tom Hibbard kept his head and held his unit in place, as did a number of other junior officers. But the militia needed help, and Brigadier Wilson sorely missed the Seneca, who could have pinpointed the Huron positions for his troops.

He worked his way to the rear of the Virginia line, and there he conferred with Colonel Ridley. "Much as I hate the idea," Wilson said, "I'm wondering if we ought to pull back a hundred yards or so and let the Huron expose themselves."

"I hate to see us suffering unnecessary losses, too," Austin Ridley replied. "But the Huron know what they're about, and if we start a withdrawal we might not be able to stop it."

The brigadier nodded grimly. "It appears that we'll just have to dig in and hold," he said.

The militia braced itself and did not yield a foot of ground.

By now, however, the French infantry had enough of battle for one day. The men of the battalion at the rear of the formation saw the Algonquian streaming back to Louisburg, and realizing they might be cut off from behind, they retreated without waiting for orders.

Once the flow toward the rear began, the tide could not be reversed, and the regimental commanders, afraid the orderly withdrawal might turn into flight, directed their troops to break off contact with the enemy.

The British regulars were too weary to pursue them and could not take advantage of the situation. The colonial militiamen were pinned down by the Huron, so only the Seneca and Mohawk were able to harass the French troops. Devoting their full attention to the infantry, the warriors sent streams of arrows into their ranks.

Golden Eagle saved the French from disaster. He quickly brought the Ottawa forward to take places held by the Huron, and then he led his own warriors across the field to hold the Iroquois at bay while the French reached the safety of the fortress.

At last the Seneca and Huron met each other in full force, but their contact was short-lived. An area that extended about three-quarters of a mile from Louisburg's walls had been cleared of trees and other cover, and no experienced warrior wanted to risk complete exposure. The Iroquois, like the Huron, were veterans of wilderness warfare and knew better than to follow their enemies into open fields.

The warriors exchanged showers of arrows, but Ghonka refused to take his braves beyond the edge of the scrub forest, and soon the two forces were out of range.

French artillery continued to thunder, but as the English, the colonials, and their Indian allies made their way back to their own lines, they were able to avoid the areas where the heavy iron balls were falling. Several hours of daylight remained after the battle came to an end.

Then a French officer appeared from the fortress carrying a white flag. Captain Jeffrey Wilson was sent to meet him.

The Frenchman proposed a truce until sundown so the dead and wounded of both sides could be removed from the field before being scalped by the Indians. Jeffrey readily agreed.

A quarter of an hour later the least weary troops of both armies came back to the battlefield. The dead were piled into carts, and the injured were either carried or helped to the rear. Men on each side totally ignored those of the other. Seneca who witnessed this strange spectacle marveled at the inconsistency of men from the Old World. Only Renno, who had learned enough about the civilization of Europeans to grasp their motives, realized that a feeling of compassion was responsible. Indians never spared the wounded, but men from England and France lived according to a different standard.

The surgeons and physicians in the English colonial camp worked feverishly to treat the injured, and long lines formed outside the medical tents, with the most critical cases receiving attention first. Meanwhile, cooking fires were lighted, and on orders from General Pepperrell extra food was prepared. Each fighting man also received a generous ration of rum.

The casualty figures were startling. The British regulars had taken the worst punishment, losing seventy men with another two hundred wounded. The militia losses were light by comparison, and the Seneca had suffered few casualties.

Members of the high command held a war council before supper, and each officer sipped from his mug of rum as they gathered at one side of the campfire. The atmosphere was gloomy.

"Gentlemen," Lord Dunmore said, "this was a very expensive day."

"Our only consolation," Brigadier Wilson declared, "is that the French losses were heavier."

Colonel Ridley removed his broad-brimmed leather hat and ran a hand through his white hair. "What I'm damned if I can understand is why de Martine ordered his troops into combat in the first place. Or why he used just his French infantry at the outset."

General Pepperrell shook his head. "I'm a mite confused myself," he confessed. "You'd think if de Martine wanted to challenge us, he'd have thrown his full strength at us from the very beginning of the battle."

"Maybe he was trying out some newfangled tactics—that didn't work," Andrew Wilson suggested.

Jeffrey Wilson had been quietly interpreting for Ghonka, who now allowed himself the luxury of a faint, rare smile and, not bothering to speak through a translator, addressed his colleagues in English. "French have war fever," he said. "Huron and Ottawa and Algonquian too smart. Only join when French fall."

The others knew what he meant by "war fever" and realized he was right. The French had been cooped up in Fort Louisburg for so long they had grown restless and would have mutinied had they not been taken into action. The leader of the Seneca obviously understood fighting men.

The Great Sachem was not yet done. "Many French die this day," he said. "Now all know France will not win. Soon Louisburg belong to us."

By the end of September the nights had grown cooler, the leaves on Cape Breton Island's little trees were turning red and gold, and autumn was in the air. The badly wounded had been transported to Boston in the fleet of privateers, which had now returned with fresh supplies.

"If necessary," General Pepperrell said, "we'll spend the winter here, although I must admit I dread the prospect. Half our men will fall ill in the cold."

"We may not have to worry about illness," Andrew Wilson said. "The fact is, whole companies of militia are talking about going home. They've already spent months here, their terms of enlistment are ended, and they have no intention of staying on indefinitely."

Even though the two were sitting alone in the general's tent, Pepperrell lowered his voice. "The French must be suffering far worse than we are, so I'm tempted. . . ."

Brigadier Wilson brightened. "You mean you're thinking of ending the siege once and for all with a full-scale attack on Louisburg?"

Pepperrell nodded. "The risks are enormous, of course. But the French lack the strength they had when we first came here. And I'd like to see us do something positive before our army melts away."

"Put the issue to the whole council, Will, and let's find out how the others feel."

The unit commanders were summoned, then polled.

Lord Dunmore was emphatic. "My men are so bloody homesick for civilization they're ready to tear down Louisburg stone by stone. I'm definitely in favor of an attack!"

"The Virginians are ready tonight," Colonel Ridley declared.

"Attack," said the New York commander, and was echoed by the leaders of the Connecticut, Rhode Island, and New Hampshire militia.

Brigadier Wilson's attitude was critical. "I'm always reluctant to run the risk of suffering heavy casualties," he said, "but we have only two choices. If we don't attack and the siege continues indefinitely, militiamen will go home by the hundreds, and hundreds more will become too sick to fight. So all that we've undergone here will be in vain. That leaves me no real choice. With full awareness of the possible consequences, Massachusetts Bay votes in favor of an attack."

Ghonka was the last to speak. "The warriors of the Seneca and the warriors of the Mohawk came to this place to fight," he said. "They have grown fat and lazy, and their hearts have been heavy. Now they will fight and will become true warriors again."

Preparations for the climactic struggle were made

the following day. Renno was summoned to headquarters and spent hours confirming the details of the maps that had been drawn of Louisburg's interior. The commander of the Royal Artillery selected several places in the walls of the fortress that, in his opinion, could be breached if they were first subjected to a strong enough bombardment. All troops were issued extra rounds of ammunition and full pouches of gunpowder.

Late in the day Renno was given an additional one hundred warriors to augment his scouting force and was ordered to allow no enemy scouts to escape back to Louisburg in the areas where the attack would be centered. At sundown he and his warriors left the English colonial camp and fanned out to scour the countryside.

Under cover of darkness the cannon were moved forward, some hauled by horses, others dragged by sweating, silently cursing men. At the same time, ammunition for the guns was carried forward.

Shortly before midnight chaplains conducted religious services for all who wanted to attend.

The order of battle having been drawn, all units moved to their assigned positions. The Redcoats and militiamen had been provided with scaling ladders, but Ghonka refused to be encumbered by them. If the preparations were adequate, he indicated, his warriors would do their part.

At three o'clock in the morning the French still were unaware of the coming attack, because of a heavy cloud cover and the zealousness of Renno's scouts, who killed seven of the enemy who were roaming through the area.

Promptly at three the artillery bombardment began and continued unabated for an hour and a half. The French cannon came to life, too, the defenders' gunners guided by the flashes of light they saw in the distance, but it was impossible for them to judge the accuracy of their shots in the dark. The British and Rhode Island gunners, knowing the wall of the fortress was their target, had less difficulty.

At four-thirty in the morning there was a lull. Renno and his warriors led the sappers forward on the run, and explosives were planted at the base of Louisburg's wall in several places. The detonation of the bags of gunpowder echoed through the night, and then the artillery began to roar again, with the bombardment continuing for another full hour.

General Pepperrell coordinated every move, and a short time before daybreak he sent his infantry forward. The Seneca and Mohawk, divided into three bands, were in the lead, with Ghonka commmanding in the center himself, and two of his senior war chiefs in charge on either flank. The Redcoats were assigned to the center, Massachusetts Bay was given the left, and the militia from the other colonies were placed on the right. Because of the British regulars' unfamiliarity with wilderness warfare, Colonel Ridley's Virginians led.

The scouts were assigned to the band on the left. Sun-ai-yee, who was in command, knew that Renno was more familiar with the area in the immediate vicinity of the wall than anyone else and granted him the privilege of taking the lead. When Pepperrell gave his signal, the young war chief sprinted forward, with El-i-chi and other comrades close behind him. Now the entire army was on the move.

The English colonial artillery continued to fire for precisely ten minutes, giving the attackers just enough time to reach their goal. Then, suddenly, the cannonade ceased.

For a few moments there was a strange, almost unearthly silence.

By the light of the first streaks of dawn, Renno made out the wall directly ahead of him. The artillerymen and sappers had done their work well, and in one spot they had made a gaping hole in the masonry. Renno climbed over the rubble into the supposedly impenetrable Fort Louisburg, his fellow warriors on his heels.

General de Martine had mustered his entire defending force for the assault he now realized was inevitable, but he still didn't know where the principal attack would take place, so his troops and their Indian allies were spread out over an area that covered the better part of half a mile. By the time the French were able to pinpoint the assault areas their enemies were pouring into Louisburg in three places.

Renno let fly with an arrow at an Algonquian warrior, impaled a French infantryman with another, and pressed forward at a sprint. He no longer had specific instructions to obey and had already chosen his goal. Ignoring the fighting that was erupting everywhere, he ran past barracks and parade grounds as daylight dawned, and when he caught a quick glimpse of the officers' quarters where Major Sir Philip Rand had lived, he hoped the spirit of his late friend was on hand, watching the attack that his own heroic sacrifice had made possible. On this day Sir Philip would be avenged.

Avoiding a developing fight between Massachusetts Bay militiamen and French infantry, Renno ran on, slowing his pace slightly only when he approached a small, one-story stone building. The private house of Colonel Alain de Gramont.

He put his shoulder to the door, and it burst open.

Standing in the living room, facing him, was a young woman—Marie, the half-breed whom he had bedded. Obviously she had been living with Gramont, and he was so astonished at the sight of a woman during a battle that he stopped short.

Too late he realized she was holding a dueling pistol similar to the pistols King William had given him, which he carried in his belt at this moment.

Marie fired, but her shot went wild.

Before Renno could react, El-i-chi's tomahawk smashed the girl's head and she dropped, dead before she struck the floor.

Renno leaped over her body and opened an inner door.

At last! There was Gramont himself, dressed as Golden Eagle but lacking the identifying bonnet of a chief.

Gramont recognized his enemy instantly. "You again! I should have killed you long ago!" He raised an arm, and a knife left his hand.

The blade grazed Renno's temple and landed in the wall behind him, where it quivered in the wood.

Renno fired one of his dueling pistols. For a moment he had no idea whether he had struck his target. Then, when the smoke had cleared, he saw that a rear door was open, and there was no sign of Gramont.

The young war chief hurried to the door, but scores of men were fighting viciously in an open area in front of a barracks. Gramont was nowhere to be seen in the confusion.

Renno had to put his personal enemy out of his mind when he saw a burly Huron war chief approaching him, tomahawk in hand. El-i-chi and the other Seneca who followed Renno into the open did not interfere. It was the right of leaders of equal rank to duel to the death.

The Huron carried a tomahawk in one hand, and Renno knew from the way he was holding it that the man was taking his measure. In a moment that tomahawk could decapitate him.

Snatching his other pistol from his belt, Renno had to rely on his long hours of practice with firearms to guide him. There was simply no time to take careful aim.

He fired the pistol an instant before the Huron could release his tomahawk. The surprised war chief crumpled to the ground.

Resisting the temptation to scalp him and take his bonnet as a trophy, Renno plunged into the melee. It was more important that he and his warriors come to the aid of the Massachusetts Bay militia.

Once again Golden Eagle had eluded him, and Renno suspected that the manitous were enjoying a hearty laugh at the expense of both mortals. It was impossible to find Golden Eagle now in the maelstrom, but surely they would meet again. Their destinies were intertwined, and the day would come when one would kill the other. But that day was not today.

Renno slashed left and right with his tomahawk as he cleared a path for himself through the ranks of French infantrymen until he reached the side of Captain Tom Hibbard. Major Doremus was lying on the ground, his kneecap shattered by a bullet. He was conscious, suffering great pain.

Tom Hibbard and several other militiamen were trying to hold off a surging mob of French infantrymen intent on capturing Doremus. Rene Gautier stood guard over the fallen major, saving the bullet in his musket for the moment when it would count most.

Renno needed to give no orders to his warriors. They formed a line in front of Tom Hibbard, their tomahawks slashing, their knives cutting. The ranks of the French thinned, then dissipated. Two militiamen carried the now unconscious Doremus to the rear.

"Thanks, Renno," Tom said. Not waiting for a reply, he shouted, "Trumpeter, play a rally!" He was taking command of the battalion, and Renno was pleased when he heard the ringing notes and saw militiamen falling into line for another charge. Hibbard was a true war chief.

Elsewhere in the fortress the situation was equally confused. The British Redcoats, like the French infantry, were unaccustomed to disorganized combat, and in their bewilderment made the situation worse. The Virginia regiment, their fire slicing through enemy formations, turned the tide in the center, and Colonel Ridley, operating smoothly in tandem with Ghonka's own warriors, forced entire companies of white-clad soldiers to lay down their arms and surrender.

Jeffrey Wilson performed valiantly, fighting with demonic fury at Ghonka's side, pausing only to relay messages from the Great Sachem to Colonel Ridley. Jeffrey fully earned the rank of senior warrior of the Seneca that Ghonka conferred on him after the battle ended.

A battalion of New York frontiersmen from the Fort Albany area led the attack on the right flank. They were opposed by the tough, resilient Huron, and the Seneca and Mohawk leading the assault had to call for help from their brothers. Ghonka promptly transferred all of his warriors to their aid, and the Seneca at last engaged in a major, direct confrontation with their ancient foes.

Renno's spirits soared, as did those of his warriors, and they fought furiously. Crouching low, they sent out volleys of arrows and the Huron answered in kind. Neither side elected to use the firearms supplied by the British and French; in this time of supreme crisis the warriors relied exclusively on the weapons they knew best.

Little by little the Huron were forced to retreat, and ultimately their ranks broke. The victory of the Seneca and Mohawk was complete.

As the braves raced forward to take the scalps of their fallen enemies, Renno hastily returned to the rear of Gramont's house, where he had vanquished the Huron war chief. The man's body was still there, untouched, so Renno took his scalp and chief's bonnet, legitimate trophies of war.

The forces of the Algonquian were disintegrating rapidly now, and their sachem came to Ghonka, extending a strip of wampum to which white clam shells were sewn. The Great Sachem accepted the token, and Algonquian chiefs quickly passed the word to their subordinates, who stopped fighting. By making an alliance with the French, the largest of Indian nations on the seaboard had gambled and lost. Their sachem solemnly pledged that his people would not make war against the Iroquois again, a promise to be kept for more than half a century.

Then the Ottawa capitulated, and although they promised only not to become active again during the current hostilities, Ghonka did not demand a long-term commitment from them. The Seneca were willing to meet them in the field again at any time. If the Ottawa had not already learned a lesson, more severe punishment would be inflicted on them if they disturbed the peace again.

The Huron war chiefs came together to Ghonka and explained to him that, in the absence of Golden Eagle, they could not submit a formal surrender. The Great

Sachem well knew their excuse was a typical Huron trick, and they were simply avoiding a gesture of submission.

But their defeat spoke for itself, and he did not insist on their further humiliation. They wouldn't have regarded any pledge as binding anyway, and the Seneca were fully prepared to fight them again.

All the same, Ghonka was relieved that he had not found it necessary to make an attempt to wean the Huron from the side of the French, even on a temporary basis. He had held that option in reserve and would have utilized it only in case of dire need. As events had developed, the Huron had been vanquished decisively, and there was no way they could now claim that the Seneca had been afraid to meet them in fair combat. The record was clear, and new songs would be composed by the women of the Seneca to commemorate the victory.

Gradually the musket fire ceased, and late in the morning General de Martine, accompanied by his staff, approached General Pepperrell under a flag of truce. Saluting crisply, the French commander in chief drew his sword and tendered it to his opponent, hilt first. "You have accomplished the impossible, sir," he said. "You have conquered Louisburg."

Pepperrell was equally generous. "Your troops fought honorably and well, sir. You need not be ashamed of them or of yourself."

The terms of surrender were arranged with dispatch. The French officers were required to relinquish their swords but were permitted to keep their firearms, as were their men. They would leave Cape Breton Island without delay, going to the mainland on boats and barges provided by the Royal Navy, and would proceed to Quebec, en route to France. Before their departure all would be required to take an oath promising never again to take up arms against Great Britain or her New World colonies.

Ghonka demanded a gesture of tribute from the defeated Indian nations. The sachems and war chiefs were required to give the victors their bonnets, and the senior warriors were forced to relinquish their ornamental headdress feathers. In this way, when they returned to their own lands, their people would know they had been defeated, and their leaders would not be able to claim victories they had not won.

The evacuation began that same day. Renno and El-i-chi stationed themselves at the waterfront of the virtually deserted Cape Breton Island town in order to keep watch for Golden Eagle, but there was no sign of him. Sensing the outcome of the battle, he had vanished without a trace, and Renno could only hope their paths would cross again.

The next day General Pepperrell's principal quartermaster made a count of supplies still on hand at Fort Louisburg and reported that provisions would have been exhausted in another month. In fact, rice, flour, and peas were already running low.

The Seneca and Mohawk were anxious to return to their own lands, so General Pepperrell agreed to allow them to depart the next day. They would march into the Maine District, then make a trail to the southwest.

That night Ghonka's colleagues paid tribute to him at a supper they held in his honor. General Pepperrell presented him with a French sword, and one by one the other commanders rose to praise him.

The Great Sachem sat stolidly, apparently unmoved by the ceremony, and he replied in a few words. "The Seneca and the other nations of the Iroquois are the friends of the English and the English colonies," he said. "Together we have drawn the blood of our enemies. We will be friends as long as I live in this world."

Later that evening Jeffrey Wilson said good-bye to Renno, promising to see him again by the following summer, at the latest. Then Ned Ridley came to the Seneca camp to bid his comrade farewell. "We'll meet again, Renno," he said. "I'm sure of it."

The Seneca and Mohawk departed silently at dawn. The Royal Navy transported them to the Nova Scotia mainland, and there they disappeared into the wilderness.

Later that day General Pepperrell and Admiral

Markham finished writing their official accounts of the campaign, and the admiral gave the dispatches to the captain of one of his sloops-of-war, with orders to carry the news to London without delay. Even though war had never been declared, all England would rejoice over the fall of Fort Louisburg.

When the privateers returned to Cape Breton Island, the militia units marched on board the transports and headed for Boston, with several of the Royal Navy warships shepherding them. The Royal Army units were to be relieved by other Redcoats whom London was expected to send to America as their replacements.

Huge crowds gathered at the Boston waterfront to greet the returning heroes. The militiamen paraded through town, their regimental and battalion banners flying, but ceremonies were held to a minimum. The men were tired after the long siege and two major battles and were eager to return to their homes. After a stay overnight, when the commanders attended a banquet given by Governor Shirley, the troops from Rhode Island, Connecticut, New York, and Virginia departed by sea, and the New Hampshire men marched home.

So did the militiamen from western Massachusetts Bay. Brigadier Wilson rode with his staff at the head of the procession. Major Doremus, who could not walk without a cane, rode in a carriage with several others who had been wounded. Then came the battalion, led by Tom Hibbard, who held the brevet rank of major.

People turned out en masse in small towns and villages on the line of march. Girls threw flowers, women and older men offered them gifts of food and ale, and in each community of consequence the leading citizens insisted on holding victory ceremonies at the town common. The troops' progress was necessarily slow, and more than a week passed before they reached Fort Springfield.

Lookouts brought advance word of their approach, and people from the entire area gathered to give the returning troops a riotous welcome. Huge victory bonfires were lighted, and sides of beef were roasted on spits on the town green, opposite the fort. People lined the High Street, and near the fort they stood three and four deep.

The applause and cheers started when Andrew Wilson and his staff appeared, but they died away briefly at the sight of the wounded. But Major Doremus's grin was genuine as he waved to the crowd, and spirits revived quickly.

Mildred Wilson stood directly opposite the entrance to the fort, and her husband saw her before he dismounted. They smiled at each other, and their kiss was as tender as that of young lovers.

"It may be that we have years of peace ahead," he told her. "I pray to God I'll never have to lead another expedition."

Nettie Hibbard pushed through the crowd and was standing at her husband's side as he leaped from his horse to the ground. Tom hugged her exuberantly, and laughed when she wept.

Captain Jeffrey Wilson searched in vain for a glimpse of Adrienne Bartel, but he didn't see her anywhere. He handed the reins of his horse to an orderly, then made his way slowly through the throngs of well-wishers, the men shaking his hand and the women kissing him.

Finally he came to the green, where the feast was being prepared by volunteers. There, at last, he saw Adrienne, wearing an apron over her wool dress and, her face flushed because of the fire, busily ladling sauce over a side of beef that two boys were slowly turning on a spit.

He stopped short and stared at her. Not even in his dreams had she been as lovely, as desirable, and his whole being ached for her.

Adrienne became aware of his stare and looked up. Her eyes met his and, as he started toward her, she dropped the ladle and began to walk slowly toward him.

As they came face to face, Jeffrey read his longed-for message in Adrienne's eyes, and there was no need for words as he took her in his arms.

Eventually they saw Rene Gautier, and Jeffrey felt a stab of pity for his vanquished rival. Then, just as quickly, he stopped feeling sorry for him. Rene's son was proudly carrying his musket, and his daughter rode on one of his shoulders, steadied by his strong hand. Clinging to his other arm was the Huguenot girl Michele. She was looking up at Rene, smiling, her eyes speaking volumes, and it was obvious that Rene was already finding consolation. Michele was exceptionally pretty, her interest in him was genuine, and Rene's future was assured.

Jeffrey slid an arm around Adrienne's waist, and she leaned against him as they went together to break their news to his parents.

Rarely had the Seneca enjoyed a better hunting season. Renno went into the wilderness every day with El-i-chi, and they always returned with game, so much of it that Ena had more than enough for the family's needs, with ample left to be smoked for the lean months ahead. Sometimes the brothers took Walter with them, and the boy was not only expert with bow and arrow but had an instinct for finding deer.

"Wal-ter," Renno told a delighted Ba-lin-ta, "is truly a Seneca, worthy of being a son of Ghonka."

Then winter came, and the young war chief occasionally went ice fishing. He took his turn with the other war chiefs commanding the sentry detail; he regularly attended meetings of the council, and twice he was sent on brief missions to other Seneca towns. He also made a journey to the land of the Oneida to act as his father's representative at an Iroquois conclave.

He continued to live alone in his own small house, although he ate most of his meals with the family. Ena openly and regularly urged him to find a wife, but there was no woman he wanted to marry. He also could not follow the example of some Seneca and allow his parents to arrange a marriage with the parents of some girl who meant nothing to him. He had absorbed enough of the attitudes of the colonists and English to insist he would wed only someone he loved.

Spring came, the women went into the fields to work, and the warriors resumed their hunting. Then Jeffrey Wilson appeared at the head of a small company of militia, bringing news and gifts.

He presented Ghonka with a portrait of King William and a musket with a silver-inlaid butt, both sent by the monarch himself, and Renno received a sword with a jewel-encrusted hilt. That night, in Renno's house, Jeffrey brought his friend up to date on what was happening in the outside world.

"You'll be surprised—and sorry—to learn that Cape Breton Island has been returned to the French. I have no doubt they'll soon be repairing Louisburg."

Renno was incredulous. "The English gave the fort back to the French?"

"They had no real choice," Jeffrey explained. "Technically, the two nations have been at peace because neither ever issued a formal declaration of war. Under international law Great Britain had no right to keep Cape Breton Island, so King William returned it to King Louis."

The ways of Europeans continued to puzzle Renno. "Then we will fight at Louisburg again?"

"I hope not. London believes, and so do my father and General Pepperrell, that the French have learned a lesson and won't repeat their mistakes."

Renno nodded gravely. "Plenty of room in America for English and French colonists to live as friends."

"That's exactly what Adrienne says." Jeffrey paused and smiled broadly. "It just occurs to me that you don't know my news. Or maybe you do, because you predicted what would happen."

"You are married to Adrienne! The best that could happen to both of you!"

"In every way. We're expecting a baby late in the summer."

Renno felt a quick pang of envy, but it passed quickly. Adrienne had married the man who was right for her.

They chatted for a time, and then Jeffrey sobered. "I had several reasons for coming out here, and one I haven't yet told you. I've brought a letter to Ghonka that's very important. I have a fairly good idea of the contents, but I'd rather let the letter speak for itself."

The next morning, at breakfast, he handed the square of parchment to the Great Sachem. Ghonka broke the seal, unfolded the communication and handed it back to Jeffrey. "Tell me the words," he said.

The letter, Jeffrey explained, had been sent by Colonel Austin Ridley of Virginia. The warlike Pimlico Indians living in Virginia, he wrote, were planning a series of raids, to drive the Virginian colonists into the sea.

" 'We will fight, if we must, but we hope there is some way to settle our dispute by peaceful means,' " Jeffrey read aloud. " 'I cannot and do not ask you to do anything that would be harmful to another Indian nation. But I write to you in the hope that the Seneca will be able to intervene, help us clear up our mutual misunderstandings, and prevent much needless bloodshed.' "

The Great Sachem sat immobile for a long time as he pondered. Then he said, "I do not know what happens in Virginia. Ridley is my friend. It may be that the Indian nations there are good. It may be they are bad. I must find out. If the council wills it and Renno agrees, my son will become my eyes and ears. Renno will go to Virginia and learn what I must know."

Renno's hopes of spending long months enjoying the fruits of his victory were blasted. He was afraid his life would be disrupted again because of a delicate, difficult mission.

It was his right, as a war chief, to reject the assignment, but he refused to allow himself that luxury. He was the son of Ghonka, a true Seneca, and when the Great Sachem commanded, he obeyed.

★ WAGONS WEST ★

A series of unforgettable books that trace the lives of a dauntless band of pioneering men, women, and children as they brave the hazards of an untamed land in their trek across America. This legendary caravan of people forge a new link in the wilderness. They are Americans from the North and the South, alongside immigrants, Blacks, and Indians, who wage fierce daily battles for survival on this uncompromising journey—each to their private destinies as they fulfill their greatest dreams.

☐	24408	**INDEPENDENCE!**	$3.95
☐	24651	**NEBRASKA!**	$3.95
☐	24229	**WYOMING!**	$3.95
☐	24088	**OREGON!**	$3.95
☐	24848	**TEXAS!**	$3.95
☐	24655	**CALIFORNIA!**	$3.95
☐	24694	**COLORADO!**	$3.95
☐	20174	**NEVADA!**	$3.50
☐	25010	**WASHINGTON!**	$3.95
☐	22925	**MONTANA!**	$3.95
☐	23572	**DAKOTA!**	$3.95
☐	23921	**UTAH!**	$3.95
☐	24256	**IDAHO!**	$3.95

"FROM THE PRODUCER OF WAGONS WEST COMES YET ANOTHER EXPLOSIVE SAGA OF LEGENDARY COURAGE AND UNFORGETTABLE LOVE"

CHILDREN OF THE LION

SPECIAL MONEY SAVING OFFER

Now you can have an up-to-date listing of Bantam's hundreds of titles plus take advantage of our unique and exciting bonus book offer. A special offer which gives you the opportunity to purchase a Bantam book for only 50¢. Here's how!

By ordering any five books at the regular price per order, you can also choose any other single book listed (up to a $4.95 value) for just 50¢. Some restrictions do apply, but for further details why not send for Bantam's listing of titles today!

Just send us your name and address plus 50¢ to defray the postage and handling costs.
